SOME EXCERPTS FROM 5 STAR REVIEWS
ON AMAZON KINDLE

...I highly recommend readers start from Book 1 and read in order. ...Nothing could have prepared me for the rousing conclusion, though that's what made Sacha all the more rewarding. The stories work independently, but the layers of growth and understanding build one upon each other towards a memorable conclusion.

Alex Prosper (Amazon.com, USA)

Author Stan I.S. Law delivers the thrilling and emotional ending of this fascinating and insightful trilogy. He brings his talent to the forefront creating these complex and lovable characters to transmit the philosophical meaning behind it all. The story is steeped in challenge, science, art, love, romance, family, the esoteric, religion, faith and destiny.

Amy Taylor (Amazon.com, USA)

...It is a wonderful story... always entertaining and captivating. Sacha is a fitting and very powerful end to the Alexander Trilogy and should leave all readers feeling satisfied with the results

Kevin Linter (Amazon.com, USA)

This book is fascinating and for me, the best of the trilogy... ...I couldn't put this book down, probably because it dealt with human nature in a way that I could understand. I heartily recommend it.

Joan A. Adamak VINE VOICE (USA)

Oh, the deep thought this book provoked! ...captivating story-line and characters that I became deeply involved with. You simply have got to check out this entire trilogy.

Mary Leckie (Amazon.com, USA)

...perfect amount of fantasy, thrill, and suspense... ...the son of Alex & Suzy is a lot more magnificent than you could imagine.

Monica G. (Amazon TOP 1000 REVIEWER)

...Such a well-written series with so many themes and intriguing ideas that I know I will be re-reading it again soon, as I am sure that I have missed much in the first pass. Highly recommended.

Trish FL Reader (TOP 500 REVIEWER, USA)

...I simply cannot say enough good things about this book or this author and I highly recommend the entire trilogy.

Mrs. B. (TOP 500 REVIEWER, USA)

By the same author

ALEC (Alexander Trilogy, Book I)
ALEXANDER (Alexander Trilogy, Book II)
SACHA—The Way Back (Alexander Trilogy, Book III)
YESHUA—Personal Memoir of the Missing Years of Jesus
PETER AND PAUL (An intuitive sequel to Yeshûa)
ONE JUST MAN (Winston Trilogy Book I)
ELOHIM (Winston Trilogy Book II)
WINSTON'S KINGDOM (Winston Trilogy Book III)
THE AVATAR SYNDROME (Prequel to Headless World)
HEADLESS WORLD—The Vatican Incident
(Sequel to *The Avatar Syndrome*)
MARVIN CLARK–In Search of Freedom
THE GATE—Things My Mother Told Me
NOW—Being and Becoming
GIFT OF GAMMAN
THE PRINCESS
ENIGMA of the Second Coming
WALL—Love, Sex, and Immortality (Aquarius Trilogy Book I)
PLUTO EFFECT [Aquarius Trilogy Book II]
OLYMPUS—Of Gods and Men [Aquarius Trilogy Book III]

Short stories

THE JEWEL & OTHER STORIES
CATS AND DOGS
Sci-Fi Series 1
Sci-Fi Series 2

Non-fiction Books by Stanislaw Kapuscinski

VISUALIZATION—Creating Your Own Universe
KEY TO IMMORTALITY
[Commentary on the Gospel of Thomas]
BEYOND RELIGION: Volumes I, II and III
[Collections of essays on perception of Reality]
DICTIONARY OF BIBLICAL SYMBOLISM
DELUSIONS—Pragmatic Realism

Poetry in Polish
[with illustrations by Bozena Happach]
KILKA SŁÓW I TROCHĘ GLINY
WIĘCEJ SŁÓW I WIĘCEJ GLINY

INHOUSEPRESS, MONTREAL, CANADA
http://inhousepress.ca

"A Book must be the axe for the frozen sea inside us,"

Franz Kafka

SACHA
THE WAY BACK
Alexander Trilogy Book Three

Sequel to
ALEC
and
ALEXANDER

A novel by

Stan I.S. Law

BY INHOUSEPRESS, MONTREAL, CANADA

Published by
INHOUSEPRESS
http://inhousepress.ca

This book is a work of fiction.
Names, characters, titles, places and incidents are
either the products of the author's imagination
or used fictitiously

ISBN 978-1-987864-06-9

Paperback Edition 2015
INHOUSEPRESS

CONTENTS

PART ONE—Innocence

PART TWO—The Search

PART THREE—The Journey

PART FOUR—The Way Back

Epilogue

PART ONE
Innocence

*"Every act of rebellion expresses a nostalgia for innocence
and an appeal to the essence of being."*

Albert Camus

1
Suzy

"It was not at all like his father,"** Suzy mused, aloud, smiling against her will. "This was no peek-a-boo. Not by a long shot."

She was desperately trying to make sense, find some rational explanation, for Sacha's behaviour before alerting her husband. She'd have to tell him, of course. Sooner or later. Or... or she could wait for Alec to find out for himself. It was bound to happen again.

Suzy recalled that she'd once referred to Alec's odd behavior as "peek-a-boo". This was way back in Montreal, when she had no idea what game her husband-to-be had been playing. At least then, she'd suspected, it might have been some kind of a game. What else could have it been? She did not believe in miracles—then or now—though since, she'd drawn different conclusions. The whole world was a miracle. Every rose, every common or garden flower, every sunset or sunrise was a miracle; although, of late, the latter was a rare occasion. In Los Angeles the mornings tend to be foggy. The sun comes out a little later, shyly creeping out of the morning mists, which drift from the mighty Pacific toward the distant hills. Or do they slide down the mountains? She forgot.

Anyway, her mind was elsewhere.

At the time of Alec's peculiar behavior, Suzy and Alec had just become officially engaged. Unofficially they practically tied the knot at least a dozen times. But it was only after they had 'permanently' moved in together that she'd first noticed his habit of shifting position. That's what she'd called his peek-a-boo syndrome. A number of symptoms, an array of inexplicable tidbits, but always connected with Alec's strange if innocuous idiosyncrasies. One moment he was there, or here, the next, virtually in the same instant, she'd see him a few feet away, acting as though nothing had happened. Since then they had both reached their conclusions of what it was all about. Whatever the truth, it was nothing like Sacha's performance. Actually, over time, Sacha had, once or twice, emulated his father's odd behavior. Well, say a dozen times, but that last one was different. Quite different.

And much, much stranger.

Suzy recalled that long before his peek-a-boo antics, Alec had displayed quite unprecedented imagination. Even as a lad. Long before they'd shared countless experiences for which there was no rational explanation. Only their shared experiences belonged to the inner world, a realm as subjective as ones own subconscious; whereas with Sacha...

Her mind drifted even farther back to the day when she and Alec had first met. When they first saw each other. She smiled at the unexplainable, at the time seemingly forbidden yet so attractive guiles of the opposite sex. They'd both been around fourteen then. She, a lithe, long-haired girl brimming with youthful confidence, he an awkward lad who had little to show for himself other than a magnificent mop of hair. It crowned his head as the branches crown a deciduous tree. She'd half-expected robins to take flight from it. And then he dove into the water and the mop was gone. When he'd come up for air, his crowning glory drifted behind him like a wake following a boat. Luckily, his hair seemed to spring back into life minutes after he climbed aboard his father's yacht. And it turned out that he had a great deal more to show than his mane.

Later. Much later.

But even then... She smiled at the thoughts she's never shared with anyone.

Her mind flashed back to the tango they'd danced at the school prom. She recalled the gaping mouths of other youths as she and Alec swept the floor with contrived arrogance. The others had been capable of little more than twitching, roughly in time with the beat. She and Alec, well, they've been dancing. Really dancing. She admitted later, if only to herself, that the relative rigidity of her movements had not been intentional. It had nothing to do with the Latin rhythms. She'd been scared stiff. Literally. In seconds they'd remained the only couple on the dance floor. The others drifted to adorn the walls.

She shrugged at her memories.

She also recalled responding to Alec's apparent confidence with stiff, jerky movements, worthy of the best professional ballroom dancers she'd seen later on TV. At the time she'd had no idea just how good she'd been. Way back when... when Sacha was not even a spark in his father's eye...

All her memories invoked smiles. It was hard to believe that when they'd met, Alec was still 'two'. In a matter of speaking. He was still Alec and Sandra. It was before he became Alexander. Until he became one...

Sacha's antics were definitely not of the peek-a-boo variety. They were more like the boo with the peek left in abeyance. There was no name for it. Unless you believed in ghosts. Or spirits? Or anything equally as absurd...

It had started, in earnest, just after Sacha's 10th birthday. To celebrate the first decade of their first-born, Grandma had given Sacha two Siamese kittens. Suzy realized later that she shouldn't have done it, but she'd called them Peeka and Boo. Guess why? They were the sweetest bundles of joy Suzy had ever laid eyes on. And although the two played havoc with the furniture, the problem didn't lie with them.

One day, Suzy was reading when the two sprites darted in front of her nose. It wasn't the first time. Only this time they jumped upwards, and seemed to land on something that enabled them to remain suspended in the air for a few seconds, before continuing their wild chase around the room. Moments later Suzy noticed one other thing. Sacha who seconds ago was standing by the window trying to attract the kittens' attention, suddenly found himself by the far wall, on the other side of the bed. Now if this were his father, Suzy would have said: "Oh no! Not the peek-a-boo again."

But it hadn't been Sacha's father. Dad Alec still hadn't returned from the university.

And then, there was the question of the kittens remaining suspended in mid-air, at arms' length from her, by the edge of the bed. Just in front of the space where Sacha appeared a second later.

This was no peek-a-boo. Sacha had not shifted positions at supraluminal speed. She'd witnessed, indeed shared in, a number of strange (to say the least) experiences with Sacha, even with Sacha and her husband—altogether, but all those events had been of the 'inner' variety. They could have been assigned to the inner, the subliminal, the imaginary realm. To joint hallucinations, if you must. We all have them, occasionally, don't we? Well, some of us. We all have stories to tell that only make sense to us. But this?

This was a physical impossibility.

At least in the realm of physics—as she'd known physics. What on Earth would Alec say? Sacha's father was a scientist. An established physicist, with a Ph.D. to his name.

Finally, Suzy gathered all her courage. She knew that she hadn't imagined things. She knew that she was sane. She'd decided to trust her visual perception.

"What happened, Sacha?" She tried to make her voice as normal as she could.

Sacha did not stop playing. The kittens held all his attention. A second later he disappeared again and Boo missed him in full flight. Peeka continued to peek from behind the chair. But no harm came to Boo. Sacha caught him in flight and gently brought him down to his chest. The kitten purred so loudly that Suzy could hear him across the room.

"What happened Sacha?" she repeated.

"What do you mean, Mom?"

"You know what I mean."

She tried to sound stern. It wasn't easy, as she had no idea what it was exactly that she was supposed to be stern about.

"You mean my... my..." Sacha obviously was missing the right words. "What do you mean, Mom?" he repeated, as though playing for time. Then, realizing that he would not get away with pleading ignorance he added: "Dad will explain."

And that was that.

For the whole of next week Suzy could not bring herself to raise the problem with Alec. Sacha continued with the game that the kittens obviously adored, but only after he'd promised not to repeat, whatever it was that he was doing, outside the bedroom doors. Suzy was worried what effect his antics might have on Alicia and Desmond. In spite of Alec's and her own tendency towards periodically eccentric behavior, neither Des nor Alec's mother gave any indication that they suspected anything unusual.

Sacha called the game hide'n seek. He would hide and the kittens would have to find him. Only Sacha's method of hiding was... unusual. He'd become invisible. And, to Suzy's and later Alec's amazement both, Peeka and Boo, continued to find him much faster then either of his parents could. The kittens knew something they didn't. It wasn't fair.

When Sacha's father was about the same age, he already showed an extremely keen, perhaps over-developed imagination. It became so vivid that whatever he'd imagined became real. At least to him—to young Alec. Long before he became Alexander.

And then the problems began in earnest.

One day, Suzy and Alec were on the terrace overlooking the brooding gray rollers drawing towards them over the endless Pacific. The waves seemed to have spent their energies and lapped the shore gently, as though exhausted after a long journey. There was no wind. All was quiet, almost too quiet. Suzy became somewhat drowsy, while Alec, as was his habit, allowed his eyes to drift towards the horizon.

It was then that Sacha disappeared.

One moment he was sitting by the coffee table playing with his Strato Set, the next he wasn't there.

Thankfully, neither Alicia nor Des seemed to have noticed the event. Neither, at first, had Alec nor Suzy. Then, slowly, Alec nudged Suzy on the elbow.

"A good trick that," he murmured, pointing to the Strato structure on the small table.

He was referring to a male interlocking piece insinuating itself into a female receptacle with perfect precision. Suzy snapped out of her sleepy state only to catch her breath. As she watched, the next piece of the Strato puzzle lifted itself from the table, remained poised in the air without any visible means of support; then it drifted towards its destination in the growing construction.

"Easy, girl..."

Alec put his hand on Suzy's arm as leaned over towards the table.

"Come on, son. That's enough of that..."

The next instant first Sacha's hand, holding the next block of brightly colored plastic, then the rest of him reappeared beside them. He seemed as preoccupied with his toy construction as ever.

"Sorry, Dad, I wasn't thinking..."

Neither of his parents made any comments. They could not think of anything wise or profound to say. Sacha was ten at the time. Ten years and three weeks. They both wondered what lay ahead of him. Ahead for them all.

In some ways, Suzy was glad. Had she told Alec about Sacha's hide'n seek frolics, she would have risked her scientifically minded husband telling her to take some time off and relax. He'd have told her that she was a little tired, that she ought to paint a little less and spend more time on the beach. And she would end up throwing an assortment of slippers at him in exasperation. And he would dodge her missiles...

Now Alec had witnessed Sacha's disappearing trick. What she couldn't figure out was why he did not seem disturbed by it. He seemed to have taken it in his stride, as though it was perfectly normal for his first-born to disappear into thin air.

"Actually, it's quite thick. I think we are in for a lengthy drizzle."

"What? What are you talking about?"

Suzy forgot that Alec had the ability to read her thoughts. Not always, and not all her thoughts—but thoughts which were 'pregnant with emotions' and which concerned him. They'd first noticed this ability of his some years ago. It was neither good nor bad. It just was.

"You thought about thin air," he explained.

"Very funny!"

Only she wasn't amused. Sacha was a perfect child. Wonderful, bright, smart, you name it. Only she wished he wouldn't... disappear. Who could tell? Perhaps one day he would disappear and not find his way back? Her eyes were turning moist. What if he...

"Don't be silly, darling. This could not happen. Nothing in the world can disappear."

"He does!"

"It only seems like it. Trust me. Sacha is perfectly all right."

"B-b-but... but..." Now her eyes were completely wet.

"I knew that drizzle was coming," he joked, but walked over and knelt next to Suzy's deck chair. She pressed her face into his chest.

"There, now… there. Trust me Sue. Just trust me."

He might try to explain to his wife what had happened, but in her present emotional state she was unlikely to understand it; and even if she did, she would probably reject his explanation. It had to wait.

For the next few weeks Suzy continued painting. She had an exhibition scheduled for the end of next month and hoped to enlarge on the number of her canvases. She wondered if she could paint a disappearing object. It would certainly be a challenge. She decided to try. She wondered too if she should share her ambition with Alicia. After all, it was Alec's mother who encouraged her interest in painting. Without Alicia she would still be experimenting with new styles, without ever developing her own.

"Name one old master, one impressionist, or even one so-called modern painter, whose work you cannot recognize," Alicia asked innocently.

"How can I name him or her if I cannot recognize him. Her. Whatever…"

"You know very well what I mean," Alicia insisted.

She did. It was a little embarrassing but Alicia was usually right. It would be less embarrassing if Alec's mother were the more experienced painter. In fact, it was she, Suzy, who encouraged Alicia to take up painting. Since then, Alicia had directed her talents towards stimulating the artistic talent latent in young people. She loved doing it and she was good, very good at it. Unfortunately she accomplished this at the expense of her own artistic development. Or perhaps, that was exactly what she was doing. Developing herself as a first-class teacher. Or motivator. Who knows what's written in the stars for us? Most people don't even try to find out.

As Sacha grew, painting became Suzy's passion. At her last exhibition she'd sold nearly half of her latest paintings. First she was flabbergasted, then euphoric, and finally decided to visit the church on the hill where Alicia and Des got married, to thank God for her good fortune. The church, a chapel really, hasn't changed. It was still whitewashed; the winding road leading up the hill to its doors was still overflowing with Bougainvilleas dressed over the low stone walls. On that little hill, time stood still. She liked that. She wondered why. Since the wedding almost ten years ago, she'd never returned there.

Perhaps time was waiting for her.

Suzy was not a religious person, but she did like the padre who refused to commit himself to any particular church. When she got to the chapel, the doors were wide open but the padre was nowhere to be seen. She realized that she'd never taken the trouble to learn his name. A most unprepossessing man. What Suzy really liked about him was his constant smile, his easy-going friendliness and complete absence of moral judgment.

Strange that, she thought, so unprepossessing—yet she could picture him so well after all these years.

She looked around.

A bunch of leaflets in a small wooden box on a table by the door caught her eye. Then she remembered. The padre offered leaflets, with telephones and addresses of, what he smilingly called, his competition. The leaflets had been laying here for ten years. Probably a lot longer. The top ones turned a bit yellow. Suzy's only interest in religion was to protect Sacha from its influence. It wasn't an act of premeditation. She did it impulsively, perhaps intuitively, yet, paradoxically, with a deep if unexplained premonition. Knowing how sensitive Sacha was she was afraid of what religion might do to him. She just felt, felt deeply, that she must protect him at all costs.

Ten years ago she wouldn't have picked up anything that had remotely to do with religion. Now, she was curious. It was with a sort of 'know thy enemy' gesture that she picked up one pamphlet. She was stunned. The list wasn't long but still, it was impressive. The churches, or sects, were listed in vaguely alphabetical order:

Baha'i, Baptist Church, Buddhism, Confucianism, Catholicism, Hinduism, Islam, Judaism, Church of Christ, Church of Christian Science or Christ the Scientist, Church of England, Episcopal Church, Lutheran Church, Mennonite Church, Methodist Church, Moravian Church of America, Orthodox Eastern Church, Pentecostal Church, Presbyterian Church, Seventh Day Adventists, United Church of Christ, The Mormons also known as the Church of Jesus Christ of Latter-day Saints...

On the other side of the circular the list continued with notes on Celtic Revivalists, Druids, International Society of Krishna Consciousness, Jainism, Jehovah's Witnesses, Quakers, Unitarian Universalist Association, Rosicruicianists, Shamanism, Shinto, Sikhism, Taoism, even on Wicca and Witchcraft. Each church or organization has been listed in neat columns and was followed by a few descriptive words, an approximate number of members, and their nearest point of contact.

Suzy was sure that this wasn't the complete list of churches. For a start, all the New Age groups were missing, and she knew they were plentiful. And what of the followers of the great Lao Tsu philosophy? And those who believed in the teaching of the prophet Zarathustra better known as Zoroaster? What of the various Islamic sects, like the Sunnites? The Shiites? What of the Sufis? And the many religions of the African continent? Of the Amazonian jungle? In fact of the Tribal, Aboriginal and Paleo-Pagan Religions? Surely, the Big Churches did not manage to destroy them all. Not yet? Anyway, these were the older, well established churches. Churches that boosted upwards of a few million members.

It's been a long time since Suzy had anything to do with any particular religion. When younger, she'd read avidly on various myths. In fact, she'd been fascinated by them. What she could never accept was what happened to those beautiful legends when they became adopted, or perhaps adapted, by the many religious organizations.

A fleeting memory made her smile.

She recalled a TV program in which a comic-strip hero, Homer Simpson, attempted to explain to his wife why he does not want to go to church on Sunday: "What," he asked, "what if we picked the wrong religion? We'd make God madder and madder!"

It would be almost impossible for an honest person to be a member of any particular church without offending so many others. Oh, she wished them all well, but...

What was it that people expected?

People who attended regular services were one thing, but so many others seemed preoccupied with pointing out what was wrong with all the other religious groups, sects, cults and churches. The Hindus criticized the Christians and the Moslem. The Moslem tried to reduced the Hindu ranks by derailing as many trains in India as they could. In turn, the Hindus were becoming more and more militant. They even dangled an atomic bomb over the Pakistan borders. The Christians were busy asserting *urbi et orbi that* they were the only true religion. The rest, they said, would go to hell.

Suzy glanced at the cross towering over the altar.

"And it's all in your name?" she whispered. There was no mirth in her smile.

Others enjoyed different predilections. The Sikhs seemed preoccupied with their headgear, and other symbols arranged surreptitiously under their clothing. Evidently, they no longer carried those symbols in their hearts. And the Jews? The Jews were so busy asserting their right to the land, which God had given them by a personal, immovable, unchangeable, eternal and inflexible Covenant that they were too busy to criticize anybody else. As long as the 'anybodies' stayed a goodly distance from the exclusive Holy Land.

Unless they were tourists, of course.

And finally there were the various Christian sects, or churches, although what they had to do with Christ's teaching she had no idea. "By this shall all men know that ye are my disciples, if ye have love one to another," she mused: or was it "for one another?" She recalled the phrase vaguely. From what she'd seen, the various groups disliked each other as water dislikes fire. Many of them thought nothing of murdering hundreds of thousands of people; others would shoot, on sight, any woman who might want to abort a one-day-old fetus—thousands of which are aborted, daily, by nature itself.

There were so many names on the pamphlets. So many churches in whose name you could kill.

There was also a brochure issued by the Church of Seven Planes, which offered everyone the opportunity to become an ordained minister, at absolutely no cost, without any need to believe in anything. Once ordained, however, you would be free to start your own church. All expenses tax deductible no doubt. Not bad work if you can get it, she mused. All you had to do was to get rid of your conscience and bingo, you were a big religious Banana. You could even wear a funny hat to impress people.

But this was the least of the world's problems.

Lately it became fashionable for everyone to accuse everyone else of being a terrorist. Mostly on religious grounds. Only she knew that the only grounds that fueled the 'religious grounds' were economic, yet people who practiced various religions seemed the most gullible, and they were the vast majority. They believed anything you threw at them, providing you did it in the name of God. Any God. Of any religion. Not that the so-called believers practiced the tenets their faith. The hardly knew what they were. But they certainly practiced pointing out the iniquities of all the others.

With trembling fingers Suzy replaced the leaflet on the table. The next moment, for no apparent reason, her knees gave way. She leaned against the nearest pew. A sudden pain shot through her, as though a sharp rod of fire had pierced her heart. Then it was gone.

When she got home everyone was out except for Sacha. He was lying on the bed, his legs bent at right angles, swaying gently as though to some strange music. He was reading. As she drew closer her heart missed a beat. Sacha had a dozen books on the bed with him. He was flipping the pages like a windmill in a gusty wind. All the books were on the same subject. She kept these books hidden in an old suitcase under her bed. She'd hidden them purposely.

She'd hidden them to protect her son.

Sacha was thumbing through the old, worn copies of her esoteric library. Once her passion, she hadn't touched them since Sacha was born. She kept them under the bed, here, to minimize the danger of Sacha finding them at home, in LA. By the time she opened her mouth, Sacha put the last book down. His face registered a mixture of amusement and disbelief.

"Hello, Mom. Do people really believe all this stuff?"

There was genuine concern in his voice. For some inexplicable reason Suzy thought she saw, in his eyes, concern for the human race. She shrugged. What nonsense, she thought. He's just a little boy.

***

2
Grandma 'Licia

There were the Baldwins: Suzy, Alexander and Sacha. There was also Alicia, Alec's mother, who married Desmond, a little over a year after Alec's father died of a heart attack. They were the McBrides. Originally, Dr. Desmond McBride, himself a widower, had two sons from a previous marriage. One emigrated to Australia. The other, well, the other was dead. The father and the surviving son hardly kept in touch. It wasn't really the son's fault. Many years ago their father made it very plain that his sons had been directly responsible for their mother's death. No one knew the details, and Desmond wasn't offering any explanations. As for Alicia, since Suzy's parents still lived in Kingston, Ontario, way up in Canada, she took on the job of being the family matriarch. A job, she thought, she performed rather well. At least, no one complained.

Her proximity to Suzy drew the two women together, as though mother and daughter, but what was even more important, as really good, trusting friends.

As for living together, it only happened during summer recesses and, more often than not, during weekends. The protracted family reunions took place at the McBrides' home, in Solana Beach, some 20 miles North of San Diego, fairly close to the Mexican border. The rest of the year the Baldwins stayed in their third-floor condo across the park from Caltech, and the McBrides enjoyed an even better view from the twenty-fourth floor of their rented apartment, only a stone's throw away from the Baldwins. Dr. McBride did not want to own two residences.

"The morre you own the more you'rre tied down. And you do want to travel, don't you, lassie?"

He hardly rolled the 'r's when he was serious. He only pretended at being very serious about taking things a little easier and enjoying life with his 'young bride'. He would enjoy the company of his bride wherever they were. Traveling or not.

The young bride was a grandmother in her middle fifties but she really did look young. In his eyes she still was, and would probably remain, a young lassie, forever.

And thus Alicia regarded Sacha through Grandma's eyes. To her, he was a miniature Alec. His father's nose, eyes, forehead, even the mop of hair... But she also saw Suzy in him. She saw in Sacha his father on the outside and his mother on the inside. There was one fundamental difference. To make Sacha truly his father's son, one would have to die the boy's hair. For while they both, father and son, sported what, in the late sixties, people called an 'afro', Alec's mop was jet black. His son, however, took after his mother. The mop, equal in size and prominence, was resplendent in pure gold. When the sun hit his hair it seemed to glow with an unearthly aura, as though radiating its own light.

Alicia soon discovered that Sacha was so very, very capable in all fields of art. He exhibited, even at such an absurdly young age, an uncanny maturity in the way he viewed art. He liked or disliked certain color combinations. At first he lacked the vocabulary to explain his preferences, later he talked fluently about the balance, harmony, and visual resonance. If an adult said the same things he would have sound stilted, or perhaps as though making an effort to impress the listener. But there was no presumptuous buffoonery in Sacha's opinions. He stated his preferences as simply as if he talked about his beloved Strato Set. He treated colors as toys. One had to arrange them in a certain relationships to each other, or they would collapse. In fact exactly like in his Strato Set.

The *Strato* was a successful marriage of the simplicity of a Lego set with the complexity of Buvös Kocka—the Magic Cube, also known as Rubik's Cube—only on a much larger scale. There was a right way and a wrong way, and only the right way pleased him. The strange thing was that, when Alicia listened to Sacha, the relationships of colours he proposed also pleased her. Only she wasn't quite sure why.

Alicia discovered this affinity for color in Sacha a little after his seventh birthday, but it took another two years before he could vocalize his preferences. As for harmony and resonance, Sacha could whistle or hum the more melodic themes from symphonies after hearing them only once. Sacha definitely displayed a great artistic sensitivity. It was as though he, himself, resonated with music and with colours.

Alicia loved looking after Sacha—though her precocious grandson hardly needed much supervision. She loved looking after him because he was such good company, even for a fifty-year-old.

It wasn't as though Alicia was lonely.

She had Suzy and Alec and of course Desmond. But Sacha was quite different. And it wasn't just his age. Sacha never tried to convince her about anything. He expressed his own views, and rejoiced in the diversity of the opinions of others. From the time he was eight or nine, she talked to him as though he were an adult. He was certainly knowledgeable enough though, admittedly, his knowledge was derived almost exclusively from books. It was theoretical—untarnished by the compromises which adults imposed on life in general. Listening to him Alicia noticed what an enormous act we put on, particularly when talking to others. Unwittingly, or purposefully, we all try to impress others with our best side. Be it with our real or imagined talents, with our knowledge of certain subjects, or just some contrived sense of importance. Some do so more than others, but we all do it.

And Sacha never insisted on being right.

"No one is ever right or wrong," he once said. "We just look at reality from different points of view." He was eight when he'd said that.

A year later, she and Sacha were sitting on the terrace, Alicia doing a watercolor, Sacha's eyes following the convoluted activities of the seagulls. He touched on related subject.

"You know, Grandma, the seagulls drop whatever they have in their beaks to attack another bird, who might have a bigger piece. Why do you think they do that?"

"I suppose they are more hungry, they want a bigger piece?" Alicia tried lamely.

Sacha did not appear to have heard her. For a while he continued to follow the birds' movements with great attention.

"They just don't understand," he said after a minute or two.

"Who doesn't understand what?" Alicia asked, her mind back on her watercolor.

"The birds. They don't understand that there is exactly enough for every one of them. And they could conserve their energy if they were satisfied with their portion."

For a moment Alicia was lost.

"Enough food, you mean?"

"Yes, Grandma. There is exactly enough of everything for everybody. It cannot be otherwise. There would be no harmony in the world if it were otherwise."

And with this Sacha went back to his Strato. In Strato things had to be just right, or the structure would collapse.

Alicia stopped painting and thought about the youngster's words. Enough for everyone of everything. If only we stopped running around. Had Sacha read something like this somewhere? Did he regard the world as a well-oiled machine set on automatic? Or did he mean that we are all looked after by some Higher Source. '...the fowls of the air, they sow not, neither do they reap...' Alicia didn't remember the exact quotation. She'd known it once. Or it could have been some parson preaching at a Sunday Service. 'Be like birds, carefree...' That's what Sacha seemed to be saying.

Only the seagulls weren't carefree. They fought for every scrap, as if some other bird were shortchanging them. How stupid. How very much like the human race.

Some time later Sacha answered her question as though he'd read her thoughts and stored them for future reference. Sacha often did that—or seemed to. His concept of time was very different from anyone she'd ever met.

"The world is set on automatic," he'd said. "But the results of the setting are not always predictable. There is the element of free will. Not to deny our destiny, only in the individuality we breathe into it."

Over the years, Alicia heard a number of such, hard to explain, statements. Most of them she kept to herself. Talking about them would be silly, not knowing if what she'd heard was really so profound, or if she just assigned extra weight to them because they came from her own grandson.

Or, on occasion, because she had just a drop too much of her favorite *Chardonnay*.

From the time Sacha started to move around, Alicia developed a passion for painting her one and only grandson. She had no idea why Alec and Sue didn't have more children. It might have had something to do with close to seven billion people polluting the world with their insipid presence. Or it may have been because someone once told her that each American child, by the time he dies, will have polluted the Earth with the equivalent of some fifty Hindu or African children. We were the world's greatest contaminators. We were slowly drowning in our own offal, our excrement. And pulling the rest of the world into the latrine on top of us.

At moments of such reflection, she was glad that Alec was her only son.

She painted Sacha in watercolor, oil and acrylic. She drew him with pastel, crayon, ink applied with a split bamboo stick, and even using an ordinary ball-pen. All her attempts to immortalize Sacha were imbued with a single characteristic. She was depicting Sacha in constant motion, as though he were in more than one place at any one time; as if Sacha were moving and Alicia was snapping rapid-fire photos of him. At first, the reason was fairly obvious. First, his palms and knees, later his feet, were in constant motion. Only when he got his first Strato Set had she managed to do some parts of him while he was actually sitting down.

Even before Sacha had shown his prodigious affinity for colour, he'd already become Alicia's favorite critic. Not with childish comments, but often with quite fascinating insights. Such insights might well have been reasonably natural from a knowledgeable adult, but had been always surprising from a young boy. Comments like... "why don't you pretend, Grandma, that I am not really here. Why don't you just paint the light reflected from my body..." Or, on another occasion: "...It's not really me, Grandma. You can't really paint *me*."

"And just why wouldn't I be able to paint just you, darling?" she'd asked.

"Because I am not really here."

"And may I ask where exactly are you, dear?"

"I'm... I am..."

But it wouldn't come out. It was good to see that even the most precocious child she'd ever met was occasionally at a loss for words. But the silence only lasted seconds. Then, the words would come at a flood.

"What you see is my shadow. My body is my shadow," Sacha offered, but his tone carried misgivings.

"I thought you said that I am to paint light reflected from you. How can you be a shadow if you reflect light?" Alicia was probing, perhaps not taking Sacha's words very seriously.

"I don't know. But both things I said are right, Grandma," Sacha affirmed, nodding his head as if to add weight to his words. "I am a shadow cast by my thoughts."

Alicia had no idea where Sacha found such ideas. It couldn't have been Alec. Her son was a physicist, through and through. She'd also noticed that from the time Sacha was born, Suzy had refused to get involved in any discussions, which were not "down to earth". Which were not firmly anchored in the here-and-now.

"I will not be a party to my son missing his boyhood," Suzy told her.

She was right, of course, but...

Alicia knew that Sacha read an awful lot. He had the ability to read at an incredible speed. There were courses on speed-reading, she knew, but to Sacha the ability was innate. On occasion she would leave a book on the table, and a short while later Sacha expressed his opinion about it. She recalled one such occasion. Sacha must have been about eleven at the time. Alicia found him replacing a book on the shelf. She was just in time to see the jacket sliding into its designated position.

"He was wrong, Grandma."

"Who might that be, my dear?" Alicia wondered what was coming. Sacha had just replaced the complete works of Shakespeare. Obviously he couldn't have read the whole tome in one session. He must have just opened it at random.

"Hamlet."

"And why was Hamlet wrong?"

"He thought that he must die to dream." Sacha threw over his shoulder already busy reaching for a different volume. It was about the time when his parents withdrew Sacha from school. The teachers said, quite simply, that they had nothing to teach him. Suzy suspected that the teachers had been repeatedly embarrassed by Sacha's knowledge. At home, in LA, Sacha read three or four books every day. Here, in Solana Beach, in bad weather he kept up the average. They made biweekly trips to the library in San Diego just to satisfy his juvenile hunger.

"He means a different kind of dream, darling."

"Then why did he say 'To die, to sleep; perchance to dream'?" Sacha quoted from memory. If Sacha had a weakness it was that all too often he'd taken the written word literally.

Alicia wasn't a Shakespearean buff. She was not in a position to argue. Even after being forced by an eleven-year-old to voice her opinion on the most famous soliloquy in English literature, which, to her later embarrassment, she hasn't recognized. Alicia preferred to read novels.

"And anyway, he was wrong to start with," Sacha added as an afterthought. "You cannot stop being. You are."

This time Alicia connected. Sacha must have been referring to the famous 'To be, or not to be,' quandary. But she still had no idea what Sacha meant. It sounded 'adult', but it could have been just a precocious child's patter. Altogether, that 'dreaming' and 'being' business was a bit over her head. Alicia took life as it came, and any notion of existential philosophy filled her with dread. She preferred a good, strong cup of tea. She loved life too much to dissect it and risk injury. Alicia was born, and for most of her life managed to remain, carefree. Like the fowl of the air, she thought smiling. She could relate to Sacha's opinion about the stupid seagulls fighting over more than they could eat, but this...?

If Sacha made sense, then it sounded a little too good to be true. Alicia had the same problem with her grandson earlier, when he encouraged her to paint reflected light. That's what the impressionists had claimed they were doing. And impressionists were her favorite artists. But to her knowledge, Sacha had never seen an impressionist's painting. There may have been some books in LA, but most of them belonged to Suzy's earlier studies. By now Suzy had moved on. By now her adopted daughter was more into expressionism. Suzy was too definitive, too precise in her opinions to develop the gentle impressionistic touch.

At Solana Beach, Alicia's favorite time was early morning. The fog didn't bother her. In fact, in a strange way it took her to her youth. She'd met Alec's father in England. And in those early days, morning fog was to be expected; especially, during the winter months. It was the substance of which Dickens and Conan Doyle were made of. Now, on those misty Pacific mornings, she'd sit alone on the terrace and wait for Sacha.

On weekends, men preferred late mornings. Alec—to catch up on sleep, Des—just to catch up. Her husband wasn't getting any younger. He was still active but at a different pace. Suzy also liked to linger in bed a little longer, even during the summer months. Perhaps knowing that Alicia would look after Sacha gave her an excuse. Or perhaps she just waited for the sun to win its diurnal battle with the moisture suspended in the air.

For Alicia it was just the opposite.

Not working in LA, and her own youngster having weaned from her embrace some twenty-five years ago, she was well rested even before they got to the oceanfront. She and Sacha spent the mornings sipping fresh orange juice on the terrace, going for walks along the beach, and occasionally taking a pre-breakfast swim. She didn't like the last option mostly because Sacha, in spite of all his talents, was quite unable to comprehend the concept of danger. He would venture into the oncoming waves, dive underneath them, and then ride them back using his body as a surfboard. Alicia could hardly look when he did that. What if the wave broke on him just as he dove under? What if he was thrown onto the coarse sand? He could be skinned alive. No. She had to play her cards in such a way that on days when the waves looked dangerous she would convince Sacha to stay on the terrace and play or just talk.

Sacha didn't seem to mind. In fact, with the exception of being told to eat certain foods "because they are good for you," he was a very easygoing child. And Sacha definitely liked to talk. Not prattle, not go on nineteen-to-a-dozen, but actually discuss whatever subject she raised. If he didn't know anything on the particular theme he would say so and nothing would induce him to say a single word about the matter. He remained mum until Alicia gave up and changed the subject herself. Otherwise, his opinions were always fresh, not to say unique.

During summer months, Alicia had organized an Art School for the local children. Not exactly a school, but a place where local children could express themselves, without resorting to pastimes that, all too often, landed them in the local jail. Until then, the children had no playground, literally no place to play, let alone get exited by the very idea of fine arts.

She was not an art teacher, but she's painted for a number of years. And she loved children. Soon she provided them with an environment in which those who wanted could find the means and opportunity to develop their talents. Originally the classes were held on the beach, or, if raining, on the terrace of her house. But within a couple of years, the number of children had increased so as to risk her terrace collapsing under their weight. Maria, the dear, dear Maria, originally a maid, a reliable housekeeper, and later Alicia's most trusted companion, arranged for Alicia to have access to the local school, to conduct her classes. Initially, no one imagined that children would want to go to school during holidays. That's not what holidays are for, they'd said. No one will come, they'd said.

"Da lady from LA don't know what she'a doing…"

The doubters hadn't met Alicia.

First of all, all children were welcome. But only those who really showed interest in art could remain. The nucleus of students has already created a cadre, who acted as the spearhead to spread the gospel of St. Alicia.

"Art," she said, "is only for the few. It is a gift. A privilege."

Alicia believed that everyone could paint. Perhaps badly, at first, but everyone had some sort of ability to create. The children poured onto the paper, or canvas, their desires, their dreams, their innermost secrets.

They were true artists.

Since turning six, Sacha accompanied Alicia to her school. For some strange reason he didn't want to paint himself. But he was there, he looked, he absorbed. What interested him were not the paintings, but the painters. Being tutored at home, he was learning how to relate to other children. In time he became a 'confessor' to most of them. He had a great affinity for making everyone feel important. It wasn't a put-on front. He hated what some called "people skills". He really loved those kids. And it showed.

And then Sacha met Benita.

She was a peculiar girl: as shy and reticent—as she was pretty. She regarded Sacha with enormous dark-brown eyes, in which wonder seemed suspended in some peculiar time-warp. For the last few weeks, she drew with pencil and charcoal at a level well above her age. She exhibited a wonderful sense of proportion, a great sensitivity of line and a mature understanding of light and shade. But for the life of her, Alicia couldn't teach her how to use colours. Once Benita touched a brush, with a few strokes she was apt to destroy the base sketch, which she'd created with such facility.

Then Sacha spoke to her.

The two youngsters sat opposite each other, mostly just looking into each other's eyes. The girl's expression hardly changed, though her irises seemed to dart here and there, as if she was in some daydream, looking at things invisible to others. It made Alicia think of REM sleep, only Benita's eyes were wide open.

Nothing happened that day, but a week later, the girl produced the most wonderful painting. Some time later Alicia asked Sacha what was it that they've been taking about.

"We weren't taking, Grandma," he replied defensively.

That was true. They weren't taking. Not as such. But in some way or another they were communicating. Alicia said as much. She'd also told him how, since Benita 'didn't speak to him', she couldn't use color.

"Oh, that?" Sacha smiled in total innocence. "It's just the way she was looking before, Grandma," he told her.

Alicia half expected Sacha to assure her that there was nothing organically wrong with the girl's eyesight. But Sacha said something quite different.

"I showed her how the birds look at things. And the bees. Then the fish. And then she understood."

Which was more than Grandma 'Licia did.

***

3
Alexander Baldwin Ph.D.

Alec did not merely love his son. Sacha embodied the world, the reality, to which Alec had aspired all his life. From the time he was a little boy himself, Alec dreamed of being able to do what Sacha did. Only Sacha did it with such facility as to deny the need for any effort. His son seemed to oscillate between the earthly and the inner realities as though they were all co-existent, as though he could change from one to another at the push of a button. At having control over his dreams, his son, Sacha, was an accomplished Master.

Alec didn't merely love his son. He was in awe of him.

And he admired him, also.

Most parents admire their children to a degree. Most parents dream that their children might accomplish what they themselves have failed to accomplish. They want their children to embody the traits, which they wished they could exhibit themselves. Most parents ended up disappointed. Either that, or they diluted their expectations to reconcile their need for success and for their peace of mind.

Alec did neither.

Sacha was so much more than Alec could possibly have imagined. Before he'd learned to walk, he could fly. Before he'd learned to manipulate his imagination, or his mind, he had taken him and Suzy a step further, to a reality that neither of them knew even existed. He raised them both to the realm of the Undiscovered Country, which seemed accessible only to the truly innocent, truly unspoiled, unpolluted by the exigencies of earthly survival. It belonged to those who never succumbed to a dualistic state of consciousness. When Alec and Sandra had reunited, they became aware of the futility of attempting to treat life as a battleground for the survival of the fittest. Alec became aware of his immortality, not here, not on Earth, but in realms that most people didn't know existed. Some saints, lamas, yogis of the Far East, and poets, spoke of them. But they spoke in parables, in symbols indecipherable to him or other earthly mortals.

It was through Sacha that Alec had learned that as long as you regard the Earth as your true home, you remain a mortal. Everything, which you regard as you, as your personality—your possessions, your talents, aspirations, desires—all that is transient. None of it is important. Living is important. The process of becoming. Nothing is important until you discover your purpose and take up the reins towards its fulfillment. No mater how simple, how seemingly prosaic. It could be a single deed, a single act of kindness towards someone towards whom you carried a debt. It could be advancing the level of consciousness of someone near you just that much, that little. But no one in the whole universe could do it for you. You and you alone had the necessary vibrations, the necessary state of consciousness, which enabled you to change that particular discord into a harmony of angelic joy.

And all this Alec had learned from Sacha.

Sometimes on their walks along the beach, their chats in LA after a heavy day of lectures, and sometimes just by observing him. Sacha was quite incapable of not acting according to his beliefs. He didn't practice his philosophy as one practices one's job or plays a piano. Sacha was the embodiment of his philosophy. He was what he said, and he said what he was. If there were a limitation in Sacha's make up, it was his inability to understand how could others do otherwise.

Sacha has still not lost his innocence.

Alexander Baldwin, Ph.D. was also known as the Mop. Hardly surprising if you witnessed the haystack he cultivated atop his pate. It may not have been as exuberant as in his younger days, but it was still voluminous enough to spot him from a distance. Although quite muscular, Alec's height and innate slimness made him look lankier and thus younger than he was. With the exception of a bout with an undiagnosed syndrome, which for a short time left Alec paralyzed from the waist down, he'd always enjoyed quite exceptional health.

In his late thirties, he could easily hold his own with men ten years younger. Especially on the tennis court. And even more so in his willingness and ability to dive, head first, into new scientific theories, which would be looked upon with caution and mistrust by his older colleagues. Except for Desmond, of course.

But Des always was something else.

Until recently, Alec had been looking forward to the day when he and Sacha would face each other across the net, or together face others in doubles. It did not appear that Sacha shared his father's dream. While perfectly fit, an excellent swimmer and an accomplished jogger, Sacha did not seem to show any predisposition towards sports for their own sake. When Sacha swam, he seemed to be examining the behavior of his body in the water. When jogging, it was mostly to keep his dad company. Even on the tennis court Sacha was reasonably proficient, but his heart wasn't in it. He did it for dad.

And so it was.

Physical activity for its own sake seemed strange to Sacha, as though redundant, certainly not requiring his special attention. When Sacha's age, Alec had already won the school doubles championship. Of course, Sacha didn't go to school. Yet, in spite of all this, there was a great deal more Alec shared with his son than with any other person in the world. Except for Suzy, of course. But even then with Sacha, Alec crossed new borders; he expanded his horizons.

"Come on, Dad, let's swing."

'Swinging', in Sacha's vernacular, was to oscillate between two nebulas and observe the differences between their expanding gasses. That, obviously, was in the Far Country. An inner realm, which Sacha much favored over the Home Planet. Sacha adopted his father's names for those two inner realities, although he thought the name for Undiscovered Country was vastly inadequate. He preferred to refer to it as a Plane, or even a Zone, something that did not limit this state of consciousness in any way. Sometimes Sacha called it the Undiscovered Kingdom, or Realm.

The Home Planet was a reality where your dreams ruled supreme. It was a place where your emotions found satisfaction, where you rested from the vicissitudes of earthly life. You could call it the realm of imagination. Like the physical reality, the Home Planet was also replete with changes. It seemed to subsist in a constant state of flux. Only on the Home Planet you controlled them faster and to a much greater degree. For ordinary mortals, such as Alec regarded himself, Home Planet was a haven as well as heaven. It was also a place where, on occasion, he and Suzy and Sacha met to impregnate themselves with tangible beauty. It was their Real Home away from home.

Sacha preferred the Far Country.

For Alec, the Far Country was a reality to be admired, to astound one, to fill one with wonder. For Sacha it was an altogether different realm.

The ever-expanding universe was his true playground. It was as wide, and as deep, and as great, and as young, or as old, as he cared to make it.

It was a realm of pure mind.

Here Sacha flexed his creative muscles. Here he could breathe life into a pattern, into a mathematical formula, a concept that was untried, as yet, by anyone.

"Here I create," he told his father. "Here I'm the Creator."

This was his true playground.

Here Sacha brought the universes into being, and dissolved them with a wave of his mental arm. He felt good here. He felt that he belonged. At least, whenever he left the Undiscovered Plane. On the rare occasions when they traveled together, Alec could do little more then to keep up. Out here his son had already outgrown his father by the time he was six years old. Later, there was little point traveling to the Far Country with Sacha. Alec's mind could no longer accept concepts that appeared to stand in direct opposition to his knowledge anchored in the lower realms.

Alec missed the freedom he once had. To a boy, nothing seemed impossible. Especially here—in the Far Country. Alec smiled as his mind drifted to the time he was thirteen himself.

It had been a very good year. It was the year he'd met Sandra. His father had bought a yacht. Later he'd met Suzy who never left his life. Not for long, anyway. And Sandra? Sandra, he now knew, was his own Inner Self. She was his Anima, that part of him which gave him life, which enabled him to travel the inner worlds almost at will. He recalled the moment when he and Sandra became reunited. It was his coming of age—the moment when he became aware of his immortality. As a boy he externalized her, and then they were one again. He would never forget that moment. A moment beyond time, eternal, yet as vivid today as when he was a lad of thirteen...

"I love you my Prince..." she'd whispered...

He recalled Sandra's very last emotive thought coming from the outside of his own being. And then he'd whispered with the same ardor:

"I love you for ever more, my Princess. You are my life."

In the next segment of eternity Alec and Sandra, became Alexander. Was it really so long ago? It seemed like only yesterday. It also seemed that Sacha was born but days ago. So it seemed...

All has changed in Alec's life on the day on which his son called him 'dad' for the first time.

"Did you hear that, Sue? He called me dad. DAD!"

"Well, I suppose that makes an honest woman of his mother?" But she looked definitely pleased. Perhaps even proud?

Alec enjoyed many inner trips he shared with his son even if, on occasion, he couldn't grasp exactly what his son was about. At least until it dawned on him that Sacha was not visiting other realms, but creating them. Traveling together was as close as Alec got to his personal concept of ecstasy. Others had different names for it. Bliss, Nirvana, Samadhi... there were others, but the terms were so subjective that they were likely to mean different states to different people.

For Alec it was also a condition wherein, at least for a while, his mind discarded all limitations.

At the Tech, the California Institute of Technology, Alec was a regular lecturer—a full professor of physics, Head of the Department. He resisted the appointment, but Desmond told him that he couldn't trust anyone else not to fill the young minds with junk.

"Don't forrrget your inspirrration," Dr. McBride continued to roll his r's when occasion commanded. "Can you think of anyone on the staff, orr anywherre for that matterr, who would admonish his own students to mistrrust his own worrds?"

For a moment Alec was lost. Then he remembered. His own role model, Richard Feynman once told his students to learn, from science, that they should doubt the experts. Dr. McBride was right. He was ready to pass the reins to a younger man. He had chosen Alec. And to plan his own future, Alec had to put in some time as professor with a full tenure. Alec couldn't refute both, Dr. McBride and Dr. Feynman. He agreed.

In his spare time, Alec continued to develop comparative theories by attempting to find new analogies between matter and energy. Or, more accurately, between matter, energy, space and time. He was also postulating different behavior patterns, which energies must manifest under different gravity conditions. As for instance the energy patterns within the neutron stars and black holes. In all his Far Country exploits he'd never come across a Black Hole. Not even from a great distance. It was as though there was no such entity in the Far Country.

Alec recalled the incident that Suzy confessed she'd been reticent to tell him about. It concerned the flying Strato blocks, or later, the Peeka and Boo behaviour. They had been sitting in the living room, after dinner, Vivaldi's Four Seasons adding to the peasant atmosphere. Suzy switched off the music and sat on a chair facing Alec. She'd looked as thought she meant business.

"Really, you must believe me, Ali, it really happened."

"Of course, darling, I've been teaching him slight of hand for some time now."

"I'm serious!" She'd raised her voice.

Alec knew she was, only he'd long given up being surprised by anything his son did or said. He only hoped that the 'unusual' occurrences would remain in the family. It was too early to expose Sacha to the possible ridicule of others. For all he knew, there might have been some sort of evolutionary quirk that was taking place all over the world.

"Don't I wish he could believe it myself," he mused, at the time.

Frankly, Alec also knew that if he continued to make light of Sacha's uncanny behavior, he would expose himself to a salve of flying objects propelled by his dear wife. Whereas Suzy matured over the years in many ways, she has not as yet gained full control over her volatile temper. When suitably stimulated, she was still apt to pick up the most

convenient missile in her immediate vicinity, and aim it at
him with great precision.

Alec, to escape injury, judiciously, and just as quickly,
chose to adopt a different stance. By politely agreeing with
Suzy's story he hoped to dissipate her tension. And, quite
honestly, he would only really believe in Sacha's purported
invisibility if and when he'd witnessed it with his own eyes.
Or didn't witness it—with his eyes, that is. If he saw that he
didn't see him.

He didn't find it easy spending his waking hours
lecturing on theoretical physics and then having his own son,
with a sweep of his tiny hand make minced-meat of the
proven, established science or, at the very least, of the
official, established version of it.

"Sacha, Sacha…" he whispered, his tone wavering
between bewilderment and admiration.

It wasn't often that his son's exploits and his work
overlapped. He remembered, how worried Suzy was when
she became aware of Sacha's disappearances. Most people
couldn't accept that it was physically possible. In fact, Alec
suspected, it had to do with light. A long time ago he'd tried
to explain to Suzy that by polarizing photons, we can make
light coming from certain angles undetectable to the human
eye.

"Light travels in straight lines. Our Polaroid sunglasses
only transmit photons traveling in a specific direction. If we
could affect the polarization of light, it should be theoretically
possible to become invisible, at certain angles," he tried
desperately.

"But how does he do that?" Suzy's eyes were growing
larger.

"I'm afraid you have to ask him that."

Alec was a little nonplused. He knew the theory but not
the practical application. That is the problem with theoretical
physics. You postulate a theory and then you must wait for
others to back it up with laboratory experiments. There are

some aspects of Einstein's theories that are only now being confirmed.

"But how does he do that?" Suzy insisted. "You must have some idea?"

Alec had some idea, but drawing a page full of equations wouldn't help. His ideas were mathematical. He thought in terms of mathematics. He told her as much.

"Don't blame me, daring, blame Pythagoras. He started it." Actually he didn't. The Greeks espoused mathematics as a philosophical tool long before the Pythagorean School. But the detail was of no consequence. "Sue, please don't worry. After all, it doesn't do him any harm, does it?"

"How do I know? I can't see him!"

There was little more he could add. He told her that as long as Sacha returned from his invisible state in one piece, she could treat it as a visit to the Home Planet or the Far Country.

"After all, the ancient myths, which you like so much, are full of people winking in and out of our reality..." he tried desperately.

"I hate esoteric history. I hate myths. I hate religions. I hate... " And her eyes filled with tears.

He had no idea what brought this outburst about. He tried to console her as best he could. There was really no use giving her a mass of equations that would, possibly, shed light on Sacha's apparent ability. He wasn't sure they would help even if she could understand them.

"There, there, I love you, darling." He stroked her golden hair. "There, there..."

Just then Peeka hopped on her knees. It helped. It was very hard to be miserable with a kitten purring on your lap. Boo was nowhere to be seen. Perhaps he too became invisible.

Suzy wanted desperately for Sacha to be a normal boy. Like other boys. Like any boy who plays and acts and talks like a boy his age.

Sacha did none of these things.

Since Sacha was born, Alec was twice more nominated for the Nobel Prize in physics, this time for the Theory of Information. All who knew him were sure that he would at least make the short list. Actually the short list is prepared not by the Nobel Committee itself only by an advisory committee, mostly professors of history and political science. The advisors do not really make recommendations but examine the suitability of the candidate, which could be an individual or an organization.

"So what do they really do, Dad?" There were very few things that lay outside Sacha's sphere of interest. He actually stopped reading a book when he posed the question. He was serious.

"There may be literally hundreds of candidates submitted. After all, the Nobel Prize in not only a sign of great recognition, but one-and-a-half million dollars US is no chicken feed either, son."

Alec was more interested in the dollars than in the recognition. Now, his name was sufficiently well known, though official recognition of his Theory of Information wouldn't do any harm, either. On the other hand, with $1.5 dollars he could do a lot of good for youngsters, who had no access to science at present. The so-called popular science was becoming much more popular than science.

"I could do with a nice sailing boat, too," he muttered to himself. He saw Sacha at the helm while he leaned back in the cockpit, propped up against the doghouse. Suzy, in the scantiest bikini, serving him a Scotch on the rocks...

"So anyone can submit a name?" Sacha wouldn't let go.

"What's that? Ah, yes. You have someone in mind?" Alec looked down at his son whose face remained serious. As Sacha did not rise to the bite, he continued. "Practically... or at least a great many people."

"Who?"

"Well, virtually all the politicians, leaders of peace research institutes..."

"No, Dad," Sacha interrupted. "I mean for the prize in science."

"That's easy. The university chancellors, professors of social science, history, philosophy, law, theology..."

"What has social science got to do with physics? Or, for that matter, philosophy or law, or theology?"

"Nothing, but I thought..."

"It's O.K, Dad. I know. So Granddad could only name you after he became the Chancellor?"

"That's right, son. Before that he was a nobody. Like you and I."

Actually Desmond was appointed the Chancellor of Caltech months after Alec became his assistant.

"And then what?" For some reason, Sacha really wanted to know. It seemed that he was less interested in who got the prize or for what, as in the process itself.

"Then, once the short list is established, the Committee of five makes their decision."

"Committee of five?"

"Yes, they are appointed for a six-year term by Storting––that's the Norwegian Parliament."

Sacha's eyes lit up. "I knew it!" he exclaimed. "I knew it," he repeated with deep satisfaction. Sacha was forming an opinion of how the world worked. Who pushed which buttons, who made the decisions, and so forth. Recently he'd been pestering Granddad and Alicia on similar subjects. He wanted to know what being human was all about.

"You did?" Alec wasn't sure what egg he'd just laid.

"It all comes down to politics. If you look at the various laureates, I bet at least half of them will be politically motivated. The other half might have a chance. It would be politically incorrect to make them all politically biased."

And Sacha dropped the subject. He was twelve years old when he'd raised it. He never asked anything about Nobel or any other prize again. Alec could have told him that past

Nobel Prize laureates could also nominate the candidates, which broadened the field. But then, he would also have to tell him about nominating privileges of the present and past members of the Nobel Committee, as well as the present and past advisors at the Norwegian Nobel Institute. That would muddy the political waters even more.

"Hey, it's their money!" he tried to lighten up.

Alec smiled as he remembered Desmond telling him about his failure to be selected for the third time for the Information Theory. It was some years ago.

"After all, m'lad, you'rrre not quite two hundred and thirty-four yearrrs old, arrre ye'now."

For a moment he remembered having been quite lost. Then it came to him. They'd talked about it the previous week. The 2002 Nobel Prize in Physics prize was awarded to three gentlemen. A 71, a 76, and another who was 87 years old. Together that came to 234 years. So if he wanted to keep the prize all to himself, and if seniority was any factor in the selection process, then he might as well not hold his breath.

As for Alec's nominations, Dr. McBride was responsible for the last one, and his good friend the Chancellor of MIT for the previous ones. Since he got a piece of the joint Prize for the work on the Unified Field Theory, twice more Alec had been bypassed for the more fashionable, less controversial trends in science. Perhaps they were political. Alec had no idea. He managed to keep his physics as far away from politics as he possibly could. Perhaps this was a mistake. Politicians awarded funds for research. They were very powerful. Sacha was right.

Alec felt disdain for power.

As for his field of endeavor, he suspected that people wanted something more tangible, something that they could measure, weigh; feel with their instruments. The Information Theory was above all that. As was Alec's preliminary work on the compressed wave theory. If you applied the principles of the two theories, much of the mystery, which stunned the theoretical physicists for generations, would dissipate. Yet you couldn't prove that the theory as such was right any more then you could disprove it. You could use it but you had to do it on faith. Scientists didn't like doing that. It wasn't scientific, they said. It was dangerous, though the only thing that seemed in danger were the well-established theories.

"Nothing, *nothing,* impedes the progress of science as much as the scientific establishment," Desmond once said. "With few exceptions, all scientists should die young. They never have an original idea after they turn thirty, anyway."

Good old Desmond.

It seemed that the old Prof. was right. What Des forgot to mention was that once past thirty, the very same, revolutionary, progressive scientists spent the rest of their lives making sure that no one upset their scientific apple cart. Any progress in science, again with few exceptions, is due to youngsters who seldom succeed against the stonewalling by their illustrious seniors. Then, when they turn eighty, the establishment catches up with them and awards them the Nobel Prize.

As time went by, Alec began to crawl into a protective shell. He was tired of repeating, *ad nauseam,* the same lectures although, by some strange twist of fate, people never grew tired of hearing them. Except for the scientists. He supposed his colleagues had heard them all before. But the 'ordinary' people, without a vested professional interest, filled the halls to overflowing wherever he gave open lectures.

Allover the world.

There have been moments when Alec wanted more. He wanted someone to pick up the challenge and take his theory a step further. Some tried. But people with enough experience didn't, and those without it couldn't. A catch 22. Perhaps young minds weren't quite ready for him yet, even as old minds were already too old.

And then, just before Sacha's fourteenth birthday, there was an incident that made Alec think again about the purpose of life. The two of them had been walking along the beach when a large motorboat run down a swimmer. The swimmer's body was scooped out of the water and thrown some ten or more yards into the air. It splashed down way behind the speeding boat. Apparently the motorboat was a hydroplane with water skis, which were lowered to raise the boat for planing at high speeds. It was at the moment of rapid acceleration that the accident occurred.

"He thought he'd hit a submerged log," Sacha said.

"How do you know?" Alec was disgusted with the boatman's behavior. He hated motorboats on principle. They were noisy, smelly and, apparently, they killed people. "The son-of-a-bitch came too close to the shore."

"He's innocent. No one ever swims that far out, Dad."

"So?" Alec was still livid. "This guy will never swim again, period."

"Oh, he'll be all right," Sacha said with confidence.

"You mean he survived this powerful impact?" Alec asked, his voice rising in incredulity.

"Oh, no, Dad." Sacha smiled with definite amusement. "No one could survive such an impact, as you call it. Our ah... bodies are much too fragile for that." Sacha still sounded amused. His callousness was getting on Alec's nerves.

"I don't find murder funny, son," he said more sternly than he'd intended.

"I'm sorry, Dad. You are right, of course." Sacha nodded and remained silent.

Even as they looked towards the ocean, a Coastal Patrol boat was speeding towards the man whose body was floating close to mile off shore. As they watched, the corpse was lifted on board. From what they could see from this distance, the patrolmen didn't even try to resuscitate him. He must have died on impact. For some reason, the body remained afloat till the Coastal Patrol fished him out of the water.

Alec and Sacha turned slowly and walked off. For a few minutes they walked in silence. Then Alec stopped again and regarded his son. He knew him to be sensitive, caring, and certainly not callous. What on earth could have amused him back there?

"I wasn't talking about the man's body, Dad."

Sacha had an unnerving habit of reading his father's thoughts. Even the most private ones—providing they concerned him. He'd said some time ago that listening to peoples' thoughts that didn't concern him would be impolite. He'd failed to explain how he knew what type the thoughts were until he'd listened to them.

Alec was trying to work out Sacha's latter assurance.

"I don't see people as physical objects, Dad. It would be like worrying about a pair of pants that are ready for disposal. It simply doesn't matter. What matters is whether the pants served you well. If they've served the purpose for which they'd been made."

"Are you comparing a human life to a pair of pants?" This was getting to be too much.

"No, of course not." There was a moment's silence. Then Sacha tried again. "As a scientist you know that the body consists of a number of chemicals held together by biochemical and electromagnetic bonds..."

"How on earth did you know that?"

Sacha was right, of course. The moment Alec asked the question he realized it must have sounded silly. Obviously his son must have read it somewhere. God knows he went through all the books at home, the local library, and the extensive library at Caltech.

"Quite," Sacha agreed. "So if you were to think of the man's body in those terms, you wouldn't give it much weight, would you, Dad?"

"You are leading up to man being more than the sum of his parts," Alec nodded in spite of himself.

"Not at all. Man is none of his parts. Any more than his old pants are."

They walked on in silence. A moment later Alec saw his son flying over a lustrous surface of an almost absurdly serene lake. They don't make lakes like that on Earth. Not even mirrors. Somehow, they found themselves on the Home Planet. Alec spread his arms, gave himself a gentle push and joined his son. They soared up and down, swirled in spiral descents only to rise again towards the enormous sun.

"Careful, son. Remember what happened to Icarus," Alec's voice was filled with joy and wonder as only the Home Planet can inspire.

"I really don't like being careful. I don't think this is what it's all about..."

Alec was still wondering if Daedalus could really have been held accountable, when he noticed that they were both walking along the beach. The moment of illusion had past.

Illusion? It was much too real for that.

Alec looked over his shoulder. There was no sign of the Coastal Patrol. There were also no people staring towards the sea, as though waiting for the next chapter of the gory incident to unfold.

"Was there an accident, back there?" he murmured under his breath.

"Was there, Dad?"

There and then, for the first time, Alec really understood Sacha's point of view. He was not like any of the people he'd ever known. He was like the others in as much as he wore a similar "pair of pants". Sacha that walked the Earth, by his side, was but a shadow of his real self. Even on the Home Planet his 'body' was a glorified version of the earthly Sacha. A version, Alec suspected, created for his and Suzy's benefit.

Sacha, regardless of his physical appearance, was still a globule of light, shimmering with ineffable light in the Undiscovered Country.

***

4
Grandpa Desmond

At first, **Grandpa McBride** treated Sacha as a wee lad. Then, as a bigger lad. And finally as a young adolescent. He didn't pretend Sacha was something special, unless one considers all children special. If he ever noticed somewhat odd or, to put it mildly, at times unconventional behavior, he didn't let on.

Grandpa Des was the only member of the Baldwin and McBride clans who did not treat Sacha as a wunderkind. Of course Sacha was bright, but Dr. McBride held that all children were bright, and remained so until adults destroyed their innate abilities. He thought that Einstein was right: "Education is what remains after one has forgotten everything one learned in school." At least that danger was over. Sacha would not have too much to forget. He wouldn't be retarded by the limitations of his teachers.

Sacha was six when Professor McBride took him on a tour of his university. They walked side by side. Each time they neared anyone, the students would step to one side to let them pass. After only a few such occurrences Sacha asked his grandfather why they did that.

"It's a sign of rrrespect, lad," Desmond answered, and caught his breath. Well, it was partially true. It was because he was a professor and they were students. The students might have just been playing safe. He did have a reputation of being somewhat of a holy terror. Alec had once told him so.

"But don't you respect them, Grandpa?" Sacha's tone placed an accent on 'them'.

Dr. Desmond McBride knew there and then that he must be very careful when he talked to the wee lad. "Of courrrse I do, laddie. Of courrse I do."

The next moment Sacha pulled hard on Grandpa's sleeve. Obediently Dr. McBride allowed himself to be pulled to one side of the corridor. The oncoming students did the same against the opposite wall. The group of students stared at the chivalrous duo with quizzical expressions having no idea what they were supposed to do. Then they nodded, bowed, and slowly sidled along the wall on their way.

"I think they really respect you, Grandpa," Sacha affirmed, when they also resumed their walk. "Only they didn't know that you respect them, too."

They had to step out of student's way four more times before Sacha let it pass. He was getting the message that if one party gets off the way, the other can pass. And the students were unlikely to take advantage of the extra space. There was no need to hold up all the traffic going both ways.

Usually, on return home, Sacha would run up to the door and wait to be let in. This time he stood to one side and let his grandfather reach the door first.

"I thank you for your sign of respect, lad," the professor said bowing to his grandson.

"Oh, I respect you a lot, Grandpa, but I had to wait because you have the key."

Alicia thought she knew why Desmond poured so much love on Sacha. It was, she thought, the guilt Desmond carried, for so many years, about the way he'd treated his own boys. In fact, just his remaining boy.

It was a bizarre story. It dated back to Dr. McBride's sons' late teens. Desmond had been busy at Caltech. Due to his colleague's illness he was lumbered with a series of additional lectures he could neither postpone nor delegate to anyone else. He'd previously promised his two sons to take them skiing to the Vale. The snow conditions were reportedly perfect. At the last moment Dr. McBride had to cancel.

The boys raised Cain about broken promises. Finally, his wife asked if he would mind if she took the boys skiing on her own. There was nothing wrong with the idea, except that Marla, his wife, was a fairly poor skier. She could hold her own on the easy, even on some intermediate runs, but that was about it. The boys regarded themselves as experts. They were good, but not that good. The last time Desmond skied with them he could still leave them well behind. Especially on fresh snow.

The lads liked to look for challenges to test their prowess. They had long planned a surprise. It was to have been for their father, but... it was not to be. Over a period of time they had saved their money to rent a helicopter. Marla and their two sons had been whisked onto pristine, virginal slopes. All that remained was the getting down.

Perhaps, for the sake of their mother, the boys took it fairly easy. Perhaps they waited a little too long, skied too slowly. The midday sun warmed up the slopes a little too much. A minor avalanche caught them about halfway down. It wasn't a big avalanche. Experts could probably avoid it with ease. They were no experts. Not on pristine snow.

John, the younger boy, died with his mother. George, who was almost nineteen at the time, emigrated to Australia after his father refused to speak to him for three months. They hadn't spoken to each other for many years although George did send a telegram for Desmond's wedding. It was terse, but it was a gesture. His father hadn't responded.

The scars ran deep.

Now Desmond was pouring love on Sacha. He had time. He was not trying to build a career to support his two sons and a young wife, to give them the best he could. That was then, a million years ago. Now, he was slowing down. But mostly, he wanted to give love. He felt a well within him that had never been used to its capacity. He tried his best. He didn't impose himself, but was always available.

Always.

On occasion, Alec would drop Sacha off at Dr. McBride's office at Caltech for a short while. He didn't abuse the privilege, and Desmond insisted that he didn't mind.

"Whenever you want to, son. Whenever you want to," the professor assured.

In fact grandpa found little chats with Sacha a lot more stimulating than shuffling papers on his desk. They must have been... Whenever Alec returned to pick up his son, invariably there was a wondrous expression on Desmond's face.

"I think I understand, Grandpa," Sacha had once said when Dr. McBride found it difficult to explain to him the gravitational field. "Gravity is like love. It is forever attracting. It neither judges nor expects anything in return. It just encloses you in its protective embrace, both the good and bad, with equal equanimity."

Equanimity? This was not at all how a eight-year-old talked. By now Alec was used to such vocabulary from his son, but Desmond didn't see his grandson often enough to catch up with the lad's reading habits. He no more expected childish patter than he could imagine that Sacha would stop thinking. His mind, Desmond knew, was a very precious thing. But it still resided in the body of a boy. Of a wee lad. And Desmond knew he must cater to both. He talked to Sacha as he would to an adult. Otherwise, he treated him as he would any eight-year-old.

"Yes, Sacha, m'son. I darrre say, it is at that." What else could he have said to the laddie? And then Desmond McBride scratched his balding head for a long time. "I dare say it is..." he murmured under his breath.

He wondered why he'd never thought of it that way.

On another occasion the professor asked Sacha about religion. He didn't want to, but Suzy asked him to find out Sacha's thoughts on the subject. For reasons Desmond didn't quite understand she didn't want to ask her own son herself. There was little Desmond wouldn't do for Suzy. She was Alec's wife, and Alec gave him Alicia. And Alicia brought a strange feeling of youth into his life. It was like being given another chance. For happiness. He'd waited for her for a very, very long time. And now Suzy gave him Sacha.

Meeting Suzy's request, he thought, would not be easy. He was not a religious man himself, and he carried no residual emotions on the subject. He thought religion was fine for people who needed it. He asked Sacha point black if he had any interest in any religion. He always asked Sacha things point blank. No matter what the subject. He was not a man to beat about the bush. He thought it a waste of time. And with Sacha, he soon found out, directness was the only way. If he tried hedging about anything, the lad could see through his subterfuge in an instant. So he asked him point blank. Sacha replied, just as directly, that he still didn't understand what religion was all about.

"I read all I could find, and there was nothing there that made any sense," Sacha said with sadness in his voice. "I wish I could help them..."

Sacha didn't elucidate what was it and just whom he wanted to help. Desmond didn't pursue the matter. He found dialogue on religious matters over his head. He felt that talking about religion was like listening to, or watching, the blind leading the blind. At the very most he thought that religion might have its place in the sanctuary of your own home. It wasn't something to be aired in public. But it was Sacha who returned to the subject some minutes later.

"And you, Grandpa, do you understand any religion?"

"No son. I don't. As for myself, when I do good, I feel good. When I do bad, I feel bad. That's about it," Desmond replied. He didn't find it necessary to credit Abraham Lincoln with the authorship of this terse creed.

"So religion is about feeling good and bad?"

"I don't know, son. I just don't know." And Desmond's voice also carried a hint of distress. As though he'd lost something and couldn't find it again. As though it just wasn't there anymore.

There had been many such exchanges, on just about every subject under the sun. Once the professor wondered if his own children, way back when, had asked similar questions. Or, for that matter, had they, or he, given similar answers. Perhaps all children have access to a source to which doors are closed once they, or we, have grown up. He reached back in his memory. Yes, there was definitely a door there, somewhere, which closed once you grew older. He wondered if the same thing would happen to Sacha.

It would be such a great pity.

How often does a man in his seventies, early seventies, have an opportunity to learn? It could no longer be from books. Not books on religion. Whatever had been put in writing had been run through the translation process of arranging thoughts into words and sentences that readers would understand. By then, the essence became too diluted. Too emaciated. Perhaps made ineffectual.

Sacha did not take grandpa's understanding into account. His thoughts came out directly, unhampered by considerations of grammar or syntax. He just let his thoughts spill out as if he and whomever he addressed were on the same wavelength. Why can't adults do that? Poets do, occasionally. Poets do not address their words to our minds, or intellects. They speak directly to our hearts. And even if we don't understand some of the words, it doesn't matter. We get the spirit of the subject. That elusive essence. They get us on the same wavelength. In this sense Sacha was born a poet.

Desmond hoped he would remain one. Forever.

Over the last few years, Desmond was getting into the habit of thanking his lucky stars. After years of loneliness in which his work has been his only passion, his only companion, even escape, he'd met Alec Baldwin. He recalled, vaguely, their first meeting.

"A beanstalk with a mop-a-top, stepping from one foot to another, as though swaying in the wind," he mused, when he first saw him.

That was Alec.

But there was a spark in the young man's eye that the professor spotted immediately. He'd suspected, and was since proven right, that Alec would venture into territories that other physicists dared not tread. At his first opportunity he had advanced Alec's name for the Nobel Prize. Why not? Dr. Alexander Baldwin's Theory of Information was as far ahead of the thinking of his own generation as Galileo's was over the thinking of the Vatican. Alec didn't get the Prize he deserved. Some well-established traditionalist got it instead, but this in no way diminished the professor's admiration for the young man. And at least, Alec didn't have to recant his theory, nor was he tortured, nor burned at the stake.

"Perrrhaps we are making some prrrogrress," the professor admitted, when he was recounting the story to Sacha. Not the story of Galileo and Giordano Bruno, but of Sacha's father.

There were other yarns Dr. McBride shared with Sacha. Always with expansive imagination, slightly exaggerated, and augmented with broad and rambling r's. The professor was proud of his Scottish ancestry and he affirmed it at every opportunity.

Over the years, he told Sacha many stories from Alec's past. He and Sacha's father had crossed the continent many a time. Fate also took them to Central and South America, to Europe, and even to Africa where the hunger for knowledge was perhaps greater than in any country. They both enjoyed making physics accessible to, what is commonly referred to as, the common people. Only there was nothing common about the people they'd met. What was common about them was their insatiable desire to learn. To learn facts, the truth—even in a very simplified form. The people seemed tired of falsehoods their TV and radio promulgated. They wanted to hear something they could believe. Without doubts.

Sacha's favorite was the tale about the trip his father and the professor had shared to Machu Picchu. When the old man spoke of the soaring tors clad in their gray, misty tonsures attesting to their longevity, the silent sentinels of the sacred ruins, his eyes grew misty, his voice lowered as though sharing some arcane secrets. Then as he recounted their shenanigans with the visiting Russian physicist at the UCLA, the professor sounded like a student himself, the spark in his eyes dispelled the previous mists, and glittered with youthful mischief. That was the time when the professor counted himself among the staunch defenders of *pure* science. Uncompromising truth. Anyone who dared to make a cocktail by mixing his beloved physics with any vintage of cosmic consciousness was in for a painful surprise. And that was exactly what he and Alec had concocted for the poor, unsuspecting visiting lecturer.

"Don't mess with physics," Dr. McBride warned his students. "God knows they are messed up enough already," he would add incongruously.

But the professor also loved the lighter side of his career. His stories grew and exfoliated with time. And so it was with the story of Dr. Goudoff, the hapless Russian.

"I almost lost my tenure, laddie," Dr. McBride declared with a chuckle. Actually, his professorship was never in any danger. But he thought this extra tidbit raised the hazard of the operation to a new level.

There was a great deal to tell, even from the years before the professor met Sacha's father. The lad listened wide-eyed, staring at his grandfather with undisguised admiration. Sacha's grandfather unfolded a world that Sacha couldn't learn from books. A world of real people struggling, as Sacha put it, to meet their destiny. He didn't venture to speculate what his father's or Grandpa's destiny might have been. Those were sacred grounds, he once said. They belonged in the sacred garden of each and every entity. It was the ground no one dared to tread uninvited. But then, almost as an afterthought, his grandfather did invite him.

"I wonder what would have happened if I had lost my tenure. Where would the currents of fate have taken me, eh lad?"

But the question was rhetorical. For a while the professor continued speculating of what might have been. None of the alternatives sounded as good as the present reality.

"Bit of luck, eh lad?" he concluded.

"You know, Grandpa," Sacha said when the professor had finished dissecting his own fate. "You would be the first to agree that time is a dimension which is very relative." Had Sacha been talking to his father, he would have said that time is a dimension of the lower realities. To the professor he chose his words more carefully. "If you are destined for greatness, it might take you a few incarnations to realize it and a few more to do something about it. When you do, I believe it is called self-realization. And by the way, we are all destined for greatness. Only greatness, as I am sure you agree, is not measured on the scale of material success. For now, Grandpa, let us be content that you are destined for immortality."

Had Sacha the ability to predict the future, he would have known that he would be voicing the above sentiment on a number of occasions. Almost word for word.

But at this time, it was the one and only time that Sacha actually sounded as if he was teaching the professor the facts of life. Or perhaps of living? But the lad, about thirteen then, noticed that his grandfather, of late, tended to bend his back a little more, to look for a place to sit down the moment he had a chance. Life, as people thought of it, was so transient. So ephemeral. Why do people attach so much importance to biological existence?

This was one enigma Sacha could not as yet master. He'd watched the youngsters at Grandma 'Licia's school, he'd watched his grandfather. There was a paradox there. One should be getting more and more detached as one grew older. More carefree.

And yet...

Sacha supposed he had always liked to watch people. He discovered that no amount of reading could tell him the truth about the real person lurking behind the mask of daily

activity. Lately the aging process fascinated him. He watched
Grandma and Grandpa. What a difference. Alicia was still in
the process of self-discovery. Her orientation was forward.
She still dreamed of new horizons, new vistas to expose to
her the mysteries of the universe. Her universe may have
been limited to a very small galaxy, but it was still unfolding.

Not so with Grandpa. Oh, he read the very latest
scientific magazines, kept up to date with the latest theories,
latest trends in his field. But really they were the fields of
others. In his own life, Grandpa looked only backwards.

"Ah, yes. I remember..." So many sentences have begun
with this verb. "I remember..."

And then followed the past, often distant past, yet
unfolding as though it were almost new. As though he'd been
not recalling the events, but reliving them. Perhaps life, here,
on Earth, was a bit like a scroll. You could roll the parchment
either way. Recall, remember, relive, or scroll it forward and
fill in the blank pages with yet not-experienced events. It did
seem flexible. At least, at the memory level. Sometimes
Grandpa even shared with him little snippets of memory from
his own, so distant, youth. From the time when the doctor
wasn't even a doctor. Nor even a student. Before he even
imagined he'd ever fall in love with physics, well before it
became his life's passion. It was like a different life. A life of
innocence where nothing mattered much.

The stories did not matter. It was the light in Grandpa's
eyes...

Sacha wondered if he, himself, was so innocent. To him
many things were important. He felt the need to learn. Not
physics, but also physics. He refused to specialize. Except in
people. People to him always were an enigma. An
embodiment of consciousness, which, as yet, didn't make too
much sense. There had to be more to all this. He didn't think
of himself as being destined to become immortal. He knew
that he was. His daily visits to the Undiscovered Kingdom
attested to that. And it was there that none of this made any
sense. Perhaps this was his problem. Perhaps if he planted his

own feet a bit more firmly on the ground, he would find it easier to understand people. But the price was too high. He would rather give up all than stop spending timeless moments up there, in the land of ineffable freedom, of luxuriant light, of merging with all other individualizations at will, even as a wave in the ocean merges with other waves.

No, the price was much too high.

And with Grandpa it wasn't just his memory. He watched his grandfather with an unaccustomed feeling of compassion. He never experienced that emotion until he saw his grandfather facing little fragments of life, which made that very life more difficult. Of no importance individually, but when rolled into a scroll of life, they added to the hardship that wasn't there before. Getting up from the sofa, climbing the stairs, avoiding irregularities in the surface of the sand on their morning walks, when it was Grandma's turn to sleep in. Or even getting in and out of the car. Such simple activities, so taken for granted for so many years. And now, almost suddenly...

"So I am going to be immortal, am I lad?" Grandpa's voice seemed to come out of some Machu Piccean fog.

Sacha realized that he'd said too much. There was no easy way out.

"You *are* immortal, Grandpa. Believe me. You are."

Dr. McBride looked at Sacha for a long time. He wondered what it was that the lad was trying to tell him. There was no doubt that the lad was a very, very exceptional child. But regardless how bright he was, was he always right? No one he'd ever met was always right. Not Einstein, not Feynman, nor any of the great men he'd met over his impressive career.

But if so, why did Sacha sound so very, very right?

***

5

Mr. and Mrs. Norman

The Normans were not the 'Normans'. They were the
JJs. In the past they've been mostly John and Joan.
Lately, it gravitated towards Joan and John. John has
slowed down. A lot. *Tempus fugit.* Things change.

The first time Sacha visited Mr. and Mrs. Norman, he
was only seven years old. Until then, the JJs came over to
spend Christmas with the Baldwins at the McBrides beach-
house. With three bedrooms they were all reasonably
comfortable. When Suzy took Sacha to visit her parents, in
June or July, he acted as though he'd traveled alone. He
thought he could have, perhaps should have. After all, it
wasn't as though he would step out of the airplane, and get
lost somewhere. Had he been given half a chance, he would
have flown the plane himself.

During the weeks preceding the flight, Sacha had spent
hours in the Public Library, thumbing through everything he
could find on aeronautics. As he became—what can only be
described as—a speed-reader by the time he was six, going
through the whole subject matter in a little over two weeks
was relatively easy. Des doubled with laughter when Sacha
called it 'child's play'. Sacha couldn't quite understand why
people would want to travel by such an uncomfortable, noisy,
spatially restricted and badly ventilated container. It felt like a
thoroughly unpleasant mode of travel. Even in the smallest
car he'd ever been in, he'd had more room to move around,
enjoyed more diverse views, and dad or mom could stop
practically at any time, for whatever purpose. In an airplane,

once you got to a certain altitude, even on a clear day, there was nothing much to see. He understood that occasionally people might be in a great hurry, but in his opinion the vast majority of people had a very twisted, virtually unreal concept of time. He had all the time in the world to play, all the time he needed for books. And even then there was time leftover for other pastimes.

Sacha's idea of seeing the far away places had been limited to closing his eyes and in the same instant being there. And until his first visit to Canada, he couldn't quite reconcile this new concept of travel with the exigencies of not only time but also space; or more accurately of distance.

"Distance is a factor of time, Mom, and time is flexible," was his only comment on the subject.

He'd learned only recently that people wanted to take their bodies, their physical bodies, with them on their journeys. For him, this need had only presented itself at that first trip to see his Canadian Grandma and Grandpa. That's where the yacht was. He needed his body for the experience. It wasn't the same as the Home Planet, dad told him. He had to find that out for himself.

Later Sacha would also realize that here, in this reality, if he wanted to see the results of his creative endeavor he was limited, in some measure, by his physical senses.

"More's the pity," he once told his dad. "After all, when you create something in your mind, you already know what the results will be."

At the time, Alec didn't quite understand his son's comment.

That trip to experience sailing was the first of what would become annual visits to Canada. Each individual trip left a lasting impression on young Sacha. Not the travels as such. Flying in a metal can was not his favorite pastime. The impressions were generated after he got there, on the expansive waters of Lake Ontario. There, from the first moment Sacha had stepped on board, the bug of sailing

infected him. He succumbed to it under the tutelage of his
maternal grandfather, John Norman. And his mother, of
course. But in the years he could still keep his balance at the
wheel, Grandpa John struck a captain's pose that commanded
respect and obedience. Mother may have been more adept at
handling the sails, in fact doing almost everything on board,
but Grandpa remained undeniably the skipper. The Master of
the ship. Grandma Joan, was indispensable to preparing
Sacha's favorite snacks when the wind permitted. She liked
sailing, but she liked it mostly because she was of help to her
husband. There was very little she wouldn't have done for
John.

Open waters of Lake Ontario were the nearest Sacha
came, on Earth, to the sense of freedom. Not just the waters,
but he claimed the wind as his own, personal playing field.
The endless horizons were the nearest he could get to the Far
Country. Even the Home Planet was not as rewarding as the
open waters. There, in the inner realm, it was, well, it was too
easy; you did not have to pay for your mistakes. In fact there
was very little payment extracted in the upper realms. Perhaps
some disappointments? You just started again, discarding
your less successful creative endeavors. Here, the rules were
quite different. Unforgiving. In some ways, more exciting.

Here you learned a lot faster.

And it was on the water that Sacha felt, for the first time,
really alive. Until then, his body was more of a hindrance. He
regarded it as a necessary evil impeding his freedom of
movement. He would forever remain grateful to Grandpa
John for letting him hold the wheel, to feel the spray on his
cheeks, to balance his stance against the waves attacking the
gunwales.

Yes, on board the *Princess*, Sacha felt truly alive.

Other than being the second kindest Grandma he had,
Grandma Joan served to diversify Sacha's insatiable need to
study people. He'd met other people, of course. He'd been
presented, not to say 'shown off', to the JJs' friends. But to

really study people you must get to them up close. You must see them react to different circumstances, to different, often trivial, events in their everyday lives. From the very beginning, virtually from infancy, he felt like an outsider looking in. He peered at people, almost desperately trying to make sense of them, to make head or tail of their behavior.

"Why do people worry so much, Grandpa?"

This was his greatest enigma. Why do people take their 'life' so very seriously? He touched on the periphery of the answer that very first time they went sailing. You had to take life seriously the way you take any game seriously. Even when he played with his Strato Set, he remembered, he tried as best he could to build something interesting.

So life was a game, but it didn't explain why people worried all the time.

By his fourth birthday, he'd noticed that people regarded their physical bodies, as their actual selves. That they identified with their physical envelopes. At first he couldn't believe his own discovery. When you're four, all things are new, all things are surprising, but this? *This* was out of this world. Or, perhaps *this* was of this world, whereas he was not. At least he didn't feel he was.

Some years later, Grandpa John had an enigma of his own to resolve.

"Why," he wondered, often aloud, "why does a seven-year-old talk like an adult?"

What Grandpa didn't know was that Sacha was equally capable of talking 'his age' vernacular to other boys. In fact, by the time he was seven, there were very few things that Sacha was not capable of—by "normal" peoples' standards.

Very few, indeed.

And thus, the trips to see the JJs became annual events. They had to be in summer, because Sacha could not imagine visiting Grandma and Grandpa JJ and not spend a week or two on board the boat. It wasn't Kingston that was his destination. It was the *Princess*. *Princess the Third*, the 36-

foot Bayfield cutter, which looked much more like a real ship of yore than a pleasure yacht.

Yet pleasure it was.

On two occasions his dad came with them. When he did, they spent the whole time aboard the ship. They actually slept there, ate there, woke up and gazed at the stars there. Sacha loved that. Again, it was that sensation of freedom that he'd never experienced anywhere else... on Earth.

"You have an opportunity to learn as few other children have, my boy. There are few sailors with Grandpa Norman's experience. He'd crossed the Atlantic, you know, single handed!"

His father repeated this admonition on a number of occasions, always stressing the 'single-handed' aspect.

Sacha wasn't quite sure what crossing the Atlantic single-handed entailed, but Grandpa John rose in his eyes to new heights. Already then Sacha admired singularity of achievement, though, for himself, he tried to narrow his many interests to manageable proportions. Whatever he did he threw all his energies into the endeavor. He offered a quiet demeanor, but he was passionate about everything he did. He did not believe in half-measures. Whatever he could learn, increased his understanding of the *Phénomene Humain*, as he remembered Theihard de Chardin had put it.

And that last passion, man, was his most powerful of all. He still couldn't figure out what it was that the members of the human race were really after.

When his son turned thirteen, Alec implanted a skipper's hat on Sacha's bushy crown. Two years had passed since John's last sail. He'd lost his sea legs. He'd lost the call of the sea. But he also found something that hadn't been apparent before. He'd gained a certain elusive air of innocence. His commanding, somewhat dominating, features gave way to a most disarming smile. It manifested in the way he looked you in the eye. Sacha thought that perhaps what they said was true. Perhaps we start and finish in childhood. Perhaps it was all meant to be. What a pity the JJs could not be here, right now, Sacha thought. He really loved his 'other' Grandpa.

"I was about your age, son, when the command of the ship fell in my lap. That was brought about by fate, after my own father had been injured. Happily, I'm still in one piece. But now your time has come. I name you captain of this vessel."

As Alec made the announcement, Suzy stood up and saluted the new skipper. It was all quite official. If it weren't for the deep tan, Sacha's blush of pleasure would have embarrassed him.

"Prepare to cast off!" Sacha said, his first words of command as he assumed his position behind the wheel. It reached practically to his neck, but he seemed to tower behind it. His eyes resolute, his smile crooked, as was his jaunty hat with captain's insignia.

The deep throb of the diesel was churning the water at low revs. Suzy and Alec walked the finger dock holding on to the bow and stern lines. When they jumped on deck and pulled in the fenders Sacha gunned the engine. The Princess moved slowly in reverse gear, then came to a momentary stop as the forward gear reversed her direction and took her out of the marina. Minutes later Sacha pointed the bow into the wind.

"Prepare to hoist sail," he said in a calm, confident voice. Like his father did, only yesterday.

Alec pulled furiously on the mainsheet, while Suzy extended the furled Genoa. As the wind filled the sails, Sacha cut the engine. This was his favorite moment. All true sailors love the eerie silence when the throb of the engine dies down.

There were no dramatic events under Sacha's first command. But it was the first time that Sacha understood the difference between crewing and commanding the boat. Everyone was carefree, looking here and there, sipping cool drinks, enjoying the fresh breeze. Only Sacha had to keep his eye forward and aft, to port and to starboard, making sure no one was on a collision course, making sure the sails were rigged just so. A good two hours later, after he had his fill, he issued his second command.

"Dad, take over the wheel, please."

"Aye, aye, Sir," his father replied instantly.

"Keep her on 210 SWS," Sacha added.

"210 SWS, she goes, Skipper."

Being called a skipper sounded very good to Sacha's ears as he went below to look at the charts. It took him quite a while to orient himself to his destination. They had agreed, before boarding, to sail to a spot some miles East of Rochester, on the US side of the lake. With the West wind, it would be a good ten-hour sail, assuming they could average seven knots. The wind was perfect, practically on a broad reach. They should make their destination by around 1900 hours. The JJs had friends there who'd invited them over for dinner. Later they would sleep on board and, at sunrise tomorrow, make their way back. But that wasn't the important part. The trip was important because Sacha was learning to be responsible for the lives of other people.

He never realized how absorbing it was. They were not in any danger, the wind forecast was 15-18 knots, an easy sail for a yacht this size. But the sense of responsibility was something Sacha had not experienced before. Perhaps he led too sheltered a life. Perhaps that was the danger of being an only child. But he was grateful to his father for letting him take the helm. He steered the boat many times before, but this was different. This time he really felt the weight resting on his young shoulders.

He pulled his shoulders back.

Alec made sure that Sacha would not fall back on his own expertise. The skipper had to rely on his own cognizance. He engaged Suzy in conversations, served drinks, stretched out at the bow, all to make sure that his son would not seek his assistance. When asked to do something, take the helm for a while or trim the sail, he would do so at once, but he would ask Sacha just how much he was to pull a sheet in, or release it.

Alec remembered his first command on Lake Champlain. The conditions had been tougher then. Much tougher. But being in charge doesn't get harder when conditions get hard. In a way, they are easier, because the range of options is diminished. You must do this or that. Sometimes, just this. Just a single option. You do it. You don't have much time to think.

A time will come when Sacha will face adverse conditions, he thought. For now this was enough. After all, he'd had a great deal more experience when he was Sacha's age. Next time, he'd make it tougher. Alec believed that there were ways in which nature provided us with opportunities when we were ready for them. Or so it seemed in his own life.

Nature obliged.

After an uneventful sail, a delightful dinner and a reasonably quiet night, the next day wind was blowing right in their face. A cold front was coming in from the Canadian North, meeting the remnants of a Tropical storm still lingering over Lake Ontario. The waves were whipped up to at least four feet. He asked Sacha if he wanted to take them back to Kingston.

"It won't be easy, son," he warned.

"Do you believe I'm ready?" Sacha was searching for confirmation.

"You must decide that, son. You must have confidence. But I won't force you in any way." He looked down at his son who was obviously in a quandary. "It could be dangerous," he added.

Alec forgot that his son did not understand the meaning of fear.

Sacha decided to beat into the wind by pointing the bow due WNW and then lay off and sail ENE with the wind on the quarter. He wanted not only to test his own skills to the limit, but he was determined to test the boat as well. It wasn't just that the wind was upwards of 25 knots, but it was gusty, with unpredictable squalls, which played havoc with the rigging.

The Bayfield 36 is a heavy boat. With 6,500 pound full keel ballast, and an overall displacement of 18,500 pounds, she sails well into the wind. But beating into 25 knots blowing at you from the North, is a challenge for any sailor.

After long hours of being tossed by the mounting seas that splashed against their port side with unremitting fury, Sacha commanded to have the main reefed a notch. An hour later, he asked his father to furl in the foresail. Alec obeyed without saying a word. He told Sacha many a time that on board one must either obey or take over.

"And taking over amounts to mutiny, son," Alec had added with not a trace of humor in his voice. "And the minimum requirement for mutiny is an impending death resulting from the captain's aberrations. Otherwise, you are apt to walk the plank."

Sacha had no desire to walk the plank, whether he was apt to be fished out later or not.

However, by that time Sacha had finally reduced sails his crew, as well as himself, have become soaked through and through. Neither Suzy nor Alec expected their son to push the boat to the limit, and therefore neither of them prepared their oilskins. Anyway, one hardly used oilskins during summer. But this? It took another fifteen minutes before Sacha was satisfied with the new rig and let his crew go below for a change of clothing.

Many tacks later, well after sunset, when they finally got back to Kingston, Sacha asked his father if he'd done all right at the helm. To an outside listener, Sacha's tone was halfway between youthful cockiness and uncertainty. Alec knew his son well enough to know that Sacha was covering up his discomfort.

"We're here, son."

"You know what I mean, Dad." Sacha tried again, his tone even less sure of himself.

"It's not the way I would have done it. But, you were in charge."

"You would have fallen off and taken it easier on both tacks, wouldn't you?"

"Yes."

Sacha had laid out the course in order to test his skills. He was so taken by his opportunity of command that he did not take the comfort of his crew into consideration. That was a mistake, a selfish one, and now he knew it.

"I guess I'm not quite ready..." he intoned sadly.

"You are a proficient sailor, son. Where you're lacking is in the humane department."

"I know."

Sacha sounded contrite. He knew his father was right. But when he'd been given command under such difficult conditions, his dark side came to the fore. He wanted to fight the elements and win. Not by using his mind or even heart, but physically. Like other humans. Like the millions of his species who fought wars, who killed or died for no apparent reason, driven by inane hubris; who in moments of emotional folly didn't seem to care about life or death. He needed the experience. Sacha had learned the meaning of ego.

"There is one other little detail," Alec added when his son looked up from intently scrutinizing his wet sneakers. "It wasn't your boat."

"Oh, my God," Sacha bit his lip. "Will Grandpa ever forgive me?"

"There is nothing to forgive. You brought the boat in, in good shape. What you must learn is respect for other people's property."

Sacha never attached much importance to physical things. He was fully aware of their transiency, of their relative unimportance in the universal scheme of things. But he now knew that not everybody did shared his opinion; that others have a right to their own perception of reality. To their own mindset.

For a while Sacha looked so pensive, so despondent, that Alec started laughing. At first his son couldn't understand what was funny.

"After all, my son, it's only a boat!"

There was no figuring adults. They took things seriously and yet they didn't. Or perhaps they knew when to stop. When not to go too far. Perhaps it was a question of balance. Yes, Sacha's eyes lit up with new understanding. Life was a game, but it was played according to certain rules.

"It's a question of balance, right, Dad?"

"Right son." And he patted his son on the back.

In spite of the sermon, which, after all, Sacha had asked for, Alec was quite overtly proud of his son. Out of an eleven-hour sail, Sacha held the wheel for three-quarters of the way. Maybe longer. The boy had staying power. He was made of stern stuff. Sacha had made a self-centered decision as to what he wanted to get out of the sail, but there was no fear in his heart, and he handled the wheel like an old sea dog. Perhaps better then I did when I was his age, he concluded.

Of course, Grandpa John couldn't have been angry. He probably would have lost track of the conversation if Sacha, or anyone else, tried to explain to him the return trip. Even two years ago John would have participated in the discussion. Four years back he would have gone with them.

And then something had happened.

Joan remembered it so well, as though it were yesterday. John had been sitting in his favorite chair, overlooking the lake when, all of the sudden, he'd lost consciousness. Not for long. A few, maybe twenty seconds, at most. This happened three more times during the same month. And then he was all right again, only his memory was gone. Not of what happened forty or fifty years ago, but what happened this morning. Or last night. Most of the time this didn't seem to matter. But then, he started having problems with speech. The words just wouldn't come out. There was one, perhaps the only compensation. It was that smile. Since those momentary fainting spells, John charmed them all with an incredibly unreserved, totally unabashed smile. It filled his eyes, it parted his lips, in a way which we can see only in the eyes, and on the lips of the very, very young. It was a smile that opened the heart of whoever he was addressing, unreservedly, and always with kindness. John, Grandpa John, became a very different man. Or perhaps he'd always been like that, only his true self was hidden behind a mask of acquired refinement, of social skills, of *savoir fair.*

Alec and Suzy tried, nevertheless, to tell JJ's about the 'slings and arrows of outrageous fortune' to which their son had exposed them. John smiled as though the only important thing was that they've all had fun.

"It was fun, wasn't it, son. Ah... I remember..." And John's eyes drifted away.

But he didn't remember. He'd forgotten his own intrepid sails. He'd forgotten the feel of the water driven by the wind splashing on his face, while he stood braving the unknown, with Joan and Suzy below, snug and dry.

"I remember..." he intoned again.

And his face lit up with a smile of days gone by, of way-back-when, of memories all mixed in a potpourri of glimpses of Suzy's smiling face, his own princess, his most beloved daughter. He loved his wife for being herself, for giving him sons, but most of all for giving him Suzy. He never stopped regarding her as the most beautiful girl in the whole wide world. And he really did remember her every smile, every twinkle in her eyes, every touch of her hand.

"Suzanna...?" Only John called his daughter Suzanna. It dated back to his love of Mozart, and the Marriage of Figaro.

"Yes, Dad. I'm right here."

But John felt she was near him regardless where she really was. Suzy owned a permanent place within his heart. He didn't feel the need to remember other things. She was his memories. She filled them to the exclusion of virtually everything else.

That's not very fair to Grandma, Sacha thought.

He cheated a little. Since he was ten or so, he'd learned to peak into the human subconscious, without anyone knowing about it. He did it not to pry, only to learn. And it didn't do any harm to anyone. Yet, he felt uncomfortable doing so. He still felt like a Peeping Tom. He did it only in cases when he suspected that it would increase his understanding of the human phenomenon. Not to learn about things, only to learn about people. He felt he needed to know the human potential in order to reach his own destiny. When the time came. Whatever it was. Or would be.

Lately, in his thirteenth year, Sacha felt more and more that his destiny would not be an easy one.

It was the first time Sacha had witnessed the ravages of aging. He'd watched both JJ's. Joan showed such overwhelming quantities of kindness—of tolerance toward her husband—that Sacha didn't know existed in the make up of the human psyche. He still regarded mankind from the outside, like a thief trying to understand the mysterious darkness before entering the unfamiliar territory himself. But he no longer felt that he was being punished for unknown offenses by being encased in a human form, reduced to walking upright, on two feet, rather then flying through space on irrepressible wings of his mind, or his imagination. That other realm was and remained his true home. This was a new field of endeavor in which he felt, more and more, he was destined to leave his mark. Before being free once again. Before he could go back.

It was a long journey.

And he really appreciated the opportunities placed in his way. The JJs., the McBrides, his parents, the boys and girls at Grandma 'Licia's school. Those he could study from up close. He vaguely remembered Matt, a giant who once looked after his father. Matt was an enigma, yet he felt a strange affinity towards that man. And Maria, whose heart was so much greater than her intellect. Perhaps that was all that really mattered? The many others he'd met were more like reflections of themselves, casting shimmering shadows on the canvas of reality. So many of them did not seem to be real people. Whatever 'real' really meant.

He sighted deeply. There was so much more to this human equation that he couldn't find in books.

***

6
Sacha

NOTES FROM SACHA'S DIARY
with dedication:
"For my Parents"

[Editor's note: Sacha was born on June 25th at 1.30 a.m. PST, in Los Angeles. From the day he uttered his first sentence, he did not appear to recognize his affiliation to the physical mode of life; he did not recognize the Earth's calendar, which has undergone a number of changes, as dictated by various religions and/or political regimes. Furthermore, Sacha refused to recognize the fact that he was actually born. He treated his arrival on Earth as just another adventure, the purpose of which he was determined to discover. In the light of all this, he started his own calendar, which begins on day one of his arrival on Earth in human form. June 25th, therefore, is day one of year one of his life.

The first entry in the DIARY is dated 4+1, evidently celebrating the fourth anniversary of his arrival on Earth. In the first notes he explains that he has no idea how long he will remain on Earth, nor whether his life here is to have any bearing on the "unfoldment of human perception". He dedicated his notes to his parents, to do with as they choose. He assures his mother and father that he has no intention of making any "profound statements", only of attempting to explain his point of view, what he calls his "perception of reality", which might be of interest to them.

He seems to have recorded his thoughts sporadically, often writing nothing for years at a time. Then, his words would come at a flood, as though prompted by some turning point in his life. Only some of his notes are included here, as others appear to be of a more personal nature. Sacha's early notes and the ideas expressed therein, those spanning the years 4 to 13, remain, for the most part, quite incomprehensible. They express a point of view quite alien to the human mind. Those we can comprehend, however, form the basis of this narration. The rest of the book is derived from countless interviews, press clippings and other sources, which at least for the present, must remain anonymous].

SACHA 13+67 days

There are things in my head I find hard to share with anyone. Even with mom and dad. Perhaps when I'll write them down, they will arrange themselves into a more orderly flow. I always find the translation of holistic concepts into a sequentially structured communication somewhat limiting. It would be like attempting to explain a painting by listing the colors used, and then describing their pattern in a lateral succession. Other difficulties I'd already covered in my previous notes. In essence, the perception of reality espoused by people on Earth is very strange to me.

Nevertheless, I'll try.

Most people I've met have given me the impression that they have some sort of problem to sort out. On closer examination it transpired that their problem had started with their first job, or with their marriage, or even later with their first child. Those people were either very ignorant or suffered from extremely bad memories.

I distinctly remember my own first riddle.

I am not referring to what people call 'previous incarnations'. We all acquire problems in the course of our existence. After all, that is what the process of becoming is for. No one can possibly imagine how incredibly boring living would be without problems to solve. It would be like living in limbo.

Like being dead.

Really dead.

I defy anyone to go for a whole week without a single problem to solve and not suffer depression. Only we don't regard most obstacles we overcome as problems. We take care of them in our stride. When we do nothing for a little while, we feel a sense of listlessness, we feel we must get up and go. We need to face a challenge—any challenge; we must solve a problem—any problem, even if we create one in order to be able to solve it. We must remain active. They say that women must be, whereas men must do. This is partially true, although man and woman's characteristics are, to a certain degree, interchangeable.

Anyway, be it any of the things I've mentioned, or something else, like playing tennis, or swimming, or going for a morning jog, all those things point out quite clearly that none of us are capable of just being. In the physical body we must be active.

We must solve problems.

SACHA 13+68 days

I have observed myself since I was a baby. This may be hard to accept, but you must realize that my body was that of a baby, not my awareness.

In the beginning, still imbued with the stillness of the Undiscovered Kingdom, I watched an idea entering my mind like a puffy cloud drifting across an otherwise clear sky. As the mental currents increased, I began to react to them. Then I recognized more ideas penetrating my awareness. They stirred me to look around, to observe reality through my physical eyes.

Next I've learned recognition.

I could tell one face from another. I'd learned to associate different faces with different things. There was the food face, the goo-goo-goo face, the silent assuring face... There had been many others to which I couldn't attach an activity at the time. And all this I'd managed just by responding to my visual, aural and, to a lesser degree, tactile senses. My problem solving at the time was limited to telling one face from another. I couldn't believe how clever the little body was. In addition, it performed an incredible number of functions quite automatically. There seemed trillions of electrochemical discharges in my baby head controlling most of these functions.

What a magnificent machine!

And yet, I couldn't figure out why I needed this machine. After all, I was doing very well without it. Up there, in the upper realms, as my mother called them.

But however we care to put it, once we enter a physical sheath, we are not allowed to stand still. Such are the laws down here. We live in turmoil of ongoing change. And boy, is that different from everything I was used to before! The greatest difference is, however, the concept of time. Up there, we are not conscious of it. We do not measure problems or solutions in terms of 'how long do they take'. Time is a very relative concept, mostly used on the physical plane. On other plains it is much more fluid and flexible than any other dimension.

By the way, I prefer the name Undiscovered Kingdom to Undiscovered Country coined by my father. After all, it is not a country, and everyone there is a King. The absolute master of his perception.

SACHA 13+82 days (cont.)

My new set of problem solving started soon after my previous life, although 'soon' is also a relative concept. It

was soon in terms of my awareness of time, which only exists
outside the consciousness of the Undiscovered Realm.

[I've changed again my name for the Undiscovered
Country or Kingdom. The reason is that the Realm is not up
there or down here. It is as much here as there, or
everywhere. We simply cannot place limitations on it. It could
just as well be called a State, though it is no longer a state of
mind. We could also call it a Condition, which is closer to the
truth, but sounds like a disease. The nearest would be to call
it a specific state of Consciousness, only we cannot define it.
That is the problem with words.]

I recall, I had to select new parents prior to my
incarnation. For my future stint of becoming. And if you think
that this is an easy problem to solve then it's only because
you completely forgot what it was like when you had to make
your choice. Most people, practically everyone, are blessed
with regressive amnesia, which is a necessary ingredient for
remaining relatively sane in the physical reality. Imagine
playing Hamlet with your head full of lines from Macbeth,
Julius Caesar and Titus Andronicus, all at the same time. Or
if you're a girl, try Olivia, Desdemona and Ophelia. Now add
to the lines all the sounds, smells, visual effects, reactions of
the   other   players,   all   crowding   your   poor   brain
simultaneously.

Look what happened to Ophelia...

A guaranteed prescription for a loony bin, although I'm
not quite sure what a loony bin is. My dad refers to most
university committees as training ground for loony bins. I
think I know what he means.

On Earth we develop the ability to draw on selective
memories. The same is true of inter-life experiences, only the
range is vastly greater.

I know, for instance, what were the main ingredients of
my previous lives, but only those that were directly
responsible for the position in which I find myself today. All
the peripheral, non-essential items, which run into billions
upon billions of thoughts, actions, and reaction, are blissfully

discarded as non-essential. The nonessential stuff is recycled for future use by others. When and if required. Thus, though I say so myself, I am sane.

Or at least, I think I am sane. Or healthy.

Cogito ergo sum sanus.

Back to my parents.

Just as with my own life, when you are getting ready for your next becoming, the essential characteristics of your prospective parents are available to you. You don't read books about them, of course, there are no books in the Undiscovered Realm. But there is a library of knowledge. Most of it is available to you by direct perception. All that is vital to universal evolution is stored there. It feels very much like your Theory of Information, Dad. I'm sure you'll develop the concept further. The lower (mental) memories are kept in the Far Country, still lower (as well as emotions) on the Home Planet. And when you are ready, you don't actually 'go' from Bardo into a condition of becoming by popping out of your mother's womb. The baby does that, you take a longer route. We descend progressively through various states of consciousness until we absorb all the smaller bits and pieces, which combine to form our personality. Or, at least the ingredients that will contribute, and give us a predisposition, to certain traits. Thanks to this set up, we get Mozarts and Hitlers alike. They both seemed to have succumbed to their inherited traits.

I hope, Dad, when the time comes, you will be able to clarify this process.

It seems to me, that when we are faced with a choice of environments, we always start with the immediate family from our previous two or three stints on Earth. It would be quite impossible, or at the very least eminently impractical, to make a selection from all the life forms which may have had influence on us. After all, we are immortal and that means, we had no beginning.

Of course, we are always conducting our process of becoming in the present, but you know what I mean, Dad. And Mom, of course.

Earth is also a euphemism because our becoming could take place on any planet, in any galaxy of our choice. What we don't realize down here, i.e. on Earth, is that there is no such thing as material reality. At least, not as a permanent concept. What we perceive as reality is an arbitrary construct, which can be and is constantly manipulated by our minds.

That much has been explained quite clearly by Jesus' teaching and Castaneda's Don Juan. Different but fascinating sources.

[Editor's note: Sacha goes on to describe, at length, how to learn to manipulate the physical reality consciously, at will. He claims that this learning process is the primary purpose of the first stage of his embodiment. He also claims, however, that for the vast majority of human beings those techniques are inaccessible at their present stage of development. The limitation is due to their inability to overcome the perception of reality as a non-dualistic concept. He assures us that the information is available in various scriptures. Below he notes some of his conclusions].

So what we have instead is only our perception of reality. The same is true, of course, of the Home Planet and the Far Country. It seems to me, that what really makes up the illusion is our inherent need for order and harmony. We must never forget that we are beings of light, and that essentially we are indivisible components of the Field of Infinite Potential. Down there, or here—since I am down there myself at present—we refer to that Realm as heaven. This is inaccurate. The Undiscovered Realm is a state of stasis with unhindered awareness of Bliss. What people usually refer to as heaven are the lower realms, primarily the Home Planet, where imagination and emotional contentment prevail.

You both experienced all three. Perhaps you can give those pursuing the subject a more acceptable impression.

[Ed. note: Sacha describes again the perceptions of realities he refers to as the Home Planet and the Far Country which are covered elsewhere in this account. Two days later, Sacha described the foibles of excessive reliance on our physical senses].

SACHA 13+84 days

Imagine what would happen to the psychological makeup of any person if they were suddenly confronted with a mass of countless numbers of atoms in a constant state of movement, swirling in all sorts of directions, seemingly, in quite unparalleled disorder. I guarantee that it would drive every single one of us crazy in zero seconds flat. What we perceive is an act of self-defense, formulated and instigated, as I have mentioned already, by our inherent need for order and harmony. We make the best job we can from this chaos, and, I must say, we're doing pretty well at times.

It does my heart good that after only a few billion years we managed to create an objective perception which we can share, most of the time, with each other. What I am trying to say is that we perceive the world we live in as beautiful as we make it. No more and certainly not less. We are the sole creators. What we perceive—is. What we don't—is not.

SACHA 13+91 days

[Ed. note: A week later Sacha returned to his thoughts leading to his present embodiment, which he'd begun relating on 13+68].

So I had to pick parents.

I was lucky. My prospective mom and dad had already found their way into the Home Planet and even the Far Country. Getting them into the Undiscovered Realm confirmed my suspicions. They were 'my kind of people'. What happened, as you might well have guessed, was that I have completely failed to lose my memory of the upper realms. To this day I am unaware why I was exempt from this prevailing amnesia. No doubt it is necessary for the fulfillment of my purpose. At any rate, I still consider my real home, no, not the Home Planet, but the Undiscovered Realm. Because in as much as the memories of intellect and imagination stay in lower strata, the memories that form your universal individuality are always with you. So retaining my conscious connection to or with my true nature, I automatically remember the universal aspects of my total existence. It's a wonder I didn't go mad in the first few weeks on Earth. And even later, if it hadn't been for my parents who were cognizant of different states of consciousness, I'm sure I would have gone bananas.

When all preliminaries are settled and we are ready to be embodied, we succumb to a deep dream. The eastern mystics call this state of 'recumbent' consciousness Bardo. We dream of the life we shall have. The dream is much deeper than any coma you could possibly imagine. As there is no perception of time in Bardo, we dream in minute detail the complete course of our 'future' embodiment. Only then we enter our physical bodies, and spend the next number of years trying to remember our dream. In this sense, our life on Earth is a dream. In fact, not even a dream but a struggle to remember our dream. That, I suppose, is our first problem.

This may sound a little complicated but I'm sure you know what I mean.

So there I was, a little bag of water with a few grams of chemicals suspended in it in a most intricate way. People call this a baby. I thought of myself as a sort of a smart-Alec guy, ready to do my bit, which I'd dreamt up in Bardo.

I knew that my real name was Alexander. Like my father's. But in Canada, one doesn't suffer from the need to build dynasties and, though living in the States, my parents remained intrinsically Canadian. Since I was born in the States, I could have claimed the privilege to be called Alexander III. But it would have been silly. To be lumbered, at such a young age, with a 'title' was as ludicrous as what some of the Europeans do. I am told they still enjoy inherited titles.

[Ed. note: Sacha next shares with us his view on some of our traditions and customs. He displays early signs of a sense of humor. Below an extract from notes he wrote later on the same day].

A great-great-grandfather might have performed a noble deed for which he'd been rewarded with a title, usually accompanied with a nice plot of land. That's fine. Why not? The king owned anything he wanted to own, so he could bestow the land and the title on anyone that pleased him. But Alexander II, or III, or... XXIV?

Again, why not? All it took was one little spermatozoon making its way into the prescribed location and, bingo, nine months later number XXV was ready and waiting.

I am not as smart as all that. I've read about it.

Oh, yes. I've read all about the generative process. By the time I was eight I'd read all the books I could find at home, and later I used all the libraries you would take me to. How else was I supposed to learn how to function in this material illusion? I've learned to scan the books rapidly, retaining virtually all that I've read. Some people call it photographic memory, but it isn't. It is more like metabolizing what you read. Like making whatever was in the books—your own. You might recall, by my thirteenth birthday, local libraries had nothing to offer.

Nothing of interest that is.

That's why originally I'd started writing this diary. Otherwise, no one would believe me. Not that that would matter much. I have a feeling I won't be around very long. Unless I fail to remember my dream. That worries me a little. Sometimes.

By the way, Sacha is a Russian diminutive for Alexander. Why did my parents choose a Russian name for me? I asked them. They said it was because I was born in the US of A.

Go figure.

But my parents did make a concession to their democratic heritage. They spelled my name the French way, with 'ch', rather than 'sh', and pronounced it with a soft 'sh' as in chef or chalet, not as in cheetah.

As for carrying on my name, dad told me a story once. There was this man who had two beautiful daughters. He was miserable because he didn't have a son to carry on his name. You know what the man's name was? Smith.

As I was saying, go figure...

So, I've been anchored in this reality for thirteen years now, and I still have no idea what I am doing here. And if it weren't for my parents, I would have called it a day. But not a day passes by that I don't learn something from them. Not the facts, or what goes under that name, but real knowledge. Understanding the concept of a human being. I know where we all come from but nobody seems to act as if they know. My parents at least have a good idea. We visit the Home Planet, my mother's favorite, and the Far County which dad likes the most. We visit them both quite often together. Neither of my parents ventured into the Undiscovered Realm on their own. It seems too disembodied for them. They seem to loose their identity. Not surprising. Most globules of light seem the same to them. It's like visiting China for the first time and trying to tell people apart. Not easy.

But the beings of light are all different.

Down here, our eyes can see only the narrowest range of vibrations, or photons of electromagnetic energy. Sandwiched between the lengthy infrared and the extremely short ultraviolet waves is the visible spectrum ranging from violet through blue, green, yellow and orange to red. This tiny portion of the visible spectrum varies in lengths from 0.000076 centimeters at the red end of the visible spectrum to 0.000038 centimeters at the violet end.

But even in the physical world, the range of an electromagnetic wave is vastly greater. X-rays, gamma rays, radio and television waves—they all are light. All made up of photons. The waves range from lengths greater than the diameter of the Earth to others so short that a billion strung together would barely span the width of your fingernail. Dad told me that, and he knows.

We know about those waves, only we can't see them.

But this is true only on Earth. Now imagine that your vision was designed to recognize all the electromagnetic waves in existence. The explosion of colour would burn our brain to a crisp in no time flat. Luckily in the Undiscovered Realm we don't have brains and there is no time. But we all possess acute awareness not only of the virtually infinite number of wavelength, but also their intensity and the combinations of the various photons in relation to each other.

We recognize them by direct perception.

When dad or mom enter this state of consciousness, they can instantly tell the combinations that are familiar to them. It is like recognizing an old friend. "You've changed, but I'd always know you in a crowd," they might say. The familiar is inherent to them. The rest...

I don't think there is anyone who can tell apart all the different nuances of light. We can all tell apart the great souls—they stand out like beacons, and we can tell those who are still struggling in the lower realms in their physical embodiments. It's tough for some of them. They've inherited, so to speak, from their previous attempts so many mental aberrations that it may take them ages to repair the damage. Often many ages.

Thank heaven we're all immortal.

There is one other thing.
Since we are beings of light, we share the characteristics inherent in light. And one of these characteristics, or attributes, is the predisposition towards order and harmony. That which we call chaos does, in fact, harbor this predisposition also. It is also this same trait, as I've mentioned already, which enables us all to perceive order in the 'chaos' of atoms all around us. The more we allow this trait into our consciousness, the easier we can influence those atoms to enter orderly and harmonious relationships. That's how healing is done. That's how some people do things, which others call miracles. It's all the same. A tendency towards order and harmony enhanced by our consciousness.

We can all do it. And most of the time we do it we seem quite unaware of it.

There is so much to learn.

SACHA 13+107 days

Only Grandpa makes any sense. He's not trying so hard, and he's done a lot of good. He never treats me with kid gloves. When I am wrong, which is often enough, he'd say so. He has vast knowledge of how the physical universe works, and his perception of the universe is very orderly.

His body is slowing down but his mind is as sharp as nails. I love our morning walks. And that time, years ago, when he first took me to Caltech... They'd treated him like a really big honcho. That was before I'd learned that the

Chancellor is the biggest honcho of all. I found it hard to realize because to me he was just Grandpa.

And a very nice Grandpa at that.

As for my own body, well, it gradually increases in size, which seems a bit silly considering I can be any size I want to be on the Home Planet. In the Far Country the time moves so slowly that you would wait forever to grow up. I really like the names dad gave all those states of consciousness. Especially that last one. It really is an Undiscovered Country, and, in a way, it can never be discovered. Maybe it is better than calling it a Realm. I would rather just call it Home.

You can only really tell things, or states, or anything, by the way they change. When something is intangible and changeless, you can't really get to know it. Not in the same way. It remains Undiscovered.

But you can feel it. Bliss is not a state of mind. It is a state beyond mind. Or beyond the intellect. Not quite the same thing. If you equate mind with consciousness then it's a different story.

And regardless of what I'd dreamt in Bardo, the Undiscovered Country, Realm or Plane is my Real Home.

SACHA 13+132 days

I remember that walk I took with dad at the beach when a hydroplane ran down a man swimming out into the ocean. There was no point then, or even now, to tell dad that the man had spent the last ten years daring himself to swim out, way out from the shore. He worked almost daily to overcome his fear of deep water, which was only a symptom of his fear of the depth of consciousness.

After all, when we say we go 'up', as in up in heaven, we really go 'in'.

He, the man, imagined all sorts of vile fish, monsters to be more precise, to grab him and pull him down into the abyss of the deep. Saint John writes a bit about them in

Revelation. The pits and all that. On the day the man's body was killed, he had overcome his fears. The swim out was only a culmination of his struggles with fear. His whole life was filled with monsters, with evil spirits lurking in the darkness to grab him. It made his life miserable. He hardly realized that his life was hell. A self-imposed hell—self-created. A hell to be conquered, mastered.

He did.

Once victorious, there was no reason for the man to remain in his body any longer. He'd done his job— accomplished his mission. But how could I have told dad all that? My dad was perfectly aware of the Far Country. But regardless of what he'd said, it was still a 'place' for him.

I've known all along that it isn't so. I never lost my awareness of where I came from. That always gave me an overwhelming advantage. I didn't rise to the Far Country from the foibles of earthly life. I descended to it from above. The various realities are distinct, with defined rules, but they all coexist in the same space-time. Only the measurements and the dimensions change. Both space and time are but elements serving us to teach us perception of the universe. But not just the visible universe.

Visibilium omnium et invisibilium.

The realities are there to help us understand, to appreciate, or... to perceive the Creative Force. None of them really exist. Nothing exists outside the Undiscovered Realm. The other realities wink in and out of existence even as whole universes do when I venture into the Far Country.

But what the Far Country really offers is the possibility of sharing our perception of reality with other units of awareness. I suppose, mom, you would still call it 'with other souls'. In the upper realms, the subjectivity of an individual outlook overlaps much more with other souls. With other individualizations descending from the Undiscovered Realm.

From my Home. My sweet and only home.

So much for now. Love you Mom.
Sacha

Sacha 13 + 364 days

Tomorrow is my fourteenth birthday. I think they are putting together something special. Probably some pagan ritual to mark the occasion. No matter. Occasions are usually fun.

Last night I had an insight. Whenever my consciousness rests in the Undiscovered Realm I never have any problems with visiting the Far Country or the Home Planet. A simple wish and the realities created by my previous visits unfold themselves, and the playing fields are ready for new experimentation. It's like being in heaven yet having all the fun normally associated with having a body. I mean the senses, and all that. All I have to do is to pick up the resonance of the mental and emotional vibrations I left behind, and there I am sitting in my favorite villa overlooking a glorious lake, or flying over the most beautiful country in the world. And when I say flying, I don't mean in a metal can, like on Earth. Just imagine... You can create all this beauty and never be in any danger of pollution playing havoc with your landscape.

Floating, suspended at the very center of the Universe in the Far Country, being master of all creation, where the stars, galaxies are but my toys, is a very different kind of euphoria. They're not what we concoct in our imaginations, but whatever our mental body comes up with, instantly becomes the hypothetical reality. All realities are, of course, hypothetical. All of them depend exclusively on our perception. And the center of perception is the heart of our being. It is where our attention resides. And wherever we direct our attention that's where we are.

But this is not what I wanted to share with you.

During the last week or two, I sensed a nagging suspicion that I am getting close to discovering the purpose of my life. Down here, I mean. And that purpose is, I'm pretty sure, to find my way back to the Undiscovered Realm. I mean, everyone always goes there, sooner or later. For a few instants of eternity. But that's not what I mean. I mean to go there and henceforth never to have to go out, unless I choose to. I might forever want to come down to physical reality to share my perception with those I love. But I would do so as an act of my will.

This time, it was not exactly so.

When I began making preparations for my embodiment, it wasn't that someone told me to do this or that. There are no bosses in the Undiscovered Realm. But it is a feeling like waking up, only in reverse. You know that if you don't scratch it, it will drive you mad. So, sooner or later, you scratch it. Only the itch is the need to come down here, and do whatever has to be done to find your way back. Or at least get closer to your permanent residence.

So when all is said and done, the only way I could fairly define my life in this lanky body with a mop-a-top would be 'The Way Back'.

**

PART TWO
The Search

*Therefore search and see if there is not some place
where you may invest your humanity.*

Albert Schweitzer
(1875 - 1965)

7
The Rites of Passage

The Jews celebrate the coming of age of their sons a year earlier. The Bar Mitzvah is celebrated at a boy's thirteenth birthday, at which time he is welcomed into the congregation of men. Sacha never felt excluded from such, even when he was three or four years old. Nor was he now prepared to forsake the congregation of women, a number of whom he held in great affection.

And then there is the Roman Catholic Rite of Confirmation. Although chronology is not observed as strictly as in the Hebrew faith, it is an occasion when a lad of a certain age is admitted to a full membership of the Church. Sacha's parents did not bring up their son in any particular faith. They thought that the inner life of any person is and should remain inner. When you rear a son who takes frequent trips to, what can only be described as, 'heaven', it is hard to preach at him; particularly when more often than not they, Suzy and Alec, found themselves learning from their own youthful prodigy.

"Why do they wait so long to welcome youth into the congregation, Mom?" Sacha's questions were not getting any easier.

"I don't know, Sacha, but I suspect that since the christening is done *to* him or her, the confirmation is to be done *by* him or her. I mean, you can decide by yourself whether you wish to be confirmed or not."

"You don't mean that, do you?"

"I suppose not if you are a pupil in a Jesuit boarding school. But I suspect..."

"Yes, Mom. But I still don't get it." Sacha looked genuinely lost. "They wait until the child loses his or her innocence before making him or her a full member. Don't they want the innocents to be their members?"

Alec, listening in silence, let that sink in, and then shook his head.

"What do you mean lose his innocence?"

"Oh, I don't mean in the moral sense." Sacha laughed out loud. "What I mean is that by the time children reach the requisite age, he or she have lost their singularity of thought. They became firmly anchored in, what they perceive as, dualistic reality."

"Which you deny?"

"Of course!" He laughed again. "You've been up there with me. You travel the inner worlds yourself. You know that everything comes from a single source and that mind is the only creator."

They had talked about this many times before. But whereas for Sacha this was an obvious, indisputable truth, Alec was rediscovering it every time he ventured into the Home Planet. Up there, it makes sense. Indeed, it could not be otherwise. If you don't create your version of the universe, it just isn't there. Until your arrival, until you accept it in your consciousness, it exists in a potential state only, even if at first sight you are not aware of its virtual nature. Then you breathe life into it. But here? It seems so much more tangible.

"Just how do you grab an atom, Dad?" He was listening to Alec's thoughts.

"I don't know, son. But to live down here, as you call it, I must accept certain rules—or I'll go bananas," he added, under his breath.

Sacha returned to the original subject.

"So why don't they call confirmation a *conformation*, as it prohibits *confrontation*?"

This time they both laughed. Suzy was less amused.

At the age of seven, Sacha was smarter than most fourteen-year-olds. At fourteen, he could sit and pass any university entrance exam, in practically any subject. A genius? Not by his own definition. He kept repeating that he has no idea "what it's all about." His head was loaded with innumerable facts, but their purpose remained very hazy. And now he'd reached the Rites of Passage, a sort of Initiation into Manhood.

In the past, among the primitive tribes of Africa, or Amazonia, this Rite of Passage had been accompanied by rigorous tests that taxed a boy's physical and mental dexterity. Sacha remembered his dad telling him about his own coming of age when he'd discovered the Princess. But what had taken his father years to discover was that in Sacha those same traits were always inherent. At Sacha's age, Alec had just discovered the good news of the Home Planet. Sacha descended to it from above. Alec was surprised by every new discovery within the inner realities. Sacha took them for granted.

"Information or knowledge, better still 'knowingness', is disseminated throughout the universes. Look at your own Information Theory, Dad. What you're missing from your equation is the fact that this information is already predisposed to fall into predictable patterns."

"Why predictable?" Alec suspected he knew, but couldn't resist seeking confirmation.

"All patterns already exist in their virtual state, and all patterns harbor a predisposition towards order and harmony," Sacha continued. "When I visit Home Planet I do not create it from scratch. As I already mentioned, in its virtual form it is already there. It is a compendium of infinite patterns both virtual as well as those manifested over eons of time. I manipulate its reality. Or my perception of it. Countless generations of individualized units of consciousness made it come into being. It is as though it had no beginning. Nor will it ever be destroyed but rather it will metamorphose into other patterns, all ready and waiting, so to speak, to come into recognition."

"Recognition by who?" Alec wondered aloud. He loved listening to his son.

"By Consciousness." Sacha was speaking quietly, as though to himself. "The potential is infinite. And while Consciousness is really One, it seems able to individualize Itself into countless components. You can think of them, or us, as rather complex sensors the One Consciousness uses to experience Its own Infinite Potential."

"Or to regard itself in its own creation..." Alec thought aloud. It took him more than thirty years to reach very similar conclusions.

"Yes, a mirror. As a sort of reflection of Its glory."

Sacha didn't imagine soul as a separate entity floating some distance over his head and directing his moves. He always knew that he is soul. Or at least a distinct wave in the ocean of Soul.

"Too many people use the Home Planet exclusively as a holiday resort," he told his dad. "It is so much more than that. It is almost anything you care to make it."

Way back when, in another reality, Sacha recalled the soft voice telling him to sit still. To sit in the light. To see the light. To feel it. Bathe in it. Absorb it. Then, after some timeless moments the gentle voice whispered... *The light is you.* And finally before the ancient teacher could say it again, Sacha understood.

"I am the light. The light is me," he recalled his own words. "I am the object of my contemplation. I and the light are one."

It was strange indeed that Sacha had always known that. Whenever he ventured into the Undiscovered Country, he was light. There, it was obvious. He merged at will with the light of others, with the light all around him. It was as though the globule of light that was his identity exhibited some surface tension, which, while being one with the light, could emerge from it and be, in a way, himself. Not as a distinct personality but as an individual awareness. After the last time that he and dad raised their consciousness to the Undiscovered Country together, dad found it difficult to reconcile the beings of light with the physical envelope.

"But we always remain entities whose essence is light, Dad. You know that?" Sacha said.

"You mean there is some kind of transformation...?"

"No, Dad. We remain one and the same. You don't stop being you just because you put a set of clothes on your back, do you?"

"Then why is our real nature so hidden?"

"Is it? I've read of many people who can detect an aura on the edges of everything that lives. I can see it in people, animals, even plants. Life is life. What do you think this aura is?"

"The real thing showing through?"

"You could put it that way. The real thing showing through. That which we are cannot really be hidden, destroyed, or transformed. The real *you* remains always the same. What changes are the masks we put on to accommodate the exigencies of different perceptions of reality."

Alec smiled.

"You talk like a professor of metaphysics," he said.

"Sorry. I know it sounds stilted. But my language comes from books I've read. Perhaps one day I'll write one using simple or ordinary language."

"Which even your dad would understand?"

They both laughed.

So aura is the spiritual glow coming through into our physical realms. We certainly have it. Alec couldn't see it all the time, but on occasion he saw the sheen, often of different colors clinging to Suzy. Especially when she was happy.

"Perhaps soul is a happy entity? I wouldn't wonder," Alec mused aloud. "In the Undiscovered Country overwhelming joy is palpable."

But here, on Earth, and even in the immediate higher realms, one falls into the trap of becoming the object of one's contemplation. You think a lot about your body, and you become your body. You are not only where your attention is, you are your attention.

In the past, whenever Sacha came down to the lower realms, he longed for that euphoric freedom he enjoyed in his true home. Now, mostly due to his sailing experience, he rediscovered the satisfaction of being here. On Earth. It would seem that his consciousness resided in a physical enclosure. Only it didn't. He no longer felt constrained by his body. He shouted for joy the first time he felt the moment of freedom. Perhaps this was his Rite of Passage. It was the time when he felt no longer constrained by the construct of his own creation.

His mind, discarding all limitations, raced with him to the very edge of the sun's corona. This was not the Home Planet. Nor the Far Country. He soared in total abandon right here and now. He stopped at the gates of the fiery furnace, then descended to the soft grass on which his body sat, cross-legged in perfect stillness. He was sitting across from an old man, an ancient, some five feet away, his face smiling in approval. Sacha was elated at having a witness to his accomplishment. It was as though he enlivened two bodies. Both physical yet one other, completely at his command. One obeying the laws of this realm, the other obeying his will.

"Is this the duality of good and evil?" he wondered.

The old man's face lit up with a smile. Who was this guru?

Sacha felt no scathing of the infernal heat on his skin. He didn't suffer from lack of air in the upper reaches of space. Nor did his body explode in the appalling vacuum. And as joyful as was the realization of having his body intact, so was the discovery that his body was an idea. That's all it was. It was an idea expressed in terms very different than those of the Undiscovered Realm. There must be a reason for it, he mused.

"There must be a reason why I assumed a human form..." the thought nagged him.

"...no more prison," his own voice reached him from a great distance. He looked down at the old man. The guru. The old man's body had risen a few feet and hovered still directly in front of him. Sacha got up and looked closer at the smiling eyes.

"There is nothing I can teach you, my son. Rather, it may be you whom I should call my Master..."

Only then the impact of what transpired really hit home.

The face Sacha was staring at was his own.

At least for Sacha, the Rite of Passage carried other connotations, other proclivities, which tended to attract more of his attention to his growing physique. The vicissitudes of the hormones began to make their presence known, and confused Sacha's idyllic dance within his youthful body. Though he gave no such impression, he was keenly aware of them. He knew from books the theory of the process. He could write a book about it. But there was no time in his agenda for the changes occurring at the physical level. At least, not the hormonal ones.

He still regarded his physical body as one regards ones house—a transient abode at best. But one could not ignore one's house. After all, one did live in it.

As far back as Sacha could remember he had always been a dispassionate observer of other people, perhaps tending to neglect himself. About his fourteenth birthday, perhaps due to those very hormonal demands, he began paying more attention to his own biological organization. He began watching, and making notes, on his own reactions to various events. It appeared that his body had a will of its own, that it was determined to react to certain events in a manner that had been encoded in its genes. He didn't like to be held in a vice of the genetic code and wondered if there was a way to surmount it. He'd already learned that the prerequisite to conquering one's enemy was to get to know him. Or it. From that moment on, he set about studying his physiology in minute detail.

He began with watching his breath.

He soon discovered that he'd been taking this seemingly natural function for granted. Not any more. By varying the rate of breathing he soon learned to raise and lower his body temperature. He wasn't sure for what purpose he might apply this ability, but it was a step forward. Then he learned to reduce the rate of his breathing so low that a General Practitioner of Medicine, not equipped with special equipment, would have pronounced him dead. He'd read about the fakirs of the Far East doing this sort of thing, and now he understood the method. This could come in useful in a number of circumstances. It could act as a protective stance in moments of specific danger. People seldom attack corpses, although at present he had no idea, who would possibly want to attack him.

No matter, it was a step forward.

Next he began watching his blood circulation. By placing his attention on his heart, and then following the cardiovascular currents coursing through his body, he'd learned that he could actually place his attention on any, no matter how small, portion of his anatomy and, to a degree, control the blood flow. On one occasion, while watching himself in the mirror, he'd pumped so much blood to his face that his mother, seeing his color, lost most of her own.

"Sacha! What's wrong darling?" she gasped.

"What is wrong with you, mother? You look as though you saw a ghost!"

It wasn't always as bad.

On that occasion he was experimenting with setting limits. Usually the purpose of following the blood flow with his attention was only to establish control over various parts of his body. He found that if he could mentally separate one finger, or his kidneys, or his spleen from the rest of his body, then he could actually affect its or their functioning. And that included the healing process. It just so happened that there was never a healthier lad walking the Earth than he was. No matter, he thought. None of us know the future. It also might come in useful.

He pursued the geography of his body until he knew it inside out. Only then did he feel satisfied that he could consciously use it or, if need be, abuse it. Though the latter was very unlikely. Studying his physiology and biochemistry he'd grown in awe of its incredible complexity. And yet, what really amazed him, within this magnificent machine there was indescribable grace, sheer beauty of the way the various systems worked in such balance, such harmony, one could almost say, in courteous consideration of each other.

"My body is the greatest miracle, Dad," he confessed, the next time they were alone.

"Isn't it going to your head, lad?" Alec said sternly.

"Dad! I meant..."

But his father couldn't stop laughing.

"Gotch'a," he said. It wasn't often the he could get the better over his own son. And he enjoyed it. Frankly, though he did his best to look hurt, so did Sacha.

In the final stage he examined his envelope as an electromagnetic construct. This phase of his research took a lot longer. He also found it more satisfying.

Some weeks later, Alec and Sacha were walking along the beach, and, as so often when they were alone, they talked about Sacha's inner life. Little wonder. They would not breach the subject with Alicia or Grandpa Des around. It wasn't a subject you could talk about to people who did not experience comparative realities themselves. You could not repeat them, nor invoke them under the, so-called, controlled laboratory conditions. You knew of them or you didn't. And that was that.

His father, in spite of, or perhaps by the grace of his sharp scientific brain, knew.

Sacha had long suspected that many exponents of pure science were much closer to understanding the workings of the universe than people who tried to find the truth in religion.

"You always had an advantage, Dad," Sacha reminded Alec, when he was backing himself into a rhetorical corner. "You can't always argue what you know. You must learn to just accept it."

The scientists did enjoy a head start. Their brain was not muddied by 90% of extrapolated, often incomprehensible myths, which they would have to sift through before finding the original thought that lay behind the parables and symbols. Scientists, with the possible exception of the theoreticians, started with reasonably objective facts and continued from there. The secret was not to discard observations, which, at first sight, didn't make sense. It took Alec years before he really accepted his inner experiences as real. In fact it was only when the odds of a triple hallucination were less likely than acceptance of the experience that he gave in. When all three of them, Suzy, Sacha and himself, perceived an inner reality which they shared without equivocation, then he had to accept it as 'real'. And that happened on the Home Planet.

"So what does it feel like to be fourteen years old? They say it is the beginning of manhood," Alec asked not really expecting Sacha to answer.

"It feels as though my body was born fourteen years ago, around nine months after Canadian Labor Day."

That was the day, night rather, which Alec wouldn't forget to his last breath. "It was a dark and stormy night..." he mused. God, it was so long ago, but when he held Sue in his arms, yesterday, it felt like... yesterday. She retained all her beauty, her wit, her sense of humor. Only her temper mellowed a little, for which Alec was inordinately grateful. He was too old to go to work with bruises. Or could it be that she'd lost some of her aim?

It was a dark and stormy night...

The two of them were anchored in Spoon Bay, off Valcour Island, on Lake Champlain. It was a forbidding night, but they didn't care. They were together. And by the time the night was over, the first spark of Sacha was with them. Alec wondered if Sacha, with all his talents, knew that.

"I really got interested in my body a little later, Dad," Sacha was again reading his father's thoughts. "But I was aware that the wheels of my becoming were already turning."

His father didn't say anything. Neither he nor Suzy had ever shared their memories of that night with anybody.

"Then why did you ask me?" Sacha again interrupted his thoughts.

Alec laughed. "You, my son, are not anybody. You are as much part of me as is your mother."

"Aren't we all...?" Sacha muttered under his breath. He wondered when the human race would realize that. Or realize their potential. Or their heritage. Or even, just, who they are. Individually.

But he didn't say any of this, though again he had that strange feeling that his own destiny was drawing closer. And, somehow, the thought did not make him happy.

Days became weeks, weeks—months.

Sacha lost track of time. He'd spent relatively long periods of time in the upper realms. Although even that didn't make much sense, because he was capable of returning to physical reality at will, at any time in relation to his departure. To be more precise, Sacha took time to consolidate the knowledge he had gained so far, without venturing into new territories.

In time he grew confident that he was in total command of his physical body. He was wrong. He still had a great deal to learn.

*＊＊

8
A Matter of Fact

Even as his father studied physics in order to understand the mysteries of the universe, so Sacha engrossed himself in philosophy and psychology in order to understand what people do with the knowledge they discover. He soon learned that his father had chosen an easier route. While the universe changed constantly, its activities left a firm trail behind. The photons from stars millions of light-years away were reaching our planet only now, and the scientists could, with a high degree of accuracy, estimate what transpired way out there great-many eons ago. As a result of their studies, they could estimate their own origins, or at least make an inspired guess about the origins of our own solar system.

Not so with the human species.

In Sacha's eyes, we all seemed bent on destroying our past and if we couldn't destroy it then we attempted to obfuscate it as best we could. Even our reputedly holy scriptures have been written and rewritten, and translated, and re-edited, so many times that each successive student found himself, or herself, further and further away from the original intent.

And then the various churches really got down to brass tacks. As the original scriptures offered little on the subject of successful money management, but a great deal on the possible exploitation of our kinsmen, a great many scholars got down to business. They set themselves up as the interpreters of the 'holy' writings and, adding their own slant to the wisdom of the ages, they converted them into superb money making machines.

The damage was thorough.

Whatever the ancient avatars had attempted to tell their contemporaries became so insidiously ensnared in hearsay, so distorted by the professional interpreters, that no amount of effort was likely to rediscover the original concepts. And this in spite of the wisdom of the ancients, who drew a veil of symbolism over the original teaching. By the time the teaching reached Sacha, the symbol was taken as fact, and the parables as a historical reality. The method employed was now called fundamentalism.

"The proponents of this method evidently forgot that fundamentalism is derived from the word 'fundamental' or 'basic', or 'bottom'," Sacha said sharing his thoughts with his father.

"You mean the ABCs?" Alec asked.

"Well, they are terms we normally associate with the kindergarten," Sacha added hardly believing his own findings.

Sacha had already read all he could find that pertained to all major religions. To discover his own purpose, he had to ascertain where he was in relation to others. No man is an island unto himself, he recalled reading somewhere. He swam in the ocean, among other fish, and they affected him. He soon learned that in the ocean bigger fish eat smaller ones, only to be eaten by still bigger fish themselves. He'd picked up long ago that the dictum 'eat or be eaten' applied to politics. Now he began to follow the appetites of religious leaders.

And the ridiculous thing was that everything he saw on Earth was in direct opposition to the currents underlying the higher realms. There, one never gained at the expense of another entity. One drew directly on the Ocean of Infinite Possibilities to create the reality one chose. There was no need for 'eat or be eaten' premise.

He thought of the silver and the golden cords.

Early on, Sacha discovered that even as the silver cord connects his consciousness to his physical body, so its golden equivalent connects his light body, his body of light, soul if you like, to the Source. We could no more survive on Earth without the silver cord connection, than retain our individuality without the golden link.

Once the golden filament is dissolved, we merge with the Source. Since he'd begun his present incarnation, Sacha witnessed one such dissolution on visiting the Undiscovered Realm. The golden globe which was about to dispense with Its individuality was immense. If most of the spheres of light could be compared to miniature stars, then this magnificent entity shone with the radiance of a billion suns. It was truly that of which It came. This resplendent Soul has accumulated an immense storehouse of universal traits. It became indistinguishable from Its Source.

And then it happened.

Its radiance seemed to grow, increase still further, until it permeated the whole realm. Sacha felt repeated waves of euphoria, of ineffable bliss, as It grew, swelled, expanded, even as a supernova expands its presence, until Its consciousness became so finely dispersed across the Undiscovered Realm that Sacha could no longer sense Its individuality. It would, Sacha felt, never be reassembled into a distinct entity again. It became one with the universe. In a way, we all are. We never really separate from our Source. But we assume individuality to experience the process of becoming. Then, ultimately, we become as the wind that cannot be felt apart of the air that it carries.

This was a rare occasion. Or perhaps we are only given to witness such an event when we are ready. When we are no longer afraid to forsake our singularity. Sacha suspected that some of us never would. Although never is a very, very long time, and one is not aware of time in the Undiscovered Realm.

For a moment Sacha found himself suspended on gossamer threads in a realm inaccessible to most humans.

Time stopped.

On such a day, as when a mature soul merges Its individuality with The Source, one can hear music of the spheres permeating the vastness of the Far Country. The music is there to be heard at all times, but it seems to swell even as the ocean swells when the moon illuminates its surface.

SACHA 15+82days

There is a paradox in heaven. Soul is. I am. I never was nor ever will be. And the same can be said of that magnificent Soul which integrated Itself with the Whole. Yet for countless eons It accumulated Its attributes of ever-greater universality, until It reached the stage of becoming indiscernible from Its Source.

In this sense that which that magnificent Soul 'was', now became integral with the universe itself. From a different perspective, it always was that. I always was that. I am that. We all are. We all are indivisible, integral elements of the universe. Not just of the manifested cosmos, but of that which hovers eternally at the ineffable border between the potential and the manifested. Yet that great Soul became and enhanced that aspect of the Infinite Potential that is dominated by the proposition that all things are inherently good, with the predisposition towards order and harmony. And beauty. After all, to be able to disperse one's consciousness across all the realms, one must have honed all one's qualities to a universal perfection.

That particular entity no longer flourishes in Its own, individualized becoming. Its being is now expressed through

all other entities. It enriches all consciousness. I, too, feel I
have become more than I have been.

And yet... I am. Eternal. Unchangeable.

Hence the paradox of being and becoming.

As I look up at the star-filled sky, I'm reminded of the
early Greeks. They called it kosmos. To them the Universe
represented order and harmony. But the word also meant 'an
ornament'.

An Ornament of God?

The eternal Being.

The eternal Becoming.

The nearest Sacha could get to his passion—the study of
human potential—were people themselves. All the books
he'd read could only take him so far, and having been tutored
at home, his contact with people at large was severely limited.
Thus, when his father said that he was flying to Boston for a
series of lectures at Harvard, Sacha asked if he could string
along. Alec agreed, and the two of them set off together.
Sacha hadn't mentioned that, at the time, there was some kind
of ecumenical congress taking place in Boston, with audience
participation. He knew his mother wouldn't approve so he
kept quiet about it.

They landed at Logan International Airport. A limousine
took them to MIT, where Alec had been invited to stay with
an old friend. From there Alec had only a short taxi ride to
Harvard's grounds. The next day, Alexander Baldwin Ph.D.
went about his business, leaving Sacha to fend for himself.
That was exactly what Sacha had hoped for. In order not to
offend anyone, he put on his best suit, and made for the
downtown Convention Center. The bus deposited him at the
doorstep. He was welcomed with open arms.

"It's youth we want. Youth!" The fat lady told him at the
gate, scanning his size and age in quick succession. "Will you
be taking part in the discussions?"

A smirk hovered on her ruddy face. She evidently had grave doubts if this puerile mop-stick might have anything interesting to say on any subject.

"I was rather hoping to, Ma'am," Sacha replied, ignoring her visible disdain. The corpulent woman shrugged, and directed him to the entry tunnel on the right.

So far, so good, Sacha thought. He'd half-expected not to be allowed in without confessing his affiliation to a specific denomination. That could have proven embarrassing. He could easily have lied, but it wouldn't be the right thing to do. It would be a bad start. He wasn't sure what he expected to find at this meeting; he only knew that he must start finding out. Somewhere.

The Batterymarch Conference Center offered two amphitheaters. He was directed to the auditorium on the right. Apparently that was where the audience could take part in the proceedings. He wondered what surprises lay in wait for him. He had no idea what happened on such occasions. He didn't feel quite at ease.

Soon he was enwrapped in near darkness. Slowly his eyes adjusted to the lurking shadows. They were peppered with people wielding more designations than he could have imagined. They all carried lapel tags displaying their titles. Every attendee flaunted a doctorate of something or other, from divinity to theology, to scriptural studies, ancient languages, backed up by philosophy, psychology and an armful of other, lesser credits. They were an impressive bunch. Sacha felt naked without a tag.

He realized, belatedly, that he didn't belong.

All the other attendees looked important. For some strange reason, a goodly percentage of them were grossly overweight. Some wore imposing apparel, with colorful hats, and big solid gold chains hanging from their necks. The gold chains supported an array of symbols. Roman and Greek Orthodox crosses, Stars of David, and a number of seemingly ancient pagan symbols, all rested, immobile, atop their

protruding paunches. For a moment Sacha thought he'd
ventured into some sort of repertory company selling
theatrical wares. Not so. These people took themselves very
seriously. Very seriously indeed.

And then a gong rang, really, a bona fide gong,
reverberating in the penumbra of the hall, like the sacred
syllable of Aum. A tall, thin, virtually emaciated speaker,
supported by an over-long staff with a round, luminous
balloon perched at the upper end, staggered onto the stage. He
seemed in considerable danger of getting entangled in his
own flowing beard that descended to well below his waist.
The poor man really was as thin as most others were obese.

Sacha suspected that he'd come to the wrong place;
either he, or the man on the podium. Perhaps both of them.
The speaker was the spitting image of a character named
Gandalf.

"Lord of the Rings!" Sacha almost cried out.

The part of Gandalf, he remembered, was beautifully
acted by a British actor Ian McKellen. His father had
inherited from his own dad a distinct propensity for all things
British. Sacha found it harmless enough and rather amusing.
It had been a good few years since they'd all seen the movie,
but the image of the man staggering on the stage, here and
now, brought the film freshly to Sacha's mind. The only thing
the man was missing was a tall, pointed hat, and the illusion
would have been perfect. Had he been even closer to the film
version, Sacha would have felt like Frodo, a hairy-legged
pint-sized hero of the book. At least Sacha's lack of pedal
hair was amply compensated if not amplified by his hairy
mane.

Nevertheless, the man did not fly off on his broom, but
Sacha was sure the strange apparition could have—had he put
his mind to it.

"Good afternoon," the sage intoned.

Sacha glanced at his watch. The time was eleven sharp. The man was obviously ahead of his time. Surprisingly, from such an emaciated body, the man's voice was deep and resonant.

"My name is Gallan Grey. I shall be speaking to you on the subject of Druid traditions and other Celtic derivatives. After I finish, I invite those of you who are within walking distance of a microphone to ask questions. Any questions?"

"Have you finished?" Sacha murmured, and bit his tongue. He really wanted to ask if those not within walking distance, could use their broomsticks, but thought better of it.

Sacha glanced at his program. Gallan Grey was a priest of the Ancient Order of Druids. He flew here all the way from England. Dad would have loved that...

The man raised his head from his notes and scanned the audience. There were not that many present. The 'real' ecumenical meeting would begin at 3.00 p.m. These were the preliminaries. Now Sacha understood why the speaker preferred to greet his listeners with an afternoon greeting. It, sort of, put him in with the big boys.

Appearances can be misleading. Once the man overcame his initial stage fright, he spoke in a fluent, engaging and interesting manner. His knowledge enriched Sacha's understanding of the Ancient Celts. Apparently there was a time when the Druids had performed the duties of both priests and soothsayers; they had advanced knowledge (according to the speaker) of natural philosophy, which led to the practice of herbal medicine. They had also supervised the moral ethos of the people, and had acted as judges in their districts. Politically their confederation had been powerful enough to foster a revolt against ancient Rome. But what really caught and held Sacha's attention was the statement that the Druids believed in the immortality of soul.

Not bad, thought Sacha. In fact, a good start.

He was glad he came. In the countless books he'd read he'd never found it expedient to read about the Druids. He selected his reading material according to its applicability to the present time. He glanced at the program for the afternoon and his jaw dropped. The subjects, as far as he could see, had nothing whatever to do with ecumenism; nothing with the notion that began nagging his subconscious. He thought that if the socio-religious systems were responsible for the most numerous slaughters throughout the ages, then perhaps, if the practitioners of religions could see eye-to-eye, the slaughter might be diminished. He wanted to see what was being done on the subject these days.

The program for today read:

END OF THE WORLD IN PROPHECY
ARK OF THE COVENANT AND THE CHOSEN PEOPLE
ARMAGEDDON UPDATED—THE MODERN VERSION
EARTHQUAKES IN THE BIBLE AND ELSEWHERE.
SURVIVAL IN THE LAST DAYS

And then, in larger letters:

OPEN FORUM

Apparently, space permitting, he was free to wander from one amphitheater to another.

There was no point in staying the whole afternoon.

"Or should I? If I keep escaping whatever I don't like, then how am I going to get closer to people? After all, they are what they are. I have no right to judge them. They are the best that they can be," he argued with himself, silently.

But he lacked courage. He was afraid to loose all respect for the human race if he participated in fundamentalists' raving about the end of the world. Don't they know that the world is as eternal as they are? How can you have an end when there was no beginning? And even a few billion years back, before the Earth became habitable to entities in their present form, didn't they even suspect that their form might have changed? Not to mention that there are other planets, other solar systems? Countless worlds, or as the Catholics like to say "Worlds without end...?"

When they're right, they're right.

Even the Druids accepted the concept of an immortal soul. How can they reconcile immorality with a beginning? Yet most, if not all, religions insisted on an ending. Maybe not today, maybe not tomorrow, but one day the world would end, they insisted. They couldn't explain the beginning so they thought that explaining the end would be easier?

I must do something, he thought.

I must do something.

I must.

Sacha sat through all the lectures.

He joined the listeners in the other hall only to find himself just as bored. On pins and needles—but he sat through all the juvenile speculations. First he amused himself in alternating from one hall to another and trying to guess what has been said before. Later he attempted to read some of the speakers' thoughts. Only now and then did they coincide with the orators' mouths. The speakers recited well-learned manuscripts, probably regarding this get-together as a free forum to advertise their books.

And what ludicrous books they were.

Sacha sat quietly, his mind wondering repeatedly what he was doing there. This was not a gathering to foster ecumenical harmony, but a forum for cranks to air their distorted perception of reality. True—it was an open forum. You didn't have to be sane to share your views. All cranks were welcome. The freedom of speech ruled supreme.

Blah, blah...

Sacha learned that the world was about to end. He was offered indisputable evidence from beautifully distorted sources, Biblical and otherwise, that his days were numbered. Yet this was not enough. He was assured that not all of us would be treated to a good dose of fire and brimstone. Some of us will be whisked up in a single swoop and raised to heaven.

"Way up there," the speaker pointed to the ceiling; where we, 'they', will await better times?

A single swoop without so much as a parachute. No data have been offered where the lucky few would return thereafter, since the Earth would no longer be there. Here? The world had ended, remember?

Sacha scanned the speaker's mind to see if he really believed in all this nonsense. The next moment he was stamped. The thought patterns in the speaker's mind were so scattered, so incomprehensibly jumbled that, try as he would, he could not detect the man's real self. Perhaps the scientists had finally succeeded in creating zombies, by sending the souls of some men to upper realms ahead of their physical deaths?

No, that wouldn't work.

What would work would be for the scientists to maintain the bodies artificially alive after the consciousness had left them. I suppose the stories about zombies might be true, after all, he mused, half-seriously.

Sacha also thumbed through some books offered for sale during the various intermissions. He would have been better off thumbing through *The Art of Motorcycle Maintenance* and the attendant Zen, or for that matter jumping through Don Juan's *Rings of Power*. Here he found mostly dissertations on the subject of flying angels, messengers of some concerned deity sitting on convoluted clouds, ready to reward or punish the faithful or the sinners, apparently with a wink and a giggle.

"Don't people have enough problems to solve in their own lives," Sacha mused aloud.

"Ours is not to reason why..." A readymade slogan reached his ears. He moved on.

Do they have to assign tasks to some dualistic, judgmental god just to satisfy their feelings of inferiority? What happened to the saying "Ye are gods?" Even the armies of scholars hadn't managed to destroy some of the truth still discernible in some of the scriptures.

"You are gods!" he wanted to stand up and shout. "You are gods, indivisible…"

His thoughts were interrupted by thunderous applause. A man in colorful attire just mounted the stage. The time was 3 p.m.. These must be the big boys, he thought. I'd better listen.

"We humbly present to you His Divine Grace…." There followed a string of other titles.

If he is so divine, then what is he doing here? Why hasn't he merged his consciousness with the Whole? How come he looks so old and worn, and decrepit? Can't he even repair himself? And if he can't, what can he possibly do for others?

Sacha knew that repairing oneself was not on the priority list of the great souls. Many were hoping to do their bit down here, and get back to the higher realms. But this? And on the top of it all, the man had a profusion of paint smeared all over his face. No wonder his grimace was filled with pain.

Sacha withdrew to the corridor.

He had enough religion for one day. Perhaps forever. Few steps away, he saw a man sitting on a windowsill. Elderly, a sad smile on his worn face, his gaze far away.

"You too?" he greeted Sacha without turning around.

"Yes, I didn't find what I was looking for," Sacha admitted. The old man's thoughts were orderly, easy to read.

"Ah, yes." The man nodded. "Perhaps up there…"

He wasn't pointing to the sky, but to a series of doors opening on the other side of the corridor. Sacha sat down next to him. The man told him a lot of things that were not advertised in the entrance lobby. He spoke quietly, explaining what really happens at such conventions.

Sacha learned that the 'real' Ecumenical Sessions were taking place concurrently with the lectures offered in the two amphitheaters. Apparently in addition to the main auditoria, there were a dozen meeting rooms, secreted about the building. The higher echelons of the dominant religions attended *those* conferences. Their attendance was limited to three representatives of a number of Christian sects, or churches; equal number was assigned to the representatives of Islam—Shia, Sunnis and Sufis. A number of Jewish denominations represented the Diaspora. Another trio were speaking for Hinduism and a dozen others were allowed to attend, with limited power of vote. Each representative could call on six consultants, secretaries and such like, who drafted the preambles in the remaining meeting chambers. A few others had been allowed in as silent witnesses to the discussions.

There was a conspicuous absence of the Buddhists. Perhaps the followers of Siddhartha Gautama didn't really regard themselves as a religion. More as students of reality. Like his father. Or perhaps they were all just a little too enlightened?

When the man finished explaining, he got up, smiled, bowed slightly and left. Sacha never saw him again.

Sacha was grateful. Perhaps out there, he thought, behind the closed doors, they made more sense than here. With a sense of unrequited hunger, he left the Batterymarch Conference Center and took a relaxing ride through Boston. He needed a break. Boston was a beautiful city, filled with beautiful people going about their business. They seemed glad to be alive. People aren't all bad, he mused, with a wry grin. Perhaps God created religions to keep an eye on all the cranks. If I ever meet God, I'll ask Her, he promised himself. I could then present a beautiful lecture on the subject.

Only he doubted anyone would come.

**

9
Apron Strings

Sacha was disgusted. He returned to the Batterymarch
Conference Center in time for the evening session. Not
that it did him much good.

The Ecumenicists, Ecumenicals, or whatever they chose
to call themselves, left a bad taste in his mouth. But they may
have served to inject some humility into his relatively
cheerful and carefree life. It wasn't their attitude. They did
what they had to do. But Sacha had learned in one easy lesson
that one is not allowed into the inner chambers of power just
because one is bright and willing. Before leaving the
Convention Center that evening, he made a half-hearted
attempt to gain entry to the inner sanctum where the 'big
boys' negotiated 'big deals'. The art of *quid pro quo* was
unknown to him. He saw no reason for compromise. If we all
strove for the best, there wouldn't be any need for such.

He was young.

He didn't have a chance.

He was asked, politely, which particular church was he
the head of, or at least held documents attesting his
authorization to speak in the particular church's name.

Unable to satisfy either requirement, he was, politely,
directed to the Main Hall, where the oversized gentlemen
(four hunks to be precise) assured him that he would be taken
care of to his entire satisfaction. Sacha replied that he'd

already been there, and there was no activity taking place there, which had anything whatsoever to do with the ecumenical movement.

"Oh, yes, there is, Sir," the second Herculean guard assured him. "There we offer microphones to anyone who chooses to have his say on any religion he or she may espouse."

"Including ecumenicalism?" Sacha asked with a good dose of sarcasm.

"Including Ecumenism," the colossus agreed pronouncing the word with a deep nod of his head.

But Sacha had already given up. In fact he was rather tickled by having been addressed as 'sir'. It must have been his first. "Sir," he muttered under his nose. "Sir Sacha," he mused. "Rather British, don't you know, old chap?"

"Well, son? How was your day?" Alec asked him on the way back home.

"Three days," Sacha corrected. "Boston is a beautiful city," he added appreciatively.

"That's it, son?"

"That, and I'd learned that I am not ready, as yet, to live among people," he added. It was a sad realization.

He was not ready to step into the 'real world'. In fact, it was a world of illusion, an arbitrary construct more fragile in its structure than a single act of faith. Sacha decided to experiment with his own miniature universe, his own body.

For his father the trip has been more successful. Two post-doctoral students asked him if they could work under his wing on theoretical research. Alec was sufficiently unspoiled to find such inquiries flattering. He had no idea how very well known his work has become.

Back in LA, Desmond assured him: "I guarantee an Alfrrred beforrre ye die!"

"Alfred?" Alec was a little tired.

On the airplane from Boston Sacha was drilling him on possibilities of studies in Canada, Europe or anywhere for that matter.

"Mrrr. Nobel, m'lad. Alfred Bernhard Nobel!" Desmond explained.

"Ah... you mean posthumously?"

"Now, now, my lad. That will be enough of that!"

To Professor McBride anyone under sixty was a lad. And some over sixty as well. He also had an arsenal of much more condescending, not to mention degrading expletives for people he didn't like. 'Lad' was his term of endearment.

A week after their return, Sacha began a new series of experiments.

Some time ago, he'd learned to control his breathing and his blood flow. This served to increase his awareness of every minute aspect of his physical body. He now decided to attempt the reverse. He decided to attempt withdrawing his attention from his physical envelope. Not completely, that would mean death, but partially, retaining just tenuous control of his physical awareness.

It took many months. He would practice not just while sitting in total silence and concentration, but during all his daily activities. And there were many of these. He also continued his studies to be able to qualify for enrollment to any university of his choice. But that would come later. He would have to be at least sixteen to be taken at all seriously. He decided to wait.

In the meantime, he was beginning to get some results. One afternoon, alone in the condo, he decided to take his exercises a step further. He sat on a straight-backed chair in his room, and watched with morbid fascination as his left hand virtually withered before his eyes. He accomplished this by withdrawing his attention, the light, one might say, or better still the life force, from his palm and fingers. He quickly restored the previous vital condition. He'd obviously gone too far.

He now attempted to withdraw his conscious attention but allow the subconscious to maintain its supervisory activities. In other words the biochemical functions continued. Next he took a long needle he'd prepared for the occasion, and pushed it through the middle of his palm until it emerged on the other side. He thought it would be easy, but it required a fair amount of force.

It worked. He felt no pain whatsoever. He was well on the way to control his physical envelope in both time frames. Forward and backwards. He could withdraw life from his body and he could restore it. This was nothing like going to sleep or even falling into a coma. This was a conscious control of his presence in and out of his body, while allowing his physique to support itself, at least for a certain period of time.

He practiced this on various parts of his body. In a way, it was a form of hypnosis. He controlled his body with his mind. It took a lot of work but each successive step was easier. He never lost his fascination with the magnificent organization of the organism. It truly was a universe in its own right. There was a time when he had little regard for his body. His attitude changed diametrically. He now bestowed on it all the respect and admiration it deserved. He'd learned to treat it kindly, one could say—with love.

"A universe of my own, right here, on Earth, amid the ocean of fragile illusion," he mused.

Nevertheless he was not his construct, but it was his to govern. In essence, he had learned to die and to come back to life. At will.

He was ready for the next step.

By the time Sacha had turned fifteen, he had already passed all the high-school exams and wrote papers on more advanced subjects. The papers had been submitted to three universities, and within three months he had been sent application forms for enrollment. For better or worse, he had never advertised his age nor the method of his studies. At the time it wasn't necessary. Now, it could prove fatal.

He felt he had to go. Anywhere. Soon.

Already for a number of years he hadn't attended any school that normal, meaning average, children attended. There was no point, really. Even is he had no interest in any particular subject, a few days before any exam of the State Board of Education, he would put the relevant books under his pillow, and the following morning he could recite pages from the text verbatim.

On the other hand, there were other subjects, which absorbed him completely.

But that wasn't the problem. His trip to Boston had shown him that what he was missing were not the studies, *per se*, but the company of other, diverse people. He couldn't mix with boys his own age for obvious reasons. Playing for an hour or two, kicking or throwing a ball or racing his bicycle were all fine. But sooner or later he and they would have to sit down and talk.

About what? The jargon changed from one year to another.

"Did ya see that dame?"

"She's got'er skirt glued on."

"Her boobs are 'bout to fall out."

"Dig those hips, they work like a pair of cylinders. Oompha, oompha..."

"Oompha, oompha, oompha, oompha..." the other boys joined.

Sacha didn't. He liked girls well enough, but he was able to think also with his head, not just his *cojones*. He also enjoyed the boys' company, but, well, it wasn't enough. He desperately needed some kind of exchange, some airing of ideas which his age group, or even those two or three years his senior, did not provide.

He had to go.

In his spare time, Sacha played the stock market. Soon, he made a substantial sum of money. He employed the method suggested by the Chaos Theory, which his father taught him when he was eleven. Patterns within patterns. He first played on paper, actually on the computer virtual desktop, just for fun. Then he borrowed $200 dollars from his father and opened an account with a broker who allowed on line day-trading. With up to forty transactions a day, he doubled the money weekly. Almost weekly. In just over ten weeks he returned Alec the two hundred he borrowed, and cashed his stocks to his account. The balance sheet, clear of all the commissions, read almost $100,000. There would be taxes to pay, but for now he felt very rich. He couldn't imagine why he would need any more. Not for now.

Next, he again needed his father's help. But he went about getting it in his own particular, if not peculiar, way. Since Alec was late coming home from Caltech, he left a cryptic note on his father's bedside table.

"I'll see you tonight on the Home Planet. Please come."

Alec sat at the same window on which he and Suzy liked to sit so many times. It seemed the last time they met here was ages ago, yet Suzy's sweet scent still lingered.

"I thought I would find you here, Ali. Are you avoiding me?"

Alec turned from the breathtaking view of green hills reflected in the lustrous lake. Facing him was his wife, exactly as she was way back, when they sat here for the very first time. This was 'their' villa.

"Sacha is coming," he said.

He took Suzy in his arms. This was also part of the Home Planet ritual. Here they were eternally young. They lingered in each other's arms like lovers who've only just met.

"If you two lovebirds ever come up for air, I have things to ask you."

Sacha stood behind the young couple that seemed completely unaware of his presence. Here and now, they were all about the same age. All three looked as though they were in their middle twenties. Sacha waited, a grin broadening on his handsome face. Somehow he contrived to look very masculine and youthful at the same time. Sacha was a very good dreamer. Or, perhaps, he just dreamt what he thought would give the most pleasure to his parents. For here, they were still his parents. Here Alec and Suzy brought with them a much greater experience of the physical realm. And it was this experience Sacha needed. On Earth he was still a greenhorn filled with innumerable data only loosely connected. Here, those theoretical facts could be connected almost instantaneously, with his parents' help. Through telepathy.

He waited for his mother to disengage herself from Alec's embrace. It wasn't the first time he'd had to wait. After what seemed like ages, his father spoke: "Did you hear someone say something, Darling?"

Suzy didn't move, cuddling even closer.

"Noooo?" She said it with an upward tilt as the Swedes do.

Home Planet was also a reality of fun and games.

Sacha was in a quandary. He had to advance his knowledge. He had to gain greater knowledge of how people behaved in 'real life'. He had to find a way of taking life in the physical reality as 'real', not just as a dream. He needed this to accomplish his destiny. He still didn't feel in the thick of things. Certain events have already given him hints, but that's all they were. Hints.

At long last, Suzy, Alec and Sacha disposed themselves on various sitting pieces—white blocks that looked like marble until you sat on them. The instant you did, the cubes adapted themselves to the contours of your body. Home Planet was like that. Whoever visited the villa would find it 'purpose made' to his or her needs.

Sacha liked coming to the Home Planet to talk about his problems. Here, virtually nothing was impossible; and also, the passage of time on Home Planet was many times slower. You didn't have to try for a quick answer. He realized recently that there was no point having all his knowledge if he didn't know what to do with it; if he couldn't apply it to something useful. Here, sharing knowledge, ideas, was also much easier. You could use your imagination to understand other peoples' concepts. All in all, it was easier to communicate. If you couldn't think of the right words to describe something, you just did your best to imagine it and... it worked. A sort of emotional telepathy.

"What is it, son?" Alec gave Sacha his total attention.

Sacha described his dilemma as best he could. Here he could even tell his mother of his interest in ecumenism without making her nervous. At least, not too nervous. She'd developed a great mistrust for religions. She grew afraid of them. She knew that her fear was not rational, but this didn't assuage her feelings. She still worried that Sacha might fall under some adverse, exploitative influence. But by the time she'd return to physical reality, back to Earth, Sacha's interests would longer be subject to first shock. The ideas would have mellowed. And anyway, up here, even for Suzy, who invariably tried to protect Sacha from the foibles of physical reality, the word 'impossible' was not part of her vocabulary.

They both listened without interrupting.

Sacha described his unsuccessful attempt to gain entry at the Convention Center to the rooms where more serious aspects of ecumenism were being discussed.

"And no matter whether I could do anything or not, they just wouldn't take me seriously. Is it just my age, or is there more to it? After all, all I wanted was to learn. At least to listen..."

"You need more experience in handling people, son..."

"And you must develop a reputation; in any field—it takes time," Suzy thought aloud.

"Studies. Mixing with your pears, which means the senior years in any number of universities..." Alec sounded pensive.

"Travel. First travel," Suzy sounded insistent until she realized that if Sacha were to travel then he would cut his apron strings. "No, noooo, studies are better," she corrected herself.

Sacha laughed. "Don't worry, Mother. I would write. Promise."

Suzy smiled but even here, which is as close to heaven as most people get between their reincarnations, a touch of sadness crept into her eyes. Sacha was growing up. Her little baby was sprouting his own, personal wings.

Sacha was cheating—just a little.

He invited his parents to meet him here but he didn't tell them everything. Oh, he certainly wanted to hear what they had to say. But what he actually did was to scan their emotional bodies. On home planet they are as easy to read as physical bodies on Earth. Reading thoughts was not the same. At this stage of his development, he could only read thoughts of which the thinker was reasonably conscious. Here, the subconscious manifested itself in the perception of the reality that formed this planet. Sacha could scan his parents' minds and learn of ideas that were merely just germinating at their unconscious level. Yet even those thoughts were coloured by the experiences they both acquired on Earth. It was as Thomas Aquinas had said: Whatever is received is received according to the nature of the recipient. He was not talking about their spiritual nature. Nature of the recipient is formulated by his relationship to the reality he or she lives in. It is formulated by our individual perceptions. This accounts for our magnificent diversity.

"I'm getting the idea, Mom."

It sounded a bit strange, because right now, as Sacha used his advanced abilities, he looked certainly more mature, if not older, than his mother. Things like this happen on the Home Planet. Your real nature tends to come to the fore. He quickly corrected the impression he was creating. He went slightly overboard and reduced his apparent years by an extra five. Suzy noticed and managed a smile.

"You are getting very good at this, Sacha. But don't think I didn't notice your shenanigans."

Alec nodded. "And—you were picking our thoughts again, weren't you son?"

"Actually more like images. I wouldn't pick your thoughts without your permission."

"Like hell you wouldn't! Particularly if you thought you could get away with it." Alec wagged a fatherly finger.

"Sorry, Dad. But you knew that I came here to ask your advice."

This time it was Alec's head that wagged from side to side but he let that go. Sacha was right. This time. He had told them that he wanted advice. He just had an unorthodox method of obtaining it.

They sat for a while regarding the idyllic landscape. The air was so clear that the mountains on both sides of the lake didn't conceal even their minutest details. As they continued to look, the crags on the right grew another four or five hundred meters. Suzy smiled. She loved paining with her mind. Their eyes could perform feats unheard of on Earth. Even at great distance, a diversity of details was readily available to their vision. No wonder the Home Planet was heaven for most religions of Earth. It was truly heavenly. Though only if you ignored its nether regions.

"I don't suppose you'd want to follow in your father's footsteps...?" Suzy murmured breaking the silence.

"Or be a professional tennis player?" Alec offered. "There is lots more money in it."

All three laughed—Suzy, a little nervously.

But they knew that Sacha was developing his very own plans for his future. For some reason, they both found this thought disquieting. They didn't understand their own qualms. Not even up here.

Not even in this wondrous Eden.

There was a lot to be done. Sacha had to submit papers, fill in application forms, sit exams, attend interviews. His schooling was unorthodox and thus his methods of application to universities also required certain originality. His father and Desmond proved very helpful. Particularly Dr. Desmond McBride who, as the Chancellor of Caltech, carried considerable clout. But even more so, Desmond's peers, throughout the world, liked him. The students were scared stiff of him, but only those who didn't put their noses to the grindstone. Those who did learned to respect him, and out of respect grew admiration and eventually a genuine liking.

Desmond had sent out letters to all his academic friends who could be of any help to young Sacha. The answers came promptly, but it still took over six months before the contacts became firmly established. Desmond was not asking for any special treatment; only for *equal* treatment. He argued that Sacha should not be penalized for his studies having been carried out at home, nor should his age be taken negatively into consideration.

Sacha's applications were principally to the departments of political science, history and psychology. As a fringe benefit, he was hoping to gain access to the voluminous libraries, which the principal universities of the world enjoyed. As for studies, his main motivation was the intercourse with the students as well as the teaching staff. He needed to learn about other people's ambitions, plans for their future, general interests. He had to find out their real passions, not just those necessary to pass the exams.

He wanted to study the students while they studied.

Finally a confirmation came from one of his foremost choices. Next month Sacha would be leaving for England. The land where his grandparents had been born and raised, where people carried umbrellas tightly rolled and tipped their bowler-hats when greeting a lady.

He was leaving, in the words of a song, for Dear Old London Town.

SACHA 15+312

It strikes me, that after almost sixteen years of sharing many perceptions of the physical reality, my parents still regard the 'inner realms', as they call them, as the produce of their imagination or overactive mind. The strange thing is that, in a very specific way, they are right. Both the Home Planet and the Far Country are very much the products of imagination and mind, respectively, but not in the way they think.

After many a discussion on the subject, I am still under the impression that they feel, no matter how unwittingly, that their emotional and mental perceptions are the products of their physical consciousness. That they are generated by their willingness to let their imagination, and/or their creative thought-streams, to have their own way.

There is no way I can find to approach the subject from my point of view, and show them that their perceptions of all realities have taken a reverse spin. When I suggested as much they instantly agreed, and minutes later reverted to the thought patterns of their previous orientation. They still associate their being with that perception which forms their physical entity. Perhaps that is as it should be. Perhaps one should identify with the object of ones contemplation. And after all, what is physical life but a contemplation of a dream we all dreamt in Bardo?

So, in a way they are right.

By contrast, I find myself completely incapable of aligning my viewpoint with their perception of reality. Not altogether, although I've made considerable progress in that direction. I've learned to enjoy certain aspects of becoming that the physical senses offer. I've also examined and mastered most aspects of my own physical body. But I can also come and go from its constrains, without jeopardizing its safety. And, contrary to my parents, I do so in full consciousness.

This is perhaps the greatest difference between them and myself. From within my true reality, the Undiscovered Realm, I am aware of my mental, emotional and physical bodies remaining in their respective actualities. What I am really trying to say is that I enjoy my state of becoming in all the perceptions simultaneously. I don't go in or out, or up or down, I am in all states at the same time. The only thing that changes is my attention. Wheresoever I place it, I am there. But since my point of origin is not the physical reality only the Undiscovered Realm, I do not lose awareness of all my other attributes.

At best, my parents regard the various perceptions (or various realities as they think of them), as attributes of their individualized soul. I, on the other hand, consider those very same perceptions as my attributes, and the individual 'realities' as products of those very attributes. It is as though they were on the outside looking in. I am inside, and whenever I must, I look out.

It seems that I shall have to suspend my attitude, to a greater degree, if I am to fulfill my mission. For I am now convinced that every one of us has a mission. I find it acutely frustrating that I still have not discovered the nature of my own. It could be the consequence of my refusal to suspend my perception of the Undiscovered Realm—even for an instant.

Yet that is where I have my being. All else is an illusion. An arbitrary construct.

I simply cannot find the right words to show mom and dad, those dear souls with whom I've shared various perceptions so many times before, that there is only one Reality. All else is just perception. A point of view.

And yet? And yet I am here, in my physical body, writing these notes on my computer. I know that I must live out my own dream. In a way, I must wake up. It seems to be the very opposite of what all people I've met should do. They must wake up to my perception of reality, even as I must awaken to theirs. Only it is so very, very difficult. Apparently, for all of us.

It is like cutting the apron strings.

On the eve of departure for England, Sacha dreamt about already being in London. The London he visited was not a pleasant place. It was rife with poverty, with the smell of open sewers that was quite overpowering. The dark, musty, and dirty streets were populated with people clad in Dickensian attire—most were torn and filthy. The whole atmosphere was an actuality Sacha had no desire to visit. Not again. He found himself being driven in a one-horse buggy. Apparently he was a reasonably well-positioned gentleman, although, on second glance, the suit he wore had seen better days. He was on his way to help... to help someone. A sick girl?

Unbeknownst to him, Sacha was taking a step into his own past.

***

10
Scholarship

Sacha **flew to London** on British Airways. People running the Heathrow Airport were not as obsessed with security measures as the armies of guards at the international airports in the United States. There was a discreet 'uniformed' presence, but the military did not flaunt their wares. His passport was checked, and that was that. He was welcomed to Great Britain without further ado.

London impressed him.

Like New York, the City was intrinsically cosmopolitan, so much so that at times he lost awareness of what part of the world he was in. Blacks, Asians, Latinos, at times seemed to dominate the Whites. In the USA they called Blacks African-Americans. Even those who had been born and bread in the States for ten generations. Darn silly, Sacha thought. And what of African Americans who were born in the USA and then decided to emigrate to Africa? Would they be American-African-Americans or African-American-Africans? Or would anybody care? Other than the AAAs or the AAAs. He supposed that back home, in the States, immigrants from Europe should have been called European-Americans. Unless they were European-Canadians, of course. As for himself, he would be European-Canadian-American. That would leave the Indian tribes who could safely assume the title of Americans without any qualification. Only they didn't. They called themselves Native Americans.

Go figure.

In Europe they had different hang-ups, but colour wasn't considered offensive. After all, no Blacks were really black, even as no Whites were white. More like sickly pale pink. But you couldn't go around referring to people as Sickly-Pale-Pinkos, could you? It would sound silly.

After installing himself in a bed-and-breakfast room in South Ken, Sacha wandered the streets soaking up their diversity. In LA, no matter what minority one met, they all seemed to have been cast in the same mold—the American Melting Pot. They complained about the same things, spoke with a similar accent, or at least employed the same street vernacular. From what he'd heard, they even watched the same TV programs. In London you could literally forget which part of the world you were in. People retained their native characteristics without flaunting them. The country of origin was their business and nobody else's. Some time later, Sacha learned the reason why. In Britain if you visited a village ten miles away from your own, you were regarded a foreigner. What's a few miles, or a few thousand miles, more or less? After all, in Old English 'foreign' meant 'outside' or 'exterior'. It did not specify outside of what. A foreigner is a foreigner. Who can tell the difference between one foreigner and another? On the other hand, most foreigners simply qualified as bloody foreigners; an appellative, reputedly illegal, though frankly no longer offensive—merely descriptive. He wondered if most people in London were foreigners.

Some months later he found that there was another reason for such visible diversity.

Back home, most people tried to create an impression of something or someone they were not. They exaggerated their incomes, their positions, the size of their houses, even the year in which their automobiles had been manufactured. They aspired to be more then they really were. Regrettably, their aspirations were limited only to their material guise. They desired not just to keep up with the Joneses, but to supplant them.

Not so in the Old Country.

In Britain if you pretended to be something you were not, you invited immediate ridicule. People were touchy about their heritage, but not jealous of others. As for your automobile, nothing was as fashionable as an old relic. The British regarded their vintage automobiles, 'cars' down here, the way the French regard their wines. Actually, there was a way you could cheat in Britain. You could *understate* your financial status. Sacha soon discovered that the Scots were best at this. He'd never met a Scot who admitted to being rich. He also discovered that Scots were among the most generous of people.

Sacha was glad he'd flown in on a Canadian passport. In Buckingham Palace resided *his* queen.

On Wednesday, the day of his arrival, he partook in a venerable British institution, the queue, to buy tickets to the Covent Gardens. The great Baranoff was in town to sing Boris Goudonov. In LA he'd read that not since Chaliapin, did any man resurrect Tsar Boris from the grave, and made him walk the stage. He got tickets for Friday performance.

The opera illustrated the struggle of People versus Authority. This struggle interested him more and more. From the libretto he'd gathered that there are only two stars in the Boris Goudonov: The Tsar and the People. Sacha sided with the people. Yet he felt sympathy for Boris. The Tsar was one against the many. Whatever his faults, Sacha felt a strange allegiance to the Tsar's paradox. History was peppered with individuals attempting to advance the lot of humanity. Not that Boris did. Yet, the many seldom wanted to be helped.

Sacha had six more days before catching a bus to Oxford.

From his room in South Kensington he could walk to see most of the famous landmarks, though to traverse the whole of London on foot would have taken him a good few months.

Taxis were out. They took too long. There was always the Tube—the Underground train—what the French in Montreal called the Metro. Perhaps a good place to observe people, if you wanted to observe them from *very* close. Sacha was grateful that oral hygiene was well developed in London. He was fascinated by people but did not feel the need to have their shirt buttons form impressions on his chest. Yet he found them amazing. Sandwiched together like sardines in a can, they managed to remain aloof, almost distant.

Very British, he thought.

So for the most part Sacha walked, or took a bus. At least from the double-decker he could see the history of the city. It was faster than walking, though not much. Not in the West End or the City, which was the way the Londoners referred to Downtown. The City also incorporated the financial district, with the buildings dating back to the prime of the British Empire.

Sacha had landed in the Old Country the day after he'd turned sixteen. He decided to celebrate his birthday, belatedly, with a pint of ale in the East End. He hoped that they wouldn't ask him to show proof of adulthood. He'd read that the East End had changed more in recent years than any other part of London. What once was *de facto* an ocean of slums had been replaced with brand new developments. "Our future lies in the East," announced the mayor, when opening the Olympia Center built by two Jewish gentlemen from New York. Or were they from Toronto? No matter. Money has no nationality.

Though in a brand-new building, the interior was designed to simulate pubs of yesteryear. Dark, musky and... noisy. That last came in as a bonus: a number of TVs had volume turned full on. The only thing missing was the smell of stale smoke.

Sacha perched himself on a stool at the end of a brightly polished bar counter, watching people discussing the latest match (still on TV) between Tottenham and Arsenal—soccer teams to which the local aficionados referred to as Spur and the Gunners, respectively. The factions were equally divided. Sacha surmised that a number of burly fans were about to add physical persuasion to win their argument. He managed a long quaff from his tall glass when, without warning, the lights went out. Next moment they came on again, greatly dimmed. He found himself sitting in semi-darkness. Unwittingly, he pulled his shoulders in to be a little less conspicuous.

He needn't have worried. As if by a wave of Hudini's wand, the pub transformed itself into an Ol' Tavern, filled with so much acrid tobacco smoke that no one would recognize him.

"Another one, gov?"

A man with long hairy arms, and proportionately as long sideburns, regarded him from a great height. The floor behind the counter must have moved up a foot or two. The publican was as impressive, thanks to his towering height, as he was disarming by the grace of his boisterous smile.

"Ay, the same please," Sacha heard himself saying.

If they were to make a movie of a tavern as envisioned by Charles Dickens, it would look exactly like this. At least judging by what he could see through the blue and yellow vapors. Not surprisingly, Sacha started coughing. Until he confirmed the smoky presence, the fumes didn't seem to affect him. Now he felt vaguely sick. Nauseated. It was evident that he'd entered the time frame of the dream he'd had just before he'd left LA.

A nightmare?

The publican put an enormous tankard in front of him. Sacha reached into his pocket and threw a coin on the worse-for-ware counter. Evidently it had been polished by thousands of elbows rubbing its surface but it also showed scars of many a battle being fought in its immediate vicinity.

Sacha was rapidly loosing his self-confidence.

The next moment he saw his own severely spotted reflection in the mirror adorning the wall over the back counter. He cringed at the thought that he must have recently lost a bout with smallpox, until he realized that it was the mirror that suffered the malady. His reflection was further sliced by shelves, and punctured by bottles and tankards, but it was clear that he was looking at himself. He was a tall man, his hair just turning gray at the temples were peeking from under a silken top hat. He must have been about forty, reasonably good-looking, with broad shoulders and elegant attire of which Nicholas Nickleby would be proud.

"Will Miss Maxine be joining you today, gov?"

Sacha felt a gentle tap on his shoulder. He glanced sideways without moving his body. A smallish man was bending low at his elbow. When erect, his face reached the elevation of Sacha's nose, which being attached to Sacha's face, could not avoid the odious confrontation. Contrary to people in the Tube some centuries later, the man's breath could kill all the roaches in immediate vicinity. Sacha held his own as studied the man more closely.

"And what's that to you?" he asked. He was surprised at the aggressive tone of his own voice.

"Thought you might want a roid, loik the last toim." The man smiled exposing the remnants of yellowish-brown teeth.

"I'll let you know." Sacha dismissed him with a wave of his hand.

Sacha vaguely remembered the man. He used to pick up floozies in this pub and take them for a ride in his hansom for, what they called in his circles "a bit of hanky-panky." He remembered the man because contrary to the man's breath, his hansom, a two wheeled, one horse, covered conveyance was spotlessly clean. A rare circumstance at best. Also the hansom was for two people only and the driver had an elevated seat at the back, which offered total privacy to the couple in the carriage.

Sacha's presence in this reality began to grow its own roots.

Since his wife died, his medical practice had lost its clientele. He or his professional services were no longer fashionable. It had been his late wife's influence that drew the elite to his elegant offices in Harley Street. Now, he catered to whoever could afford his, considerably reduced, fees. As for social life, there was no money at all. Except for a bit of slap'n tickle.

At this very moment a young woman festooned appropriately in a long dress and bodice that squeezed her none-too-flamboyant pulchritude as high up as it would go, barged into the tavern. After a quick glance around she pushed two men roughly to the side, and made for the stool on which Sacha was sitting.

"A spin 'round the block, luv? Fer ol' toim saik?"

She sounded like a bad imitation of Elisa Doolittle.

"And just how did you know I was here?" he smiled. The girl had large blue eyes filled with professional innocence that belied her chosen profession.

"I can tell when ya're around, gov. I can just tell..." she teased. Her 'I' sounded more like an 'Oi'. Then a hurt pout formed on her full lips. "Oi missed ya somethin' awful, Oi really did, luv. Somethin' awful."

For a moment she was busy wiping a non-existent tear with her sleeve.

"Oi did, Sir," she confirmed, just to make sure Sacha, or whoever was the tall man she was tempting, got the message. Sacha realized that he would never have given his real name in such surroundings. It wouldn't do any good for his shrinking practice.

Sacha threw another coin on the counter and allowed himself to be led outside the tavern. The girl held on to his elbow, while the man who previously offered the services of his hansom led the way. He felt a little like a lamb being led to slaughter. He knew he would succumb to the girl's charms. He was that lonely. He also knew that he was risking contracting a disease if he went too often too far. But what did he have to lose?

Outside the air hit him with a wallop, but the visibility did not improve. A wet white blanket embraced him with penetrating coolness. The last sound he heard was a distant plaintive wail of a river foghorn, reaching him from some errant scow groping its way along the Thames. The moan was followed by a surprising pain in his neck.

The fog thickened into absolute darkness that prevailed until he opened his eyes. "I must have lost consciousness. Momentarily," he thought.

He found himself slumping over the counter. He was delighted that he could breathe. Not exactly the fresh breath of the Pacific, but nevertheless real air. Carefully, to avoid the pain in his neck, he straightened up. He was back in the twenty-first century. The argument for and against Arsenal and Tottenham got a bit rowdy. One of the bottles, or some other untoward object, had landed, probably quite accidentally, at the back of his head. It would be sore tomorrow. He put the incident down to experience.

I'm learning, he thought. And then he remembered the time-warp. He decided not to drink any more. He simply wasn't used to British ale. Or any ale.

He never found any need for it.

A week later a bus took him to Oxford.

Sitting back, he relived some scenes from Boris Goudonov. The opera was everything he'd imagined it would be. And he was right. The Tsar was one against the many. He was a tyrant. He was also the loneliest man in the world. Why did I choose to see this particular opera, he wondered? Am I not lonely enough all by myself? Like attracts like, he mused...

He dismissed the cobwebs before he had a chance to start feeling sorry for himself.

They say that accidents don't happen and that there is no such thing as a coincidence. If so, how come he arrived in Oxford on the last day, just in time to enroll for an exam for a scholarship? He decided to play a hunch. Thanks to Dr.

McBride's connections he was allowed to sit, and thanks to his own efforts, he had already passed the entry exams. But he decided to sit for them again. Just for fun. If he passed, he would qualify for a resident's grant. He would live on campus and be paid for it. He couldn't resist the opportunity. Not that he needed the money, but it may well have been the only way to gain admittance to, what Desmond McBride had called, the bursary.

Oxford was unique. There were more than three thousand post-graduates in the Arts and Humanities alone. Out of a total of 16,500 students, a quarter came from overseas. They represented some one hundred and thirty nationalities.

A month after his arrival in England, Sacha was declared the youngest winner of the recently forged Bertrand Russell Liberal Arts Scholarship. More so, he had won the scholarships against tremendous competition. That was the beginning. Within a week he'd learned that all he had to do now was to qualify for the Blues, the rowing team, and his reputation would be established. The studies were coincidental. In fact, he had to be careful not to show off his knowledge. Nobody likes a show-off. Not the students—not the teaching staff. He recalled mother telling dad, "Nobody likes a Smart Alec, Alec," she'd said. The phrase stuck in his mind.

The next three years passed like a whirlwind. Sacha had joined all the societies he could think of. He ran, rowed, threw the javelin, and played chess. He also studied. This last for appearances only. He also paid close attention to make sure that he was always in the first five in his year. Not first, but also not lower then fifth. This too created a challenge. Except for the final thesis. There he could finally be himself.

Finally, Sacha left Oxford as an honorary member of the Royal Society. They were threatening to actually put his name up for Fellowship of the British Academy. He escaped just in time.

The British cherished their titles.

But what Sacha cherished much more, were the memories of the town itself. He defied anyone not to get lost in London at least once. Not so in Oxford. He could embrace its scale. The Departments and Colleges were scattered all over town. When time permitted, he loved just walking the historical streets, many free of traffic, or strolling the alleys of the University Parks maintained with meticulous care. Only the English knew how to maintain their gardens. When he wanted solitude, he would walk to Christ Church Cathedral and the adjacent Meadow. But the greatest love he reserved for the Bodleian Library. There he consumed the tomes as fast as he could get them.

"Here comes the Canadian Glutton..." he heard whispers as he approached the counter with a half-dozen books under his arm. "He swallows books whole... cover and all..."

This too was part of the process of learning.

Next, his insatiable hunger took him to the Sorbonne. There he'd spent a whole year observing, learning, and soaking up what made people tick. Day by day he was becoming more proficient. He was a postgraduate now.

Some say that Paris is a city of lights. To Sacha, Paris was a city of couples. Whereas in London he was aware of history at every step he took, in Paris his attention was directed towards people. In London people were busy. They went about their business, and they minded their own business. Paris was a city of lovers. Sharing was in their nature. They strolled among impressive buildings, past and present, seemingly designed to boost, with their unabashed monumentality, their national egos. The English loved their countless dainty gothic churches. Early English, curvilinear, decorated, finally Tudor, but all small, parochial, scaled down to simple human needs. The French preferred huge, towering cathedrals, where heaven and Earth met well below the apex of the soaring arches. Yet it was here, surrounded by this splendor that, yet again, Sacha realized just how lonely he'd become. As he strolled along the banks of the Seine, he was the only human who was alone. Nineteen and alone. In Paris––it seemed wrong. Everyone else had their arms entwined around each other. Ignoring the monuments, they were lost in each other's eyes.

SACHA 18+273 days

The problem of loneliness was not easy to resolve. Back home, we were a very close-knit family. When I first arrived in England, I telephoned home, particularly my mother, on a weekly basis. I soon found, and poor mother agreed, that somehow the telephones seemed to increase the distance between us. They emphasized how long the 'long distance' really was. Also, they did little to free myself off the apron strings.

We agreed that we would rely on regular meetings on the Home Planet. With dad's help, mother became quite proficient at it. What people do not realize is that she and I can meet there, without it affecting, in any way, my presence and awareness in the physical consciousness. It is as though only a part of me wandered in the inner world. I had to remind myself that my true self is equally present in all realities simultaneously. My ability to expand my attention appears to have grown accordingly.

Nowadays, when I call, it is mostly for the sake of Grandma and Grandpa, who are, as yet, unable to take advantage of the inner realities. Dad and I also make use of email, though only to discuss specific subjects for which there are no good equivalents on the Home Planet. Subjects that are implicitly 'down-to-earth'.

As for my sense of loneliness, it was the body I inhabit, my sensual awareness, which appears to be demanding its rights. It seemed to be calling for a human touch. How very strange. It seemed to have a will of its own.

As for the French language, it did not really come to Sacha naturally, but he metabolized an excellent vocabulary. The rest, he felt sure, would come with practice.

The French academic community considered themselves the best in, well… the best at absolutely everything. He found that even the professors succumbed to national pride, and thus were subject to the guileful machinations of flattery. They seemed to need it as moths need light. Sacha offered it freely. His increasing ability to thoughts helped. Sacha amused himself by fulfilling some of the haughty men's dreams.

"You present by far the deepest insight into this matter, Professor. If I may say so, people at Oxford are years behind you in understanding the intricacies of the dilemma," he offered with a slight bow towards a fastidious professor on some relatively inconsequential matter.

The professor held that only *La France* had ever produced any philosophical concepts of value.

"*Oui, cher Monsieur*. You may say so indeed," the professor dismissed the matter nonchalantly, with a wave of his hand. Yet the lecturer was quite unsuccessful in concealing his delight.

From that moment on, the snide remarks that the professor directed at the British, Americans and even Canadians seemed to dissipate into thin air. His animosity towards everything remotely English may have been dating back all the way to Henry II, who in 1167 banned English students from attending the University in Paris. Be that as it may, Sacha became the fastidious professor's favorite student.

Sacha's stay in Rome was as rewarding as it was uneventful. He visited every museum, craned his neck at countless domes in countless churches, cathedrals and temples. What else can one do in Rome? A week after arrival in the City of the Seven Hills, Sacha had to face the inevitable. He'd noticed that he suffered an indefinable disquiet when entering the gates of the Vatican. Not that there were any actual gates, but he felt a strange unease as he approached the inner City. For some reason, as he walked along Via della Conciliazione towards the Basilica of Saint Peter, he sensed an inexplicable foreboding. It was as though a cold wind chilled his bones; only the wind seemed to come from within. "Don't go there," it seemed to say. *Don't go there.* "Why?" he asked himself. "What are those buildings to me?"

The ancient stone walls lining the street with elegant Renaissance rhythm yielded no answer. Perhaps Sacha felt the power radiating from the throne of Peter. An enormous, unbending, indomitable power. It worried him. He felt a great danger emanating from the magnificent Basilica, from the very nerve center of the most powerful Church in the history of man.

SACHA 19+102 days

I always thought that power is the opposite of love. Love and hate are reverse sides of the same coin, indifference is its absence. But power is at odds with the very concept of love. It imposes, commands, enslaves. Never in my life have I hoped so much that I was wrong. If I could pray, I would have prayed. But prayer is attempting to influence the order of the universe. It is a dangerous game to play. Unless it is an aspect of your particular destiny.

He put his notebook away and kept walking.

His feet moved slower with each step. For two thousand years this Power he was now facing was virtually ruling the civilized world. Then Mohammed came on the scene, and the Church Empire began to recede. But the Church fought back. With people who offered their love and life, but also with sword and mayhem. Crusades, inquisition, followed. The opposition was destroyed ruthlessly, without mercy.

In the name of the Father and the Son and the Holy Ghost.

Suddenly Sacha felt very tired. He came here searching for light, he found gathering darkness. He'd been walking for hours. He found some steps, sat down and listened to his own thoughts.

SACHA 19+102 days, cont.

I cannot really study the Italians. I can live with the Italians. I have to. When in Rome, do as the Romans... They know how to live. They try to live their dreams. I also noted that the closer they get to il Papa the less seriously they take him. It is a truly strange relationship. They love him, practically adore him, some even respect him, but they don't take him seriously. 'He does what he does, and we do what we do', they claim. 'Live and let live', they insist.

La dolce Vita.

Aren't they right? I feel a peculiar kinship with them. I wonder why?

Yesterday I attended a lecture on dreams by a man claiming to be a follower of Carl Jung. There was a question period. I asked the lecturer why he regards perceptions of some realities as more true than others. It took him a long time to understand my question. I told him that we all 'travel within', a function he referred to as dreams, only we don't regard these 'imaginary' travels seriously. I asked why does he regard the inner experiences, such as dreams, as unreal, whereas he takes the physical life so seriously. Isn't physical life constantly hovering on the very edge of unreality?

He smiled for a long time, studying me as one would an alien. But did not answer.

I put it to him that physical consciousness is a preset dream, running to its fulfillment, interrupted only by our ineptitude and inability to discover exactly what that dream is really about. I found I was unable to convey my concept to him, nor to the listeners. I was unable to share the perception of my reality with others. They and I are still too far apart.

Again, I felt lonely. I visited mother in her dream-state. I asked her why people couldn't understand my words. She didn't answer either.

I miss you, mother. I miss you badly. But I know that I must do this on my own. Whatever 'this' turns out to be...

Sacha walked another hundred yards towards the Basilica. There, he stopped. He couldn't go any further. The next day he left Rome for Madrid. He'd visited Mecca many times in his inner travels. Now he wanted to meet the people who had built the Alhambra. Or at least partake in the evidence they'd left behind. He wasn't disappointed.

For the rest of the year he wandered the streets of many European cities, large and small. With each passing day, he felt more detached. He felt like a stranger in a strange land. He didn't belong in this world. He admired it. He loved the people. Some of them were living their dreams, even if they did so at the subconscious level. But still, he didn't belong.

Five years had passed since he'd left home and it all seemed for naught.

He'd read somewhere that what history teaches us is that over thousands of years, people have learned nothing. That people walk in circles, forever chasing their own tails. Perhaps this is as it must be, but he refused to accept it. Perhaps we are not allowed to stay in the upper realms. But who is it that allows us? Sacha never encountered anyone in any realm who told him what to do. He was always relying on his own self. Perhaps such self-reliance comes only with time. Time, down here, was a very important commodity. It was part of the eternal circle. Or, perhaps, we all rely only on our inner self, only we don't realize it. We want to pass the buck—to have someone to blame for our mistakes.

So many questions...

Sometimes, as he stood, forlorn, on the bridges spanning the Vistula, the blue Danube or the meandering Moskva, for some ephemeral moments he hovered in the bliss of the Undiscovered Realm. Bridges over dark, pensive waters had that effect on him. But as always, all too soon the magic was gone. He missed his true Home.

Perhaps once we graduate from this vicious circle we don't have to come here anymore to partake in the eternal procession of past mistakes. We shall bathe eternally in the ineffable light of the Undiscovered Realm, descending now and then into the opulent creative streams of the Far Country, or the sensual beauty of the Home Planet. Perhaps others will come up from the animal kingdom and take our place, sustaining the physical reality, while we move on.

Only now and then, just sometimes, one or two of us might come down to give a hand to those who are still struggling. After all, at the root of our perceptions, aren't we all one?

Perhaps. Perhaps...

***

11
Self Realization

"**Why am I here?**" It wasn't the first time that Sacha asked himself this seemingly innocuous question. His ability to withdraw into the inner sanctum of his being, of his awareness, did not seem to supply the answer. Recently, it was as though his inner travels felt more like escapes from his responsibilities. They were wonderful, sublime, indeed at the deepest or highest level ineffable—beyond time.

"There, I just am," he told himself.

Yet, he always came back. He had to. He thought he was beginning to understand why.

"Perhaps if all people had the ability to escape into the higher regions of awareness, they would have no stimulus to try. To strive. To cross new horizons. They would become static. As though in limbo. Almost dead. Perhaps..."

There was no one with whom he could share his ideas. He was alone.

He'd spent the last three months in LA, with his parents. He hadn't seen them for just over five years. They could easily have met a dozen times during his self-imposed exile, but Sacha had insisted on walking his own, often painfully lonesome path. "I must, Mother," he'd told Suzy who missed his physical presence the most. "I must find myself, and I must do so on my own."

They met frequently within the Home Planet. Only there, no one changed, no one grew older. Not really. You wallowed in your acquired knowledge, but you did not cross new horizons. You were whatever you wanted to be. You could even grow horns or a tail and pretend you were a devil. All things were possible. All it took was imagination and belief. Belief that you can. Belief in yourself. Was the Earth that much different? It took longer, but the principle underlying your creativity, the creation of the reality you wanted to perceive, was essentially the same.

"Watch me fly!" Sacha sprinted to the edge of the precipice pushed off and took wing. His head thrust forward like a rising star, his arms alongside his body, his palms acting as airfoils.

"Watch me fly higher!" Suzy smiled, as she soared over the highest peaks.

"Watch me be the first to get back!" Alec shot down past them like a bullet.

"Watch us all being happy together..." Suzy concluded. She needed togetherness the most. Each night she was hoping to see her son—at least in her dreams.

On the Home Planet they were all children. Carefree.

But when Sacha flew back to LA, by a very noisy, very solid jet, Suzy and Alec couldn't believe their eyes. Sacha left a boy—came back a man. Not just older, but a man confident in his views, behaviour, even posture. In height he now matched his father. Suzy had to stand on tiptoe to stroke his golden mane. She didn't mind. She was proud of her son's looks. He was beautiful.

"Really, mother..." Sacha muttered. But the happy mother had no idea what he was mumbling about.

Sacha smiled. His mother has forgotten that he could read her thoughts. What's more, he'd never attached much importance to his physical appearance. Clean and proper was enough for him. But beautiful?

Apart from visiting his parents, Sacha had two other items on his agenda. He wanted to see the McBrides, particularly Grandpa. His father had told him that old Des was getting on. He was still sharp but he could not sustain anything for very long. He simply got tired. He and Grandma 'Licia still sauntered along the beach on weekends—only a lot slower. Desmond was no longer the Chancellor. He gave occasional lectures as a visiting professor. They were always fully attended. But his drive was missing. He was passing the torch to the next generation.

Sacha caught up with them on the beach.

"Look at that youngster go!" Des would remark, pointing to a lad on a surfboard.

Only then he noticed Sacha standing next to him. Two tears rolled slowly down his cheeks. He stood, helpless, unable to control himself. "I m-missed you, l-lad," he stammered. "I guess, I missed you," he confirmed, wiping his tears away.

Alicia took Sacha in her arms and, for a while, refused to let go. "You'll stay a spell, won't you, Sacha. Say you will stay?"

Alicia hasn't changed. She had that rare quality of remaining invisible, yet always there when needed. Sacha vaguely remembered Matt, a large, towering man, who had once looked after his father. He had the same elusive quality— –a trait more common among women than men. She looked after her husband with total commitment. But she never allowed him to think that he was slowing her down. She pretended that it was she who couldn't quite keep up the pace. She thought that Des hadn't noticed her subterfuge. He had, and he was grateful. He referred to her as his angel.

The last item on Sacha's agenda was money. He did pick up a few Euros, here and there, but he needed more money. He felt the need to rely on his own abilities. To be financially independent. In Oxford he'd spent practically nothing, but the European whirlwind cost him plenty. Travel wasn't cheap any more. Nor were convenient hotels. Or even B&Bs.

Sacha didn't need much, but money makes the world go round, and he wanted to go round the world. He could have earned the extra cash in Europe, but day-trading on the stock market was much faster, though it was virtually a full time job. He repeated the method he'd employed the first time he'd made a hundred Gs. It didn't come as easy this time, but he managed to make enough to satisfy his immediate needs. He didn't plan for the future.

He still hasn't decided if he had a future.

Finally he was ready. They all saw him to the airport. All five of them. Even Maria wanted to come. He promised that this time he would come back sooner.

"Much, much sooner, darling. Much sooner," Suzy pleaded.

"Godspeed, lad," Des whispered. He took his departure the hardest. He loved his grandson dearly.

Sacha's carryall was duly x-rayed and then he passed the point of no return. Once again, he left tears behind.

He flew economy. What seemed like a week later he landed in New Delhi.

"Why am I here?" he asked himself for the hundredth time. His eyes followed the ever-changing kaleidoscope of colors through the window of the rickety train. He chose this method of travel to develop a greater feel for this part of the world.

"Up there..." he mused. He adopted his father's thinking of the Undiscovered Realm as 'up'. He often mused of his home when alone. "Up there, there's only one color, even if it is the sum total of them all. It is the full range of colours reassembled into their original form by the prism of my soul. Funny that..." he thought, smiling. "I never realized that till I got down here. We take so much for granted, even there..."

It was beauty he felt with his whole being. Up there, he was part of it. He was beauty himself. Could this have been what mother had meant?

"So why am I here...?"

The window darkened as the train entered a tunnel. A tunnel with no light at its end.

"Self discovery." He peered into the smoky darkness. "I am here on a mission of self discovery."

Yesterday was different.

Crowds, smells, noise, but particularly crowds, endless crowds, never-ending crowds of people. Crowds, smells and noise were synonymous with India. At least in New Delhi. The capital of a billion people. Sacha dreaded what Calcutta might be like. He had no desire to go there. It was said to be much worse. Calcutta was for people in search of money and—for saints. Like Mother Theresa. Only she was dead. He wondered how many people die every day in India. How many die on the streets. He wondered how many are born. He wondered how many thought that it was worth it. To be born that is. To live. Here.

At 5 a.m., just after sunrise, you breathe deeply. The rest of the day you try to hold your breath. Literally and figuratively. Yet in the midst of all this there is beauty. Richness of nature, richness of art, richness of human spirit, though that last must be earned. He'd asked a swami, a local guru hardly distinguishable from the dust on which he was sitting, what would two weeks at his feet gain him. The old, skinny man with deep-set eyes replied: "Peace of mind. A new way of life. Happiness." But only if he, Sacha, obeyed the rules. If he neither touched, nor looked, nor even thought about the female members of the Ashram.

Detachment.

Detachment from all things physical. Wasn't it easier to raise your consciousness to the inner realms? You didn't have to leave your physical body. Just believe.

Just believe. Didn't someone once teach that?

The teaching of the majority of teachers dates back some 3500 years. It was given to mankind by Krishna, the physical incarnation of Vishnu. A God. An all-pervading Preserver. The most important God of the Hindus. Maybe Vishnu resides in the parts of the Undiscovered Realm that still remained undiscovered. After all, it is Infinite.

Sacha'd read the Bhagavad Gita. The "Song Celestial." He'd read it all in LA. The Hindus, or mankind, was given this poem about the same time Moses got his Ten Commandments. It was a good time for mankind.

What happened since?

Sacha'd spent two days in Delhi from where he only just escaped with his life. An ancient taxi narrowly missed a head-on crash with a bus carrying, what looked like, a few hundred natives. They rode everywhere—on the roof, hanging out through the windows, balancing on fenders.

The driver reassured him: "You're alive? No problem."

Perhaps the driver was right. As long as you escaped with your life… You needed your life to fulfill your mission. Your destiny. If you didn't—you would have to come back. Again. And again.

If I only knew what my mission is…

He bit his teeth.

Later he saw an elephant walking down the street. Atop it carried two tourists and a driver. Slower, but much safer than a taxi. You stayed alive longer.

That was another reason why he'd decided to take the train. To stay alive a little longer. He smiled at his thoughts, and then grew pensive again. To learn of my mission. My purpose. My *raison d'être*.

The wobbly train—that must have seen better days at the time of the British Empire—finally arrived at its destination, within a day's drive to the foothills of the mighty Himalayas. The name of the town was Varanasi. From what Sacha's heard, the place boasted a double claim to fame. The first was that the Beetles once came here. The second—Buddha had chosen this place to give his first lesson. Sacha came because of the latter reason, but the first brought in more tourists.

Or so they said.

Actually, Buddha had preached his first sermon some twelve kilometers north of Varanasi, in a place called Sarnath. Sacha looked forward to paying homage to the land on which the Enlightened One trod so many years ago. Varanasi also experienced a transformation. Until fairly recently, till 1956, it had been called Benares. The name had been changed abruptly, perhaps in homage to Varuna and Assi that still flowed north and south of the city in a loving embrace.

Sacha got off the train at the Kashi station on the far side of the city. He arrived just in time to see the long graceful prows of countless boats, silhouetted across the Ganges against the setting sun. The boats seemed to hover at the edge of time. Floating, suspended, in a world of their own. After a long while, Sacha decided to walk back towards the town center.

Ashrams were anywhere. Good places to stay for a night or two. The cots were hard but clean. They didn't cost much. Anyone could stay if they obeyed the rules. Usually the no-looking-no-touching-no-nudity type of rules. Why are those people so obsesses with sex, he wondered?

The Far East is plentiful of gurus.

"Namaste", he heard everywhere. "Welcome," in English. The real Sanskrit meaning is "I bow to the divine in you."

Inside, some men sat perfectly still in *Padmasana*, the Lotus Seat, others rotated their bodies clock-wise in the graceful *Laukiki-mudra*, while waiting for their guru to appear. Other acolytes stretched their backs in the pose of *Paschimottasana* or, or the easier *Dhanurasana*, while others still, particularly women, oxygenated their brains while resting in *Sirshasana*, an internationally known aid in beauty-culture. Sacha preferred not to stand on his head, regardless of the purported benefits. He had problems enough remaining on his feet.

Sacha had two main reasons for coming to this country of contrasts. He hoped this ancient culture would help him clarify his destiny. His second reason was more flippant. He wondered if yogis could really manipulate time and matter. And space.

So far neither of his quests were satisfied.

The rishis, the swamis, the gurus, exuded eastern philosophies with an amazing diversity of colour, tone and inflection. It became apparent, confirmed rather, that every man must follow a different path. Even at the feet of the same guru, in the same ashram, the receiver metabolizes the teaching at his own rate; within the context of his own accumulated dross. The dross of life. Of Karma.

And then there was the country itself.

From Varanasi Sacha took to the hills in a rented car. At least, according to the driver that came with it, it once was a car. In the West it would have fetched a small fortune. As a relic. The road soon lost its paving to the ravages of time. Also of climate. During the winter this road was closed. It was impassable. The man drove slowly, stopping very three hours to stretch his legs, drink some water and chew on local pancakes. Sacha told the driver to take enough food for three or four days. They stopped at Sarnath, rested, and then continued northward. The mountains loomed on the horizon, some 150 miles north of Varanasi.

The Himalayas were very real. Physically real. Hard. They imposed themselves on the sky with absurd authority. Sacha wondered what mind had created such monsters. They represented a peculiar mixture of adamant power and sublime beauty. He always thought that beauty was gentle. Not here. Here it was hard, impenetrable. Uncompromising.

Then he remembered the Far Country.

The stars were like that. They moved, yet were immovable. They were beautiful, yet unforgiving. From afar, they were as cold and as hard as diamonds. From up close, they consumed all with the fire of detached indifference. An oxymoron, until you experienced their enigma yourself. They contained both sides of the equation. They were in no man's world.

They inhabited the lofty worlds of gods.

On the second day, they spent the night on a broad plateau, about 3000 meters above sea level. Here and there Sacha noticed peculiar white pyramids—like the giant termite hills that pepper the waysides of Brazil. His driver told him that the white cones were ancient sarcophagi; graves protecting the ashes of past lamas. Strange. They burned their bodies then tried to preserve the ashes. By first darkness they pulled up to the side of the road. It was still warm enough to spend the night in the open. Sacha took the final look at the panorama, and fell asleep almost at once.

He woke in the middle of a moonless night.

He felt cold and decided to take a walk to improve his circulation. To warm up. He approached the peculiar white cones silhouetted against a darker background. There was a man sitting in front of one of them, his feet crossed in *padmasana*. The man was neither young nor old, yet, in a peculiar way, he was both. Sacha felt that the man knew many answers. Only he wasn't sure if he, himself, knew the right questions.

"As a spectator, you are where your attention is." The man spoke in measured, very precise, accentless English. "You can go anywhere, into any time..." he was responding to Sacha's stream of thoughts. There were so many of them...

"Isn't my physical body in danger when I am absent from it?"

"You should be the last man to ask this question." In the darkness Sacha thought he detected a smile. It was neither condescending nor scolding. Just amused.

Of course Sacha should have known better. Each time he'd ventured into the upper realms, particularly into the Undiscovered Realm, he lost all awareness of his physical body. It's not that his body was or was not in danger. It was simply that the physical body was of absolutely no consequence. It was as if he could create any number of such bodies, should the need arise.

"Are you afraid for your body when you dream, or sleep?"

Funny how the monk, for surely, this must have been a monk, made it all sound so easy. In or out of his physical body the man was very knowledgeable. He must have been one of the departed lamas whose dust lingered, hidden within the conical structures. Of course Sacha wasn't worried about his physical body. He hardly knew why he'd asked the question. He never gave his body any serious thought. He recalled how Grandma was nervous when he dived into the oncoming waves of the Pacific. It seemed as though that was a million years ago. Time was so fluid...

"Then how do I contact others? I can, can't I?" Sacha was thinking of Father Pio and others who appeared simultaneously in different parts of the world. He felt that he needed this information. He just didn't know why.

"You contact their mental bodies. Or their astral sheath. And they in turn translate this communication to their senses. Actually, the physical body, the senses, are hardly aware of this. When you dream, your dreams are vivid, but how often do you remember them in your waken state?" The man spoke in soft monotone, as if he didn't try to convince Sacha of anything, but merely stated facts.

"Can one manipulate time and matter with one's mind?"

The same smile of amusement appeared on the young man's face. This time the smile was clearly visible and the man wore a face as young as his own. As they talked, the lama became more and more visible. Only the light did not come from any external source. It came from within the man's being. By then his face was really young, or better still, ageless. Yet it was the same face only adorned with the innocence of youth.

"You do so all the time, don't you?"

"What do you mean?" For once Sacha was lost.

"Reality has its existence in the present. Past and future are figments of your imagination. You manipulate them to arrange events in a sequence suitable to you."

It all sounded too easy. Yet, thinking of some past events, Sacha knew that the monk was right. He did, on a number of occasions, do things, which altered his perception of the reality he was in at that moment. Not just sleeping or dreaming or traveling to inner realms, but even right here. On Earth. He changed things to fit different patterns. Anyone could do it. If they only believed they could...

This time Sacha smiled, his teeth showing in the darkness. Miracles? Why bother? They're so childish. If I want miracles I just go to Home Planet, he thought with a broadening grin. Now, there you can see miracles! Only nobody else can. Except mom and dad. And obviously many others only he'd never met them. Not so as to know them on an individual basis. Yet there must have been many others. Someone had to maintain the reality for others to share. And yet, his dad still thought that Home Planet and the Far Country had reality only in your head.

"All reality exists only in your head," the monk said quietly.

Gradually it dawned on Sacha what people meant by miracles. They were stuck in a certain mindset they couldn't change. When someone changed it for them, they thought it miraculous. Yet it was the simplest thing to do. All it took was a little faith. At the time, Sacha had done it intuitively. Now he understood what it was that he'd done.

Still, the laws in the inner realms were more permissive. Exacting, but still, easier to obey. The beauty was also more intense. The dreams—more vivid. He felt that people there did not believe in miracles. They all created their realities consciously. Not by accident. Not by trial and error. Well, not all the time. Sacha wondered why he never attempted to see other people there...

"Then why are we here?" he asked, instead. He thought he knew the answer but still, he wanted to hear it. He wanted to travel the world, to sails through a storms, to visit the Far Country. He wanted to...

"...experience the mode of becoming." The monk finished his thought for him.

But there was more. There had to be more. You couldn't have so much fun—all for free. Surely, one had to give back something. Anything? Otherwise there would be a state of imbalance. One would feel like a parasite. A taker...

"There is also your destiny," the monk's lips didn't move yet the words rang in his head like a Buddhist gong, reverberating on and on. It grew and receded, like the essence behind the holy syllable of Aum. "You pay by fulfilling it."

"And what is my destiny?"

"It is written inside you. When you're ready you'll know."

There is a time to play and there is a time to pay, Sacha thought. He hoped his account wouldn't be too overdrawn. On the other hand, he was keen to do it—to experience the joy of restoring the balance in his own life. The physical life, where balance was a fundamental law underscoring all duality.

The next moment he found himself in the car. He still felt the cold. He closed his eyes and changed his view of reality. The windows in the car became misty with the difference in temperature. He grinned. If I raise the temperature any more, I'll have to open the windows. The monk was right. We manipulate reality all the time. We just don't know it. And if we did, we wouldn't believe it. And then Sacha closed his eyes, again, and slept till the first light.

His driver didn't bat an eye.

Next morning Sacha decided to drive back. There was little more he could learn here. He had a feeling that finally, after this entire search, after all the books, and travels, he was nearing his destination. Manipulation of time and space was of little interest to him. He knew he could do it. He still wasn't sure if it had anything to do with his destiny, but he knew that he could. Everyone could. It was a question of one's point of view. Or the way of looking at reality. You might say, of faith. Whatever you really believed in—was. The patterns you created would remain, obeying the laws of its reality until you changed them. We do it all the time. We translate one form of energy into another, or matter into energy, and we are not even surprised. Yet reality is like that. It is flowing, ever changing, metamorphosing itself. With or without our influence. We just step in, give a little push, and the waves continue to expand in ever increasing circles. Hence the universe.

And what of God?

He closed his eyes and saw the lama's face.

SACHA 20+117 days

God is 'I' without physical, emotional or intellectual limitations. Without body, without emotions, without the intellect. God just IS. Like the sum total of all realities. Like the Reality that spans the universes, oscillates Itself into supernovas and collapses into massive black-holes only to feed the universe with a different form of Itself. With equal ease. Yet, in essence, It never changes. It is like an ocean that entertains countless billions of different waves, currents traveling in diverse directions, yet always remaining an ocean.

Perhaps, ultimately, I am the only true reality.

The only Reality.

He wrote the notes in his pocket diary and went for a little walk. The last peek at India. Then he sighed, smiled and continued towards his car. There he stopped once again. He wanted to add another memory.

SACHA 20+117 days, cont.

It was the second time that I'd met myself face to face. Why is it that we must travel thousands of miles to find that that which is right before our eyes is within us? The moment I got back to the car, out there on that freezing mesa, I knew that the lama wore my own face. My face in different stages of my development. I wonder how long I've spent in India. In which life it was. Was it difficult? Had I perceived that life as difficult? Did the ashes guide me to wisdom I'd once had and lost? I could probably find answers to at least some of these questions inside me. Yet it seems that finding the answers right here and now is part of my mission. Perhaps we must learn to function in all realms, in all perceptions of realities.

There is still so much I must do.

Another thought struck me on the way back from the plateau seemingly frozen in the hoary past. If the lama and I are one, what of everybody else? Would others find their own faces in his ashes?

Does it matter?

***

12

You're Never Alone

The next ten months Sacha spent wandering all over southern India and later Japan. The last three weeks he'd spent in China. The People's Republic wouldn't grant him a visa for a longer period. Yet even in such a short time, China surprised him tremendously. He found it just as crowded as India, and Japan for that matter, but he also found, in the land of the rising sun, a paradoxical feeling of space. The Chinese gave an impression of being extremely well organized. Even disciplined. He doubted that this could have been imposed by a relatively totalitarian regime. Relatively—because at the onset of the Age of Aquarius, Uranus ruled with a powerful hand. Few people realized that democracy is but a thin wedge rising from an ocean of autocracy on the one side, and anarchy on the other. The torrents of fate were gradually dissolving the old ways to make room for the new. New ideas and new people to apply them.

The systems, the methods employed by the old power structures, the ideological concepts based on the principle of centralization, were dying. The Third Reich, the British and the USSR Empires, the Chinese Communist Oligarchy itself––in fact all attempts to centralize power have been destined to fall. Even the American feeble attempts at the beginning of the twenty-first century to 'unify' the world under its watchful wing were already showing signs of weakness. The same was becoming true of the once all-powerful

international business conglomerates. The age of the
individual was coming to the fore. To avoid anarchy, the new
system required specific personal traits.

And the Chinese had them. They were more disciplined.
It was in their nature. Sacha felt sure that they were destined
to inherit the Earth.

Apart from that, the Chinese philosophy always appealed
to him. Not the modern schisms, nor even various outgrowths
of Zen Buddhism. He loved the depth of wisdom hidden in
the ancient poems of Lao Tsu. Confucius he'd found more,
perhaps altogether too, pragmatic. More practical, in a strictly
worldly sense, but over-concerned with the result. Lao Tsu
appealed to Sacha's heart. He thought that perhaps the Old
Master was the last great poet the Chinese race had spawned.
Not that he'd read that many Chinese poets. But perhaps one
that is truly great might be enough to sustain a nation. Sacha
thought Lao Tsu's philosophy as pertinent today as it had
been centuries before Christ brought us his version of
malleable reality.

Sacha found his visit to China intensely interesting. Yet,
in spite of their hidden promise, the Chinese were not yet
ready for the final step. Sacha felt the radical metamorphosis
was imminent. He could feel its scent in the air. Alas, there
was no time to study them any further. His time was up, as
was his visa. Sacha bid them a silent success as he made his
way back to New Delhi. He'd promised to see a friend there.
A searcher, like himself.

A searcher, not a seeker.

Sacha held that a seeker was one who yearned for
spiritual life. For inner life of some sort, beyond the
limitations imposed by physical reality. Sacha was the very
opposite. His inner life was his nature. He was searching for
sense in his outer existence, searching for his particular,
unique place on Earth.

So was his friend.

It seemed that whereas the direction Sacha was pursuing
in relation to his own environment steered him towards the

exigencies of the world known as The West, his friend was gravitating to becoming his alter ego in the Orient. They met and communicated on the inner planes of perception. They also talked English, face to face, in the old town of Delhi. New Delhi had been constructed to replace old Calcutta as the national capital. But Delhi, old Delhi, was a town as old as most in the vastness of India, and it was there that Arjuna chose to live and advance his knowledge. It was the first time Sacha'd met somebody trapped in a physical form. Even as he was. Arjuna also found Home Planet, the Far and the Undiscovered Countries his natural habitat. It brought Sacha great joy. He no longer felt quite so lonely.

"Could it be that life is no more than an eternal search?" Arjuna'd asked Sacha on the first day they'd met.

"For what?" Sacha replied. "Searching for what?"

They both laughed.

Sacha felt it the moment it happened. He was convinced that the greatest evidence that at some level of perception we are all One, or at the very least effectively and indivisibly interconnected, was his immediate sensing that Desmond needed his help. Sacha suspected that we all have an affinity for one or two, perhaps more people, who in turn are tied to two or three others, until the whole world exhibits a matrix of emotional or mental relevance as strong and as unbreakable as to render us into a single organism.

Perhaps, he thought, filaments of emotions stronger than we imagine connect some of us. Though physically he was the farthermost away, when the consciousness of Desmond McBride decided to withdraw from the material world, Sacha was the first to sense it. He was ready to leave India anyway, but even a supersonic jet, had one flown from New Delhi to Los Angeles, could not have brought him to Desmond's side in time.

Yet, Sacha did make it.

He got there in time for Grandpa's departure. He got there in a manner in which he could help more than by being there physically.

When Sacha arrived, Desmond was still sleeping. His grip on life was tenuous at best, but his body was still breathing regularly, if not exerting his lungs to capacity. Alicia was also asleep on the bed separated from Desmond's by a common bedside table. They pulled their twin beds apart only last year to ease the chore of making them up in the morning. The king-sized linen was just too unwieldy to handle.

"So this is the end?" Des had asked at the time.

Unbeknown to all but Alicia, Des was an incurable romantic.

Sacha connected directly with his grandfather's mind. There was neither time nor any need to attempt to revive him. Desmond had a long and, for the most part, good life. By Sacha's terms of reference, this was a joyful moment. A sense of anticipation of an impending liberation. Of freedom such as few men have ever imagined.

Last year, just after Sacha's visit, Alicia had taken Desmond to Australia. His son, George, welcomed him as the long forsaken father. He must have gathered, after so many years, that his father had spent a lifetime of emotions on his mother. On his first wife. There was none left, till Alicia had slowly rebuilt them.

Desmond's son had been right. His father had given too much to his wife. What remained after her death was a deep-set, indefinable anguish. So many years ago...

It was the kind of pain that leads to total indifference. On their arrival in Sydney, there was a feast waiting for him worthy of a king. Not to mention a queen who'd engineered the long overdue reunion. George and his wife, and their two sunburned children, treated the elders like visiting royalty. The McBrides had dropped in on the McBrides only for a weekend. There was no telling what the meeting might bring.

No telling if a gulf of such pain could be bridged with equanimity.

But in Alicia's eyes it looked promising.

Everyone played their part. The past was never mentioned. They rejoiced in the moment. When it was time to go, Desmond's son announced a surprise of his own. Politeness demands that we see one's guests to the front door, the porch or at best the gate at the end of one's garden. George, though alone, saw them to Solana Beach. It was the first time he'd ever visited his father. They both needed gestures of reconciliation. Yet, sadly, these remained mostly gestures—a mild anesthetic applied to still festering, if slowly healing, scars. They contrived to bring peace to each other.

But after all these years they had too little in common. A week later Desmond drove his son to the airport. Both shed a tear, both held each other, both swore to keep regularly in touch. And both breathed a little easier when the departure gate closed between them.

It had been too long. Just too long.

In the months following the reconciliation, Desmond grew a little more pensive. More introspective. Alicia thought she might have made a mistake by bringing them together. She shouldn't have worried.

"You know lass, I would find it very difficult to die if it weren't for you. Very difficult."

She didn't ask what he'd meant. She thought it obvious. They didn't exactly read each other's thoughts, only Sacha could do that, but they could detect each other's emotions with such accuracy that the actual thoughts became secondary. They'd grown very close. As though they'd spent their whole lives together.

And now Des was dying.

Sacha never questioned whether it was by accident or design that he'd returned just in time to take Grandpa across the great divide. He'd responded to his inner voice the way people respond to a voice blaring on a multi-amp speaker.

Now, at the deathbed, he had to wait until Desmond was ready. At the right moment when the silver cord snapped like an over-stretched string on an angelic harp, he surrounded his Grandpa's awareness with a halo of golden light. He held him with warmth generated by his own love.

Like most people in this moment of truth, Desmond appeared worried. Then slowly and carefully Sacha had raised him to the Home Planet.

"Where am I?" Desmond asked, his eyes as wide as a newborn baby's.

"You are almost home, Grandpa. You are almost home..."

Sacha could only help the freshly liberated consciousness to find its own level. Sometimes the souls stayed here for hundreds of years. Sometimes they soon rose to the Far Country. Only a few rose all the way. Others bode their time in the lower strata, yet realms so much higher than physical consciousness that most regarded themselves as having arrived in heaven. After all, on Home Planet you could sate virtually all your heart's desires. Providing, of course, you knew how to desire. How to create with imagination.

"What do you call this place?"

"My mother and father call this the Home Planet."

"You mean we're not on Earth...?"

He finished the sentence but only just. Sudden realization hit him with a force which most people find overwhelming.

"I'm... I am..."

"...you are very much alive and well, Grandpa. Only not on Earth. Well, it is a different Earth, Grandpa. You left your physical prison and are free to satisfy all your desires."

Desmond examined his arms and legs. They seemed to him in perfect order. "My b-b-body?" he stammered. "B-but... but... w-why...?" No one ever seemed to understand why they died.

"You don't get to choose when or how you die, Grandpa. You only get to choose how you live."

Desmond looked around and then grabbed Sacha by the hand.

"Alicia?" he whispered, his eyes filled with concern.

"She knows. I told her. I am also with her this moment."

"You are here and there?" Desmond's scientific mind refused to accept the paradox.

"Space and time are a dualistic concept created to facilitate perception of material worlds. In fact, we are all everywhere at all times, Grandpa. We just don't know it. Not yet..."

"But time and space..."

"...are figments of our imagination. Look!"

And Sacha changed the panorama in front of them with a sweep on his hand.

"Can I do that?" His mouth hung open. "I mean here..." he added, his gray, shaggy eyebrows rising in disbelief.

"You can try, but I would rather you started with your own body."

Desmond was still wearing his pajamas. Imaginary pajamas. Pajamas he expected to wear on stepping out of his bed. Deathbed. He shivered. Sitting in 'Alec's villa' with the most glorious view of this incredible country, he looked and felt profoundly incongruous.

"How do I do it?"

"Just imagine what you would like to be wearing." Sacha couldn't help smiling.

On his deeply lined face, Desmond still carried evidence of years of care and concern. But the most incompatible item with this reality was his whole body that showed unmistakable signs of prolonged neglect. In addition, he looked lost, and embarrassed, and helpless. The next moment he was covered, from head to toe, with an abundance of lustrous white linen.

"Too much, eh, lad?" This was the first sign of his humor returning. Rapidly. The next instant he was wearing a flowing Roman toga. "I should have been wearing one of these at my oral exam, a century ago," he quipped.

"Now tr-r-ry your-r-r body," Sacha mimicked his earthly accent.

"What?" Des either ignored or didn't notice the joke. There was no sign of his former Scottish accent. He was too busy trying to make head and tail of his new surroundings. Hardly surprising, Sacha had to admit, with a boyish grin.

"Your body. Wouldn't you prefer to look younger?"

Desmond didn't question his youthful mentor. He closed his eyes as though to utter abracadabra and opened them with a shout and a chuckle.

"It tickles a little," he confessed. He now looked like a young Roman patrician ready to deliver his doctoral dissertation. Yet, he was still unmistakably Desmond.

"I think I am going to like it here," he muttered. Then his face lost his boyish enthusiasm. "Are you sure Alicia is all right?"

"I'd better check," Sacha agreed. Being here and there was one thing, but the focus of attention was another. "Experiment, Des. Walk. Use your young body. If you want to eat, create food. If you want to fly... well, we'll leave that for another time.

Sacha wondered what Desmond's reaction would be to the Far Country. People didn't usually progress all the way 'up' at the moment of 'death'. In fact, a lot of Desmond's physical reality was still lingering on Earth—the 'real', solid Earth 'below'. Hence, his retention of physical characteristics when he first got here. Not to mention his pajamas! Likewise, his concern for Alicia. There will be moments when he'll miss his morning cup of coffee, his drop of the hard-stuff towards the end of the day. In time he'll develop new, much broader interests without the attendant emotional ties. It was just too easy to change one's perception of reality here to become attached to any specific part of it. Perhaps that is why suffering on the Home Planet was virtually impossible. What you didn't like, you changed. Usually it takes the equivalent of forty earthly days before the transfer of consciousness is complete. But it varies. After all, the concept of time here is quite different. By the Home Planet's standards, Desmond would be fully adjusted in about a year.

But the Far Country would really be much more Desmond's cup of tea than the Home Planet. With his knowledge of physics, he could really have fun there. Providing he doesn't allow his learning to hold him back. He would only lose his erudition after his spell in Bardo. And no one had any idea when that would happen.

When Sacha was about to leave him, Des looked up at his young friend with concern.

"Am I here all alone?" He looked around.

"Look again," Sacha admonished.

The next moment the streets of this wondrous city seem filled with people, strolling, standing in groups, chatting, laughing, as carefree as can be. The next instant they dissolved into thin air. "It's all up to you," Sacha repeated patiently.

"What happened?" Des asked, his eyes once again filled with awe.

"This reality, like any other reality, is what you make it, Des. It doesn't really exist. What gives it actuality is your perception of it. Trust me." Again, Sacha smiled. He didn't realize how new and incredible Home Planet must look to people who lost all memory of their previous visits here. "And anyway, here I'll see you for as long as you like, as often as you like," he added.

"But isn't this a place for the dead?"

"Ha, ha... No, my youthful Grandpa! This is the place for the living. The place for the mostly dead you've just left behind!" What a strange question, Sacha thought. What bizarre concepts of life people evolve on Earth. They really forget their true identity. I wonder why I didn't? Or my friend in India?

India! My body's in India...

Desmond still looked unconvinced. Sacha wanted to transfer his attention to other matters but he decided to try once more.

"Do you feel dead, Des?"

"I've never felt more alive!" he answered, surprising only himself. Sacha was already gone. It didn't matter. Grandpa Desmond was already in the process of realizing that not just his body but he, that which made up his awareness of being, was also no longer that of an old man.

By then Sacha's attention was elsewhere.

A second later Alec and Suzy appeared out of thin air at both sides of the young patrician wrapped in his white, luminous toga. Both new arrivals looked as young, or younger, then they had been when Desmond had first met them. Neither Suzy nor Alec recognized professor McBride. Not with their eyes. After all, here he wasn't a professor. He was a willing beginner. They both saw to it that he learned fast.

Sacha, who'd witnessed some of this from afar, sighed wistfully. What a pity that Alicia was not ready to join them, he thought. But he didn't create the rules. And there were rules here. There were rules in every realm. It took an eternity to learn them. And then one was free.

So they said...

"You know, Grandma," Sacha was sitting on the edge of the bed holding Alicia's emotive hand, "we never listen to what Her Majesty, our Queen, has to say. She gives her Christmas or Easter Messages, and we assume that that's her job. We wish her well, but we don't really listen."

Alicia didn't agree. She'd always listened to Her Majesty's messages. Alicia thought the queen was a wonderful, wonderful woman. Actually Sacha knew of Alicia's sentiments regarding Her Majesty. That is precisely why he chose this route. He continued before Alicia had a chance to question his judgment.

"But there was an occasion when we should have paid close attention. It was at the service for the people who died in the bombing that Islamic extremists committed against humanity in New York. Her Majesty didn't attend, but she had sent a letter. Towards the end of the message, she wrote that grief is the price we pay for love. I think there is truth in this statement. I thought you might want to know that, Grandma."

The truth of this statement was only in the physical, dualistic reality. But that is where Alicia was trapped at present. That was where she needed help.

"He's gone, isn't he?" she asked. The question was rhetorical. She knew.

"Yes Grandma," Sacha echoed her emotive thoughts. "He loves you very much. I never saw such love in a man..."

Two tears formed at the corners of her eyes, and then ran slowly along her cheeks. After all, sleeping or not, her body was the expression of her emotions. Her sorrow would not be denied. Slowly she opened her eyes. She turned towards Sacha to thank him. She was surprised that he wasn't there. Sacha had already withdrawn his emotional sheath. But not his presence. He would always be there. She'd never been, nor ever would be, alone. None of us are, he smiled. Ever.

And he embraced her with a caress of pure, quite invisible to the human eyes, golden light.

In earthly terms, at about this time his body, his physical body, was boarding an airplane that would bring him back to Los Angeles. The loving, earthly home. A home where he would see his family. Only Grandpa would be missing. Poor Alicia. Would she understand?

Sacha's meeting with his friend was fruitful. They agreed to do their best to find out how many more kindred individualizations such as themselves walked the Earth at present. They suspected there must be a good number. After all, there was so much to do. They both were in their middle twenties and still had difficulties in formulating their exact destiny. Actually Arjuna was a few years older, in human terms, than Sacha, but it didn't seem to matter. Their thoughts oscillated between them, often without uttering a sound.

"Perhaps we are not supposed to know the future."

"Perhaps we should follow our intuition wherever it takes us."

"Isn't our intuition our silver cord?" Arjuna asked quietly. His English was coloured by a slight Indian accent. It seemed to add an esoteric flavour to their exchanges.

Outwardly, Arjuna was always quiet. He had not chosen the path of learning in universities as Sacha had. He chose instead to find the truth within himself. It was more the Oriental way. Sacha belonged to the West with equal intensity. He thought that the truth within should remain within. He thought that we are here to learn to perceive the truth by the rules established and controlling this peculiar reality.

"Why else would we be here?" he asked Arjuna.

But his friend had no answer to offer. He withdrew into the realm of light as though lacking air. A moment later luminescence returned to his dark, lustrous eyes.

"Why indeed, my friend. Why indeed?"

Although Arjuna had spent a few extra years in the material reality, he still couldn't resign himself to accept what his physical senses told him. Perhaps there was too much suffering, too much injustice, too great an imbalance in his world. He desperately wanted to go back home.

"And what of your destiny?"

They were both acutely aware of Bardo. The dreams had been dreamt. Now, they had to be recalled. Played out. Those were the rules.

"Who created these rules, anyway?" he asked wagging his shaggy head from side to side like a disenchanted poodle.

"They've been around for as long as I can remember," Sacha said with mock conviction. In spite of their temporal dilemmas they were both acutely aware of being immortal.

Arjuna, a name he shared with his hero from the Hindu scriptures, did not strike anyone as being a man with a mission. Of course, everyone has a mission. But the consequences of some missions affect broader numbers. They create wider ripples in the fabric of spacetime. Sacha had recognized a soul mate, if one could call him that, by his aura. The sheen surrounding Arjuna was such that he was clearly visible in the darkness of a moonless night. They both laughed when Arjuna confessed that that was also how he'd recognized Sacha. Yet, at the time, not one other person had been able to detect their eerie luminosity. It was true that some people had the ability to detect auras, but that was only when they concentrated. When they were actually looking for one.

It wasn't natural for them.

Having met, for a little while Sacha and Arjuna felt embarrassed by their unique characteristics. For Arjuna this was second such meeting. Sacha began glancing over his shoulders to see if anyone was watching him. Arjuna laughed. He'd once met a swami, a Hindu teacher, who had recognized his aura. The teacher himself was sporting an impressive glow of his own. Yet, when he'd met Arjuna he'd prostrated himself on the dirt road and had asked to be taken on as an acolyte. Arjuna found this experience profoundly embarrassing. It had taken him hours to convince the old guru that he was himself but a beginner on the path. That he knew nothing. That he could not teach anyone anything.

At the time it was true. Almost true.

Arjuna was blessed with intrinsic knowledge, but he wouldn't have known how to communicate it. Yet he doubted that the old seeker believed him. He was forced to enter the man's mind and open his own consciousness to him. After that the man seemed satisfied, though only partially. He looked as though he suspected that Arjuna was hiding something from him.

Anyway, already then Arjuna went through the process of acceptance of his own aura, while Sacha had to overcome his self-consciousness only now. It wasn't easy. He felt that he carried a big lamp on his head that he couldn't hide. Much bigger than his mop of golden hair. It took him a good month to finally accept that his lantern was not visible to the masses. To people at large. And if someone did see it, the chances were that he or she would be a friend. As was the case with Arjuna.

On parting, they agreed to call on each other, in case of need. Now that they met, they both had the ability to do so. It is difficult to contact someone on the mental or emotional plane if one could not recognize him or her. Just like... on Earth.

"I'll see you my friend," Sacha said a little sadly, embracing the dark body of his soul mate.

"I shall always be with you, Sacha. You know that?" Arjuna replied, his tone as much a question as it was an assertion.

Sacha did know it. But physical perception places its own demands on our appreciation of what we recognize as reality. Sometimes we all need an assertion. It is habit forming. But, he knew that too.

***

PART THREE

The Journey

"Always go too far,
because that's where you'll find the truth."

Albert Camus

SACHA-The Way Back   181

13
Reunion

The whirlwind, which had blown Sacha around the
world, was over. Sacha returned to Los Angeles on the
last day of July. He found both apartments empty. He
should have called. He decided to spend a few days in his
parents' LA condo, to recover from jet lag, and to get used to
the pace of the Western world. On Friday he took a bus to
Solana Beach. He felt sure he would find his parents there,
keeping Grandma company. They would not have left her
alone. Not now.

Almost a week had passed since Desmond died. Passed
away, they called it. It was more like passing inward,
although frankly, he was still here. There is only one
Absolute Reality, and it is here and now. You can't pass away
from it. There is nowhere else to go. Sacha sighed, a distant
look creeping into his eyes. It was here and now yet, like his
father, when he thought of the inner realms, that far away
look clouded his vision.

If they could only see it, he mused. If they could only see
it...

By now, Desmond's body would have been cremated or
buried. Just as well. Sacha had absolutely no interest in
discarded bodies. They had their uses, they were necessary

under certain conditions, but that was all. He did not understand why people attached so much importance to their remains. Or the remains of their dear ones. After all, it wasn't as though they hadn't mistreated their bodies throughout their stints on Earth.

Or that nonsense about religious relics. They ignored, if not actually abused, their saints, and then worshiped their bones. How quaint. How very primitive.

Sacha knew exactly where Desmond was. He was not interested in rites that people maintained and cultivated for the sake of some ancient pagan tradition. As far as he was concerned, there was no death. Although, he had to admit, in the physical realm there was sorrow and grief. Usually caused by attachment to things, or perceptions, to which we had no business getting attached to, in the first place. Sacha found such attachments intensely illogical.

The atmosphere in Solana Beach was somber. Although Alicia, in her innate wisdom, shared many of Sacha's views, well… she was also very human. And humans have a tendency to develop a fondness that leads to attraction that leads to affection that leads to grief. Sooner or later. No matter what the great avatars of the past had attempted to teach us, most of us persist in the same old ways. Buddha had insisted that attachment is at the root of all suffering. We continue to suffer. We continue to become attached.

Sacha learned on his travels that this was one of the peculiarities of human nature. People felt the need to attach themselves to things or ideas they knew were transient; or to people, for that matter, and then suffer for having lost them. It seemed that this was the price one paid for the fascination of becoming.

Sacha walked from the bus station.

A rucksack on his back, like the globetrotter he'd been so recently. A vagabond—without a reality to call his own. As he approached the villa, he regarded it with affection. Am I forming an attachment, he mused? For a short while he stood still, soaking up memories of the years he'd spent here as a baby, his first tentative steps in human consciousness, his total inability to reconcile his true nature with the reality perceived by his physical senses. He'd come a long way. The Undiscovered Realm remained his true home, but he'd forgone his frequent escapes to the other realms for the sake of spending most of his time here, on Earth. It wasn't easy.

The door was open.

He found Maria busy in the kitchen. Poor Maria. "I'd completely forgotten about her. Dear, dear Maria." He owed her so much. He reached out and gently stroked her black hair hanging loose over her shoulders. She recognized his touch instantly. She caught her breath. Soon her breathing became steady. He held her in his arms in silence. By the time he released her, her eyes were filled with tears of joy.

"Señor Alejandro! You look magnificent!"

Maria was the only one who, since his last visit to Solana Beach, decided to call him by his 'proper' name. She thought that since the designation 'Sacha' was a diminutive, it smacked of familiarity. He was unable to persuade her otherwise.

Sacha had little idea of how he looked. He supposed it was all right to look 'magnificent'. Or even less than magnificent, as long as one could function efficiently in one's body. He decided to take a long look at himself, at the first opportunity, in a mirror. Although he continued to carry an electric shaver with him, once he'd finished his studies, he'd stopped shaving, In LA he'd found that his shaving machine didn't work. He had no choice but to perform preliminary sheering with scissors. Finally, he snooped around, until he had found his mother's safety razor, which she'd probably used on quite different parts of her anatomy. Once he'd removed years of outgrowth, he decided that he looked human enough so as not to scare his parents.

"Why thank you, Maria. You look lovely, too," he assured her.

"No, Señor. You know..."

"Yes, Maria. I know. How is Grandma taking it?"

"I do not know. It is as though she hardly notices. Only the Señora is even more kind to me..." And her eyes once again filled with unrestrained tears.

"There, now, she knows that he's all right where he is now..." he assured her.

"But how can we be sure?" she asked haltingly. Maria was a Catholic, and Catholics are never sure. To them most things are shrouded in mystery. They rely exclusively on faith, not on knowledge.

Sacha placed both his arms on Maria's shoulders and gazed gently into her dark eyes. For a few seconds neither moved. It was as though they'd been cast in a single mold. Solid. For those few seconds Sacha had altered his and her perception of time. The next instant Maria looked away.

"I understand. Thank you Master Alejandro," She spoke hardly above a whisper. Then she shook her head, sighed, turned, and went about her business.

Sacha followed her with his eyes. Funny, he thought, that people accept communication at their mind level as completely natural. She didn't even ask me how I communicated the news about Desmond to her. Funny that...

Sacha found the rest of the family on the terrace. All three sat looking into the ocean, seemingly lost in thoughts. Peeka and Boo sat facing each other on the rail, probably catching some well-earned rest. As Sacha entered, Boo opened one eye. Peeka was too busy dreaming. The sun was getting ready to slip behind a ponderous cloud that was forming high over the horizon. The bottom edges of the billowing vapour were already refracting the reds of the Pacific sunset. The top was still bathed in pure gold. Sacha stood motionless transfixed by the intransigent beauty. Within seconds the phantasmagoria of light and shadow would be over.

In the next instant, the darkness of the cloud became ominous. I'm just in time, Sacha thought. He walked behind his mother's chair and kissed her cascading hair. They all looked up. It was as though the mists that surrounded the terrace were swept away with a single breath.

"Sacha!" It was a shout of joy. "Sacha, my Sacha..." This time she whispered. She sat frozen, unable to move.

Alicia was the first to recover but Suzy's arms were already reaching for Sacha's neck. She held him without speaking. She was dreaming of just such a moment. Who says your dreams didn't come true?

Alec stood up and waited his turn to embrace his son. For a while the two men were locked in a silent bear hug. It was Sacha's physical proximity they all missed. They met in the inner realities. That was wonderful. But this was different. It was tangible. It was solid. It was, well... it was physical.

At last Sacha disengaged himself from his father and knelt before Alicia's chair. She sat, a smile of blissful contentment on her lips, her eyes dreamy, as she witnessed the reunion of the three people she loved most. She looked at Sacha as though she'd last seen him only yesterday. She had. Even if only in her dreams. Every night.

"Thank you my love," she whispered, so that only Sacha could hear. Her dreams kept her going. She was no longer as resilient as when she was younger. As she was when she'd lost Alec's father.

Sacha rose and kissed her on both cheeks. She seemed not to have changed at all. A touch of gray mingled in with the gold, but that was already there a year ago. She was still beautiful. No wonder Desmond's thoughts returned to her when Sacha accompanied him to the Home Planet. She looked as fresh, as joyful as though Desmond was sitting right next to her.

In a way, he was.

Maria's smile appeared in the doorway. She brought a tray of glasses with a jug of red liquid. The fruit had sunk to the bottom while cubes of ice jingled on the surface. It was her famous Sangria. No one, no one in the world, made Sangria as good as did Maria.

"Maria, you forgot one glass!" This was Alicia.

There were four glasses on the tray. Maria shook her head. Alicia made as though to get up and get the extra glass herself. Maria quickly withdrew and got the missing tumbler.

"That's better," Alicia approved. "Surely you want to hear what my grandson has to say?"

"Yes, Señora. *Gracias.*"

Maria was more formal than usually. Could it be Sacha's presence? She seemed in awe of him. She poured out five glasses and sat at the end of the terrace. Alicia gave her a stern look and she moved her chair closer. Grandma smiled and said nothing.

"OK son. Let's hear it!" Alec leaned back regarding his son with a critical eye. Judging by the expression on his face, he approved.

"The beginning, the middle or the end?" Sacha asked.

"You choose!" Suzy also couldn't take her eyes away from her son only there was nothing critical in her eyes. Just love, love and more love.

He was her only son.

During the next three hours, and two more jugs of Sangria, Sacha sketched out the last eleven months, which took him on a wild jaunt across the Far East. He related items that he thought would be of interest to all of them. While his parents enjoyed some awareness of the inner states of consciousness, Alicia would probably not be able to follow. Nor would Maria. Being awfully nice women did not qualify either of them to reach beyond their present destiny. This made them neither better nor worse. Sacha had learned long ago that every human being, every living creature, has a purpose. The universe, even the transient, ephemeral universe would collapse if a single atom were to be removed from it. Only metamorphoses were possible in all realities.

Some recognized this as evolution.

Sacha told them about his first impressions of India. He gave them a whirlwind tour of Japan and China. He tried to sketch the atmosphere of abundance, not so much of wealth as we measure it in the West, but the abundance of nature and of human spirit.

"I strongly suspect that most swamis who sit cross-legged in the omnipresent dust on the sides of the endless, unpaved roads know more about the workings of reality than the vast majority of priests, imams or rabbis. India is a strange country blessed with quite incredible progress in fields that are still in kindergarten in the western world," he concluded.

Last night he was reviewing his diary. He remembered some of his notes, scribbled hastily, as though he'd found the subject distasteful. Or maybe just a little painful.

SACHA 21+ 36 days

The downtrodden gurus, regarded by many as freaks, never cease to amaze me. I have attended postgraduate courses in philosophy and theology at Oxford and the Sorbonne. Lectures given by established scholars, priests, monsignors, doctors of theology. I've listened to sermons in churches and cathedrals of England, France and Italy. Yet none of the sacerdotal scholars could compare their grasp of reality with those emaciated swamis. The lecturers all sounded like phenomenologists, arguing for the sake of argument. They relied exclusively on externally acquired knowledge. They never crossed any new ground. They sounded as though they tried to convince themselves of their own perception of reality.

Perception is perception. None is better than any other. It defines your universe and for you it represents the truth. But only some knowledge advances you forward. The knowledge of others reduces you to gasping for air in a

prodigious whirlpool of time and space of your own making.
Virtually forever.

Those half-naked gurus with their faces smeared with
sweat and dust, also exhibited infinitely greater
understanding of the sacred and secret teaching of the Bible,
the Koran and of their own scriptures from which they claim
to have derived their knowledge. The difference is, I think,
that they confirm their findings by practice, and adjust their
perception of reality accordingly.

Even though he still searches for his exact purpose, I'm
glad Arjuna has been embodied among such people.

"But what exactly do they teach?" Alicia's tone sounded
dubious.

"They teach about life. About being happy. About
finding your purpose." Sacha spoke as though thinking aloud.
"But it is not as easy as it might sound. Every person listening
to them hears a different message. I don't know if they do it
intentionally or not, but I found it quite fascinating." Sacha
remembered peeking into the minds of students as they all sat
in a broad semicircle at the feet of various teachers.

"But isn't the truth just one?" Suzy asked.

She tried hard not to return to the subject which had been
dear to her in her youth and then left her with a feeling of
great emptiness.

"I'm not sure what you mean by truth, mother. I am the
truth. So are you. Truth is our indestructible essence. Truth is
changeless but our perception of it varies from one instant to
another."

"Wouldn't you say that the truth is the Whole," Alec
offered, stressing the word 'whole'.

"It would be if any one of us could ever embrace the
Whole. It is beyond our mind, our emotions, even beyond any
individual consciousness. You must become the Whole to
know the Whole. And should you do that you would no
longer be you."

Or, for an instant of eternity, just before merging, you could perceive your own true nature, he thought. But there was no point saying that. Not yet.

They shared the silence that followed Sacha's words with the mounting wind. Clouds, a short while ago hanging over distant horizon, have swollen to cover most of the western sky. Soon the first drops of rain would start their irregular tattoo on the terrace roof. How many times had they all sat together, just like this, and watched the fulminating clouds approaching them across the endless waters. So many memories. Perhaps this is the greatest trap. We become attached to our own memories.

Even as I am to India...

When Suzy left to help Maria with supper, Alicia moved her chair closer to Sacha's. Alec, sitting on his son's the other side, was happy to just listen without interrupting. Suzy extracted a promise from Sacha that he wouldn't say anything interesting till she returned. Sacha assured his mother that he had absolutely nothing interesting to say. His mother didn't like that.

Alicia looked at Sacha as though trying to remember a familiar face. She wasn't really aware of his nocturnal visits. Not enough to carry them intact into the light of day. But they did help her. Enormously. They stabilized her enough to carry on with her life. Towards her destiny. As best she could.

"What a pity you missed Grandpa. He would have so liked to see you, now that you're all grown up," she said at last.

She'd forgotten that Sacha was here less than a year ago. She saw an almost indiscernible difference in Sacha. His last ten months did not advance his factual knowledge, but he had rubbed shoulders with people the way you cannot do in Europe, or in any part of the Western world. Here enjoyed, or suffered, clearly defined, what many called, psychic spaces. We respected each other's rights to privacy. Out there, few things were private. Particularly in India. Oh, there were some rich people as depraved, or as attached to their worldly possessions, as here. But percentage-wise, those were few. The vast majority had nothing to protect. Not even their psychic space.

Whatever the reasons, those last ten months had turned Sacha into manhood. In Europe he'd matured intellectually, now his metamorphosis was complete. He had learned to respect people who never asked for respect. Who didn't demand, let alone expect, that favorite misnomer of the West called 'dignity'. The people he'd met possessed certain nobility, a distinction that did not come from their possessions or position, but from who they really were. From their soul? They called it their Atma. Their true being. Some gurus said that you have the body you think you have, the body others think you have, which they call your mental body, and your real body, the Atma. That last was where the respect was accorded. All peripheral appurtenances were shunned by many, perhaps most.

It was a strange country.

East and West... Sacha wondered what forces created two cultures so diametrically opposed. The need for balance? It wasn't a question of which was better, which worse. Just so very, very different. Would they ever overlap?

He smiled at his recurring thought: ever is a very long time... It's as eternal as now.

Suzy was back.

Alec got up to offer her his chair, next to Sacha. Suzy, looking out to the ocean repeated almost word for word Alicia's concern.

"What a pity you missed Des. He would have so liked to see you..."

Most of Suzy's memories of other realms were also stored in different realities. On her return to Home Planet, she found everything familiar. Yet here, it was like remembering fragments of a dream. Alec had already developed a much better recall. He'd had a lot more practice.

"It's all right mother. I didn't miss him. Nor he me," Sacha said it so that only his mother could hear him.

Then she remembered. He brought her and Ali to Des' side in his hour of need.

"Thank you, Sacha. Somehow I knew it, though it's so hard to understand."

"It will come. Patience is a divine virtue," he murmured.

His mother never suffered from abundance of patience nor, for that matter, of self-control. She smiled at Sacha's words, then leaned over and kissed him. Again. Yet she remained saddened. There was so much she'd missed.

"Don't try mother. Just feel it. Feeling is like the gravitational force. It is omnipresent. It affects everything, even though you can't see it. So few of us realize how very dependent we are on it."

Sacha thought that being with one's parents was the nicest dream one could have on Earth. It was the only place in the physical reality where everyone gave without asking for anything in return. There was no need for miracles here. Life at home was characterized by the same traits as chaos. Not as in a mess, but in the ancient Athenian sense—by a constant, never-ending predisposition towards order and harmony. At home, with the people one loved in a particular way, this trait was translated into a predisposition towards helping one another.

After dinner, they continued chatting on the terrace. The oncoming gale gradually dissipated itself somewhere in the vastness of the Pacific. The rain, such as it came, was perfect for watering the plants, for cleaning the dust off the roads, for refreshing the previously heavy air. They retired well after midnight.

Sacha had one more chore he'd reserved for his homecoming.

Already in bed, he reached out with his emotive tendrils and carefully prodded Alicia's mind. She was already asleep, but not yet deeply. Her condition was perfect. He was hoping she would be perfectly relaxed but not completely unconscious. In this state the mind is most receptive to new ideas. It would likely accept that which it would reject when wide-awake.

"Grandma?"

A moment later Alicia took a deep breath. She thought she'd hear Sacha's voice.

"Grandma, don't wake up. This is me."

Ahh, finally I'm asleep. I love dreaming about my little Sacha.

Sacha immediately adjusted his configuration to fit Alicia's dreamy perceptions.

"Will you come with me?"

Where?

"Far, far away, to a place you've never been before..."

Little Sacha had loved it when she used to tell him stories about far away places. They invariably began with words 'Once upon a time....'

Lead on, darling. Grandma will go with you wherever you want to take her...

Next Sacha opened Alicia's mind to the reality of the Home Planet. He led her here and there, holding her hand, pointing out the beauty of this realm. He then looked up at his grandmother and tried his luck.

"In this country, Grandma, we can be anything we want to be?

Of course we can, sweetheart.

She was still humoring him. So far so good. Sacha tried again. "Would you like to be young like when you were twenty?"

She smiled as though remembering a long forgotten dream.

"Oh, do it then, Grandma, do it, please do it!" He danced around her in small circles.

Oh, all right darling. I am now as young as I was when Alec was your age!

And in that very instant she became young again.

"I love it, I love it, I love it, Grandma!" Sacha assured her.

It was time. It wouldn't do to bring Alicia here to meet Des when he was a sprightly youngster, while she an advancing widow. Now it was worth a try. After all, anything can happen in a fable, let alone in a dream.

And in that instant Desmond, still in his Roman toga, appeared as though from nowhere.

"What...?"

Desmond? Is that you?

"Lassie...? You were never *this* beautiful. Except in my dreams..." Desmond took a pace back not believing his eyes.

Neither of them noticed when Sacha withdrew. The two youngsters—not as young as Sacha in this particular dream, but youngsters nevertheless—would not have noticed if an earthquake destroyed the whole planet.

Sacha admitted to himself that he cheated a bit. But what's the point of having powers if one didn't use them at all? He only hoped that, on waking, Alicia would retain some of the memories of the dream he tried so hard to make a success. Anyway, he could do no more. If it worked, two entities in this vast universe would be a little happier than they were before. And surely, that was worth a try.

It was an eerie feeling to lie down in one's own bed. After the hard cots of so many Ashrams, his old bed felt truly palatial. Admittedly, Sacha was not prone to make new or maintain old attachments, but he observed his own body with all its accessories, including his mind and emotions, and he noted that most people couldn't help being what they are. The bed you knew for many years felt good. It gave you a feeling belonging. It gave you a sensation of safety. Safety from what? Safety from all imaginary danger. Safety for your transient, ephemeral, organism, which subsisted in a constant state of ferment and change. Trillions of electrochemical reactions per second maintained it in, what we liked to call, the condition of being alive. Sacha knew that there was no body as such. There was only the instant of birth followed by the instant of dissolution. A condition of continuous transition. A condition of constant transmutation, alteration, regeneration, conversion and substitution. Each single cell would be replaced on an ongoing basis. No one lived *in* his or her body. The body was never there long enough for anyone to take up residence.

Sacha tried to visualize what it would be like to suspend time so as to make his body a permanent abode. He dismissed the thought the moment it crossed his mind. The idea abhorred him. A prison in a constant state of decay.

"Never", he said out loud. "Not for an instant!"

Sacha knew where the problem lay. Once we lose conscious awareness of who we are, we became a byproduct of the dictates of our body. Yet he seldom met a person who expressed the slightest interest in *who* they were. *What* they were seemed all-important. How they appeared in the eyes of others.

"What will people say?"

"What impression am I creating?"

"W

as this or that good for my image?"

People he'd met as good as admitted that all that existed in their perception of reality was an image. Yet they fought, tooth and nail, to sustain that ephemeral, ever-changing impression. They lied, cheated, stole, abused and murdered in the name of that image. In the name of a wisp of their distorted imagination. Not all people were like that. But, from what Sacha's observed—the vast majority were.

Unable to create an image they could abide in, they reached out and created gods in the image of their inflated egos. Gods that magnified their own limitations, even their iniquity. Gods that punished and rewarded arbitrarily, depending on which religion they belonged to. And to assure their superiority over others, they acclaimed a single God.

Not a single God for all men, but just for those few who'd accepted and worshiped their particular version of divinity. My God is the only God, they said. You shall have no other gods before me. God is one, they acclaimed, providing it is mine, not your God.

The human condition...

And when their true self, their real indestructible nature, desperately attempted to get through to their disfigured consciousness to make itself known in their sleep, they dismissed such truly Herculean efforts as ravings caused by having overeaten at supper.

"That could be true, on occasion," Sacha murmured his understanding.

But there were so many other occasions when the inner voice was screaming, calling for a new vision, demanding to be heard, not to be ignored...

"I'm a realist," he or she announced proudly. "I believe in what I can see and touch and smell and hear."

They could not see. Neither could they hear. They were the blind leading the blind, the deaf preaching to the deaf. They were transient vagabonds waiting for a free ride.

Sacha's thoughts kept sleep away from his eyes.

Did they act thus on purpose? Why did the human body create such a reality? Was it so on other planets throughout the universes? Why am I limited to just one physical reality, one Home Planet, one Far Country? Or was this condition of the human race a byproduct of millions and millions of years of drifting away from our true nature, tempered and influenced by the body's need to maintain an image of pseudo-immortality? Perhaps all creation strives to emulate its creator. Like father—like son?

Only God, in whatever form or definition, did not cause attachments. If God be theirs, indeed *our* Source, then It is both the potential and the manifestation of such diversity, with changes occurring at such an incredible rate, that only the very instant of creation subsisted in the present. And God IS.

All else was no more. Or remained not yet perceived by Its own mode of becoming.

I must do something.
I must help them.
I must...

***

14
Not Bread Alone

Even as Sacha fell asleep there was a nebulous smile of surprise on his face. As he slowly drifted away from the physical awareness he realized how very human he'd become. "Other planets?" "A single Home Planet, a Far Country?" He was close to forgetting that whatever he perceived with his senses, regardless whether the senses were physical, emotional or mental, he perceived the product of his creation. Not even that. What he perceived was the product of his creative will. He, and he alone, gave his perception reality. It couldn't be otherwise. He reinforced this fact by raising his consciousness to the Far Country. In the next immeasurable fraction of eternity, the wonder of the universe appeared at his fingertips. He closed his mental eyes and dismissed his own creation. The next instant he was suspended in the vastness of impenetrable darkness. A void without thoughts or feelings. Without an echo. If hell existed this was it. A reality without creation. An emptiness of mind, of emotions. An absence of light.

With a mental shiver he restored the glory to the universe. The cosmos.

The ornament of God.

Next morning Sacha was back to his usual self. He knew who he was, and was getting very close to knowing why. The all-important *why* of life. He was determined to find his particular path without cheating, by rising to the

Undiscovered Realm where all memories, past and present, coexisted in perfect harmony. There is no sequence of events in that illustrious reality. No sequence, no time. Neither past nor future. It is a realm from which Mozart and other soul travelers drew their inspiration. It is a realm wherein such as he could hear whole symphonies in a single magnificent chord. It was the Source of all.

From the viewpoint of the highest realm, you were wherever you placed your attention. You experienced on whatsoever you placed your attention. You experienced by direct perception.

He knew that by drawing on the unfathomable reserves of the Undiscovered Realm, he would not learn how to control his own mind and body in the physical reality. He would not become a master of all the realms. He would not be the best that he could be. And thus his contribution to the Whole would be diminished. That he simply couldn't afford. What God was to some people, the Whole was to him. It was the Eternal Source, the bliss of indivisible oneness, the enigmatic bliss of eternity. In the palm of his hand. Not to keep, but to share and spread among all who developed the capacity to understand the meaning of love. The meaning of oneness.

That much he'd learned in Bardo.

Furthermore, memories stored in the ineffable fabric of the Undiscovered Realm were only those that concerned the universal traits. The successful results had been recorded for others to draw on. Not methods on how to obtain them. All other memories were kept in the lower realms. And those realms were his to create. As was the reality with which he was struggling at present.

There was one other reason for Sacha's return to LA, to Solana Beach. Sacha was broke. Flat broke. And his moral code did not allow him to sponge off other people. He had to pay his own way. He decided to ask his father for advice.

"Can you think of a way I could earn a decent living doing something constructive?"

"Why would you want to, son? Can't you make your usual chaotic exercise on the computer and..."

"Dad, I said constructive. I know how to make money, but it seems abortive to be rewarded for doing virtually nothing."

"Using your brain is hardly nothing, Sacha. Isn't that what I've been doing all my life?"

"You know very well what I mean," Sacha would not give in.

There was a moment's silence. Alec regarded his son with concern. Twice he opened his mouth as though to say something and twice he held back. There was something eating at Sacha, and Alec had no idea how to get at the problem that his son might be facing. It was only then that Sacha began scanning his father's thoughts.

"I am twenty-two, Dad. What did you do when you were twenty-two?"

"Not much more than you are doing now, I suppose?" Alec didn't know where Sacha was going with this.

"And here I am, a wunderkind, a prodigy with a string of letters from Oxford and the Sorbonne behind my name. I'm capable of memorizing a book just by putting it under my pillow. I'm capable of healing my every ailment, of speaking a dozen languages enough to speed-read their literature, of polarizing photons dancing around my body... Dad! I am totally useless! I don't have a single achievement to my name. I am nothing. A failure. An absolute dismal failure." Sacha's tone was becoming quieter, until the last words were uttered in a frantic whisper.

Alec was stunned.

The list of abilities, which Sacha had enumerated, was hardly Alec's idea of failure. He thought that to have done, seen, learned by Sacha's age all his son had learned, was a tremendous achievement in its own right. He thought Sacha was indeed a prodigy that had come to fruition—a child's promise that was fulfilling itself in a marvelous way. What else could Sacha possibly want?

And what of the guidance he'd provided within the inner realms? Did he count that for nothing, too? Was not his mind reaching where no man's mind had reached before? Was he not daily crossing new horizons, conquering new unknowns, finding answers to which most men couldn't even formulate questions?

Alec knew. He met his son in the inner realms often enough. Whether Sacha was capable of inducing hallucinations or just wondrous dreams, Alec's own perception of reality became twice as exciting as it ever was. Did that also count for nothing? And what of...

"Dad..." Sacha cut in.

He was following his father's thoughts. Dad wasn't wrong. All his perceptions were on target. He did open new ways of regarding reality. He did create new horizons, cross new unknowns. But what of it?

"I may have helped you and mother, maybe even Grandma and Grandpa, a little. But do you really think that I possess these abilities for the sole purpose of opening the door to the unknown a little wider for four people? Four wonderful, loving, dearest to me people? Is that my destiny?"

Alec didn't answer.

"Is that why I was born...?" Sacha asked quietly.

But this time there was more sadness in his voice than despair. Yet he knew he could not resign himself to just helping his family. No matter how wonderful they were. There was a swell in his heart that was ready to burst and flood the world. There must have been a 'real' reason why he'd been called at this moment in history. His inability to verbalize these feelings was getting him down. They sounded conceited. Pompous. He needed help and none came.

Not even from his father.

"Son. You once told your mother that patience is a divine virtue. Shouldn't you practice this attribute yourself?"

Sacha froze, and the next moment he doubled over with laughter.

"I love you, Dad! With a single sentence you have released my tension. You made me free again." He hugged his father with unrestrained emotion. "But I warn you, Dad. The moment is close when strange things will begin happening. Don't be surprised, Dad."

"Son," Alec regarded Sacha now holding him at arm's length. "Nothing you do will ever surprise me. That much you've taught me yourself."

"What is it boys?" Suzy joined them on the terrace. Peeka landed on her back in a single leap. Boo looked jealous. They seemed to have spent half their life on the terrace. "Anyone for a walk?" Suzy was wearing a flattering one-piece costume that was the *dernier cri* in LA. She ignored Alec's wolf whistle.

"Or a swim?" Sacha added. "Only I don't have any swimming shorts..."

"Your father has a dozen," Suzy assured. Actually Alec had three pairs.

"Give us five minutes," Alec said, disappearing into the house, pulling Sacha behind him.

Suzy looked in on Alicia, but Grandma preferred to read. She was feeling a little tired of late. She wasn't sleeping as well. Or perhaps she was hoping too much to repeat her dreams of Des.

"I'll see you when you get back," she waved Suzy away with a smile.

It has been years since the three of them walked barefoot on the sand together. Years, since Sacha returned home, without announcing another impending departure. Suzy had learned to count her blessings. She felt, as only a mother could, that she could not hold on to her son for much longer. She was unable to explain, let alone justify, her feelings, but lately a sense of impending disaster, of inexplicable foreboding intruded on her carefree disposition. She kept her qualms to herself, but she tried more and more often to escape to the emotional protection of Home Planet. It didn't always work. She kept forgetting that the first condition for success in such ventures was a state of carefree relaxation. You had to accept your fate in order to free yourself from its impositions. Sacha once told her that you could only escape your fate by fulfilling it. It didn't make sense, at the time, but taken in the perspective of immortality it wasn't absurd. You couldn't really escape your fate. If you didn't fulfill it in your present life, you would have to do so later. Or later still.

And that was precisely what kept her awake in the early hours. She would think of Sacha's fate. All she saw were blank images. Yet that eerie nondescript vacuity seemed to hide ominous consummation.

Now that Sacha was here, she managed to dismiss the clouds gathering in her heart. She shook the cobwebs from her troubled mind and smiled at her son.

"You remember our walks down here, Sacha?" It was a silly question. Of course he remembered. His memory was infallible.

"You wouldn't have me forget, Mom, would you?"

"It was over there," Alec pointed towards the horizon. The three of them looked afar and saw nothing.

"It was there that the motorboat struck the intrepid swimmer..."

"A hydroplane," Sacha corrected. "You were quite angry with me, Dad, if I recall?"

"W-well..." Alec sounded a little flustered.

"You couldn't forgive me for comparing a man's life to a pair of trousers," Sacha reminded his father. "Have you changed your perception of reality since that time, Dad?"

"To be honest, son, not until you woke the both of us to Desmond's whereabouts, a few days ago. It was only seeing him, different yet unmistakably him, that your view began to make sense," Alec admitted.

And then Alec stopped and stared at his son with undisguised wonderment. "That was a few days before your fourteenth birthday. How did you know all that?" There was an unspoken "then" in his question.

"Sometimes I think that during our lives we continually forget things. And as we forget everything then we move on," Sacha answered.

"We die," Suzy insisted. "I, too, saw Desmond. But he died," she persisted haltingly.

"He did," Sacha's tone was conciliatory. "He died to his world. To this reality."

"I know..." Suzy was still struggling. Her recall of experiences on the 'inner' was still not as good as Alec's. "I know that we are all immortal. That we cannot die. Not really. But we do die..."

She was thinking was that blank fate surrounding her son that was clouding her vision again. The next moment she stopped and threw both her arms around Sacha's neck. "You will stay with us a long time, say you will darling. Please say you will?"

Sacha did not answer. In the past he'd hold his mother even as Alec usually did when Suzy had problems controlling her emotions. Now he stood helpless, his arms dangling on each side, not knowing what to do.

When Suzy finally smiled, Sacha tried again.

"Time is not of importance, mother. We are always together. Always..."

He hoped his mother would learn to reconcile her emotions with her mind. He couldn't tell her anything she didn't already know, but refused to accept. If he did, she would not be able to metabolize it. We really only learn from within. From the outside we only search confirmation to reassure ourselves. Surely, Sacha thought, surely this should be argument enough for anyone to accept our true nature?

"I'm all right now," Suzy said.

Regardless of how she felt, Suzy now looked her usual sunny self. Seeing his wife was in control, Alec returned to the previous subject.

"Did you ever check on that guy, I mean later?" Alec was thinking of Sacha's 'check' on his grandfather and imagined his son would have followed up on the hapless swimmer.

"Dad! There are more individualizations of consciousness than there are stars in the sky. Each time we become fully aware of anyone, we must place our attention on him or her. And usually, for real communion, we can only do so one at a time," Sacha sounded a little exasperated.

It was at this moment that Sacha understood why some great souls decide to merge with the Whole. It was the only way they could offer all they'd accumulated to the totality of cosmos. To the Whole. The rest of us can do so only one at a time.

"I guess you are right, son. Sorry. Wasn't thinking."

A minute later Alec looked perturbed again.

"You said, then, that the fellow who drowned would be all right. But what happens to the guy who hit him?"

Sacha read his fathers thoughts before he spoke them out loud.

"What happens to any one of us?"

Three pairs of eyes followed a single tern hanging over the ocean. It swooped this way and that, as if he'd lost his bearings.

"We continually create our reality," Sacha said when no one took up his question. "We perceive what we want to perceive. If the man felt guilty he'll pay his dues. If he accepted his fate humbly, then he would have learned his lesson. You can't have it both ways, Dad. There is no arbitrary deity sitting in judgment above us. Had Judas accepted his fate with humility, he probably would have been spared. I am talking about the mental anguish he suffered which caused him to take his own life. Although there is no one sitting in judgment over us, we are all indispensable pieces of the cosmic jigsaw puzzle. At a certain stage, we become our own judge and jury. We must find our place, our destiny, and fulfill it as best we can."

"Even if it means murder or treachery?" Suzy would never accept it. Not in this life.

"If you accept it, mother, then there is no murder. There is only the current of fate. If you accept it, you become a conscious instrument of the Whole."

Sacha was thinking of Arjuna's struggles. Not his friend in India, but the 'original' Arjuna in the Bhagavad Gita. It was not a premise that was easy to accept. He struggled with it himself. The problem was that if you made a mistake and reached beyond your fate for personal gain, you would pay for it dearly. No one said it was supposed to be easy. When the prophet of yore said that 'ye are gods', he forgot to add that to be gods you must act like gods. And gods don't make mistakes. We do.

"So he might be all right, or might not be..." Alec smiled against his will.

"It is as Einstein said, it's all relative," Sacha chuckled at his own pun.

"Or as Desmond would have said, leave Alberrrrt out of it," Suzy finally joined in the fun.

But Sacha was right. The only way you could make it easy on yourself was to completely negate the demands of your personality and merge with the exigencies of the Whole. To achieve this, you would have to become universal in your outlook. A tall order for people who have been taught that strong personality was a good thing. They have been taught great many other things that put brakes on their development.

"You know, Dad, I'm beginning to think that if everyone left everyone else alone, the world would be a better place."

This didn't come out right. What he meant was that if people stop telling other people what to do, then that which people would start doing would be more universal in nature.

"I agree son. Not with what you said only with what you had in mind."

Suzy looked up, surprised. Alec translated Sacha's thoughts. She was great at picking up emotions but not abstract patterns of thought. When she finally understood, she nodded repeatedly.

"I've been saying this for years. Perhaps not as precisely. But that was one reason why I stopped reading all those books on religions. Too many of them felt all wrong."

Sacha refused to be drawn into this discussion. His own views were as strong, but much less complimentary. But more than anything, he felt great compassion for people who were led by the nose by countless blind shepherds.

"In order to be an immaculate member of a flock of sheep, one must above all be a sheep oneself," Alec murmured under his nose.

"What's that?" Suzy thought she'd heard a similar, if not the same, sentiment expressed before.

"I was just quoting Einstein," Alec admitted. "The old Albert had a good head on his shoulders."

The next moment Alec experienced that rare and wonderful flash of memory. He recalled the exact words Sacha had said after Coastal Patrol fished out from the sea the body of the poor man who had just overcome his own nemesis. His inordinate fear of the deep. The man had won and died in the same instant. Sacha had said: I *don't see people as physical objects, Dad. It would be like worrying about a pair of pants that are ready for disposal. It simply doesn't matter. What matters is if the pants served you well. If they've served the purpose for which they were made."* Suddenly Alec felt very proud to be Sacha's father.

On the way back to the villa they all walked right along the water's edge, until Suzy pushed Sacha into an oncoming wave. This started a veritable bedlam. The three acted like ten-year-olds, trying to topple each other into advancing breakers. Alec won the greatest number of successful pushes, but Suzy was the best at screaming. Sacha hasn't been so happy since he was three.

That evening Alec was going to drive to LA. He was to give a free lecture tomorrow, and didn't feel like getting up early in the morning. Suzy turned in early. She was emotionally exhausted. Alicia lingered at the dinner table for a while, but then she, too, retired with a good book. She loved having the children around. They took turns at spoiling her. Yet, she still felt a little tired. As you grow older, rather then grow more immune to the vagrancy of fate you become less resilient. At least Alec and Suzy had each other.

Sacha didn't need much sleep. In a way, often he was busier when asleep than during daytime. Pure consciousness never sleeps. But that night, it was not to be. Fate extended her gaunt fingers and took him into her adamant, unpredictable embrace.

The fog was still stifling. His head and neck hurt as though an army of ants made a meal of his neck and left bare bones exposed to the sopping sky. He was lying prostrated just below the eaves of the tavern where he'd had a few drinks. Surely, just one or two. He seldom if ever drank any more.

He tried moving his legs. They wouldn't budge. He was pinned down. It was still too dark to see what was immobilizing him. The lamppost on the corner cast a spherical halo no more than a yard or two in diameter. The dirty yellow gaslight hardly sauntered near enough to be of any use.

"A stupid way for a physician to behave," he scolded himself.

After massaging his neck he managed to prop himself up against the wall. Memory was coming back to him in little snippets. A smoky interior, a drink or two, a dirty mirror, a man tugging at his elbow, Maxine, a forlorn foghorn and then... and then darkness...

His eyes were getting used to the darkness. He looked at his legs still straight out in front of him under a soft heavy load. It was a human form. He bent forward and pulled the body towards him. He recognized Maxine's face. She must have lost consciousness for some reason. She was completely pliant.

He put one hand behind her head to hold it up. There was something warm and sticky behind her. He was a physician. He would know that texture anywhere. It was blood. He pulled his legs from below Maxine's body and laid her out on the cold pavement. Next he took off his cape and covered her body. She was quite cool and her pulse was weak. Very weak. Not at all the Maxine he'd met before. The last time she'd been bubbling with life—to overflowing.

"Was it good for ya, luv...?" Her voice reached him in a conspiratorial undertone as though she didn't want anyone else to hear. "Was it, gov? She needed to know. Was she worried about a just reward for her efforts?

"Don't talk. You're hurt. I'll get you to a doctor," he replied in half-whisper.

What the devil am I saying. I am a doctor. My God, what can I do?

He felt around the cobblestones to see if he had his bag with him. It wasn't there. He wouldn't have brought it with him to this place. They would only steal the contents. They would steal...

He searched his pockets. His wallet, his watch and the heavy gold fob chain his wife had given him for their first anniversary, even his wedding ring, were all gone. He then remembered the hansom driver. He was nowhere to be seen. Was he the culprit?

He looked down at Maxine. She rested quietly, probably still hoping that she made it 'good for him.' What an incredibly honest woman. She's bleeding half to death and she's worried whether she'd carried out her part of the bargain.

He sat down again and lifted her head onto his lap. She seemed to be breathing normally. How on earth was he supposed to help her here? He wanted to lift her and take her into the tavern. He looked behind him. The windows were already dark. He took off his jacket, rolled it into a pillow and put it under Maxine's head. She smiled up at him.

"Ain't goin' already, luv... are ya?" she whispered.

The door to the tavern was no more than ten paces away. He walked over quickly and knocked on the heavy oak door reinforced with iron bars. Evidently there was need for additional protection. He knocked again. There was no answer. This time he banged the wood with all his might. There was movement inside. A male gruff voice came through a Judas' hole.

"If ya don't stop bangin' my door, I'm gonna set the dogs on ya."

"There is a woman hurt. I need to bring her in. I am a physician," he said assertively.

"Sure ya are. And I am the queen of Sheba. You've 'ad enough fer one night. Now, you rowdy son of a bitch, bugger off!" The sound of a man spitting was followed by a shrill whistle.

Almost immediately a herd of dogs growled in the darkness. It was no use. He made his way back to Maxine. He remembered the publican. He must have been a small man to elevate the floor behind the bar so high. He was probably afraid to open the doors to anyone. This was not the best of neighborhoods.

"I'll get you to a hospital, little girl," he spoke quietly as he gently lifted Maxine's lithe body from the wet pavement. She didn't resist. She hung limp in his arms, her head resting against his chest. He carried her to the lamppost. There, in the dim gaslight he looked at her lovely, youthful face. Her eyes were open. They were beautiful, strangely innocent eyes. Only there was no life in them. No life at all.

Sacha woke up covered in sweat. His jaws were set. For the first time in his life he decided to peak into his own past. If he could. By an act of his will.

He was rewarded with short, colorful flashes. Images as though painted on glass, which constantly changed shapes. The pictures were accompanied by fragments of knowledge. Of understanding.

He saw a tall, gaunt man working in a different parts of the East End of London. The man was a physician who had forsaken his fashionable practice and catered only to the poor. He never asked for money. He'd been attacked a few more times. It did not dissuade him. He kept telling himself that if he hadn't been there, in that tavern that night, Maxine would still be alive. He couldn't save her. He was trying to save everybody else.

Sacha shook his head. It all became very clear. He knew exactly what he had to do.

After all was said and done, Sacha returned once again to the stock market on the Internet. Let's face it, he reasoned, no one lost in this game. For every buyer there had to be a seller. And vice versa. It wasn't as though he had insider information about Initial Public Offerings. He played fair and square. It took a little longer but nothing would make his mother happier if it took him a whole year. It very nearly did. In a way, it was his first holiday in twenty-two years.

***

15
Mother's Town

What now? Every man, woman and child must translate their own, individual insights into a plan of action. He or she may be wrong. But a time comes when fear of making a mistake must be overcome. Sacha had reached this stage.

He had to act.

There were preliminaries that had to be done. In the Far East, it was an accepted practice, even for Buddhist monks, to sustain themselves with a begging bowl. In the West, while one might emulate this method to barely stay alive, it hardly sufficed if one's field of endeavor covered a larger area. Sacha had to prepare himself for all contingencies.

By the following June, he finally reached the state known as financial independence. It meant that the income from his investments was equal to his projected expenses. He transferred all his assets to his father's account in exchange for Alec keeping it alive, and wiring him money as needed. After some objections presumably for form's sake, Alec overcame his reticence and agreed. It could have been just a bit embarrassing for Alec to receive a large sum of money from his son who was just twenty-three years old. A mere stripling compared to the years of effort he'd put in himself to develop his own position. In spite of Dr. Alexander Baldwin's stature in the academic circles, and his undeniably successful career, Sacha's father had not 'put aside' anything substantial for old age. It seemed that Sacha, unwittingly, took care of that.

"Dad," Sacha argued over Alec's objections, "what you have given me already cannot possibly be translated into money."

What Sacha had in mind was that any 'normal' parent would have sent his delinquent son to a psychiatrist, or had him certified and committed for the rest of his ineffectual life. If it hadn't been for his father's own youthful 'fancies', as he'd occasionally called them, Sacha would not have been afforded the freedom to develop in his own particular, curiously eccentric, way.

What Sacha did not tell his father was that the investment account he'd opened initially had been registered in the name of Alexander Baldwin, a name he legally shared with his father, with the power of attorney reserved for himself. That way Sacha had the wisdom to avoid any transfer duties on which the menials of the various governmental agencies would gladly lay their greedy fingers. Legally, the capital was his father's already. As for Sacha's projected expenses, the amount was relatively modest. As modest as his needs.

Alicia's needs were quite different. Just before Sacha left for another of his quests, she wanted to learn his 'trick' as she called it. The trick of staying at home, playing with the computer and ending up a millionaire.

"You are a millionaire, darling, aren't you?"

"Hardly, Grandma. I don't need much money," he said with a mischievous smile, as though he had the world by the horns. But then he got serious and tried to explain the system he'd used on the Internet. He tried hard.

"It's just work, Grandma. Anyone can do it," Sacha insisted. He'd spent hours trying to explain his method to his grandmother—to no avail. Either he was an inept teacher, or Alicia an inept student. And then he reminded himself, again, that each one of us serves a different purpose. We are endowed with different talents. We shouldn't venture into other fields until our mission is fulfilled. Unfortunately when it is, we... die. A vicious circle. That's why they call it the Wheel of Awagawan—the Wheel of Life, Death, and Rebirth.

But there must have been a reason for Alicia's apparent need. Sacha prodded his Grandma gently until she confessed that she felt guilty that throughout her life she lived like a sponge off other people.

"First your grandfather kept me. Then Desmond. It doesn't seem fair," she concluded.

"I can't speak for your first husband, Grandma, but from what I hear from Dad, you made *his* father a very happy man. What was the going rate for happiness in those days? As for Desmond, you gave him more than you could possibly imagine," Sacha assured her.

"Perhaps, but not in financial terms," she insisted.

"Did Desmond ever ask you to contribute?"

"Don't be silly. He would have been too proud for that."

"Then...?" Sacha prodded, but Alicia was driving at something that she didn't want to readily admit. Actually Sacha knew that Grandma had inherited her first husband's estate that made her virtually independent.

"You wouldn't understand," she stated categorically.

"Try me," he gave her his best boyish grin.

She remained silent for some minutes. Then the words came out in a flood. The crux of it was that she wanted Desmond's son to have some tangible memory of his father. She wanted exactly the same for Alec and Suzy.

"He never really knew his father. He only saw his anger, then his agony, and finally his sorrow. But that wasn't Des at all. It's so unfair..."

Sacha gathered that Alicia deemed it unfair to both, Desmond and his son.

"And you too, Sacha," she continued. "I want you also to have something to remember Desmond by, and…"

Sacha listened patiently. Grandma had to get all those pent up emotions out of her system. She must have been stewing on them for some time now. Finally she stopped, sighed deeply, and looked up at Sacha like a wounded cocker spaniel. Sacha tried hard to keep a straight face.

"I wish you would leave me out of the equation, Grandma. My memories of Desmond are as fresh today as they ever were. I don't need material reinforcement. As for my parents, surely they are fully independent and they reserve a special spot in their heart for Des. I'm confident that they will treasure their memories for as long as they live… a lot longer, than you can possibly imagine…" Sacha grinned at his thoughts. "Now Desmond's son, that's another story. But why do you want to give him material memories?"

"What else can I give him?"

This time Sacha sighed. Why do people always think that the transient, material things are those that last? The very reverse is true. Even emotions last longer. Ideas last longer still. But love lasts longest of all. When you leave this Earth, you take it with you, yet it lingers on, and on, often for ages. Some say it never dies.

"You will think of something, Grandma. You always do."

The next day Alicia set about painting Desmond's portrait. Months later, Suzy told him that Alicia was on her eleventh painting. Each one depicted a different facet of Desmond's personality. She must have known her husband inside out. She must have loved him even more. Suzy told him that she'd never seen such diversity in the face of a single person. There was the stringent intellectual, the prolific ideas man, the devoted father/protector of all his students, the man of a great sense of humor, a practical joker, a devoted husband, a loyal friend and family man.

"Why do you paint so many of them," Suzy had asked.

"Because none of them show the true Desmond," Alicia replied. "They are like flashes of nearby objects seen through a window of a moving train. Fragments. And Desmond was so much more than a series of flashes. I must capture them all at the same time."

Sacha had a good idea what she would do with her paintings in her own good time. Dear Grandma…

Recently Sacha was growing more aware of his power over the elements, over physical reality, yet he was very hesitant to use it. It seemed wrong. He felt that his power belonged to another realm—that its efficacy might too easily be abused here. He felt he had learned the iniquities, the dark side, perhaps even the boundaries of human nature, but refused to take advantage on his knowledge. This, too, was a vicious circle. He continued to regard people as globes of light. For him their aura was more important than their facial features. Their external appearance was no more than a dust cover on a book. It gave you a first impression, but it told you little or nothing about the quality within. The difference was that Sacha knew their true nature, whereas people themselves made little effort to discover it themselves.

In many of them, the light within was very dim. So many protective layers covered it, making it almost indiscernible. The aura they displayed was of a dirty dark shade of brown. There was no joy in it. Not even hope.

Sacha felt lost.

Escaping into the higher realms brought him temporary relief. Seemingly, he would spend hours suspended in the vastness of space, inhaling the beauty of stars being born, new universes spewing from the mysterious entrails of gigantic black holes which countless ages ago swallowed innumerable galaxies. In the fullness of time, new life would evolve on new planets, seeded with the complex atoms born in the fiery hearts of countless stars. He collapsed time and witnessed new ornaments of God coming into being. Far Country was his only real solace. The only realm where he felt all-powerful, confident; where he didn't look for solutions, but acted on impulse. His individual thoughts crossed millennia of time, traversing light-years in the blink of an eye.

Such was his playground.

Such was the glory of the Far Country.

And then, for a timeless moment he would cleanse his mind of all thought and rise to the Undiscovered Realm. Here no one created, no one thought of great universes. Here he felt oneness with all of them. He was light within light. He was life, consciousness itself. He was eternity encapsulated in a single sphere of light.

Yet no matter how long he remained in those august realms, how wonderful his experiences within those wondrous states of consciousness, he always returned to physical reality, to Earth, in exactly the same place, at the precise moment of his departure. To his mother's delight, he no longer suffered from the peek-a-boo syndrome. He'd left that to her cats, purring happily on the terrace rail of Solana Beach villa. But he couldn't escape his destiny, any more than other creatures walking this valley of tears. No matter how hard he tried. After all, it was his own dream he was living.

"But what happens when I don't know what my particular dream is?" he mused sadly.

There were moments when Sacha envied his own parents. They were happy, contented with the niche they'd created for themselves. He could choose to live their innocuous life of contentment. Only, about then, he was beginning to experience a deep sense of frustration. It was time to embark on his own journey. Not as a youth, with little or no responsibility, but as an adult. He had to understand as a man.

He wasn't sure why he'd picked Montreal. He knew he had to be on his own. Montreal offered at least a tenuous link with the past. It was his mother's town. Long ago, his father has adopted a cosmopolitan frame of mind. But for mother Montreal was a city where she'd been carefree; where she had spent the innocent years of her life. It might give me a crutch, Sacha thought, something to lean on, in an hour of need.

In the hour of decision.

He found a B&B near the center of town. It guaranteed at least one meal a day. He seldom used public transport, preferring to walk. The *Centre Ville* location was necessary for his purpose. He spent the next few days walking the streets, watching, absorbing, determined to familiarize himself with the soul of *Ville de Montréal*. It was principally a French city, although the language spoken was far from the French he'd enjoyed at the Sorbonne. It was a parody of a language, a nasal goulash of mostly French, but a great many English words thrown in to add spice. Only the result was not very tasty.

No matter. He didn't have to talk; he mostly listened.

The city had a distinct flavor of its own—and not just the language. People seemed to display a lighter demeanor. They got wholeheartedly involved in local political squabbles as though their life depended on them. The next moment they would share a Molson or a Labatte, and transfer their allegiance from politics to *Les Canadiens*, or another hockey team; all with the same intense, overtly shallow yet deeply emotional passion. Finally, they would agree to meet for another bout of verbal abuse... in great equanimity. Sacha recalled that Italians were also like that. They didn't take life all that seriously, either.

In late afternoon he took a stroll to the top of Mount Royal: a lush verdant bouquet, smack in the middle of the city. Here, one could get lost in the richness of trees and foliage—a veritable jungle. By contrast, from some of the lookouts, on a clear day one could see the distant mountains of Vermont, in the USA he'd left behind.

He spent his first few evenings in a small terraced cafe on *Rue Saint-Denis*. He ordered *eau mineral au citron* and tried to eavesdrop on the conversations taking place at the adjoining tables. The local vernacular really wasn't easy to grasp, but after a few hours and four more bottles of mineral water, he began to pick up its rhythms. They tended to tilt their sentences upwards as if asking a question. And the pronunciation wasn't that impossible once you got used to it. Sacha was a very fast learner. It was fun to pick up, what to him was virtually, a new language. But he wouldn't dare express this sentiment aloud. Both his parents had warned him that the *Quebecois* and *Quebequoises* were very touchy about their culture.

Very touchy, indeed.

On the third day he took a train to Kingston, a smallish town in the adjoining Province. He'd promised mother to see the JJs, at first opportunity. Grandma Joan was overjoyed. But only after he'd introduced himself.

"If it weren't for your hair, Sacha, I would never have suspected it was you!" she assured him.

And then she took him in her frail arms, stood up on her toes, and insisted on kissing both his cheeks, stroking his hair, patting him on the back, feeling his muscles and generally making a thorough inspection of his physical condition.

"Will I pass?" he asked finally.

"Oh, I am sorry!" she smiled, evidently quite unaware of her detailed scrutiny. "It's just that you were a boy. A lad. We loved you so much. Of course we still love you... Oh, come in, do come in..." And she led him by the arm to the living room.

"Can I say hello to Grandpa John?"

Her face lost some of its luster. "You don't know? Suzy didn't tell you?"

"Tell me what, Grandma?"

"John had a stroke last week. Since he already suffered from Alzheimer's, they kept him at the Lakeshore General. They said it was for observation, but... I couldn't possibly cope anymore."

As she talked, her eyes left his face and drifted towards the far horizon beyond the Lake Ontario. Her eyes seemed to be probing somewhere, out there, where the sky met the earth, or water. Sacha felt she longed for release. Release from fear? The last few years with John must have been very trying. As joyful as she was a minute or two ago, now she looked drained. Sacha suspected she would rather die than go through those years again. Yet it was not *her* death, she feared. It was John's. With her next breath, she said as much. Consciously or not, it was a cry for help.

Sacha did not respond immediately. It never crossed his mind that people could be afraid to die. He suspected that fear of death was almost exclusively a fear of the unknown. That, and the ensuing loneliness for those left behind. If only they knew that we are never alone…

Perhaps when he would eventually come face to face with the end of his journey, he would also experience fear. But he was too young to even think about that. In both cases he'd witnessed so far, he'd experienced death as a *fait accompli.* Desmond was already on his way, and Maxine… well, in that reality he hadn't had the power to influence her mind. Maxine's death prayed heavily on his own conscience. Even now.

As he'd done before with Maria, he held Joan at arm's length and focused her attention with his eyes. He showed her fragments of his own reality. Of his own perception of the universal reality. Of the actuality of Home Planet. Joan wouldn't have learned how to realign her understanding in an instant. Usually, it took a lifetime. But for some time she would wonder why she would experience successive waves of inexplicable inner peace. Waves of an unconditional sense of acceptance—not to be confused with resignation.

Sacha could only heal the symptoms, not the disease. The disease was a state of mind we all create, painstakingly, over successive embodiments.

Yet in the days to come, Joan imagined she saw a strange light within John. It was not really a light but a warmth, a luminescence that was at odds with his physical condition. She became convinced that whatever John presented to the outside world, to the doctors and nurses, even to her, was not the real John. It was just, well... it was just his shadow. She rediscovered the John she'd known and loved. The real John.

Arjuna would call it his Atma.

The next day Joan asked Sacha if he could take a look at Princess III, the 36-foot Bayfield yacht moored at the Kingston Municipal Marina. He'd sailed the yacht before, as a youngster.

"I suppose we'll have to sell her. It's been years since we... since John and I put a foot on her deck. We kept her in case you or Suzy and Alec would want to come up."

They did come up almost every year, while Sacha had been gallivanting around the world. Both his parents were seasoned sailors. Sacha wondered if he could handle the boat on his own.

"John could do it," Joan assured him. "I went with him, of course, but I was much better in the galley than at the helm. That's why he installed the automatic pilot and brought all the lines to the cockpit."

Sacha remembered. He thought Joan was underestimating herself by a long shot. On board, always composed, she inspired an air of confidence. That was of enormous help to any crew, visitors, and even the captain himself.

The following morning Sacha walked down to the dock. He found the yacht in Bristol shape, if in want of a little TLC. He unwound the long hose from the finger dock and gave the Princess a good shower. He then went over the wet deck with a long brush, and hosed the decks again. That's all she needed. A little TLC.

He set out about eleven a.m.. He was only taking her out for a few hours, so didn't bother to check the weather forecast. Anyway, the wind was Westerly, 10-15 knots. What could be less demanding? And, to make things even easier, he didn't hoist the mizzen. The main and the Genoa would do just fine.

Two hours later he was barely within sight of the shore. The wind was steady if slightly stronger in the open sea. That's as it should be. He set the automatic pilot, stripped down to his shorts, and sat back to enjoy the sun.

His mind wandered ahead.

He hardly noticed that the winds began gathering strength. The cumulus clouds dropped lower, darkened their edges and stretched all the way to the far horizon. He was heading directly into the approaching storm—a storm as irrevocable as the darkness that seemed to engulf him. Only minutes later the clouds amassed directly over his head. The waves churned, smashing against the bow with tempestuous anger. The wind whined and whistled ominous warnings.

"I must trim the sails..." he thought.

The clouds now tore apart and spat a tremendous flash of light, followed by a clap of thunder.

"I must..." Another thunder. "Must I?" The Princess was healing to port heavily. "I must, surely I must... But why me? Surely there are others..." "Isn't there another way?"

Sacha shook his head and slapped his face with an open palm. The waters were as calm as minutes ago. Overhead, the same joyful cumulus clouds were reaching higher and higher. The sun shone with a serenity of a peaceful day.

He switched off the automatic pilot and turned the boat around. He'd had his sail. He knew that no matter how far he would attempt to run, he would not escape his destiny. The clouds on the horizon were his to face. To conquer.

He stayed two more days with Joan. They visited the hospital together and took a few walks. They also telephoned Solana Beach and chatted with Suzy and Alec. His father was planning another lecture tour. Suzy decided to visit her mother for a few weeks. Alec always gave lectures, in summer, to all-comers. He really wanted to spread the knowledge in his chosen field. It was his gift to humanity. That's all anyone of us can do. Share our perception of reality, and hope that it will make someone else as happy as it makes us. What else was there?

On the way back to *Montréal*, relaxed by the regular rhythm of the railway wheels, Sacha had a unique vision. He saw the very beginning of the world. A sort of Eden. There were no stars, no galaxies. Man seldom looked up. He was content to live in the here and now. Later, as man's thoughts were multiplied, as exemplified in Abraham, man created little points of light. Astronomers added nebulas, gaseous clouds and a great variety of galaxies. Sacha was in love with galaxies. He thought of them as jewels in God's crown. There were the Spheroidals, the Sombreros, the Whirlpools... there were countless numbers of them. Each one totally different. Each created by a single mind, a single soul basking in the reality of the Far Country. Finally came the black holes that swallowed all previous efforts and forced man to start again.

It was in one of the great cycles, eons ago, that man first understood the concept of black holes. It was then that he'd decided to place our little planet, our Earth, in the most inconspicuous place he could think of. Around a small sun on the periphery of an average galaxy. The Milky Way. Man thought he was buying time to achieve his immortality before the black hole would swallow him again.

That's why we are here, thought Sacha. Why we perceive reality from such an assiduously circumspect place. And yet we still think of ourselves as gods.

Or at least, that gods take special care of us.

Sacha was getting to know Montreal fairly well.

On his return from Kingston, he walked the streets at night. There were the homeless, the disenchanted, the drug addicts, the derelicts discarded by society. No one really wanted them. They did not contribute to society. They even endangered the image of the town they lived in.

He walked the streets in the early hours. There were not many people around. Not many witnesses. It was a good time to help people.

He didn't heal anyone.

He quieted the minds of people in distress, removed the dross, momentarily suspended their lack of faith, and allowed their own light to heal them from within. He felt that was as far as he could go. If anyone had suggested that he was performing miracles, he would have laughed. He would repeat the words he spoke to his grandmother when she asked him how to raise money on the stock market on the Internet. Anyone can do it, he'd said then. He felt the same way about helping people to heal themselves. Anyone could do it, if they would only change their perception of reality. If they would only suspend, even for a moment, their misbegotten ideas fed to them, through countless millennia, by organized religions.

There was no god healing them from afar. What divinity there was had always been, and is, hiding within their own hearts.

And then Sacha grew pensive.

"Why can't they understand my words?" he whispered. But no one answered.

No one even listened.

***

16

The Red Lights

The first day of the second week after his return from Kingston brought Sacha to *Rue St-Laurent*. There were many famous Lawrences, spelled with a 'w'. Montrealers could have named their street after any of them. There was Ernest Orlando Lawrence who won the Nobel Prize in Physics in 1939 for his invention on the cyclotron. They've been spinning atoms in ever increasing circles ever since. Sacha's dad could write a book about Ernest Orlando. There was, of course, Gertrude Lawrence whose charm and magnetic personality captivated vast audiences. There was James, the American war hero, admittedly south of the border, but there was also Sir Thomas Lawrence, the English portrait painter who took over from Reynolds, and who's vision of children adorn the walls of many museums on both sides of the Atlantic. Perhaps, even the walls of the *Musée des Beaux-Arts, de Montréal.*

There have been other famous namesakes.

But the French Canadians have always been obsessed with naming everything they could think of after saints. Their streets, villages and towns, even country lanes immortalize the names of numerous, long-dead, seldom venerated, Catholic saints. Men and women alike. And so it was with Saint Lawrence. In the year of Our Lord 285, this diminutive Roman is said to have been roasted to death on a gridiron. Perhaps it is from the red embers that the street took its name.

For, over the years, the *Rue St-Laurent* of Montreal became the Street of Red Lights.

The number one street in the Red Lights District.

Sacha remembered how his father, when only thirteen or so, had created in his mind Princess Sandra, who turned out to have been his father's higher image of himself. His Atma. Apparently, within a year, young Alec became reunited with his Princess, becoming Alexander. Sacha had suggested to his father that perhaps it was Sandra who created him, not the other way round. No matter.

What Sacha really envied was his father's youthful ability to create a companion who was virtually omniscient, practically omnipresent, and omnipotent. The only problem was that in most of us, this Princess abides only in a potential form. She, the Princess, or her counterpart the Prince, are potentially omniscient, potentially omnipresent and omnipotent.

Potentially.

In his own case, Sacha would compare himself to the Prince. He was fully cognizant of the potential within himself. He identified himself with his inner nature. He could even exercise a great number of traits that seemed beyond the scope of average men. But that didn't help. Even fleas have their fleas. And lately Sacha felt as if he was chewed upon, devoured, from within and without. He was struggling. He found himself escaping into imaginary realms, into dreams and visions, without conscious control. This had nothing to do with the Home Planet or the Far Country. Such experiences, as he suffered of late, belonged in the domain of psychiatry. He felt that Dr. Freud would have had a feast day with his subliminal experiences.

Sacha had to face problems that he didn't know existed. He was facing the unknown. When he ventured into the minds of the derelicts of society to offer help, he was deeply affected by their depravity. His own perception of reality elevated the men he'd met at least to his own level, even if just potentially. He was no more than a messenger. The message had a life of its own.

He had the highest possible respect for man's potential. He never imagined men, or women, could sink to the levels of subhuman impulses. He hasn't learned, as yet, to remain only a spectator—a passer-by. To be non-judgmental. Yet if he didn't learn, soon, to detach himself emotionally and mentally from the quagmire he'd discovered in the minds of those unfortunates, he would succumb to their maladies himself. He would be drawn, inexorably into their festering infernos.

It was a trying time.

SACHA 23+202 days

Am I swept by the events of my own creation? Sometimes I wonder if the reality I perceive has an objective base. Am I the only one who discerns this abysmal malignancy, or am I witnessing reality in which others really have their becoming?

Yet, try I must. I must try harder. Whatever the resolution, I sense that I am on the right track. That my intuition will guide me in my endeavors. At least, for as long as I remain tied to my physical body with the insubstantial yet virtually unbreakable, infinitely elastic silver cord. For most humans the cord is protected by the instinct for self-preservation. For me it is part of my perception of reality. I cannot break it without destroying my dream.

When Sacha first began wandering the streets, he felt somewhat lost. Now that he directed his steps towards *St-Laurent*, his perplexity grew exponentially. He saw children selling their bodies for whatever they could get. A few dollars, a hot meal, a reefer, or a sniff of white powder. They searched ecstasy in a pill, escape in a bottle. Some of them had not yet reached the age of puberty. They were the innocents, the martyrs of the present age, roasted on the gridiron of human depravity.

Sacha never found anything demeaning about sex, nor in the expression of sexuality. Without it, he reasoned, he wouldn't be here. But the perception of sex depended on whether you were the taker or the giver of pleasure. He was not concerned with the body of the delinquent children at all. There were armies of physicians who could fatten their bank accounts catering to those. His concern was for the vibrations that the self-centered attitude brought to the world.

To the fabric of spacetime.

Yet he couldn't force his will on anyone. He thought that the unfortunates, who sought and paid for the services of 'working girls', were even more depraved. Even if they didn't cheat on their wives or lovers, they succumbed to their base instincts to the exclusion of everything else. Animals responded to their instincts. The humans sunk below theirs. They were the hardest to help.

He once saw a man sitting in his car for a good half-hour trying to muster enough courage to drive another fifty yards to give in to his desire. People, such as he, as that man, didn't know that all desires are merely perceived. Imagined. They occur when stimulated by some associations and then are fueled into a conflagration by our imagination—till the flame is too strong for us to control. Then, we say, "I couldn't stand it!" "It was too strong for me!" Some of us even blame the imaginary creations of our fertile imagination. "The devil made me do it!" we aver, with a straight face. We seem unaware that the tempter and the tempted are always one and the same.

In a sense, all of us, no matter how insignificant, always spoke the truth. If we allowed ourselves to procrastinate, to wait before we act, our natural defenses would crumble. We'd start as humans, go through the stage of animal instincts, and then sink to the level of demons that no longer perceive any light within themselves. We become as dead, as though our silver cord's had been severed.

Only it hasn't.

Gradually, rationality returns to our perception. We feel depraved by our own weaknesses. We become desperate. We search for an escape. Then, we return to *St-Laurent* hoping to loose our identity once again.

A vicious circle.

Sacha followed some of these unfortunates through their nefarious cycle. He gathered first hand experience of what hell was like. Some claimed that there was only one Creator. That god created heaven and hell. They forgot that we were the sole creators of all realities.

The only gods.

Later, Sacha witnessed the same man returning to *St-Laurent* on three successive days. On the third day, Sacha prodded his mind. The man yielded. All Sacha did was to show him what his perception of reality will be, or would be, one half-hour later. The man turned the key in the ignition and left. Sacha did not see him on street of red lights again.

But mostly Sacha tried to help the girls, if only because they were younger. It was too early for them to die, to become zombies, the living dead. Often he was successful. He approached each girl individually. He tried to assess her mental state. Some were too far gone. They've already acquired a slew of sexually transmitted diseases, AIDS— more often then not. They would soon die and try again. Later. Much, much, later… After another long stint in Bardo.

Sacha's decision to concentrate on younger girls was a matter of judgment. He reasoned that if a girl began her spiral descent at a really young age then, if she survived, by the time she was an adult, she would have accumulated so much negative karma that all of her next embodiment would be an unmitigated hell.

He knew that no one died before his or her time. One could cheat death, but no one could cheat on his or her destiny. He recalled his father telling him about an airplane smashing itself to smithereens killing all on board—all but one. Two hundred and seventy-three people died and one walked off unscathed. Destiny would not be cheated. That is not to say that one could not take one's own life. But it would an exercise in abject futility. We would only sentence ourselves to dream the very same dream again. On the other hand, destiny is disposed with infinite, remorseful patience. It will keep us in our physical bodies as long as such bodies are capable of supporting our consciousness. Whatever our perceptions.

"Don't ever forget," he told one girl, "you are your consciousness."

Usually Sacha did little more than to project a vision of the probable future that the girls were building for themselves. No one knew the future. But the telltale sings were unmistakable. After exposing the young mind to the ominous possibilities, many girls chose to try a different route. Some slipped back, but most succeeded. Most of us seem to think that we, and we alone, can get away with 'things'. We might for a while. But sooner or later we must all pay the piper. Sacha didn't mince words.

"This is the universal law," he made it clear, "and the law cannot be broken."

Towards the end of the fourth week, a beautiful girl caught Sacha's eye. She looked about seventeen. At first he thought she was just another subject for his ministrations. But then he stopped short. Although she wore the uniform of her profession, she still didn't seem to belong on this street. The extra short, extra tight skirt and an equally tight bodice exposing as much of her upper charms as is possible without actually being arrested, did not match her face. Her bearing was upright, almost proud, her smile direct. She stood out from others, even other teenagers, possibly less fortunate than herself. It was the first time that Sacha was actually approached by a girl. Usually he chose his ground from a short distance, or managed to dodge into the shadows, and if not, he would polarize photons hitting his body and hide within a cloak of invisibility. Actually this ability had saved him more than once from possibly unpleasant consequences. On half a dozen occasions, oversized pimps had threatened to teach him a lesson, unless he left *their* girls alone. Apparently Sacha's method of opening up the girls' perception, to alternate realities, was not good for business. He also helped some other derelicts that had been taught a lesson by the goons for not paying the full amount to the girls. Sacha had no reservations about the punishment being well deserved but, left to themselves, the culprits would have died in a state of dismal depression. Such badly timed deaths were one of Sacha's principal concerns.

Over just a few weeks, he'd learned from three other girls that some local flesh merchants were circulating a story about a troublemaker who was muscling in on their territory. Apparently Sacha has been roiling the waters, disturbing the established system. He was the purported troublemaker.

The roiling culprit.

Last week, one of the girls had actually shown him a luckily rather bad photo of himself, published in the local rag. The article that followed made up an amazing story about a disappearing Robin Hood who protected *les* girls from the hands of their atrocious villains. The funny thing was that Sacha had never taken a single penny from, nor given to, any of them. Whatever he was, a Robin Hood he was not. He dealt in quite different currency.

Sacha glanced again at the youthful vixen facing him. This girl was definitely different. She didn't even look as though she was in dire need of his help.

"Buy me a drink, *Monsieur*?"

A usual enough gambit.

She spoke French. They all did though some of them found their way here from different parts of Canada. Some even came from the States, the Caribbean, and Middle East. For all of them, a smattering of French was good for business.

"Why?" he asked. He was so taken aback that he didn't even attempt to probe her mind.

"It's my birthday," she replied, her saucy tone accompanied by a broad smile.

There was something very familiar in that smile. Sacha couldn't put his finger on it but he felt that they'd met before.

"And just why should I believe you?" He played for time.

"Can't you tell? I am not wearing any makeup!" She wasn't insulted by his question; rather surprised at his lack of powers of observation.

There was that smile again. She was definitely a lady of pleasure. Not yet spoiled, not depraved. But she was a lady of pleasure. Sacha peeked into her mind. He found innocence mixed with curiosity. Not a combination one expects from a prostitute. Sacha decided to trust his instincts.

"Where would you like to go?"

"Anywhere will do. But..." she scanned Sacha from head to toe, "you don't belong here," she said knowledgeably. "Let's buy a bottle of wine and go to my place."

Had I been wrong about her? He gazed into her eyes but all he saw was an expectancy of pleasure. Not quite knowing why—he agreed. They stopped at a couple of stores where Sacha made his purchases. She waited outside. *Les* girls of *St-Laurent* did not like to advertise their presence in establishments flooded with light.

A half-hour later, they climbed a steep stair to her small third floor *Plateau* apartment. She pointed Sacha towards her sofa and made for the bathroom.

"Make yourself comfortable, while I freshen up."

She didn't need any freshening up. She had all the vitality, the irresistibility of youth, which is seldom seen even outside the confines of the strip of *St-Laurent*. No matter. On the inside she must have been more mature than she appeared to be on the outside.

Sacha took the opportunity to uncork the bottle, unwrap the cake he bought for her, and installed eight candles in a little circle. He looked around for matches. He couldn't find any. Could it be that the girl didn't smoke?

"Where do you keep matches?" he asked.

"You are not going to smoke on my birthday, are you?" she sounded hurt.

"No. Where are they?"

She told him. Before she came out of the bathroom he'd lit all the candles, poured out two glasses of wine and, as she'd entered the room, he sang in his best baritone the first line of "Happy Birthday." The last thing he expected was to see tears in her eyes. She stood at the door to her tiny living space looking completely vulnerable.

Sacha fought hard not to peek into her mind again. He used his ability to help people, not spy on them. Instead he walked up to her and took her in his arms. She looked as though she needed a hug. The moment he embraced her, she collapsed against his body. He picked her up, as gently as he could, and carried her to the sofa. Her head rested against his chest, the rest of her body hang limp over his arms.

And then it hit him.

He'd carried a girl like that once before. She too had been hanging limp, as though lifeless, as he carried her towards the lamppost. Her name was... her name was Maxine. Sacha felt a shiver passing up his spine. Hair stood up on his neck.

Am I given another chance?

"What happened?" She looked up at him like a baby looking for comfort.

"What is your name?" he asked.

"Deborah. What happened?"

Deborah. Not Maxine. Oh, I'm being stupid. That was another life.

"You fainted..." he replied.

"I know I fainted. What happened?"

Sacha remembered Maxine's dying whisper word for word: *Was it good for you, luv?*

Only then did he realize that he was still holding her in his arms. He put her on the sofa and sat next to her. There was no other furniture except for a small table and two wicker chairs by the window. It all looked simple, clean and proper. Not really, "good for business," he thought.

And then her eyes fell on the wine bottle, the glasses but mostly on the eight candles burning brightly in the middle of her birthday cake. It all came back to her in a single flash.

"You're not a John, are you?" she asked scrutinizing his face.

Sacha had spent many a night on the *St-Laurent*. He knew what a John was. He shook his head.

"I knew it! I knew it!"

Deborah had recovered completely. The very young can do that. She shot up from the sofa, clapped her hands and did a little exotic dance that looked like a cross between an Irish jig and a whirl he'd once seen the dervishes perform in India.

"I knew it... I knew it!" she sang again. "I knew I would have a real birthday, and I will!" The next moment she stopped. She looked at Sacha again and asked, this time shyly. "May I ask what your name is?"

He told her.

"You are very kind, Sacha. I think I am falling in love with you," she actually blushed. "You don't mind do you?" There was that innocence again.

Deborah had been walking the streets since a little after her fourteenth birthday. She'd been sent out by her foster mother. She didn't mind. It was better than watching her foster father drinking around the clock. Going to school was no fun either. The other kids gave her a rough time just for living in a foster home. There were seven of them, the children that is. The children were her foster parents' only income. A small stipend, per child, from the government. That, and whatever Deborah brought in from the street.

At first she'd brought all her money home, and had given it to her foster mother. This went on for a little over a year.

Then the foster father tried to beat the money out of her to buy himself more booze. That was when she'd left. She didn't pack her things. She didn't have any. She just left. She's been "on the street" ever since.

Most of this Sacha learned from her as they sipped the light Chablis and munched on the birthday cake. Some of the story he got by scanning her mind. Like the part about the beatings by the foster father. She hadn't told him that. Was she that proud, he wondered?

"Why did you make me tell you all that?" she asked finally. "I've never spoken about my past to anybody." She sounded surprised.

"What happened to your parents?"

"They both died in an auto accident the day after we came over from England."

So that was her accent! It was already Canadian but there were those quaint British overtones.

"And you were left with nothing?"

"The baggage was lost in transport. My fosters tried to recover it but failed. I was lucky they took me in."

Those were her actual words. After her twelve months with the depraved, spurious pseudo-parents, she considered herself lucky. Her love of life must have been incredible. Still was.

For a while they sat in silence. Later Sacha had learned that she now considered herself an expert. In her profession that is. Would she stay in it, he asked?

"I try not to look too far ahead. If I have enough to eat and keep this flat, I'm content. I don't invite Johns here. I share a pad with my girlfriend for that."

No wonder she considered herself an expert. She'd been a prostitute in her previous life. Not that she knew that, of course. Evidently she couldn't break out of the cycle. Sacha knew that Maxine had died in his arms. There, he'd been too late. He would not make the same mistake again. He would not let her contract an incurable disease and die, as Maxine had died. On the street. Or worse. When you don't break out of your cycle, it's always worse the next time. The extra difficulties are supposed to help you. Often they do. They act as a stimulus.

Sacha was amazed at her inner light, still glowing with the innocence of a child. He'd seen such light in no one with the possible exception of John Norman, towards the end. Not the last time he saw him, but the time before. But that was different. Light has brightness that you might almost measure in lumens, but it also has color and tone. There is a joyful light. There is no sad light but there is light less joyful. After that, the light continues to dim so much that its qualities become indiscernible.

Light and love are almost synonymous. There are degrees of both, at least in the way we perceive them. Love is one, but there are degrees how deeply it can manifest itself. The same goes for light. People have long discovered that white light incorporates all other colors. There are also pure colors and some that are left with a desire for purification. Sacha was delighted by what Deborah had to offer. She radiated more joy than people with fat bank accounts. That's assuming people with fat bank accounts were joyful. Sacha hadn't met any. They seemed to manage on their own.

"Would you like to make love?" she asked very quietly. When Sacha didn't answer she added: "I'm eighteen now. You don't have to worry."

For some reason Sacha thought he detected a plea in her voice. The idea never crossed his mind. Judging by her aura her body was obviously not harboring any disease. The next instant he was ashamed that he thought of her in those terms. In terms of an object that is to be examined before purchase.

"It is your birthday, Deborah. We shall do whatever you want to," he heard himself say.

For the first time in his life Sacha found himself over his depth. He bandied arguments with professors at Oxford and Sorbonne, he compared visions of reality with men who had dedicated their lives to the subject, yet here and now he was lost. He had no choice but to let her take the helm.

"I've never made love before..." she whispered.

For crying out loud! She was speaking the truth. In her heart she was a true, unspoiled, uncontaminated virgin. She was a child in need of love. Make love to her meant love me. You can love every part of me. Including my body.

Sacha found making love to her, the actual physical contact, the nearest thing to leaving his body. An OBE, an out of body experience, they called it. Only... he was one hundred percent aware of his body. His emotions, his senses rose and took both, Deborah and himself to a different plane. A plane he'd never experienced before. He rejoiced in his new discovery. He came here as a teacher and he ended up learning. So this was sex... This was what so many searched for under the red lights of *St-Laurent*. They searched, paid, and left wanting, their hunger unquenched.

Yet, he had found it.

He held her body as gently as father would hold his daughter, as passionately as a lover would embrace his dearest mistress. His consciousness was making random leaps from one facet of her personality to another. At one particular instant he became so engrossed in her being that he in turn swept her emotions to the Home Planet. It all happened outside the normal frame of time. They soared together, they hovered on the fringes of the Far Country, and they came back united as though a single mind bound with a single emotion. It lasted only for a briefest moment but it was intensely real.

"What was that... that..." she asked, awe in her eyes shining with pleasure.

"That was the real you," he answered.

It wasn't supposed to be like that. She'd needed warmth. Even if it was artificial, fractional, insincere. Like so many confused souls pacing *rue St-Laurent* in the early hours of yet another forgettable day, she wanted to lose herself. She found herself at the momentary threshold of Nirvana, in a fragmentary instant torn out of the fabric of time, in which to cease being, in which to forget the reality she refused to accept. She offered her own self in exchange. She was prepared to try her best to give Sacha pleasure. All for a little warmth. She tried giving love the only way she knew how. Instead she'd met her own self.

"You are the perceiver and the perceived. You are your attention," he told her later. "Wherever your attention is, you are there. If you think yourself in hell, then that's where you are. When you think yourself in heaven, then all you must do is imagine it and believe."

Deborah's perceptions were as innocent as those of a newborn baby. All things were possible for her. The religious, the pious, the saintly, would call her a sinner. A Jezebel. A harlot. She was none of these. She would have no idea what they were talking about.

Nor would Sacha.

***

17

Once More LA

There is one way to break the habit, and that is to remove its cause.

Sacha did not return to his B&B for three days. He stayed with Deborah. During the day they went for walks, ate at local cafes, visited a few art galleries. They talked and talked until Sacha felt that he knew her the way he knew himself. He purposely did not venture into her subconscious because it was important to him that Deborah uncovers the darkest corners of her mind herself. Sometimes he prodded, but only with a word or two. After the three days Deborah sounded as though her past was no longer a mysterious chasm to be afraid of, but a fragment of her existence which no longer had anything to do with her. In a way, she was starting anew. Only neither of them had any idea where that new way would take her.

At night Sacha walked the streets alone, while Deborah remained at her apartment. He suggested this course of action and she agreed without a word. She seemed to have developed instant trust in Sacha's word. Whatever he said was law. Contrary to other teenagers her age, she didn't need to reassert her ego by negating whatever the adults said. She went through two, almost three years of making all her own decisions. To have someone to make them for her was like a sort of holiday.

But it didn't last. It couldn't have.

As for Sacha, there had been two more near escapes from the Vice Squad and one incident with a pimp. The latter was a particularly brutal man. Sacha had been forced once again to use his skills of becoming invisible, thanks to which, rather than retreating, he continued to examine the man's mind. There is a strange light hovering around a human form when he or she is about to vacate the body. Sacha had seen it before. The pimp displayed this particular, if dull, vaguely violet luminosity. Sacha had gently insinuated his thought patterns into the man's subconscious and showed him a different perception of what he was doing. He made him aware of possible consequences of... pimping. He did so on the man's own terms, from the man's own point of view. An ignorant witness might have thought that Sacha went too far. The man attempted to cross the street before he managed to recover from the shock of a higher perception invading his consciousness. Still in a daze, he was hit by a speeding car. Sacha, there and then, raised him gently to the Home Planet. It would have taken the ex-pimp hundreds of years to be able to perceive the glorious reality on his own. He wouldn't know how to keep it. But at least the poor man would not start in the abysmal depth, which are known to ensnare some that venture into this reality unprepared.

Towards the end of that week, sipping cup after cup of coffee in her little flat, Deborah grew discontented. Sacha had been expecting as much. He'd sensed the wind of change. It had to happen, sooner or later. As for himself, no matter how little sleep he needed, he couldn't continue in his present mode for much longer either. They've reached their first crossroads.

"I feel like a kept woman," she said.

Sacha looked at her in disbelief. Each time he thought he'd fathomed her psyche she came up with new surprises. But he refused to argue. He knew how she felt.

"Can't you think of it as a holiday?"

"I did. Until now. I've never had a holiday that long," she replied with a straight face.

"But aren't I staying in your place... for free? Isn't that enough?" he asked. It was worth a try.

"It would be if you didn't do it just for me."

There was no doubt in her voice. No room for maneuvering. This eighteen-year-old refused to be a kept woman. She was too honest. She had to pay her own way. Sacha thought that they didn't make them like her any more. Not even in the East End of London.

He needed time. "Can you give me till tomorrow?"

"Of course." But her facial expression said, "and not a minute longer."

The next moment her eyes misted. Sacha, though implicitly embarrassed, succumbed to his own weakness. After all, he was very young himself. In spite of his own avowed principles, he peeked into her mind. Almost immediately he regretted having done so. He found pain where so recently there was only pleasure. Her heart cried out in silent emotive plea: God *please don't make me give him up. Please God... please...*

And after that he sensed mostly sorrow. Sorrow and a little fear.

The next day he took Deborah to the passport office. She resisted under the pretext that she had no intention of going anywhere.

"I can't afford it, Sacha. And you know how I feel about taking alms."

"I need a secretary," he lied.

"I am not a secretary," she replied.

"A companion?"

"They are a dime a dozen." Then she muttered under her breath, "I'll introduce you to some of my friends..."

Sacha pretended he didn't hear that.

"I'll marry you," he said.

"I'm not the marrying..." She leaned against the wall. "What did you say?"

"I said I'll marry you. If you will have me, of course. I have a little money put aside and we could afford to live together for a while. Then I would make some more money and..." Deborah knew nothing about Sacha other than that he was a man who did her kindness. Who didn't insist on *quid pro quo*.

"You would marry me? Don't you know what I am?"

"I know *who* you are. And well, you don't know much about me either."

"No Sacha. I most certainly will not marry you. I love you too much to lose you." Her mind was made up. "You were the first man, the first human being, who treated me as a person. I am not going to lose you. Can't we be friends?"

Deborah had stories to tell about marriages that would make Sacha's mop turn gray. She regarded marriages as legalized institutions for mutual abuse. Sacha learned later that her own parents were none too skillful at creating marital bliss. Perhaps that was why she believed herself to have been lucky to have been given a bed to sleep on at the foster home. Even if just for a while. The ridiculous thing was that she'd never given any indication that she thought life dealt her a raw deal.

Sacha recalled his father telling him about Stephen Hawking, regarded by many of his peers as the most brilliant theoretical physicist since Einstein. Hawking, after being confined to a wheel-chair for over twenty years by the Lou Gehrig's disease, in the *Acknowledgments* to one of his books had written: "Apart from being unlucky enough to get ALS, or motor neuron disease, I have been fortunate in almost every other respect." Sacha thought that Deborah would have made Hawking proud. They both exhibited indomitable spirit that refused to dwell on the dark side of life. In addition, although Sacha had traveled the world, Deborah seemed to know as much about human nature as he did. More, in some respects.

"How much would you do for a friend?" he asked after recovering from her answer.

"Name it!" Freshness returned to her eyes. He knew that he could ask for virtually anything. Anything that would not impinge on the remnants of dignity she still retained.

"Come with me to Los Angeles."

"But why? I don't know Los Angeles. I don't know if I can make my way there..."

Her last sentence followed the path of what the musicians call *decrescendo*. To extend the metaphor, it also registered a pronounced *diminuendo*. Her tone of voice lost something of its assurance and volume.

"There are some people there I want you to meet."

"But..."

"It's important to me," he said more sternly than he'd intended. And when she still didn't react he added—this time softly: "For a friend?"

She leaned her head on the back of the sofa and closed her eyes. Even now, in full daylight she looked two or three years younger than her age. It's a wonder she hadn't been arrested for underage soliciting. Assuming there is a good age for prostitution. So far she'd survived the tribulations of her imposed profession. Imposed, not chosen. Sacha knew that this time he had caught her in time. There was no way he would let her slip through his fingers again.

"Is it a deal then?" he asked hopefully.

"You must find me things to do. I don't know if there is anything that I know how to do. I've never really done anything. I mean..."

"I know," he cut her off sharply.

He took her face in his palms. Slowly, still smiling, he raised her head and looked intensely into her eyes. She saw the infinite potential swirling within her being. She saw the countless possibilities waiting to be explored. Not any particular ones. It was like hearing whole symphonies compressed into a single chord.

"The world is there for you to conquer. I can't do it for you, Deborah. But I know that you have it in you to do whatever you want."

She remained motionless, breathing deeply. Finally she looked away from his eyes and let her lids protect them from further invasion.

"No one ever told me that," she said, as though in a dream.

No one ever did. Nor could anyone—except for Sacha.

And then, as though coming awake for the first time in her life, she whispered in disbelief: "Who are you...?"

Three days later they left for LA.

There was another reason why Sacha thought it wise to leave town. It would allow things to cool down a little. The last thing he needed was the reputation of an avenging Zorro. And the paparazzi tended to hang on like well-trained fleas. Or pit bulls. Once they bit they wouldn't let go. He'd decided to remove himself from the biting scene for a while.

Sacha telephoned ahead. He said that he'd met a friend who needed looking after. Could she stay with Alicia for a few days?

"It would mean a great deal to me," he told her.

Alicia agreed at once. There was very little she wouldn't do for Sacha. Anyway, since Desmond had died, she had time on her hands. All her life she'd been looking after someone. It was what made her happy.

In LA Sacha took Deborah directly to Alicia's apartment. Grandma drove back from Solana Beach just to pick them up. Eventually, he would take Deborah to meet the rest of the family, but for now Sacha entrusted her to his grandmother's care. They arrived late and Alicia suggested they both stay the night. Sacha excused himself under some lame pretext. He lied.

"Must go to parents condo. Things to do..." he lied cryptically. He was very bad at lying. Of course, he always had things to do. It's just that this was not his underlying motive. What he found hard to admit to Grandma was that, somehow, he was embarrassed to sleep with Deborah in his grandmother's house. Together, that is. He was even more embarrassed not to.

His parents had just left on one of his father's lecture tours. Finally they could travel together. He was glad that he would be able to tell them about Deborah in his own good time.

"You're not going to leave me here for ever, are you?" There was a mixture of fear and plea in Deborah's voice. She felt at home among the cutthroats of *St-Laurent*, but felt quite ill at ease in Alicia's apartment.

"I'll be back before you know it," he assured her. "Now have a good rest and don't let the bedbugs bite."

"You have bugs here?" Deborah's eye grew larger.

Alicia shook her head. "Only when Sacha's around. Once he goes we shall both be all right," she assured her young visitor with a grave face.

It was at this moment that Deborah decided that she was going to like Alicia after all.

There was another reason why Sacha had chosen Alicia to look after Deborah. His grandmother had an incredible affinity for dealing with, for the want of a better word, difficult children. Deborah was hardly a child. But she qualified in the difficult department. Not for the usual reasons. But her set of values, her whole ethos, while fundamentally sound, was not adapted to the so-called civilized society. Even though the civilization we all admire and cherish left a lot to be desired. In LA alone, last year, more than 550 people had been murdered—so much for freedom and democracy. Sacha felt that Alicia could look after this disparity in Deborah's education. The rest would come later. He soon learned that he'd made the right choice.

The following day, over breakfast, Deborah told Alicia about her past. Having confided in Sacha, she regarded her early life with a strange detachment. As though she'd been freed from a tremendous burden. Alicia wasn't shocked. At her age it would take a great deal to shock her. And she half-expected Sacha to come up with something 'unusual'. But she advised Deborah not to advertise the story of her last few years.

"Promise me, little one, that you'll never, *never*, tell that to anyone. Never again."

Deborah agreed. She wasn't quite sure why. After all she didn't steal, or cheat, or lie. She'd earned an honest living. That couldn't have been wrong. But Sacha told her—no—he'd *asked* her, to listen to Grandma. And she promised she would. And Deborah had not learned yet how to break promises.

As with the children in her art classes Alicia, for reasons she'd never quite understood herself, accepted Deborah, Debbie, just as she was. There was neither judgment nor displeasure in her admonition. She thought it best for Debbie. Alicia sneaked in surreptitious—sneaky would be a better word—questions over dinner and during breakfast, and came to some conclusions. Even after just a few hours, Deborah seemed to her the most innocent girl she'd ever met. Certainly more so than she'd been at seventeen herself. At that age she's been preoccupied with boys like every good, healthy, vital seventeen-year-old. For Debbie, boys seemed furthest from her mind.

Alicia thought she knew why.

Sacha visited them daily. They talked, joked, went for long walks. After dinner, he left. He needed his nights for himself. His parents were still away. But, once again, Sacha was beginning to feel the strain of a double life. He convinced Alicia and Deborah to go to Solana Beach.

"I'll join you as soon as I can."

"I've never seen the Pacific," Deborah confessed, her eyes shining. Their walks had not taken them as far as the waterfront.

Deborah was gradually losing her feeling of being 'a kept woman'. It was easier with another woman. Sacha had known that. And anyway, Alicia was halfway to convincing Deborah that without her she simply wouldn't be able to cope.

"I am not as old as I look," she lied. Alicia looked a lot younger than she was. "But it's all getting to be a bit much for me. I wish I had someone to help me."

"Couldn't I help you?" Deborah's smile lit the whole room.

The impasse worked. Alicia worked hard not to show a smile of victory.

"Are you sure it's not too much for you?"

Deborah had absolutely no idea what Alicia had in mind, but she was determined to help her in whatever it might be. Alicia spent hours trying to make up all sort of chores. And then she hit the jackpot.

"You know, my eyes are not as good as they once were. Do you thing you might read aloud to me?"

She could relax. The chores took a second place, while Deborah's reading skills improved on a daily basis. Alicia was a very sneaky woman. Both her husbands had known that. Deborah was yet to discover just how sneaky Alicia could be when she put her mind to it.

Three days later the LA press discovered that Sacha was back in town. Someone who had nothing better to do, must have looked him up on the Internet and discovered that he was Alexander Baldwin Ph.D., a Member of the Royal Society. All new members had their pictures published and one could look them up. Assuming one would want to sift through the vast electronic files. They had to dig back over five years to sate their appetite.

Unlike the doctorate of his father, Sacha's degrees were in philosophy, sociology and political science. But this was not what put the paparazzi on Sacha's trail. Nor was it because of his reputation of an avenging angel *de Montréal.* This time the sin he'd committed had been that of having saved a child involved in a car crash. An army of reporters, headed by cameramen from the local TV station, immortalized his ministrations. Had Sacha been unsuccessful, no one would have bothered. Unfortunately, Sacha knew exactly what he was doing.

In Sacha's reality there was nothing wrong with children dying. Not as such. It only meant that their karma had been very easy to discharge. But when a child dies before she is aware of her conscious mental processes, it simply postpones the resolutions she'd assumed for that particular embodiment to the next one. It seemed like a waste. There was, of course, the aspect of parents, both emerging from the accident unscathed, fulfilling their karmic obligations. But this time they were both convinced that they'd already lost their little girl. Their debt had been paid. Sacha never attempted to interfere with someone's karma before examining his or her subconscious.

Sacha did not accept that there was good and evil in the world. There were only different perceptions of reality. The universal ones were incorporated into the fabric of the Whole, the parochial—recycled. Like garbage that could be reused again, perhaps, in a better form. That's all. No great mystery.

Yet there was seldom a black and white situation. His philosophy of life was relatively simple: we all must make our own decisions based on our knowledge, and act on them. After all, we are the sole creators of reality. We perceive whatever we perceive. It cannot be otherwise. Yet, Sacha would not have been able to live with himself if he didn't try to help whenever he could.

Perhaps he was becoming all too human.

But the attention of the press was unfortunate. Sacha spent his nights continuing the work he'd started in Montreal. He helped only those who had sunk to the bottom of society. Who'd already been rejected by all. Only here, in LA, he didn't restrict himself to the Red Light District. He'd gone back to the work of his early days in Montreal: the derelicts, the drug addicts, and those who had given up. It did not matter what their physical needs might have been. Financial, health, self-image, it was all the same. He scanned a prospective vagrant, he did what he did by opening his eyes to his potential, and he withdrew. Sometimes, only sometimes, he also healed his or her body. The way he always did. By preparing the ground for them to heal themselves. After all, we all are just what we imagine ourselves to be. Again, it cannot be otherwise. Or as his dad used to quote his personal idol, God does not play dice with the universe.

And now, thanks to the omnipresent ladies and gentlemen of the media, it was time to leave town again. Also, Suzy called Grandma Alicia. He parents would be back in LA in two days. He still found it hard to tell them about Deborah. Particularly his mother. And he still had no idea why.

He'd once read a book many talk about but few have read. He'd read a book that said that birds had their nests... and foxes—their holes. He wondered if he would ever again find his hole. His lair. A place he could rest. He took the flight back to Montreal by a circuitous route to mislead the paparazzi. For a while he succeeded. But to those who had taken the trouble to find out, Sacha's *curriculum vita* was impressive. His parents' address was already swamped with requests for Sacha to speak at a number of university campuses. Even two or three evangelical churches offered him their pulpits.

Sacha hated publicity.

What the paparazzi dug up about him was radically different from that which the American audience had heard before. This included the theses he'd written way back when. At that time, they had all been published. Locally. Now, his views were being published again. In the process they were enlarged, popularized and generally made more marketable.

Suddenly, Sacha became the talk of the town. All because he had saved one baby who'd been pronounced dead by two inept physicians. No matter that the physicians were wrong. The paparazzi wouldn't let go. Like pit bulls.

His dad asked him, by phone, if he intended to honor any of the invitations. Or even answer them.

"Do you think I should, Dad?" He badly needed advise.

"I'm afraid son, you are the only one who can answer that question. It's your life."

And it might prove a good way to lose it, thought Sacha. They were already twisting his words. Only he could straighten them out. Would they understand him then?

That night he wrote in his notebook.

SACHA 23+253 days

I am not a man. Nor a woman. Nor am I a child with a vague awareness of an immortal soul. I don't have a soul. Not one of us has a soul. I am soul. You are soul. Or at least an individualization of the Whole. Of the universal mind. More than a mind. You are an individualization of the infinite potential. Am I to give lectures and tell them that? Is this what people want to hear? Will anyone listen? Should I tell them that many of the principle religions of the world have been lying to their people for thousands of years?

How long would I survive?

Would it matter?

The following two months, in Montreal, had been trying. Sacha worked around the clock, ignoring sleep, seldom eating. He felt and acted like a driven man, as though his time were running out. His feelings were entirely irrational. He had an arsenal of powers—he thought of them as abilities— which would offer him ample protection in virtually any imaginable circumstances. Yet there was that nagging feeling that he was approaching a point of no return; that everything he did was sweeping him towards an irrevocable fulfillment of his destiny.

"But if so, then why am I not filled with joy?" he wondered. "Why is there anxiety in my heart as if danger was lurking at me from every corner, day and night?"

The dark street corners offered no answers.

Three times he had to change his lodgings, but this was not enough to explain his sense of foreboding. Each time he'd moved to a new place, a rooming house, where they would ask fewer questions. Where rental payments were made in advance. Where people didn't talk about their problems, didn't invite conversation. In a most inexplicable way he felt a strange kinship with those furtive shadows of men. For that was what they were. Shadows of their former selves. Sacha had managed to salvage a few of them. Their bodies recovered some of their aura. Yet there were so many of them, so very many. He was becoming constantly tired... so tired, and there was so much to do.

There was so much to do...

Is this really what I've been sent down here for? Is this my own dream?

**

18
The Danger Signs

Sacha had to go back to LA. It didn't really matter
where he practiced his peculiar mode of mental and
emotional medicine, and in LA he was needed for other
reasons. He was also becoming convinced that whatever he
did, wherever the succession of events took him, there he
would find the next chapter of his destiny. It was unfolding
with such consequence, such inexorable determination that
he'd given up attempting to reason out its contrivances, and
allowed himself to be swept by its tide.

During the last month in Montreal Sacha had acquired a
new ability.

It had been thrust upon him by necessity. For the first
time in his life Sacha discovered that he could sense not one
or even three or four states of consciousness at a time, but
that he could 'read' a whole crowd of people simultaneously.
Not their individual thoughts or emotions, but the ethos, the
common vibrations of a whole bunch of them. It was as if, in
addition to each individual karma, they also shared a common
reaction to their previous embodiments. As if people who
shared certain karmic aspects joined hands, or rather minds
and emotions, rather like men and women who choose to
become engineers, or teachers, physicians, or picked music to
give substance and expression to their lives.

There was an intangible cognitive connection between
them, and Sacha could sense it. Armed with this perception,

he could, to a degree, influence their common behavior. Not in any magical or miraculous fashion, but he could both sense and impose certain ambiance towards which a particular group of people reacted in a predictable fashion. He imagined what a marvelous card it would be for a politician. Some leaders and actors behaved as though they shared this ability. They called it charisma, or charm, or just a superb ability to "read the crowd". No doubt it was a field to be exploited, if not abused, by anyone seeking power.

Nothing was further from Sacha's mind.

He discovered his new ability quite by accident. A bunch of bullies, somewhere between middle teens and early twenties, were just beginning to vent their ire on another youth that Sacha had helped some days ago, and who'd lost interest in belonging to this very group of hooligans. There was no time for Sacha to set about adjusting the various states of consciousness of the individual members of the depraved bunch of thugs. It was then that he detected a common thread between them. Not just anger at the emotional level, or irresponsibility at the mental, but a common thread at much higher levels of cognition. One could say that their individual auras, uninspiring as they were, displayed a similar, virtually the same, color and intensity. Sacha instantly attuned himself to their particular vibrations and then proceeded to purify their resonance, then their colour, and even their degree of brightness.

In no time the hooligans picked up their victim from the ground with hardly a punch having been thrown, and walked away, as though losing all interest in their vicious designs. Sacha had no idea if the positive effect would last, but he was glad that the lad he'd worked on before had escaped unharmed. As for the others, what a minute ago was a gang, transformed itself into a loosely knit camaraderie in search of means to satisfy their vacuity.

Whatever else had happened, they were all, at least partially, reawakened to their potential.

Then, with the suddenness and unpredictability of a bolt of lightening from a cloudless sky, the inevitable happened. Overnight, Sacha developed a following.

He began being recognized on the streets by the needy, the sick, even those who normally wouldn't venture from the furtive shadows. They began to seek him out. To tell each other where he might be, at any time, any day. They seemed to have joined some unspoken alliance, a brotherhood, and kept their eyes and ears opened for Sacha's arrival. It wasn't that difficult. Their mentor's golden mane seemed to light the paths he walked.

Once again Sacha realized that it was time to go.

During that last week he'd worked only at night, but almost openly.

There was so little time.

He worked mostly with the destitute. He attempted to explain to them that wealth is a state of consciousness, and then tried helping them to metabolize this axiom. He tried to tell them that wealth has nothing to do with worldly domains. That even material independence is the result of a state of consciousness, and not the rationale for it. Whether they understood him or not, he felt that he became adored by some, mostly those on the fringes of society, hated by others, usually those who were well to do. Why?

"There are proper organizations, authorities, churches, duly registered charities committed to this sort of thing!" claimed one reporter. She'd failed to explain "what sort of thing?"

"People will stop their contributions, their donations to the proper organizations if this character (sic) is helping the derelicts for free..." asserted another.

Now this was closer to the heart of the matter. Canadian charities and churches, combined, run an annual budget into billions of dollars. No one should be allowed to interfere with such a golden goose. No one!

Heretofore, no one had.

Not one of his detractors would have guessed that Sacha extracted payments of a different sort. He expected people he helped to give up the states of mind that brought them to their present condition. Just their state of mind, but on that he'd insisted.

"Whatever you perceive as reality that will manifest in your lives," he'd declared firmly. It appeared that many believed him. From among those who did, seldom had he encountered anyone slipping back into his or her "old ways".

Sacha had other compensations. When working one-on-one, he derived inexplicable joy from just observing light returning into the heretofore-dull eyes. The stooped backs would straighten; the chins were thrust forward, daring the world to deal them any cards not of their own making.

They found, or recovered, faith in their own selves.

Some men and some women bent to kiss his hand. Not in worship since Sacha inspired in them the very essence of equality, but as an act of gratitude.

"How can I ever thank you, Sir?" Many of them didn't even know his name.

Others asked if they could help still others. Anyone. They felt the need to pass on the good news. The good news that we, and we alone, are the creators of our reality. That it all is—all that we perceive with our senses—merely a state of mind...

Many understood it. The vast majority did not. This was a hard premise to metabolize. It did not deal just with our own subjective self, but with the reality all around us. The majority still preferred to look up to the governments, or churches, or do-good organizations, for guidance. Those organizations talked a great deal about human dignity, but they destroyed its remnants by allowing people to continue relying on handouts; but no longer those few whose eyes lit up in understanding. The chosen few? Those who understood that it had always been their choice whether or not to become the chosen people.

Towards the end, Sacha tried hard not to attract attention. He never gave his name, and when leaving an area he made sure that he hadn't been followed. Yet the news spread like wild fire. The press, other media, they all seemed ready to pounce and grab their pound of flesh. More articles appeared, more questions had been asked.

"A saint or a charlatan?"

"Medicine without a license?"

"A natural psychiatrist or a fraud?"

"Would you trust anyone who lives in hiding?"

And then there were the inevitable warnings from the clergy who seemed concerned for the good of their people. For the good of good sheep.

"Beware of false prophets!"

"The devil comes in many forms!"

And many others. Many. All within the past week.

It was definitely time to go.

And then came moments of doubt. All too soon. For the thousandth time Sacha staggered under the magnitude of his endeavor. He had moved away from his home in LA to protect those he loved most. He lived surrounded by beggars asking for redemption. He taught them how to redeem themselves. The only true redemption. It all seemed futile. The more men he helped, the more came. Seemingly there was no end to human misery. Yet, there were so many churches that claimed to offer succor. Why did so many churches remain empty? Why didn't these people seek help there? Why didn't they ask the priests, the clergymen, the imams, the rabbis to help them? Were all religions such abysmal failures?

Even as he was?

SACHA 23+323 days

How can I help people free themselves from slavery when they are determined to remain slaves? They pray to gods, to divinities, who show no interest in their welfare at all. Why won't they believe that the only god they will ever encounter is the almighty king, the ruler, the councilor within their own hearts?

Why can't they understand my words?

Sacha remembered the Ecumenical Congress he'd attended in Boston when he was just fourteen. And for the umpteenth time he felt a flash of understanding as violent as all the previous bolts combined.

Once again he felt that his understanding of his mission in life was finally becoming clearer. It had been a long and arduous process. He was pealing off layers that the exigencies of survival on Earth had imposed on him. Finally he'd returned to his origins. Once again he regarded the whole physical reality as an arbitrary construct of human mind and imagination. Even as he looked at various events in his own life, he noticed their fluidity, as though they had neither beginning nor end. They seemed to hover in the matrix of spacetime, tenuously, seemingly toying with a temporal experiment, only to be re-absorbed into the Whole when no longer required.

It had been a long journey.

Gradually his mind was clearing. The cobwebs accumulated through years of progressive tiredness, recently by sheer exhaustion, were beginning to clear. There were three things he had to do before leaving Montreal. First, he went to a barber. A hairstylist, they called it here. Some style! He emerged a half-hour later clean-shaven, his golden glory clipped to a fashionable quarter of an inch crew-cut. He looked like a skinny marine in civvies.

When he'd returned to his rooming house, he changed into his one and only good suit, packed the rest of his meager belongings into a single carryall, and caught a bus to the University of McGill. He presented himself at the Faculty of

Religious Studies as a postgraduate, interested in furthering his studies in theology. There was a tremendous shortage of applications for this particular department. After the administration staff checked his credentials on the Internet, he was admitted on the spot. He would be billed later, the clerk assured him with a wink. No doubt. Next he thumbed through a telephone book in search of an organization that would suit his purpose.

There were the Pax Christi, Pax Mundi, the Caritas, and indeed a good many other trusty organizations. Too good, too well established. He went to the university cafe and sat at the only available computer outlet. A half-hour later he'd found his quarry.

A bus deposited him at its door. The sign etched in two-inch high, elegant Roman letters, stated their business. It looked clean and proper. The inscription, in Latin, said:

BONAE VOLUNTATIS

He remembered some but not all of it. ...*Et in terra pax hominibus bonae voluntatis... por tua immensa gloria... Laudamsus te...* There was more but he'd read it some two decades ago. Anyway, it did not really matter.

The brass plate on the door assured all-comers that this was a place for people of Good Will. Probably not as impressive an address as sported by some better-known organizations, but an established society nevertheless. A young lady smiled at him. Perhaps more lady-like than young. The smile she offered seemed a little tired. Perhaps bored? Or maybe she just worked too hard.

Sacha gave the place an once-over. There were some pamphlets on a shelf near the door, a few chairs—a little worse for wear, and a good-size desk with an inquiring face behind it.

"Can I help you, Sir?"

He explained that he was a visiting research fellow at McGill University and the pressure of work didn't allow him to check on various charitable organizations. He had come into some good fortune, and was hoping that she might suggest some alternatives, or, better still, take his donation and pass it on to the appropriate quarters.

The woman's face was rapidly loosing its lassitude.

"May I ask how much you wish to donate, Sir?"

"I would like to start with $5,000, and then I would increase my donations as funds become available. I would need a receipt for tax purposes, of course."

"Of course!" The remnants of tiredness evaporated into thin air.

The place and the woman looked as if they both needed the money. For a moment Sacha wondered how come the recipients of human generosity never asked what motivated the donor. Perhaps it didn't really matter. Perhaps they just didn't care. And then he wondered why there were so many needy people in the world? Or maybe *Bonae Voluntatis* really *was* a charitable organization and they were discreet, and they didn't ride Mercedes-Benz limousines while other people were starving. By Sacha's definition of reality they may have been just ignorant, but not necessarily dishonest. He wrote the check while the young lady filled out the receipt. He was almost ready to leave when she asked causally.

"Would you consider joining our organization, Sir?"

Sacha took a deep breath. It worked! And it wasn't just that. Never had he been called 'Sir' so many times in such quick succession. He hesitated for form's sake. This was the only reason that had brought him here.

"A membership?" he did his best to sound surprised.

"We offer a membership to those who are interested in our work. I'm sure yours would be approved in no time, Sir. No time at all."

"I am leaving for Los Angeles in a few hours. I shall be back later, of course. Could you send me some staff? Some reading material?" He'd already read all he wanted to read about the organization on the Internet.

"Of course, Sir. But you might care to fill in the application form and it would be processed while you are becoming acquainted with *Bonae Voluntatis.*" Her tone of voice was almost begging.

"That would be acceptable. Just in case my business takes a little longer, you might care to send me my membership card to my LA address." He patted his pocket as though looking for his business cards.

"Just write it on the application form, Sir."

She was a smart girl. A credit to her organization. Sacha filled in the essentials and, looking at his watch, turned toward the door.

"Thank you, Sir. You'll get all the documents in two or three days," she assured him.

Sacha thanked her and left. He hadn't asked *what* documents. All he needed was an affiliation, a membership in an organization that was already established internationally, but not broad enough to have its own, well established hierarchy at the top. From what he'd read on the Internet, *Bonae Voluntatis* fitted the bill precisely.

For now, his job in Montreal was done.

He indulged himself in a taxi to the P-E. Trudeau International Airport. It was a quiet ride. He actually managed to sleep for twenty minutes. He decided to fly out on the first available flight. If there was waiting involved, he was prepared to sleep in any position for as long as it took. He had a lot of catching up to do.

He made the next plane to LA by ten minutes. They waved the formalities of a three-hour waiting period. His gentle prodding of the attendants and the security staff's subconscious helped somewhat. It was cheating but he felt he'd earned a little rest. And to sleep in LA, in his own bed, even a few hours sooner was a temptation he could hardly resist.

He fell asleep the moment his back relaxed against the softness of the reclining seat. It did not matter that there was hardly any legroom; or that the loudspeakers were blaring completely redundant security information. Nothing mattered when he could finally close his eyes, and no longer be forced to remain alert for danger from unexpected quarters. Here, contrary to the reality of fear and distrust the security guards tried so hard to instill on the passengers, he felt completely safe.

For the first time in so many days and nights, there was no danger at all.

Suzy, her eyes narrowed in a blissful smile, picked him up at the LA International. Soon her face would be aglow with joy. But not immediately. She looked at him, then looked away, and only on the second take fell into his awaiting arms. His crew-cut had changed him virtually beyond recognition. The mop was his trademark. Holding her close, even as Suzy fought hard to hold back her tears of joy, he assured her: "It will grow again, mother. I promise..."

By then she wouldn't care if he'd shaved his whole body. He was home. Finally, at long last, Sacha was home. Her home. Next to her, better, she was in his arms.

After another long hug and a dozen kisses interrupted only by more hugs, Suzy confessed that she and Alec had been hoping for this day for years. Christmas was coming and they had hoped against hope that at least once, in so many years, they would spend the Festive Season together.

They were well on their way home before Sacha broached the subject of Deborah.

"Of course! How silly of me," she exclaimed. "You called us ten times from Montreal but you never explained how you two had met?"

Alicia was a marvel. She must have learned a great deal by now, and she'd kept it all to herself. Deborah was unlikely not to have blurted out her past. After all, she did not recognize her late profession as anything she should be ashamed of.

"How is she?"

"Oh, I have no idea. Alicia and Debbie are in total cahoots about everything. They are acting like mother and daughter, a grandmother more likely, but Alicia looks at least twenty years younger. I strongly suspect that soon they will be the same age!"

All this was delivered on a single breath. Sacha concluded that Deborah was OK. Good old 'Licia. Good *young* Alicia. Surely she must be well over seventy by now. What an incredible woman.

"Are they in town?" he asked thinking the duo might be in Solana Beach.

"They are everywhere. Everywhere!" Suzy insisted. "They drive to the villa for a day or two, then into the mountains, then down to Mexico and back to us for a late supper, only to return to Solana Beach that same evening. I tell you Sacha, I have no idea where mother finds her strength. I really don't."

First with the first Granddad, then with the second, and now with Deborah. It seemed that Deborah was just what Grandma had needed.

"The other day Alicia asked me all about your schooling. I gather that the young lady you brought from back home has some catching up to do. Mother makes her study everyday for at least two hours. Apparently she learns quickly. And you know she speaks that wonderfully atrocious French. I just love it!"

So they'd *really* met. I wonder what Deborah would say if she heard herself described as a young lady.

"Did she ask about me?"

"When she was here she wouldn't talk about anyone or anything else. Frankly, son, I think she has a crush on you. A sizable crush."

"Do you mind?"

"Whatever you do, Sacha, I don't mind. I don't think it would make much difference if I did, would it?" This time Suzy's tone lost some of its bubbly luster.

"I would never do anything to hurt you, Mom. Surely, you know that."

This wasn't a question. It was an affirmation that didn't allow for argument. Sacha had moments when he spoke like that. Whatever he said—just was. On such occasions, his voice had a ring of authority. It was there when he spoke of things he had to do. He had to be true to his path. To his destiny. Apparently, it did not allow him much latitude.

Soon they were home. Alec was still at work but a car was parked in their visitor's spot. Sacha recognized it as Grandma's. He was a little nervous. He had to face Deborah not on his own ground. Recently his ground consisted of back alleys of the red light district.

They didn't bother with the elevator. After a three-hour sleep on the airplane, Sacha ran up two at a time, with Suzy taking a more leisurely tempo. On the third floor the entrance door was open. He hardly had time to say anything before Deborah planted a king-size kiss on his lips. Only then did she step back to look at him.

"Where is your crown?" she asked, her eyes as large as a newborn baby's.

"I lost it on the way." It was almost true.

But she didn't really care. Sacha was back. Her savior, her deliverer, her... her...

"Your friend, most of all," he finished her thoughts for her. He got into the habit of doing that with her. Her subliminal innocence made it easy.

"Will you be staying?"

She didn't pull any punches. Somehow she already knew that any relationship with Sacha wouldn't be a normal one. She was prepared to take whatever she could get; even if it lasted a week or a day.

"A while, kitten. A little while," he said slowly.

He couldn't lie to her. She was, well, she was too pure to lie to. One peek at her inner being and her consciousness attested to that. And now she'd even discarded the old dust jacket. What remained...

As absurd as it may sound, he thought she was, now, too innocent. Especially after his last few weeks in Montreal. She didn't act. She seemed to have discarded any and all masks we all wear on occasion. That very honesty made her vulnerable. Very vulnerable. Despite the many years of hardship, she'd dropped her guard. She would be easy to hurt. And that might mean the end of her. But she was truly innocent. Innocent off all crimes. And innocence put all men, young and old, at a disadvantage. The world was like that.

He didn't know how long he would stay. He was rapidly loosing control of his life. Recently, greater and greater currents were taking over, and he felt he was little more than a pawn caught in their interplay. He had no complaints—he'd chosen this route. But she hadn't. He felt responsible for her.

"I'll stay as long as I possible can," he added.

Just as Suzy emerged from the staircase, while Alicia appeared in the doorway. There was the usual exchange of hugs and kisses. They were family. Families are like that. Sacha wondered if Deborah was family or his lover. In spite of his habit, he didn't dare to probe her mind on this subject. There were matters in which she had a right to privacy.

Before they had a chance to enter the condo, the elevator door opened and Alec came out with outstretched arms.

"Son!" he shouted on the top of his voice. Then his tone changed. "You are my son, aren't you?" He ran his hand over the top of Sacha's head. "I am so glad you are home, my boy."

And then they all talked at once.

Sacha managed to slip out of the lobby, into the hall, drop his bag on the table and lead the way into the living room. There were fresh flowers on the table, more on the window shelf. Suzy had already laid out the dining table for five. Everyone was expected. Everyone was to share in each other's joy. This was the time for celebration. Her son had come home. At last.

***

PART FOUR
The Way Back

"We are all visitors to this time, this place.
We are just passing through.
Our purpose here is to observe, to learn, to grow, to love...
and then we return home."

Australian Aboriginal Proverb

19
Jail

The joyful reunion lasted till the wee hours. Finally, Alec told Sacha that he'd taken the liberty of changing some furniture in his old room. He took Sacha by the arm and led him to the old jungle. The walls were still painted (and repeatedly repainted) all over by Suzy from the time he'd slept there as a baby. The room looked smaller somehow, and the exuberant flora took on a new, almost menacing mystery. Even though Sacha stopped there now and then for a night or two, the lianas and exorbitant exotic foliage that covered the walls and ceiling seemed to constrict the room as though cutting off any escape. For just a moment he felt trapped. The feeling passed almost as quickly.

In the middle of the room, headboard against the far wall, stood a brand knew king-size bed.

"I don't know what ah… your plans are, son. But your mother and I…"

"It's all right, Dad. But it's not up to me, you know."

"Tell me about it. It never is!" Alec smiled remembering his younger, much younger days. He'd always proposed, Suzy had disposed. Actually that wasn't quite true. Suzy had her moments of quite unabashed spontaneity.

That was not quite what Sacha had meant. Knowing that he was no longer a master of his destiny, not in the strictly physical and thus predictable sense, he worried what effect being with Deborah might have on her emotional life. Surely she must still be in a relatively delicate mental state. Alicia seemed to have done wonders, but... well, only time would tell.

"Thanks, Dad. Your blessing is appreciated."

And he meant it. He'd learned some time ago that his parents' early days did not follow the established course of their own parents. They did not go through the accepted procedures associated with mating. On the other hand, hardly anyone did these days. There were the usual spring and other rites, of course, but they had little to do with the previously established mores. In fact, the mores were no longer established.

Around two a.m. Alicia got up, kissed Deborah on both cheeks and wished her a good night. The two women must have spoken before. Suzy and Alec saw Grandma to the elevator, while Deborah and Sacha lingered at the table.

"You don't mind do you?" she asked a little nervously.

Sacha did not answer immediately. He was again reticent to peek into her mind. He had no idea how he ought to act.

"You don't have to make love to me," she said when the others seemed to dally in the hall. "I just hoped to have you to myself. Just for a little while..."

"You sure?" It wasn't a very bright question. He wondered why with Deborah around he became tongue tied and mentally disjointed.

"It is the only thing I am really sure about, Sacha. This, and that Alicia and your parents are the most wonderful people I've ever met."

But instead of a smile of joy two great tears made their slow descent down her cheeks. She didn't wipe them off. She looked down at her hands resting in her lap and waited as though for the judge to pass sentence.

"I told you that we shall do whatever you want, remember?"

"Actually, it was I who had said that," she corrected.

That did it. They both looked at each other and suddenly they were standing, Deborah nestled in Sacha's arms, Sacha kissing her moist cheeks. Someone had been clearing his throat in the hall for quite a while, before either of them heard it. Reluctantly they pulled apart. "So this is what being in love is about..." Sacha marveled. He'd read about it, but this was different. Quite different. It was as close to the Home Planet as anyone on Earth could get. And then some...

They both ran out to the hall to wave Grandma good-bye. Sacha offered to drive Alice home but she refused.

"I know someone who's been waiting for you a long time. I am not going to be the one who makes that someone wait even a second longer."

And this promise was accompanied by the biggest, dirtiest, possibly the sexiest wink Sacha had ever seen. Alec hid his face in his hands in order not to laugh. He remembered his mother from way back in Montreal. She was indeed quite an actress in those days. Even if she never walked the boards.

It has been said that, when you are looking at a piece of great art, time stops. There are degrees of beauty that defy time and reject any and all constrains imposed on them by the precepts of modern science. They absorb your attention to such a degree that you are no longer able to share the reality of mere mortals. You are swept into a state that ordinary people tread with great caution. It is the nearest thing to being in heaven.

Sacha was in such a state for the rest of the night.

Tiredness, longing, constant vigilance of the past year or so were gone; swept as one sweeps the autumn leaves. They were part of a different time, a different season. His mundane preoccupations had been relegated to the inanimate past. They belonged in illusion.

There was another realization that came to him that same night. Sacha finally understood that being on Earth is not just a "necessary evil". Once past his boyhood, he never really believed it. He felt extremely human at the helm of The Princess; he enjoyed using his body when swimming,

running, performing all sorts of sports at Oxford, yet all that
had nothing to do with this. This experience was more
sublime than its forerunner in Montreal. There it had been a
moment of discovery. This was more like fulfillment. It was
in the domain of the gods.

Or else, it was the human version of bliss.

Over a real, eggs-and-toast and unlimited-coffee breakfast,
Sacha and Alec discussed the mail Sacha had received during
the last three month. Alec was still trying to avoid straight
answers regarding Sacha's possible involvement with the
religious organizations, but Sacha's views had crystallized
somewhat over the last few weeks.

"Though I am not going to enjoy it, Dad, it seems to me
that, if I have something to say yet keep it to myself, then I
would be shortchanging those who want to hear it. Don't you
agree?"

Alec recalled his first lecture tour. South America,
Machu Picchu, the relatively youthful Desmond looking after
him like a mother hen. Sacha had no one to look after him.
No one was even close to his son's competency in the field
that Sacha had apparently chosen—the field of the intangible,
of the ineffable, the transcendent. Yet, after talking to
Deborah, Alec had learned that somehow his son translated
that knowledge, that most peculiar expertise, into a physical,
or at least a down to earth, science, which he, again according
to Deborah, practiced with an inerrant hand. In his own early
days, Alec had, on occasion, escaped into the inner worlds in
search of adventure. Sacha seemingly brought those same
worlds down to Earth.

Lately, Alec's own escapes into the esoteric remained
limited to periodic ventures into the realm of imagination, the
Home Planet. Less often he was swept into the realm of pure
mind, the Far Country, where not only all was possible to
imagine, but there were no limits set on his stream of
thoughts. The phenomenal realm where pure thought was the

creative impulse. But after those moments of near-ecstasy, he'd returned to the 'real world', where he reverted to being a hard-nosed scientist, where whatever he couldn't measure by some means or other, did not really exist. After all these years, Alec still felt that living on Earth, in the tangible, tactile, solid universe was his lot. He continued to 'just live', and he'd learned to like it.

His son was different. Sacha visited the Earth most people recognized as real only occasionally. Most of the time he seemed to roam realties as inaccessible to Alec as to any other man or woman he'd ever met.

Sacha was very different.

It just so happened that Sacha was not actually asking dad for permission. Not even for advice. His path was clear to him. What Sacha was doing was preparing his father and mother, and in a way all his family, for the days to come. He knew that once he went into the open, new events would unfold at a very accelerated pace. His father was a very clever man. He would not only suspect what might well happen but he would look after his mother and Alicia. And, Sacha hoped—he hoped dearly—after Deborah.

The still pure, still childlike, yet so mature Debbie.

So very guileless... so very mature.

"I suppose you are right. In any other field I would be sure," Alec still wavered. "But, as I am sure you know, the field you have chosen is responsible for more death and mayhem in the world than any other."

Did dad actually suspect something? He was an accomplished traveler of the inner worlds. Did he have a premonition?

"No, son. I am not that good." This was the first time Alec actually read Sacha's thoughts since his son's return. It might have been that Sacha was becoming ever more proficient at broadcasting them. Consciously or not. "Be careful," Alec said quietly. "Be very careful."

Alec did not sound happy. He was young enough to remember his own youthful vigour. When you're young you always think you are indestructible. That there is nothing you cannot do. And then Alec smiled at his own thoughts: in Sacha's case, this just might be true.

"Thank you, Dad." Sacha sounded as if he needed a vote of confidence. "I certainly hope you are right."

The rest of the day Sacha spent with Suzy and Deborah. They, too, seemed to have hit it off. He was glad. Very glad. Whatever has been gathering on his own horizon did not offer a country cottage with a white picket fence. And Deborah deserved so much more than he had to offer. Yet he was too committed to his destiny to waver now. And destiny called on him that very night.

Sacha knew what he had to do. There were a number of preliminary steps necessary to achieve his purpose. Also, there were reasons why he had to accelerate his schedule.

That evening he'd accessed the Internet and e-mailed letters to nine organizations which had offered him a platform to air his views. Next, he punched his Internet day-trader's personal code and made some adjustments to his investments. The word 'day-trader' was a euphemism. Trading on the world markets never stopped. There was always 'day' somewhere on Earth. Day-trading referred to the speed at which one got into and out of the market. Usually a lot less than a day. Finally, after supper, he changed into his 'working' clothes, a blue shirt with well-worn jeans, and excused himself for 'a while'. Deborah smiled but there was no mirth in her eyes. Her full lips formed more of a resigned grimace than her usual joyful radiance. Sacha hoped he would not be the instrument that destroyed her innate happiness.

He walked four or five blocks before he'd found the right opportunity.

There was a group of beggars, vagrants or just simply homeless people, who gathered under a fly-over bridge. They were neither together, nor apart. Yet, a common, invisible thread connected them. He addressed that collective link.

First one, then two more, then the remainder of the group sauntered out of their hiding places. They followed him, slowly, some twenty paces behind.

Sacha led them to the parking lot of a large food store. He opened the rear service doors and let the two-dozen beggars in. They ate their fill, took some stuff with them, and left. Sacha activated the alarms, and stayed behind to get arrested. From the police station he telephoned home that he'd been unavoidably detained. He actually laughed aloud when he'd said that. Nothing could have been closer to the truth. The following day he was given a lecture by a judge, who unwittingly helped Sacha accomplish his objective. Sacha wanted to get into the prison system to learn about its inmates.

He was given two weeks. More, he'd read in the judge's mind, would have placed unnecessary burden on the already overcrowded prison system.

Sacha found the jail fascinating. So many people there were simply lost, and there was absolutely no one who offered them any help, who would even point them in the right direction. On the day of his arrival, two multi-denominational padres had visited Sacha. They called themselves chaplains. They tried hard to show Sacha the error of his ways. They were good men. They were also the proverbial blind bent on leading the blind.

Sacha studied the minds of his inmates. He was amazed. Many of them had a greater grasp of the truth then a number of professors at Oxford. He decided to remain incarcerated for a while. He needed to really understand all facets of the human psyche. There were truly innumerable patterns. Yet most of us seemed to fit into a groove that we had traveled before. It was up to each one of us to find our own, individual path. In fact, this was, and is, the most difficult part of one's journey. Perhaps that is why people continued in the same cycle, age after age. They'd built up traditions, customs, even morality, all to protect their status quo. But most of all, the vast majority preferred to follow their leaders rather than step out on a limb.

The prisoners filed out into the prison yard.

Sacha looked around. With a grin, he recalled Paul of Tarsus 'doing time'. Sacha felt he was in good company. But it didn't last.

The police informed Alec of Sacha's whereabouts. Instead of sounding worried, Alec sighed and murmured under his breath: "It's started. Heaven help Suzy and Deborah." "And mother," he added after some thought.

Grandma loved his son as much as they all did. The four of them were spending the evening together. Somehow it felt easier, when Sacha was in LA, even though not actually at home. They all worried about him yet, strangely enough, not one of them would actually say so. Suzy seemed the most nervous until, to Alec's amazement, Deborah had set her mind at peace.

"If Sacha wanted to, he could walk out of that jail in ten seconds flat," she assured her. "I wouldn't be surprised if he couldn't walk through walls!"

Then she told Suzy of Sacha's ability to make himself invisible. It struck a bell.

"Of course!" Suzy let out a huge sigh of relief. "He'd been doing that since he was four or five years old. He was playing with his Strato... It drove me crazy at the time..."

There is a reason for everything, she finally realized. There most certainly is where her Sacha is concerned.

Deborah was becoming a very smart girl. She'd discovered Sacha's Internet account. After all, Sacha and his father shared both first and second names. By sheer luck, she'd also discovered his password. It wasn't that difficult. He'd chosen PEEKA. Poor Boo had been left out. She'd e-mailed his broker. The man e-mailed back providing evidence that Sacha had recently acquired a controlling interest in the Supermarket he'd broken into two nights ago. You can't rob yourself, she thought.

The next day she got Sacha released. The lawyers offered him their services to sue the system for compensation. He called them hypocrites.

"You are the system," he said good-naturedly. "Sue yourselves."

He thanked Deborah for her efforts and excused himself that same evening again. He returned to jail, only this time as an uninvited guest. It is incredibly easy to gain access almost anywhere when they can't see you. You might set off one or two alarms, but soon things would get back to normal. It just takes a little longer to find the right opportunity.

He continued his work with the convicts—mostly with men who had killed, often in anger, in a moment of weakness. In a single moment in which they'd lost control of their dark-side. He wondered how often we forget that physical reality is a dualistic reality. That, under certain circumstances, we are all capable of dire extremes. And yet we all are so quick to judge.

Others.

Sacha couldn't do his work during the day. To talk to those people, he had to drop his cloak of invisibility. They didn't always react to mental contact only. They actually told him that most of them heard voices often enough. A sort of self-defense mechanism, they said.

"Otherwise you'd go nuts, here," one man assured him after Sacha opened his mind to the source of strength within his own being. The next moment a guard was making his rounds and Sacha had to disappear again. After the guard left, Sacha's contour became once more visible. The man wasn't surprised.

"Some of us even see disappearing men," he'd said.

Sacha was on the verge of giving up.

"T'is OK, man. Just kiddin'," and the man grinned from ear to ear.

Two other convicts he'd come across had killed no one. They'd never carried a gun, nor partaken in an armed robbery. Nor had they hurt or injured anyone except for some slightly bruised egos, a little wounded pride. Though they may have been indirectly responsible for insurance premiums being raised by a few bucks for a few thousand customers. Those men were completely amoral. They neither suffered nor had they ever felt joy. They were constructs of pure intellectual energy; men who chose to match their wits against the combined efforts of the greater Los Angeles police force. All they needed was awakening to other facets of their own being.

Although they presented an easier task for Sacha, the men paid dearly for years of neglect of their emotional body. When Sacha reinstated their capacity to feel, the flood of emotions they experienced made full-grown men cry like little children.

Once Sacha came across a prison guard who was venting his ire, on a groveling inmate, with a nightstick. Sacha could not reveal his own presence, so he scanned the man's mind. It was filled with hatred. Not just towards the inmates, but the world at large, including his wife and children. Sacha had neither chance nor time to find out why. But there was a glimmer of humanity left in the unfortunate man. He had two huskies. Two dogs he'd raised from puppies and regarded as his only friends. Sacha planted the aura of his favorite dog around the man on the receiving end of the guard's nightstick.

The guard raised the stick for another sadistic blow. The weapon remained suspended in the air, wavered and then fell from the guard's limp fingers. Would it change the guard's mind? No one could tell. No one knows the future. We can only hope.

There are people who think that dogs and other animals do not have auras. Sacha had met a student of theology at the Sorbonne who'd claimed that if there is such a thing as aura then only human beings could have it, because only human beings have souls. At the time Sacha didn't attempt to convince the student otherwise. There is a fundamental difference between people not aware of being blind, and those who insists on maintaining and exacerbating their blindness. The first group is silently crying out for help. To help the second group would break the universal law of free will. Sacha knew that before he'd learned to walk.

There were other cases with which he wasn't as successful. There was only so much you could do with a hardened mindset. He had to try. He thought it imperative that a new way of thinking, a new conceptualization of reality be made available to people at all levels. It would be up to them, later, to carry on. To spread the good news. Wherever it would take them.

One man had baby blue eyes. He was small, slimy and unpleasantly soft. The sort of man whose hand you would not want to shake. He gave an impression that he wouldn't hurt a fly. He didn't. But he had dispatched from this world his mother, his wife and two children.

He was quite mad.

There was no room in the institutions for criminally insane. They gave him triple life, the sentence for the two children to be served concurrently. Maybe his children were twins, thought Sacha with grim humor. Possibility of parole had been set in a few hundred years. Sacha wondered if repairing the man's mind would be doing him a favor. He would have to face his acts in a new light. That might really drive him crazy. On the other hand, not doing it would only postpone the process of realization to a later time.

Sacha always wondered where some religious people got that idea that you could murder a dozen people, then sigh deeply, say that you were sorry and retire on a silver-edged cloud in the never-never land. The Christians have evolved a complex theology in which they claim that someone else died for their sins, and therefore they could escape the consequences of their actions with impunity. Sacha wondered if they also thought that someone else would go to hell for them, a destination they freely advocated to all 'unbelievers'.

It took millennia to develop such mindsets.

They also thought that we had but one single life, a single embodiment, and thereafter we either lazed around forever, or we fried for an equally ridiculous duration in some bottomless pit. Those people had read the same scriptures Sacha had read; yet Sacha concluded that we had to pay our debts. To the last shekel. The last talent. That nothing was ever for free.

Or maybe they haven't read those books at all?

Then there were other believers who thought that we had many lives. That we died and were born again. They were both right and wrong. We have just one life. In fact, we are never born nor would we ever die. The real 'I' does not have a body he or she could destroy. Nor could It perish by Itself. There is nothing to sit on a cloud, and there is nothing to burn in hell. Or anywhere else. But we do have to pay our debts. It is a question of restoring balance.

Sacha thought that that was the problem with religions. Each one of them offered a little bit of the truth, but not one presented the big picture. All religions taken together were like a jigsaw puzzle. If you studied all of them at the same time, you got pretty close to the truth. But not many people did that. Some were forbidden to do so by their religious leaders.

The blind leading the blind...

Sacha scanned the little man's mind and withdrew immediately. He may have been wrong about that idea of hell. The man's mind *was* hell. His placid, vacant face was a mask concealing agonies such as Sacha had never encountered in anyone. The man was still in physical consciousness but he'd lost all sensation of time. He thought he'd stay here, with his memories, for all eternity.

Gingerly, Sacha probed again.

This time it was a little easier. Apparently there were oscillations in the man's psyche. It seesawed between despair and total numbness. Like a leg going to sleep. There were moments when the man wasn't human at all. When he was truly dead. All of him except for his physical body. Sacha prodded this numbness and planted a few sparks, an echo or two, which the poor creature might remember. In a few minutes the man opened his eyes. He looked around and saw Sacha. He cringed.

It took all of Sacha's powers to maintain his own equilibrium. Slowly, very slowly, Sacha caressed the numbness that just as slowly began to respond. When Sacha left an hour later, the man was crying. He'd experienced feelings for the first time in forty years. The rest was up to him.

"Where are the priests, the chaplains, the psychiatrists, the social workers?" Sasha murmured into the somber darkness cut by jarring, exposed bulbs of the common space.

Billions of dollars had been spent on building bigger and better prisons. Better for whom? Armies of guards have been trained to vent their frustrations on the sick, lonely, often quite helpless people. The convicts had to pay for their crimes. And who would pay for society's crimes that had failed to provide those same prisoners with a sense of self-respect? Who'd failed to lend a helping hand, long ago, before it became too late?

Who were the people who took pride in the way we treated those who needed our help most of all? We don't even kick a lame dog, do we? But we kick people when they sink into the gutter. We kick them when they become too weak to get up by their own strength. Some professional do-gooders refer to them as brothers.

But they treat them as lepers.

Sacha got back home in the early hours. He crawled into bed and lay back. Deborah didn't say a word. She knew he had his work. Just as she did, once. She gently stroked his short hair, until he left his body. This time he rose directly to the Undiscovered Realm. He longed for home. His real home. A realm wherein all individualizations of the Whole are replete with light and love. Where they all *are* individualizations of life and love. Where they feel one with each other.

And with the Whole.

***

20
Deborah

"You shouldn't have done it,** Deborah. I wasn't suffering, you know. I was just visiting," he remonstrated her gently.

Actually she knew that, but by the time it came to the forefront of her awareness the 'damage' had been done. This was the first time they spoke about his release from jail. She looked as though she'd been naughty and would be punished for her transgressions. Sacha could only smile.

"That will come later," he said, wagging a stern finger.

She giggled and cuddled up under his arm.

"I know. But I missed you so..."

The press was so nagging that Sacha was ready to escape back to Montreal. He was playing with the idea of changing his name. It wouldn't work, he realized. In Montreal they didn't know his name but the paparazzi had a field-day anyway.

The next time he and Deborah went for a walk, just to be alone for a while, he'd been recognized from the newspaper photos that were splattered over his corner of North America.

"Aren't you the man...?"

"Yes ma'am, I most certainly am. And you, I am sure are the lady..." Before the 'lady' recovered, he and Deborah were some distance away.

Then, someone started a page for him on the Internet. He wanted to issue a disclaimer but had second thoughts. He offered to cooperate with the page-makers providing they let him maintain anonymity in private life. He was thinking of his parents. The idol-makers agreed at once. They also lied. In spite of all that Sacha had seen and experienced, he was quite incapable of losing faith in human nature. "If you don't give them a chance, how can you expect them to choose the right course?"

One evening, the four of them went for a drive. Suzy and Alec returned home alone, while Sacha and Deborah moved in with Alicia. Just for a change. Grandma was overjoyed. So was Deborah. They fell into each other's arms as though bridging the gulf of time that separated two dearest friends. Actually they've seen each other only four days ago.

"Were they treating you right, little one?" Alicia looked at Sacha sternly.

"Oh, Grandma, you look wonderful. Just wonderful!"

No one in his or her sane mind would question the veracity of Deborah's assurance. Alicia had no such intention, either. She was as good for Deborah as Deborah was for her. Alicia was good for Deborah because she, in spite of her knowledge, treated her as a perfectly normal teenager. And Deborah gave Alicia a new lease on life. After Desmond's death, Alicia was lost. She felt useless. After she'd lost her first husband, Alec's father, she went for a European tour. Now she was no longer willing to give up the comforts of her home. She was also much less resilient. And this was again where Deborah came in. She had enough resilience for an army, and more than enough for the two of them. Sacha enjoyed just looking at the two women together. They intermeshed, complemented each other, almost combined into a single unit greater than the sum of its parts. Even their auras displayed similar hues.

And both of them continued to learn from each other.

When Sacha went out in late evening, the two sat together, sometimes even holding hands, feeding each other strength to overcome their fear for Sacha's safety. They weren't sure what they were afraid of, but they were. Perhaps it is a woman's lot to worry when men go out to war. And, in so many ways, this was exactly what Sacha did. He said he went out to learn, but really he was fighting ignorance and indifference.

Once Deborah had asked him why did he do what he did. At first, he didn't appear to understand the question. He couldn't understand her lack of understanding.

"I help them because, at a certain level of being, they and I are one. By helping them, I help myself."

She'd listened with such attention that she seemed dead to the rest of the world. She didn't just love Sacha. She worshipped him.

"There is really only one consciousness," he continued. "We are just its individualized expressions. Without us consciousness just is. With us, you could say that consciousness is life. Because of us, you and me, and all the inhabitants of the whole biosphere, it lives. It changes from passive to an active mode. It experiences the joy of becoming."

"But what about you? Don't you deserve your own life?"

"I have my life. I am fulfilling my dream."

He could have said I don't have life, life has me. He could also have said 'I am life'. He could have told her that when he'll withdraw from this body, it will no longer be alive. To explain to her the dream of Bardo would have been more than Deborah could absorb at this moment. Perhaps later he would explain. Right then, she'd taken his assurance in the literal sense. It meant that he lived the way he wanted to live. She had never really dreamt of anything. She never imagined that if she had, her dreams could possibly come true. But if she might dream, if she really could, she would dream...

She stopped. She had no right to include Sacha in her dreams. No right at all. He'd already given her so much. More than she could ever imagine, or dream for that matter, if only she knew how to dream.

They talked for hours.

Sacha slept a short while during the day, and then, while still waiting for answers to his e-mails, he was relatively free. He continued to work at night. It was the only way for him to learn more without attracting publicity.

Deborah remained for him a constant source of surprise. Also, of inspiration. Even at her youthful age, after her tough beginnings, she could have become as hard as nails. Again and again he realized that, in many ways, she was mature well beyond her years. Yet against this background Sacha discovered in her a gentle, inexplicable vulnerability that made her desirable beyond his wildest imagination. If anyone or anything had the power to dissuade or divert him from the course of his chosen destiny, it would have been she. Only she was no Jezebel. She was a mature woman as vulnerable as a newborn baby.

Sacha also realized that, in many ways, she was more vulnerable now then when he'd met her. For at least one previous life, and almost eighteen years of this one, she has been busy attempting to overcome the vicissitudes of half-life. Of an emotional and, to a great extent, intellectual starvation. And on that day in Montreal she had been born again. Born to a world, to a reality she did not even suspect existed. And yet her previous and present lives belonged to matrices that existed all over the world, side by side. Perhaps both perceptions, of both worlds were blind. Blind to each other. And this gulf of mutual exclusion was protected by the organizations that benefit from such disparity. Another pitfall of duality.

"What is sin?" she asked him, one day. She was reading an article in a LA newspaper. Sacha watched her as she wagged her head from side to side, as though at odds with whatever she was reading.

"Why do you ask?"

"It says here that we are all sinners. What are sinners?"

At eighteen years of age, Deborah had never been to church. Or synagogue, or any other institution of religious persuasion. Except, perhaps, in England, when she was too young to remember, let alone understand. Whatever her other faults, she'd never sinned. She couldn't have. She had no idea what sin was. She'd heard about God, of course. People always said 'good God', or 'for Christ's sake', or even more often 'God will punish you for this'. This last she'd heard often enough, back in Montreal. Mostly when she had insisted on full payment of the agreed amount for her services. For a while she'd thought that God was a crooked accountant who was cooking the books in favor of Johns. She didn't like God at all.

"The word is a translation of a Greek word used in archery. It means missing the mark. Not quite hitting the bull's eye," Sacha offered, watching her intently.

"And if you miss the bull's eye you are sent to hell?"

He smiled. The same old story. Religions made up tales to control their faithful. To them the truth was of little consequence. The important thing was to keep a tight grip on the wallets of those who believed in a particular faction. Sacha remembered a marvelous example of this contention. Until the twelfth century priests, bishops, even popes, had married. After all, what could be more natural? And then the leaders at the top of the ecclesiastic hierarchy had noticed that their organization was loosing out on clergymen who were leaving their assets to their children. In other words, on parents who had been trying to help their own flesh and blood. This wouldn't do. All money, all worldly domains were to be left to the Church and to the Church alone. The priesthood rebelled. Soon a new rule had been introduced into the sacerdotal ranks. The rule of celibacy. Now no children would inherit the fruit of their father's labor. Oh, the clergymen would still have children, they do to this day, only the little bastards wouldn't inherit anything. After all such children were illegal. The Church called them illegitimate. In the eyes of the Church, it was as though they haven't been born.

"Hell and heaven, and all realities in-between, are states of consciousness. No one can send you to hell. You have to make your way there on your own," he tried to explain.

"Can I go to hell?"

This time he laughed outright. It wasn't her ignorance that he found disarming. It was her innocence against the background of her past. It seemed that the truly innocent are protected no matter where they find themselves. They say that you cannot cheat an honest man. Well, he thought, you cannot really corrupt an innocent child. As for 'going' to hell, corruption is a self-employed and self-fueled malignancy. You can even catch it, like a virus; but if your heart is pure, the disease will not take hold. No matter how hard some people try to pollute you. And there are many that do.

As for Deborah's innocence, Sacha's definition of the term was not of the usual usage. He thought of innocence as a state of consciousness, which, in Biblical terms, Adam and Eve lost after eating of the Tree of Knowledge. To Sacha this event defines the moment in the development of human psyche, when we began to differentiate between good and evil. When the Edenic singularity was split into a dualistic reality. This was the true, the real loss of innocence. We now recognize our moral discernment as a positive attribute, as, for the purposes of accelerated learning, they indeed are. Sacha wondered how many of us regard the concept of duality in this light?

Hence Deborah's innocence.

To choose—one must have a choice. In Deborah's life there was little or no choice. As a result, her life was virtually devoid of compromise. She did what she believed as right, regardless of the price she might have to pay. In fact such a payment did not figure in the equation. She conducted herself according to a code of honesty that was head and shoulders above those who would look down at her from their sacerdotal heights. Deborah could not understand the concept of sin.

When Sacha got up from a short rest following one of his nightly forays, Alicia gave the young couple time to enjoy each other, before spending any time with them. And even then, she took pleasure in just sitting there, on the side, listening to their discussions, watching them over the top of her half-moon glasses perched on the end of her nose. An open book would rest on her knees, but no page would turn for as long as the youngsters talked on any subject. Only sometimes would she butt in and then mostly when asked.

"What would you have done, Grandma?"

The question concerned a man who insisted that Sacha follow him to his house and heal his dog. He spoke through an open window of his car. Obviously he expected Sacha to drive behind him. The dog, he said, was fourteen years old and had a good year or two in him yet. The man saw Sacha's picture in a newspaper and the story beside it claimed that Sacha had the power to heal animals. It was rather an amazing story, because in all his life he'd only healed one animal, and that was in India. No one here could have known about that.

It turned out later that the story said that he helped the downtrodden, whom others treated 'worse than dogs'.

"How far was the house?" Alicia asked, in her practical manner.

"The other side of town," Sacha replied.

In truth he had no idea where the house was, but had it been close, he would have probably tried to help. Even if it was against his better judgment. Of course, Sacha didn't have a car, either.

"Then I would tell the man that we all have a term on this Earth, including dogs, and it was not up to us to decide who should live or die."

Sacha loved his grandmother more with each day. This was roughly what he had told the man. What he'd also done was to quiet the man's anxiety by showing him that his dog didn't suffer. That dogs like man go to a better place when they vacate their bodies. This wasn't quite accurate but it served to give the man peace he obviously sought.

Deborah looked up at Sacha. She always looked up to him. Not just at him. Sitting or standing, he was a foot taller than she was.

"You are a very wise woman, Grandma, if I may say so." Sacha smiled his appreciation.

He felt better knowing that when his time came, Deborah could draw on Alicia's innate wisdom. It wasn't just a question of knowledge. Sacha thought of wisdom as that strange blend of knowledge and love. One tempers the other, and only then it shines with the truth.

Deborah was buoyant. She clapped her hands as though applauding Alicia's answer.

"I knew it! I knew it! That's what I would have said." And then her radiant face got serious. "Only I have no idea why..." she confessed.

In a way, Deborah shared Sacha's propensity for truth. It was not acquired from books, although Sacha probably read more books than anyone alive. It was an inherent feeling, rather than knowledge. A characteristic that many women share. Many, though a lot fewer than claim to possess this gift. Alicia may have been born with innate knowledge, but at her age it would be hard to distinguish between inborn and acquired wisdom. That she possessed it, was self-evident. The rest was of no importance.

"So what happens to us when we die?" Deborah was in her questioning mood. She was buzzing from subject to subject like a bee or a wasp as her name implied in the original Hebrew.

"What do you think happens?"

"Nothing much," she asked, nodding her head.

"That's pretty much the truth," Sacha agreed. "Whatever you were here, in this body, you pretty much continue in the other realms."

"Other realms...?" This time she looked up and held his eyes. She did that whenever she deemed something important.

Sacha glanced at Alicia. She knew. He could speak openly.

"You recall Montreal? That was one realm. This, right here, is another. How do you find they differ?"

She was taken aback. How do they differ? Was he mad?

He read her thoughts. He couldn't help it. When Deborah got exited her emotions were screaming aloud. He couldn't possibly miss them. Actually the only people he had problems reading, like that man in prison, were those who either had no emotions to speak of, or had them under great control. Thoughts and emotions were not the same thing, but emotions were like fuel to thoughts. They ignited them and kept them coming.

"I see you think I'm mad. But let me ask this question in another way. How have you changed in the context of those two realities?"

"Why... have I changed?" This time she looked at Alicia. "Well, have I?"

"You don't detect much difference, do you. That's how it should be. The point I am making is that in two realities as different as Montreal and Los Angeles, you are the constant. The realities change, you remain basically the same."

"And that's what happens when we die?"

He nodded.

"But that means that we don't die at all. We just change..."

"...we just change our point of view. Our perception of reality changes, and that empowers us to do things which we would find difficult here."

Alicia moved closer. She'd listened with the same intensity, as did Deborah. When one is soon to become an octogenarian, such subjects are of some interest to one.

"We keep our bodies too?" Alicia asked with a degree of distaste.

"No, Grandma. We can design our own bodies. Don't forget that for many years, down here, we all designed our bodies. We have a storehouse of genes and we manipulate them into a shape and form we desire. We can increase our strength, we can eat well, not abuse our bodies with smoke and booze, and we can look as good at your age as you do."

"Don't be cheeky, young man. Thank you all the same." But she didn't buy it. Not all of it. It was a little too good to be true. Sacha looked keenly at his grandmother and asked very quietly: "Do you remember the dream you had the day Desmond died?"

And the next moment Alicia's face lit up like a thousand suns.

"It... it's... It is true then..."

She didn't ask how Sacha knew what she'd dreamt. It was the dream she wouldn't forget for as long as she lived. She didn't ask how Sacha knew all sorts of things, but had long decided never to question his words.

Sacha wondered how come Alicia had never asked about his grandfather. Her first husband. But he wasn't around when Grandpa died. She wouldn't have known how to ask him then. Or now, for that matter. Or maybe his life force was held in abeyance, during his last stages in Bardo. Anyway, subjective truth becomes more obscure with time. It even changes, depending on our perception of reality. And that changes also. Memories are so arranged as to protect the present. The only 'time' when you are really alive. Today may be an arbitrary construct of your awareness but the past is just an illusion. No two people would describe the same event of five years ago in the same way. They might agree on fundamentals, but not the details. Memory protects us from living in a mirage.

And this is what would ultimately save Deborah.

The past, no matter how true, would become hazy under the veil of time. In a few years, she would reject the notion that such a reality, as she'd experienced in Montreal, really existed. It would be at odds with the present. People who dwell on the past are seldom happy. Even if they attempt to dwell on pleasant memories. It is unnatural. Against our true nature. And our true nature, like truth itself, has its being only in the present.

When he talked to Deborah of these and other things, he arranged his thoughts in a pattern that would be easier for her to absorb. And Alicia would help, if necessary. His own time was drawing to an end. This was his last holiday during which he worked nights only. Soon he would bare his soul to the world. He would be admired by some, reviled by others. Such is the nature of dualistic reality. We all serve to restore the balance.

But he felt sorry for those who would chose to be on the wrong side. Whichever side that was. He was not here to judge. He was here to share, to set free.

As so many others before him.

Deborah's head was resting on his shoulder. She sighed as he moved her gently, placed a pillow under her head and covered her feet with a light blanket. He then walked up to Alicia and kissed her cheek. She held his head in both palms for a little while, as though to draw him towards her.

"Thank you, my boy," was all she said.

And Sacha walked to the door, on tiptoe, and let himself out. There was a man standing on the other side of the street. As Sacha moved to the left, the man followed his footsteps. A minute later the man had lost him.

Sacha dissolved into the night.

***

21
A Stranger in a Strange Land

There was a book by this title. "Stranger in a Strange Land." By Heilein. Robert Heilein. The hero of the novel was a Martian. Born on Mars but of Earthly origin. Sacha was not born on Earth either. His body was. Sacha was not born at all. You might call his birth the moment when he became fully aware of his own individuality, but that was further back than one could remember. That anyone could remember.

Sacha suspected that the Undiscovered Realm was truly infinite. When you cannot be defined in terms of either time or space, you are infinite. Like the present. The Eternal Now. While the physical, emotional and mental worlds have temporal limits, the Undiscovered Realm is forever.

Of course no one knew for sure.

If you knew that would mean you've reached the end. The border. No one ever has. Sacha suspected that no one ever would. Or even tried. Neither in spatial nor in temporal sense. There was neither time nor space in which one could travel. The Undiscovered Realm, his Real Home, was a state of consciousness.

Sacha heard, he knew not whence, that some ancients had suspected that at a certain level of perception, the globes of light, which had their being in that reality, all merged, periodically, into a single Conscious Entity. They became One. For countless eon they remained indivisible, and—at the end of time—they became individualized. There is a subtle difference. If such a proposition is true, and there is no way of proving it, then even in the Undiscovered Realm there is a form of becoming. True, the principal becoming is taking place through the perceptions generated or experienced at lower realities, but the consequences of such, the end results, did or would influence the Undiscovered Realm itself. It has been said, among those ancients, that the diversity of expression of the Whole was, periodically, turned inward. Even as each individualization periodically returned to Bardo to dream of new realities, so did all individualizations return to the Whole. It absorbed Itself into Itself. Perhaps there, the Whole also dreamt of new universes, new forms of expression.

Yet as far as Sacha could gather, in the Highest Realm, there is no periodicity. No cyclic succession. In a way, all the components already are One. Only there, wherever 'there' is, within the ultimate Unity, he suspected that there is no more differentiation. At the outer limits of the Far Country one lost the remnants of one's personality. One left it behind. In the Undiscovered Realm only individuality continued and only so as to assert its integrity with the Source that permeated each aspect of Its own expression. Sacha never lost the feeling that his true self was alien to the physical existence. He was a stranger here—on Earth. It was a reality that he could enhance enormously with his perceptions, with his state of mind, but in most respects it was inconsequential, transient, almost sad. He had to continue reminding himself where he was, and why he was here. And yet, in direct contradiction, he had to fulfill his mission in order to free himself from his own personality. From that which kept him apart.

In order to return to his true home.

Permanently? Only the Whole is permanent. Even if, as the ancients predicted, oscillating. As the day and the night of Brahma. All else is transient.

I am a stranger in a strange land, he told himself.

It was time for action. The nights grew longer; the days shed their light earlier in the evening. Winter was coming. Would it prove to be a winter of his discontent? Or a winter of success and ebullient glory?

A winter of fulfillment...

A letter from *Bonae Voluntatis*, care of McGill University, had been redirected to LA. There was some extra postage to pay. No matter. It said what Sacha wanted them to say. There were words of gratitude for his generous donation. It said that his membership was approved (card enclosed) and, would he be available to represent the work of *Bonae Voluntatis* in his area? In the southwestern United States? After he finished at McGill, of course. Or was he traveling often enough to initiate some organizational notions even now? They needed his help badly. There was so much to do. Etc., etc., etc..

They were right about the amount of work, though not quite of the genre they'd suggested. Within three days of receiving the *Bonae Voluntatis* membership, his offer to speak at two universities, three charitable organizations and two churches had also been accepted, approved and the dates fixed.

Why am I doing this?

It was time for action.

He requested and was given air time on TV. The local stations contacted their national counterparts and he was about to address the nation. Some of the nation. It was an Educational channel. PBS TV. Nevertheless, after the very first broadcast his fate has been sealed. His fame was beginning to follow him wherever he went. He had to employ all the tricks, yes tricks he'd learned from the Far Eastern gurus, to dodge the many begging him for help, advice, financial assistance, healing, even absolution. When he agreed to give a talk in the local Anglican Church, ten thousand people arrived. Loudspeakers have been installed outside; the streets had been blocked for hours. Other churches followed.

What am I doing here?

SACHA 25+ 168 days

Desire, on Earth, is regarded as a yen, as a means of satisfying an inner or outer hunger or longing. Buddha said that desire is at the root of all suffering. Not so in the higher or inner realms. Once I shed my physical body, desire is the expression of my creative will. I create to enhance the universe I perceive with my higher senses. There is no yen or wanting. My creation is as detached from me as I am, from the fruit of my desire. I don't own it. I enjoy it and offer to share it with my successors. When I depart, I might long for the state of mind—never for the fruit of my creation. Or is this what Buddha has been talking about? The state of mind?

Christmas came early this year. Not that the date had changed, but people began celebrating the Nativity a month before Sacha had arrived in Los Angeles. By mid December, the street decorations looked tattered, their fragments floating on the streets, swept by the winter winds carried by El Niño.

El Niño. More people swore at the name than rejoiced in it. It brought unaccustomed storms, challenging the dry, hot Santa Anna blowing in the opposite direction. El Niño mounted and drove the waves of the mighty Pacific until they reached far inland, until the Christmas decorations had been torn from trees, from lampposts, from people's front porches. The seacoast was no longer a desirable destination for the holiday-makers. They preferred to stay way inland, celebrating their Christmas on the golf courses, just to be sure.

And this year, El Niño blew with singular and spectacular premeditation. Like never before. El Niño, the Child born at Christmas. The Child hated by many.

It was time for action.

"I know who Jesus was, but why do we celebrate Christmas?"

Only Deborah could ask such a question and make it sound inoffensive to other people's sensibilities.

They were sitting at Sacha's parents' family table. It was the season of Good Will. Two policemen were stationed at the entrance to the condominium building. Suzy drew the curtains to hide her little gathering from the outside as much as possible. Rather than getting together on Christmas Day, Sacha suggested they might meet on the Eve of Christmas. It was an old European custom anyway and here, in the USA, it assured greater privacy in case the people outside had designs on his presence. They sat to dinner when the first star blinked at them from the darkening sky.

"Do you celebrate Christmas?" Suzy asked just as innocently. She had no desire to hurt Deborah, but frankly she had no idea what religion she practiced. If any. They never talked about it.

"I do whatever Sacha tells me," she replied.

"And what might that be?"

"To be myself. Not to compromise. But mostly just to be myself."

Alicia who was listening to this exchange smiled her most surreptitious smile. It only registered in her eyes that grew brighter, more joyous.

"I thought that Christmas was a season of joy," Alec put in. "We don't go to any particular church, but at Christmas we feel a stronger link with each other. This in itself gives us extra pleasure."

Alicia's eyes approved that also.

"And you Grandma? What is your slant on Christmas?"

"I am of the old guard. I still remember when we all went to church, at midnight, to celebrate the Holy Mass. The church smelled of incense, of burning candles, and just a little of JJ. The Irish whiskey. But the occasion was something I only gave up when Alec died. My Alec. Alec Senior. He was a traditional man. He drew his strength from old customs. He thought that even the lowest of the low got better on Christmas day. Like Scrooge..."

Her eyes reached out beyond time, beyond their little family circle. Alec's father never saw their Los Angeles home. He was born in England and died in Canada. Still as an expatriate. Poor man, she thought. He'd been so good to me...

"It seemed that Alec Senior celebrated Christmas practically every day," Suzy mused, the memory invoking a wistful smile.

She too remembered Alec's father, the tall, masculine man who always treated Alicia as a princess. A little like her father had treated her. She was looking forward to flying next week to be with her mother. Her dad probably wouldn't recognize her. Four years ago, except for Sacha, they were all here, together. Even the cats. Now dad was dying, mother was alone in Kingston, while Peeka and Boo stayed with Maria. Not quite enough to be joyful about.

Sacha got up and walked up to the window. He parted the blinds a little and peeked outside. What a marvelous thing it would have been if they'd listened to the teaching of the forgotten child. To the teaching of El Niño. If they hadn't turned the celebration of Christmas into a spending fiesta, but gathered to celebrate his words. Every word the man had spoken applied as much today as it had then, on the sun-baked hills outside Jerusalem.

Buddha, and Krishna before him, had tried their best. There had been others. Many others before them. Jesus wanted to limit his teaching to his own people, but Paul wouldn't have it that way. He'd spread the word and in doing so had diluted the intensity of the teaching. He adapted it to other people to make it more acceptable. He tried his best.

But it couldn't have worked.

The teaching sounds like pure theory until it is grounded in the past of the Jewish people. Many prophets had manipulated matter. They had shown the illusion of all that is material, physical, transient by definition. Many had prepared the ground for the man who would show that the only reality is within you. Within your very own self. That whatever you truly believe in becomes real. Your personal, glorious reality. (Be careful what you wish for!) Each one a creator unto himself. Unto herself. Whatsoever you believe in... The objective reality is not of this world, he'd said. He called it his kingdom. And your kingdom.

All to no avail.

Not even the Jews believed him. And those few who call themselves Messianic, they do not create their own reality either—they wait on their Master to do it for them. Like children wafting in the wind. Helpless, resigned to their own inadequacy. Yet the man had said that there would be others who would perform even greater acts of creation. Of manipulating matter and energy by their minds alone. But only if their minds are firmly connected to the universal mind. To the Whole.

I don't belong here. Why have I dreamt so much in Bardo?

"What is your understanding of Christmas, Sacha?"

It was, of course, Deborah. She was after the truth, not just impressions. She wanted to hear his voice. Lately Sacha spoke on television, in churches and organizations, but at home, he hardly opened his mouth. It was as though he'd already said everything he had to say. As if there was no more. Or maybe he was simply tired. More and more he looked and sounded as though he didn't belong among them. Even among his own family.

He seemed a stranger in his own home.

"I have no understanding... I'm just trying to remember..." He was still facing the window.

Only then he became aware that all four of his nearest and dearest looked towards him. He felt their eyes boring into the back of his neck. He felt embarrassed.

"I'm sorry," he said. "My thoughts took me to a different..." He didn't finish. What was the point telling them now about Bardo? They were here to celebrate. To be merry. And by an act of his will Sacha had once more come down to Earth.

"Christmas is the time of good will. My grandfather was right. Even Scrooge changed his ways at Christmas. That is the power we place on the word. It creates a different reality. A reality we all long for, but are often too weak to sustain for the rest of the year. But we can always try."

We can always try. Why can't I try a little harder?

Deborah was the first to notice that Sacha was under a great strain. He presented a calm enough face, an outward serenity, but his attention was elsewhere. "You are where your attention is," she remembered him telling her. Deborah wondered where he was. It was obvious to her that public appearances drained him physically as well as mentally. She had no idea why. She went with him a few times. He'd always sounded so composed. So radiant. Even happy. He sounded as though he just opened his mouth and the words spewed out without the slightest effort. But did they really? And was he really as happy as he looked? Or was it all a mask he put on for the masses. Did he present a different mask to the many, and a different one to the few?

"Sacha," she thought intensively. "Sacha come back... please Sacha..."

He took the five steps towards her and took her in his arms. He'd never done so before with other people around. Except for Alicia. But time was past for the form for form's sake.

"I'm sorry, my love. It won't happen again. Promise."

It didn't. Sacha was as unable to break a promise as was Deborah. The concept was simply absent from his make up both, as human, and as a Stranger from a Strange Land that he was. For the rest of the evening, Sacha was the soul of the party. He talked freely, he joked, he sang carols in his passable baritone. He even did some party tricks—like lighting candles on the Christmas tree without matches. Suzy always attached a few 'real' candles to the branches in honor of her father who'd hated the 'artificial' lights, as he'd called them. "It's all so commercial," he'd said. It also reduced the number of fires, she mused with a smile.

No matter. She loved her father.

Actually Sacha didn't actually light the candles 'by magic', although he probably could have. What he'd done was to divert their attention, become invisible, and lit them very fast one after another. By the time they looked at him, he was sitting again in his chair. The human mind usually refused to accept things that do not fit into the established pattern of understanding. Or of that which reaches outside their particular perception of reality.

It really didn't matter how he did it. He did it mostly for Deborah. She clapped her hands, and was on the verge of performing another exotic jig. Only Suzy beat her to it. She thought Sacha was about to peek-a-boo, and when he, according to her, remained in his chair, she was overjoyed. She got up, spun on her heals, sang out 'peek-a-boo' on the top of her voice and dropped back into her chair. The third bottle of wine may have had something to do with it.

"See? I can do it too!" she giggled.

Alec and Sacha knew what Suzy was talking about. Alicia and Deborah both gave her an amused if slightly baffled look.

Only Sacha hadn't remained in his chair. What stayed behind was his astral body. His projection. Alec would have loved to incorporate this ability into his Information Theory. Subliminally Sacha dropped his father a hint. But the human mind did not as yet invent mathematics for this particular conjecture. In fact there was no theory postulated as yet for any of the powers Sacha had acquired over his short life-span.

Sacha read his father's mind.

It will come, Dad... It will come.

Alec received him loud and clear.

Sacha thought that manipulating reality was a fitting way to celebrate Christmas. Wasn't this what Jesus did when he'd changed water into wine? Or walked on water? To Sacha these were party tricks. What mattered was that the motivation for and the results of the tricks met their intended purpose. Even if they just brought joy to the people you loved.

And then the dinner was over.

They left the presents till tomorrow. "Some customs should remain English," Alec insisted.

Not one of them felt like moving. There was an atmosphere in the house that was hard to define. They were all joyful. At times exuberant. Yet, there was a tenuous cloud making itself known to their inner sentience. El Niño, pounding the window panes, imposed an inexplicable, persistent susurration that every beginning must have its inevitable end. That whatever is born, must die. And the death of the Child born tonight was none too pleasant to contemplate. No one mentioned it. Yet they all knew, with knowledge that can only reach one from deep within, that this was their last Christmas together. There was an air of finality. They sensed, each one of them, that Sacha was with them only in passing. Like a comet that illuminates the sky with its flamboyant beauty and then returns into the depth of space.

Yet… no one mentioned it. No one dared.

Alicia stayed the night with them. She was given the room she'd once slept in, over Christmas, so many years ago. The room that usually served as Suzy's studio. Alicia didn't mind. She even enjoyed the smell of fresh oil on canvas. Actually Suzy used mostly acrylic, but it made no difference. Alicia loved whatever it was.

Deborah and Sacha were now accepted as a couple. Suzy wouldn't dream of suggesting a more traditional, let alone a permanent arrangement. Not after her own peek-a-boo mode of behavior with Sacha's father, way back in Montreal. She would never believe that the 'young couple' had made love in two successive embodiments—some centuries apart.

Sacha was in two minds about leaving Deborah alone on Christmas night. Later, the decision was taken out of his hands. Since that night they'd met, on *rue St-Laurent*, Deborah hasn't drank anything stronger than coffee. Today she had more than three glasses. The moment her head touched the pillow, she'd given herself up to Orpheus' embrace. Whatever she dreamed about, the smile remained on her lips till early hours. By then Sacha was back. In the meantime, he could not have forsaken those who needed him most on this Special Night of the year. Again he opened a single door at the back of the supermarket. Only this time he took out the provisions himself. People outside carried his bounty as far and as wide as they could. Later Sacha paid for every single item he'd taken from the supermarket with good ol' American greenbacks. To the last cent. After all, there were other shareholders.

Never had so many celebrated Christmas Eve in the streets of LA.

Later, Sacha walked the street for a few more hours. There were not many people. Even the usual vagrants celebrated Christmas by getting drunk. Each according to his means. He met them, he filled their heart with good will, with as much joy as they were capable of accepting. He was surprised how very receptive people were. It was as though they've been waiting for him. Waiting for the magic of Christmas.

When he returned home, he no longer felt like a stranger in a strange land.

It was a very good Christmas, after all.

***

22
First Signs

"**D**on't forget, son," said Alexander Baldwin, Ph.D., speaking as an expert in the field, "that there is a well known maxim among the physicists. It postulates that for every action there is an equal and opposite reaction." He let that sink in while searching Sacha's face for the desired effect. Alec was worried about a possible backlash from Sacha's lectures in which he refused to hold anything back.

"There are areas, Dad, in which we cannot compromise," Sacha replied, his tone unrepentant.

"And if the same holds for the less tangible aspects of the physical reality," Alec continued, as though he hadn't been interrupted, "and mystics assure us that the dictum 'as above so below'..."

"...or that whatsoever we bind on earth shall be bound in heaven, as well as the other way round, still holds in this day and age," Sacha continued reading his father's thoughts before Alec had a chance to speak them, "than I'd better watch my step."

"I was thinking more of your back, son," Alec smiled, but his tone was deadly serious.

Sacha had a good idea what to expect. And all he could expect was that equal and opposite to whatever he said or did would be initiated by somebody, and promptly thrown in his face. He was determined to dodge the counter attack for as long as he could.

In the first few weeks following Christmas, Sacha had appeared seven times on local and national TV programs. He'd also made eighteen personal appearances at various gatherings that had been attended to capacity.

He didn't preach.

He assured everyone who listened that he had nothing new to offer, no new insights, new gospels, nor new catechism. All he was doing was reminding people what had been given to humanity ages ago, reinstated and confirmed periodically by various wise men that we called mystics, prophets, saviors or avatars. That was all. Where he differed from other speakers mounting the pulpits—whom he jokingly called his competition—was that, when called upon, Sacha did not shy away from demonstrating the veracity of his convictions. He put his deeds where his mouth was. Brethren from various sacerdotal persuasions did not look kindly upon his inerrant abilities.

For them, Sacha spelled danger.

When he met doubters he scanned their minds and planted afterthoughts, as to where and how they veered from the straight and narrow. When he was accused of pretending to be a doctor without a license, he denied any such thing, and claimed that while physicians attempt to cure from without, healing always comes from within. He assured everyone that all he did was to help people find the healing power within themselves. He said that if he failed to open people's minds to this truth, no healing occurred.

Unfortunately for the objectors to his 'trickery', there had always been some people around in need of physical help and, whenever possible, he tried to oblige. On a few occasions, but only on a few, the results had been spectacular. The paralytics walked, the dying recovered on the spot, the blind recovered their eyesight. This also involved manipulation of perceived reality, of course, but he knew of no way to explain this fact to people at large. Even on, what he called, a one-on-one basis, it wasn't easy. And the few healings mentioned always took place following a one-on-one contact. The others just bore witness.

Usually Sacha preferred to open one's mindset and let nature take its course. It was a little like tuning a violin. No one would dream of playing the fiddle, no matter how well they played, unless the instrument was well tuned. People failed to do the same to their perception of reality. Their minds were badly out of tune.

Once he'd been almost run over by a car driven by a hysterical woman. She wanted to see if he would disappear or otherwise escape her 'experiment'. After a few weeks in jail and a few months of biweekly sessions on a psychiatrist's coach she was certified sane. Sacha could have done it much faster, but the result would have been virtually the same. At the time, she'd been whisked away by the men in blue.

During the fourth week after Christmas, the problems started in earnest.

First Sacha had noticed a marked increase in dog collars among his audience. They sat innocently enough, amidst the many, but toward the end of his talk they would slither their way towards the microphones, positioned among the listeners, and begin asking him questions regarding his stand on religion.

The questions had been of the category: 'Did you stop beating your wife, Sir?' Dammed if he did, dammed if he didn't. Whatever he answered could be used against him. The clergymen may have been jealous of his evident following, or simply mistrustful of his confidence. Yet, at the same time, they seemed to be feeling him out to see if he might be swayed to join their particular ranks, enhance their particular sect, and wave their spurious banner.

Only the boys in black cassocks hadn't shown any interest in captivating Sacha by their dubious charm. They'd laid claim to their own source of infallibility. There was no need for Sacha's ravings, they'd implied. They as good as insisted that only one authority had the power to heal and that was the power of Jesus. While Sacha refused to be drawn into a discussion regarding the source of healing, he had suggested that some have the humility to act as channels. He enumerated half dozen names including the Brazilian named Jose Pedro De Freitas who had become known as Arigo, the German Bruno Gröning, the American Evelyn Monahan, and the Hindu sage named Sai Baba, as just one example from the Far East. He'd named others as able, if less known, healers from around the world who did not invoke the name of Jesus to accomplish their healing. Belatedly Sacha remembered—what he'd always known though it had slipped his mind at that moment—that the majority of the healers he'd named had been successfully destroyed by the jealous ministrations of the medical profession, with able and enthusiastic assistance from various ecclesiastic authorities.

Bad examples, he thought. Bad examples nearly all of them.

Yet he couldn't help smiling.

The priest who questioned Sacha's unclaimed powers however had not been amused at all. Sacha's answer did not insult him, he'd said. It insulted the Authority of the Holy Mother the Church.

Go figure, as his night-street friends would say.

Go figure...

SACHA 24+216 days

So many among us do not know—let alone experience— those elusive realities that wait for us to be noticed, to be accepted as part of our fundamental kingdom, as our birthright. How few of us have retained the ability to soar to lands of unprecedented beauty where form and color respond to every whim of our imagination. And fewer still can draw on our memory of domains still higher, the domains of pure thought, where we had once lingered for years, ages, before returning to Earth where a fraction of a second hardly passed us by. Time is yet another limitation we choose to impose on our perceived kingdom. We impose it, we even believe that it's real. Yet ideas converted to thoughts linger for countless centuries, are passed on from one generation to another, seemingly indestructible. Ideas brought to us by Krishna, by Buddha, by Socrates through Plato, by Jesus or Mohammed, still stimulate man to action, force man to look up, towards the stars, to the intangible, ineffable, yet so very real Undiscovered Realm.

How can I find words to tell them these inalienable truths in words that their senses will not discard as fables, as ravings of a man gone mad? Perhaps gone mad with longing for his true home.

The omens are not always clear.

Not for the first time Sacha experienced moments of fantastic clarity of mind, followed by hours of darkest depression. He seemed to sink so deep as to well-nigh lose all hope, and then, as if by magic, he catapulted himself into the realm of light like a comic book hero escaping from an inescapable chasm. For a while, such moods oscillated at a fantastic and unpredictable rate.

At times, Sacha also sensed portents of tremendous power. It welled within him until nothing, nothing at all, seemed impossible. It came to him in direct proportion to the realization of his purpose. An hour earlier he might have felt as weak as a kitten licking its wounds after a losing battle in a dark alley. His moods, which he barely managed to keep within his grasp, swung like Foucault's Pendulum; only he was measuring the velocity of his Inner Light as It was refracted by his three lower forms of perception. By the mental, emotional, and physical sheath which constricted his true nature.

At other times he would spend hours on his own. People who saw him in those moments, usually wandering the streets at night, probably thought he was praying. His face was locked in a blissful smile, a beatific detachment of ineffable serenity shining from his half-closed eyes. He called those times 'retreats into the desert'. In truth, these were moments when he retreated to the Undiscovered Realm, seeking energy and strength. Towards the end of this period, he'd been tempted to manipulate people. To exercise his mounting power, albeit in self-defense. It would have been so easy. So very easy.

It also would have been wrong.

This is not why I am here...

After three weeks of such fluctuating existence he'd finally reached a state of balance. He'd won his personal Armageddon. The final battle. From now on he became a pure instrument of his own destiny. Of his own dream.

He was no longer afraid of anything. He knew that nothing could happen to him without his acquiescence. He felt free to respond to his inner voice without any allowance for the consequences. He was even free to perform what others regarded as miracles. Not just healing, but employing other talents he'd acquired over the years. When he resorted to them, it was merely to make a point.

"You all can do this. All of you. It is not my power. It is power that is omnipresent. It is equally available to every single one of you."

No one believed him. Many believed in him, but not in his words.

***

His purpose was now abundantly clear to him. Everything in his short life led him to this moment. He'd found a way to convey his perception of the world to the world. At least to the Western world. He now knew that was his destiny.

His message was simple.

Some man, who had learned to listen to his inner self, had initiated each religion. Through this inner self he, or they, could contact the Source of all knowledge. His father, Alec, had been right. Information is omnipresent, at all levels of perception. Some men even reached the awareness of the golden cord, their link with the Whole. They'd gained access to the universal knowledge—to wisdom that lay beyond time and space. But the dissemination of that knowledge had been assumed by others. By other men who, while great by human standards, still hovered on the outer boundary of physical and thus dualistic reality. At least that was their avowed perception.

Each such teacher had been given one segment of the great picture. Each prophet knew that the human race was not ready to absorb the concept of the Whole. They promulgated the portion assigned to them, a vision of the Whole adapted to the mentality, and the ability of the particular people to perceive that aspect of the Totality.

It could not have been otherwise. Our ability to metabolize wisdom is always limited by the rate at which we can absorb it. This, too, is true at all levels of perception. This is why evolution is so desperately slow.

Yet now the time has come to unify all those fragments of reality together. To destroy the parts not by eliminating them, but by fusing them into a greater, higher form of perception. The time was at hand when people would realize that the Whole is greater than the sum of Its parts. It was not Sacha's intent to destroy any religion. He felt it was his destiny to unify the diverse discernment of truth, for each one of them, each religion, held a fragment of truth. His destiny was to open people's eyes to their true nature.

But his detractors did not know that. Had he told them, they would have laughed in his face. Truth wields an enormous power. Even a fragment of truth, a portion assigned to some primitive people, can hold a man in a vise as unrelenting as his will to survive. This fact alone explained the need for free will. The freedom for man to look beyond the horizons imposed by his forefathers.

Sacha had long scrutinized the history of man.

This inordinate power of truth explained why different religions clung so fiercely to their particular fragments. They claimed god is one, without knowing what god is, or even what the concept of unity really entails. They assigned human traits to an imagined divinity, human attributes distended to Olympian heights, in order to have an image worthy of their worship. The bigger the better.

Why can't they understand my words?

SACHA 24+216 days, (cont.)

I meet so many here, on Earth, in this reality so replete with self-imposed limitations, who choose to abide in shackles of their own making. There are so many here who seem to have lost all memory of the Undiscovered Realm— their only permanent reality. The only Source of ideas. How can I show them that wherever we take our inspirations to give them form, so as to be able to share them with our neighbor, we never really leave our True Home? We abide ever there as pure consciousness, ever ready to bring forth new concepts, new impulses, which our more tangible selves would translate into thoughts, which would then linger for countless generations, growing, evolving, expanding our perception of reality.

If those forms do not find fertile ground, they will wither and die...

Yet the lower realities impose restrictions in direct proportion to their materiality. And what is more, the greater our personality, the further we are apart. We are set apart from other individualizations of the single, omnipresent Whole. Why is it that the lower we descend the greater our resistance to new concepts, new ideas? Why is it that we set limits to our own potential with such fervor yet discard the gift of life eternal with disdain?

Why can't they understand my words?

***

Sacha looked down at the faces raised towards him.

Their eyes hungry for something intangible, something they all knew, felt, that was intrinsically theirs, yet something they could not quite grasp. Something as yet hidden from them.

"How can I help you?" he asked in tacit whisper.

Each one perceives the truth in his and her own personal way. There is no limit I can place on the perception of the Whole. I cannot chop it into fragments tiny enough for them to swallow. If I could only show them. But they are too many. Their auras span too great amplitude to imbue them with a single image. And, after all, unbeknownst to most, diversity is a divine trait.

"My god is more powerful then your god," the Hebrews have claimed for many generations. Is he? Just how many gods are there?

"Allah is one, sing the Moslem. They are right of course. But what of Krishna? Is he Allah too? One billion people claim he is. Are they all wrong? Everyone of them? And what of god manifested in the eyes of a new born baby? Is that some other kind of god? A lesser god? Allah is one—only who will define which Allah?"

The silence was such that Sacha could hear his own heart pounding. They all wanted to learn. Most of them. Most searched, hoped, almost begged. Could he feed them the truth in morsels big enough to gulp down one bite at a time?

"Divinity cannot be measured," he spoke hardly above a whisper. "Neither in size nor in power. Divinity just IS. It is the Isness within everyone of us."

Will they believe me?

"God cannot be measured," Sacha resumed again. "Nor imagined. Nor embraced with thought. No matter who or what you choose to perceive as your god."

There was a wave of heads as Sacha raised his hands, as though to embrace them.

"You build temples and mosques and churches in which to protect your gods from unholy eyes. From the unbelievers. From the profane. Why do your gods need protection? Each one of you claims that your god is omnipresent, yet you lock him up in places of worship you can control. You think of god as power. Don't you know this power is equally distributed throughout the universes?"

This last sentence was directed at the clerics pressed together into a single faction, an amorphous body at the back of the hall. They held allegiance to different faiths, even different sects, but they felt safer together. They all shared the uniqueness of placing themselves between the people and their gods. The go-betweens. The ten-percenters.

There was a cold wind blowing from those pious people. Not really hatred but closer to anger. Anger that Sacha was upsetting the established system. There was room enough for all churches, they thought in perfect unison. Usually at war, here they practically held hands in prurient amity. They were merchants of the same trade. Their minds were the only minds Sacha could read at random. Their auras displayed amazing similarity.

"After all," they thought virtually as one, "people make enough money for all of us. So why roil the water? Why aggravate the situation? If God didn't like what we are doing, He wouldn't let us go on. Would He? Yahweh or Allah or God is Almighty. They are all almighty. He guides us all in our doings. In our going out and our coming in. God sees and approves all that we do. We and we alone are His servants."

So why roil the water?

Their anger was growing.

SACHA 24+ 219 days

I felt their thoughts. I am still not breaking through their self-imposed barriers. I must find a way. I must explain to them in words they will understand that ideas remain just abstractions until they are converted into, and disciplined by, thought. And thoughts remain just theories until embraced with emotion, fired with imagination. Only then they acquire form, tangible and palpable, euphoric in their beauty, which we can share with others. Artists and poets have known this for ages. We might almost stop here. Yet here, on the Home Planet, life is so beautiful, so carefree, that there is little stimulus to rise higher, to reach forever greater discernment, greater understanding.

I must find words to tell them that this is why, and it's the only reason why, we must finally descend to Earth. Only man has the power to reach for the stars. Only man has the privilege to rise above all limitations and realize his own potential. Here, on this ball of dust, we start by crawling on all fours, we lift ourselves by sheer effort of will, we stagger, fall and rise again, until we find strength enough to remain standing. Finally we walk upright, proudly, as though suspecting our true nature.

Yet so few of us reach out for the sky, where our hearts ever long to take us. Fewer still rise to the stars where thoughts flitter at the edges of our consciousness like transient universes. And fewer still return to their True Home, where light blends with light, were there is no you and I, just we, as one, together, forever united. There, in the bliss of being, we dream once again of ideas only to venture once more into lower cycles, a spiral which, we hope, will create a vortex that in turn will draw others to those higher realms, waiting so patiently for their arrival. There are so many prodigal sons, so many prodigal daughters, yet to see the light burning within their own inner selves.

How can I tell them that?

How can I explain that the essence of life is bound by the cycle of living?

How can I find the words they might understand?

"You have twenty-one requests for healing, over seventy letters of gratitude and praise, seven threats, and one hate letter. I count it apart from the threatening letters because it is different. It is not based on religion. Frankly, I can't understand it."

It was late afternoon. Deborah was staring at the computer screen, her forehead furrowed. She was reviewing Sacha's morning's email.

"You will have to look at it yourself," she added.

"I thought you didn't want to be my secretary?" Sacha smiled. Without her help the volume of e-mail alone would swamp him. "Show me that last one," he asked.

Deborah directed her mouse at the scroller and the offensive letter came up. The moment it appeared on the screen before Sacha even saw it, he knew the culprit.

"I'll see him tonight. He is right to hate me," Sacha commented enigmatically.

Deborah gave him a long look but didn't say anything. As far a she was concerned, Sacha was always right. Except for the volume of his work. He hardly slept three or four hours a night. A night and a day, for that matter. How long could a man go on like this?

Sacha hoped he wouldn't have to go on like this much longer either. As for the hate letter Sacha suspected it would come, sooner or later. He scanned it on the screen for form's sake. It wasn't signed, but to Sacha the sender was obvious. Later, that same night, he stole into the prison for the last time. He remained invisible until he reached the little insipid man who murdered his mother, his wife and two daughters. He was sitting on the concrete floor, facing the wall opposite, his face hidden in near total darkness.

Sacha waited till the man became aware of his presence. Then, before a stream of hatred which he managed to convey by the electronic mail could well inside him, Sacha showed him the destiny which his mother his wife and his children had been dealt. He showed the man that all four of his victims had been responsible for taking other peoples lives in their previous embodiments. Their cards have been dealt, by themselves. He, the murderer, helped them find peace. He helped to liberate them from their terrible karma.

Sacha could not have told the poor man all this on his previous visit. First, the man hadn't been ready for it. Second, the men's mindset had been turned completely on himself. An extreme case of egocentricity. And, also, the man was in a mental and emotional condition wherein concepts of karma would not have taken hold in his psyche.

Next, the man had his own karma to discharge. And finally, the disconsolate creature had been on the verge of self-immolation. Not physically but at the mental level. He had to recuperate his sensibilities to some degree, before he would be able to understand the next step.

Now it was done.

"You came after I spewed my venom at you?" The voice was a mere whisper in the darkness. Yet even his hushed tones conveyed traces of disbelief.

"It wasn't your venom. It belonged to a man you are no more," Sacha murmured. He preferred to keep the subliminal connection to a minimum. Otherwise the man might think later that he imagined it all. As for his words, this was not the time to tell him that all that really changed was his perception of reality. That who he really was and is, will forever remain indestructible.

"That's true..." This was all so new to the poor wretch. "Who am I?"

"You are whoever you want to be. You are a man who can help others with your understanding," Sacha whispered.

For a while neither of them spoke. The man had never asked who Sacha was. That alone spoke volumes of his mental and emotional condition. But Sacha always regarded the message more important than the messenger. He doubted though that the man knew it. He was wrong.

"I thank you, whoever you are," there was total conviction in his tone. "I shall not let you down."

Sacha was never more sure of anything in his life. The man would not let him down. Whoever he was.

The following morning a registered letter was delivered for Sacha, care of his father. It was a request for him to represent the *Bonae Voluntatis* at the Ecumenical Congress that was to be held on the West Coast. It was going to take place in San Francisco, but after reports of multiple street-marches being organized by exponents of free love and other varieties of sexual expression, the organizers decided to move it to Los Angeles. *Bonae Voluntatis* had been awarded two tickets and if Dr. Baldwin could possibly find time to attend, they would be very grateful.

There was a *post scriptum*.

"We have been watching with great interest the lectures you have delivered in and around Los Angeles. We congratulate you on the depth of your perception."

The PPS asked simply, "When can we hope to see you in Montreal?"

Sacha looked up at Deborah reading over his shoulders.

"They either don't understand what I am talking about, or they really want me to represent them."

"Will you?"

"Yes, my love. I shall. It is precisely what I am going to do." He didn't explain any further.

So the time has come.

He sighed deeply. Suzy and Alec were in the living room, busy with their own stuff. Deborah stayed next to him whenever she could. So little time. Soon she will not see me. Soon she will have to cope on her own. Probably with Alicia. Alicia needed help. I'll make Debbie promise to look after her. She will like it. They like each other. They are good for each other...

Why am I going on like this?
I must be becoming very human. Perhaps… I really am.

Somehow when the storm hovers over the horizon, we don't really believe it will reach us. We think that a butterfly will flap its wings somewhere over the Brazilian rain forest, and by the process of fractal augmentation the winds will blow the clouds away. We hope that the inclement weather will find a different course to vent its fury.

But that never happens. Virtually never.

We all carry our burdens, sometimes joyously, sometimes wearing us down to the very limit. But we always survive. Well, most of us. Some, those very unfortunate amongst us, must roll time back to prehistory, and start again. But this almost never happens, and when it does, the entity undergoing such a fate is not aware of what happened to it. It merely continues as though nothing had happened.

The Whole is not merciful. The Whole is mercy itself. It is all things to all men.

To all men of good will... As Lao Tsu said, Tao is impartial—it always favours good men. Destiny functions in mysterious ways—yet always, unerringly, for the universal good. Sacha smiled as he glanced again at the letter from *Bonae Voluntatis*.

For all men of *bonae voluntatis*.

***

23

The Debate

Sacha was not a theologian. By all human standards
he'd ever encountered, he was a confirmed atheist. He
had no reason to accept that there was anyone or
anything outside his own self that directed his life in any way.
Of course, he recognized 'self' as his light body, the
consciousness that resided permanently in the Undiscovered
Realm. At the same time, no man thought of himself as more
insignificant in relation to the Whole as he did. He also had
total faith in the benevolence of the currents underlying all
realities—currents, or laws, which manifested in the visible
and the invisible universes. He believed, unflinchingly, in the
power of love, although he might differ greatly as to what this
four-letter word meant. For Sacha, love was first and
foremost the unifying principle, a force that held the
individualized units of awareness, bound together. Nothing,
nothing man did or didn't do, could diminish the integrity of
the Whole. There was nothing man or any other
individualization could do to detract from, or to diminish, Its
completeness. That which is complete, that is holy. What is
one with the Whole is perfect.

Quite simple, really, he thought.

From the moment he flitted in and out of his mother's
womb, even before he was born, before he became Sacha, he
found it difficult to accept the evident constraints imposed on
him by his physical body. He found them as difficult and
trying as anyone of us. Yet, at some level of his awareness, he

felt sure that he could overcome them. He had always suspected that physical limitations were only imaginary, that his true self could never lose its absolute prerogatives. He also grew convinced that men like his father would, in time, extend the boundaries of physical perception to heretofore unheard of levels. Later, much later in his life, he'd accepted that his physical body was necessary. After all, it was his physical embodiment, or more accurately his physical consciousness, which was instrumental in fulfilling his destiny.

And his destiny was drawing closer.

It was approaching as adamantly as the storm clouds gathering from the direction of prevailing winds. A storm as great and as inevitable as any man witnessed on his journey towards his destiny.

Sacha knew from observation and experience that the more universal the aspirations, the greater the resultant joy, satisfaction, and ultimately bliss in their fulfillment. He'd already learned that in the East End of London. He knew it to be true at all levels of his awareness. It sounded like a simple dictum. Universality versus parochialism. It was a much simpler concept than the complexities, intricacies, not to mention implicit and explicit mysteries, concocted by many an orthodox theology.

He had to convey this axiom to all who would listen.

The actual time for the Debate had been selected on Madison Avenue. It had been estimated that by extending time-slots on TV, they could cover a larger audience from the demographic as well as psychographic point of view. The demographics defined *who* has spent money on the items advertised. The psychographics dealt more with *how* they'd spent their money. Regardless, whether it was on junk food or expensive cars. All in all, there was more money in junk food. According to Marx, or Engels, it used to be religion—now junk food has become the opium of the masses. And the masses had more money than any Marxist had ever dreamt of.

The leaders of religions swore to reverse this ungodly trend. Or, at the very least, to exploit it.

The advertising executives had decided to direct themselves at a demographic audience in the 18-49 age group, but to include the 50+ for the psycho-graphic angle. They had to. All the baby-boomers were now well over 50 but they still had the money. It was in the extraction of money that Madison Avenue specialized. And they were good at it. Like a good dentist, they knew how to pull, hard, no matter what the pain. They even became adept at making up stories that acted as an anesthetic.

> "You need (whatever we have to offer). You'll find it indispensable... It is for your own good... For your health, happiness, satisfaction, peace of mind... It will make you sleep better... It will reduce your obesity... It will give you abs, buns, pecs, (or other selected parts of your anatomy) of steel... For every ton of junk-food you buy, we give you a free sample of laxative pills guarantied to restore you to your previous contours..."

To quote the late King of Siam: et cetera, et cetera, et cetera. There was no end to their generosity.

Finally, after innumerable committee meetings and worldwide market research, they arrived at the ideal time for the Debate. By a complex system of 'live', 'taped live', and 'presently being taped live' as well as instant and not-so-instant replays, they were assured of preferred airings in different time zones. Not just in the USA, Canada, Central and South America, but in every country of Europe, Africa, Middle and Far East, people would, or at least could, listen to the Debate at their most propitious time. Prime Time—the time when people were relaxed and willing to watch and listen to the advertisers displaying their wares.

The advertising agents also worked in close cooperation with ACL, the Associated Churches League. During the last two years, various churches, sects and familiar charitable organizations, had finally learned that they can pull in more money if they cooperated. Secret negotiations had been conducted, compromises had been forged in signed contracts between interested parties, the gods, or at least the theological definitions of gods, had been realigned to suit everybody. Outside the select few, the gray (sometime crimson, sometime black, and sometime white) eminencies who run the church businesses, decided to attempt to live in harmony. It didn't work yet, but there was hope. Money was a great unifying factor. The rest of the various believers continued to fight each other. The faithful wouldn't fight on their own, of course, but with a gentle push, a little skillful manipulation, the struggle for theological supremacy was easily reawakened. The sheep needed a push to become goats. But it was worth it. And it was good for business. Competition never hurt anyone.

But times changed.

There were undercurrents; clandestine trends among some of the League members, who attempted to exploit the power of religion for their own, political ends. The League would not permit this. It was not good for their image; it undermined their authority, and, let us be quite honest, it wasn't good for business either. And business was very, very important. And necessary. The major religions, the religions that counted, had inherited an enormous burden imposed on them by history. There were tens of thousands of churches, mosques and synagogues, ancillary buildings, not to mention works of art, collections of precious metals, priceless jewelry, voluminous libraries, and all gods' bounty, which needed upkeep. There were also traditional organizations that were, at least in name, sponsored by the churches. There were also the hungry to feed, the ignorant to teach—at least a little reading and writing. These were the duties the churches took upon themselves. And in addition, the churches swore to fight the murderers of the unborn, the purveyors of sexual exploitation or prostitution; pursuers of unjust wars, abusers of... there were so many irons in the ecclesiastical fire.

Business was extremely necessary.

The Debate was to be limited to the three principal religions of the West (and the Middle East). Sacha thought it didn't amount to much until he realized that each of the major religions enjoyed countless schisms that had to be harnessed. Let the Hindus and the Buddhists take care of their own business, they told him at *Bonae Voluntatis*. To others, who pointed out this obvious inadequacy, this self-evident racism, the League replied *ex officio* that there was only so much the League could do. They were only human, etc., etc. And when that hasn't silenced the professional critics, the League spokeswoman said that there was not enough money. The critics understood instantly—lest they were asked to contribute.

And after all, the Christians, the Moslem and the Jews shared a common thread. They all began with Adam and Eve, they all called Abraham their father, and they all believed in One God, even if they invoked His presence by different names. If these three could unify under a single Authority, all would be well. Or at least better. At least for now.

It would be good for business.

Sacha didn't mind either. He knew that, left alone, Arjuna would do his best. He met his old friend from India periodically. They always chose the Home Planet. At higher planes the distractions to the mind were too great. In the Far Country they both spun universes with their mental fingertips. How could they have talked of Earth?

But that was another story.

At Oxford and the Sorbonne Sacha acquired a number of letters that qualified him to take part in the Debate. There were, however, many others of equal qualification. *'The Debate of the Century'*, as billed by the Ecumenical Movement and their Madison Avenue agents, was the first step towards clearing the way for the new Millennium. The millennium foretold by so many oracles and prophets. By the Book itself. At least, according to some interpretations. The fact that the millennium had begun some time ago was dismissed as a mere detail.

"God created time," they said. "God will adjust it if and when He deems it necessary."

Quite true. Over their combined history, the Churches adjusted time at least four times between them. In God's name, of course.

Thus having letters behind your name does not a ticket of entry make. This is why Sacha had joined *Bonae Voluntatis,* in Montreal. He had already suspected, then, that with the United Nations holding court on the Asian economical debacle on the East Coast, the Ecumenical Movement would prefer to keep as far away from there as possible, lest they were accused of some political mongering. Sacha expected that being qualified and residing officially on the West Coast, all he needed was a membership of an established international charitable organization to be allowed, if not actually be invited, into the building.

He was right.

He wrote back to Montreal that he would be more than glad to report on the proceedings to the *Bonae Voluntatis* in due course. He got back a lapel tag that displayed his name in prominent letters, and sported his photo that they must have lifted from some digital TV program. He was now able to enter not just with the masses but, if there be such, the Holy of Holies. Later he found that this precaution didn't prove necessary. This was not Boston, and he was no longer a fourteen-year-old. All participating members had equal access to the main hall where the Debate would take place. In fact there were no open tickets for the general public. Your very presence cast you among the select few. Whatever other entitlements, the membership of a recognized international charitable organization gave him access to the great leaders.

To get a better seat in the auditorium, the Sorbonne had given him an extra edge. After all, it was the Sorbonne's theological reputation that raised it above other colleges in Paris. Following all this, he'd never found out who was his counterpart, or colleague, from the organization he was representing. Perhaps there wasn't one, after all.

As for the advantages of the Sorbonne, Sacha had been aware of such when he'd decided to study there. All roads lead to Rome, he'd thought at the time. If you only let them carry you in their indomitable current. But some get you there faster than others.

Other than all of the above, Sacha had no idea what to expect. He had acquired a reputation outside the academic circles that preceded him. He traveled extensively and shared his views with all who were ready to change their lives sufficiently not to fall back on what caused their original distress. He called congenital blindness the primary illness of the world. He was not referring to physical blindness.

He was long past working incognito. And news, in certain circles, traveled fast. He was ready. The gathering clouds swept his destiny directly overhead.

There were many speeches. They were all intended to rubber stamp the previous agreements, signed and sealed behind closed doors. This occasion was designed for the masses. The select many. For the world at large.

Urbi et orbi.

The orations had been delivered by tall men, and by men who were short. By men who were fat, and others who were skinny. A good touch that, thought Sacha. Everyone had someone to identify with. Some men had long beards, others who were clean-shaven. Some wore crimson—as the blood of martyrs, others black—as pure intellect, and others still wore robes as white and as innocent as the wings of the doves of peace. They all expressed their learned opinions on the advantages of ecumenism. They all sang the same song, in perfect unison. The orations had been well rehearsed. No money or business aspects had been mentioned. It was all very grave and earnest, very compassionate and catholic, very loving, understanding, thoughtful, generous, considerate and kind. It was all above board.

Listening to them Sacha wondered why it was that so many such compassionate members had chosen to murder each other, with no rancour or mercy, for thousands of years.

This was the first mystery Sacha was unable to resolve.

Then the microphones were passed on to the lesser representatives, or perhaps to children of a lesser god. They did not represent the churches, but had served the church causes, those of compassion and loving and generous understanding. Members who might, in time, improve their lot sufficiently to contribute to the greater glory of the church. Any church. Of the Unified Churches. Perhaps, in time a Single Church? United under a single banner?

There had been even more speeches from the representatives of these organizations than from the eminencies of the churches themselves. Nevertheless, for the most part, they gave depth to the Ecumenical Movement. The sacerdotal representatives spoke in the name of God. The lay members—in the name of the people, in the name of the children of God, of the masses ever willing to follow their leaders like good, obedient, meek and servile members, on whose backs the Churches of One God rose to such unprecedented glory.

They had been given ten minutes, each. And Sacha was among them.

And then, it was his turn...

Look ... he said.

And with an effortless ease Sacha's body began to shimmer, dissolve and then reintegrate itself on the podium.

Then his mouth moved but his thoughts were projected directly to each man and woman present. Their auras were so similar. They all, or nearly all, responded to the same vibrations. Each one of them heard Sacha speak in his and her own language. Yet it was so natural that not one of them became aware of what was happening.

Later, much later, they didn't believe it either.

Sacha spoke as a Catholic, as a Southern Baptist, a Lutheran, and a Quaker. He spoke as a member of every Christian sect present. Then he spoke as a Muslim—as proponent of any and all Islamic sects that had joined forces in this Ecumenical Movement. He quoted vast passages *verbatim* from the Holy Koran and related them to the Christian teaching. Finally he spoke as a Hebrew. There were many different mindsets among the Jews, yet each saw the advantages of the Ecumenical Movement. There were as many Jewish sects, denominations, not present but listening over the airways, as there were Christian and Moslem, yet each calling themselves Jewish. The Diaspora. He showed them all what they all shared. Sacha confirmed the teaching he'd already promulgated by equally exhaustive evidence from the Old Testament. Even from the Talmud. He demonstrated the irrevocable interrelationship of all faiths, all creeds, and their interdependence in the process of arriving at the perception of reality. He gave substance to the real reason for the Ecumenical Movement. Not the agreed secret contracts that would remain secret 'as all things of God must remain secret'. Or so they said.

And yet, his whole dissertation lasted no more then the allotted time.

Time is so flexible. Even on airways.

The human brain, the wondrous physical expression of our mind, is able to absorb and metabolize concepts at an astonishing rate. It all depended on how it is fed. This same rate of absorption was true for each man, woman and child who turned on their TV, regardless what channel, what language, or which part of the world they were in. Light travels around our globe in just over a tenth of one second. Thought waves do so many thousands times faster. A time lag not perceptible even to our subliminal senses. They all heard him simultaneously. Regardless of time zones. That was how it was meant to be. That was the reality Sacha had created, and sustained for just a few minutes.

And then he drew his bow across the strings of their innermost memories and by a single tone, a single anabolic vibration he resuscitated their latent memories. Archetype memories so deep, so anchored in the eons of time that neither man, nor women even suspected their presence. And finally he spoke again. The moment wouldn't last but it would linger enough to reseed their minds with their own memories.

Regarding God.

In the Undiscovered Realm, there is no perception of any Overseer. Even the awareness of the gold thread, of golden filament, of connection, is not so much to an external Source but a gentle yet persistent tugging at our inherent Interconnectedness. Of being intrinsically One. The wondrous thing is that each one of us can draw on the Whole for our strength and vitality. It is ever-present. It is omnipresent. It is unresisting. It is nonjudgmental. It is ours for the asking. The extent to which this can be accomplished is not dictated by the Whole, but by our ability to do so. On the time scale of eternity, none of us are equal—but we are all endowed with equal potential.

In this sense, there is little difference between the Undiscovered Realm and the physical consciousness. All realities are coexistent. They all exist here and now. What changes is our perspective, our perception of truth, or our subjective reality. Do not trust those who insist on imposing an external Force on each and every one of you. Your Force comes from within you.

You and you alone are the heirs to this ability. No one can take it from you. It is your inheritance.

Then the objective reality reverted to what his listeners called normal. Only now people became aware that Sacha had risen to his feet.

All the gods, of whatever religion, are little more than the personification of human, or if you must, superhuman attributes. We cannot conceive of a god unless we endow him with our own nature, with our emotional and mental make up. As we develop, our gods develop. What you call god is no more than a fragment, an insignificant aspect, of the Whole, and such a god has no being other than in a mode of becoming. The modes vary from species to species, but also from galaxy to galaxy. Some gods are so great that no one on Earth will conceive of them for millions of years to come. But even those gods are only as great as the mode through which they find their expression. And they all remain mere expressions of the Whole.

As Sacha spoke, his body rose some ten feet into the air. It hovered over the aghast audience. This only lasted a brief moment but in people's minds time seemed to have stopped.

And then Sacha released their perceptions and waited. His father told him that for every action there is an equal and opposite reaction. He didn't have long to wait.

"Trickery!" shouted an obese minister of some Eastern denomination.

"Basta! Basta!" echoed an equally fat man hiding behind a scarlet flowing cassock.

"Enough of this nonsense!" screamed an irate cleric.

"What of my Personal Savior?!" a woman's voice screeched from the back of the hall. She didn't even need a microphone.

"Heresy!" chanted a chorus of some other equally devoted sacerdotal brethren. They stamped their brightly polished shoes to add weight to their convictions.

"An insult to the memory of the Prophet!" loudly agreed a group of turbaned representatives.

"A devil's advocate!" a man spoke his lips pressed into his microphone.

"Enough of zis mockery! Zis is not a burlesque!" shouted a man with a strong Jewish accent. "No more tricks!"

An old man, his hair as white as the robe which covered his sparse body, slowly rose to his feet. Men in scarlet robes supported him at each elbow. Concealed ultraviolet lamps cast their oblique rays on his white robe, giving it a heavenly sheen. His eyes darted over the auditorium to assure that he had the attention of the many that gathered to hear him speak. His sermon was to be given later, but he felt the power of the spirit commanding him to rise to his feet right now. Then, with eyes directed towards Sacha he spoke into a battery of microphones in front of him.

"In nomine Patris et Filii et Spiritus Sancti... BEGONE!"

He issued the command in Latin, Arabic, Hebrew and English. The command was followed by a wobbly sign of the cross cutting the air with a trembling hand towards Sacha still hovering above the auditorium.

Exhausted by the effort, the patriarch collapsed into his armchair. He did not intend to attend this session. He'd empowered his right hand, Cardinal Giordano Lucius to speak in his name. At the last minute something inspired him to come. A sign from the Holy Ghost? He suddenly remembered that one of his titles was the Ecumenical Bishop. He had to come. And now he'd done his job. He saved humanity from the devil himself. The devil in man's form had to be silenced. Thousands of years placed truth squarely on his shoulders. On the throne of Peter. The throne of infallibility.

He would protect it with his life.

Moments before Sacha projected his astral body to hover over the auditorium, he'd polarized the refractory photons to make his actual body on the podium invisible, but also to strengthen the image he'd projected upwards. Now he withdrew his projection and carefully, still invisible to those nearest him, left the auditorium. What else could he have done? Those people didn't want the truth. They wanted power.

Even as he walked along the corridor outside the convention hall, he heard elated voices rising in volume and intensity. The select few found one they could follow. He, the frail old man, showed them his real Power. The Power to cast out devils. The Power from God Himself. He was anointed to be their leader. The leader of them all.

"Il Papa! Sanctissimus Papa!"
"Alhamdulillah!"
"Abba! Rabbi! Rabboni!"
"Father! The Holy Father!"

Sacha heard many other acclamations, in many other languages. The finger of God, they cried. The Messenger of God! The Shepherd anointed amongst us! And then more Il Papa, and Father, and the exulted Rabbi.

Evidently the good sheep have found their shepherd. A unifying force. A fatherly protector. It worked, Sacha sighed in relief. They will listen to one man now, they will join forces to eliminate all minor heresies, and become one. It will reduce the confusion in the minds of people. It would be their first step.

A single head is easier to deal with than a multi-headed Hydra.

Sacha was about to reach the outside when four strong hands pinned his arms and led him to a room under the auditorium. The ecumenicists were very well organized. They've been prepared for trouble. They knew there could be some maniacs with exulted egos. There always were, on similar occasions. They would not permit any troublemaker to upset or ridicule the proceedings. After all they, the priesthood, represented God—in so many ways. They were the true leaders of humanity. Nor would they allow their dignity to be put at risk. Human dignity was what mattered. Each man had a God given right to worship in his own God given way. Providing they did not impinge on the rights of others in doing so, of course. This and this alone was the purpose of the Ecumenical Movement. For this reason alone there was a need for a Central Control Authority. They could weed out the undesirables. The reprobates. Once unified, their political clout would be greater than that of any secular power on Earth. They would not just represent God, they would be Gods themselves!

In all humility.

The following morning every daily newspaper carried news about Sacha on the front page. They had to. For some unknown reason no one was able to tape his TV appearance. Millions upon millions of people heard him. Had seen him. They've even seen his body rising and floating above the main podium. But they couldn't record him. They didn't know that they could not, as yet, capture subliminal thought-waves.

The pace at which the prosecution advanced was fantastic. The ecclesiastical authorities manufactured masses of evidence, so bizarre that even the prosecutors had trouble believing it.

"I'm not here to show the way. I'm here to help you discover your way," Sacha answered at the preliminary meeting when accused of misleading people into false, revolutionary byways.

To an accusation that he was driving people into psychosis he replied: "I am trying to help you make heads and tails of disjointed events. There are none such. Everything, every minute detail in your and my life, has a purpose. And it always leads you towards the fulfillment of your purpose, your destiny."

He didn't tell them that the fulfillment of each individual purpose could take thousands, perhaps millions of years. Up there, in the Undiscovered Realm, there is no time. Duration is of no consequence. Only the purpose. Only the need to raise the awareness of one's true nature. To widen, even just a little, our perception of reality.

Sacha thought he'd done that.

***

24
The Trial

Dozens of people that Sacha healed over the years lined the benches in the outer hall, ready and eager to testify against him. He'd healed them, and now they were sick again. This was the devil's work.

Sacha was helpless. No matter how hard he tried to help some of them, many had reverted to their old ways, bringing various diseases back into their orbit. Only those who wanted to help themselves succeeded. Sacha had made mistakes. He loved them too much. He felt too much compassion for his fellow man. A very human trait. One cannot live in physical consciousness and not make mistakes. It is a dualistic reality and all things are relative. No matter how hard one tries, one cannot change men who do not wish to change themselves. Such is the nature of our species. Such is the universal law.

Such is the principle of free will.

Sacha suspected the truth for some time, but it was becoming more evident as the trial grew closer. There was only one way he could fulfill his destiny. He'd thought he'd already met it. Not so. He'd only laid the ground. He'd prepared the ground for the final chapter.

The actual trial was to take place in Rome. There was no particular reason for it, but it seemed fit to use Peter's throne from which to render the final verdict. After all, it was also the throne of *Il Papa. Sanctissimus Papa.* The Holy Father. The Shepherd of us all. He alone saw instantly through the devil's subterfuge. He would expose the false messiah.

As the date of the trial approached, more churches were
eager to add their accusations. Within a few weeks the New
York bestseller list carried a dozen titles naming Sacha the
'Incarnation of Beelzebub' and 'Satan Incarnate', among
others. He was also accorded the lead role in such burlesques
as 'The Day of the Antichrist', 'Satan Walks' and 'The
Devil's Disciple'. Other even less complementary titles have
also been bandied in his direction.

Sacha didn't really mind. What little he'd heard of the
outside world, he found it all vaguely amusing. Perhaps he
was not capable of taking any or this seriously? In the sixth
week of his incarceration Deborah was allowed to see him.
Strangely enough, neither Alec nor Suzy have been accorded
visiting privileges. Perhaps they were hoping to get some
smut on Sacha? Anyway, Alicia told Deborah to fly to Rome
immediately.

"Never mind the money," she said. "I'll go myself or you
will go for me. Which is it to be?"

Deborah went. It was she who told Sacha about the New
York Best Sellers.

"Am I really that important?" He sounded almost
pleased. The tone of his voice implied: "Little *moi*?"

Sacha was in excellent spirits. He always was when his
path was clear. When he knew exactly where he was going. It
was the uncertainty that he found trying. He had lived in a
human body for almost twenty-six years, after all. Deborah
found his good spirits contagious. She did warn him,
however, that not all sects that had initially invited him to
speak did so in good faith.

"Why are they so sneaky?" she asked, her mind not yet
ready to accept the reality of duality. Sacha had told her that
only goodness is real. Evil is the product of our ever-
changing perception of missing the mark.

"It is in their nature. Birds must fly. Scorpions must bite.
Some men have it in them to be even as Judas was."

"And they cannot escape their destiny?"

"Being Judas is never your destiny. You become Judas by avoiding it."

"But you said...?"

"I said it was in their nature. But only they can create nature in which they find their being. Only they can create their perception of their reality."

She seemed more satisfied.

"Will they kill you?" she asked. Her tone was normal, conversational. She simply wanted to know. She wanted to know if Sacha already knew his future.

"We all die, sooner or later. Sooner or later we all shed these bodies and return to our true home."

"Can I come with you?"

Sacha did not answer. Instead he took her face in the palms of his hands and stared into her eyes. It didn't last long. But from that moment on Deborah would have the ability to meet him on Home Planet whenever she chose to.

"You cannot come with me," he said. "But you now know that I shall never leave you."

She could not explain her knowledge, but she never doubted Sacha's word. She would gladly leave her body also, and follow Sacha wherever he went. It was not to be. The next moment Sacha extended his aura. She'd accepted the new reality as though it were the most natural thing. They were sitting on a polished rock, a white stone giving under their weight, looking at rolling hills descending gently towards a brook winding its lazy way through a deep valley. It was a picture of serenity itself.

"And I can come here on my own?" she asked him. "And meet you as you are now?"

"You did come on your own. No power on Earth can lift you here against your will?"

She believed him.

"When you get back, talk to my father. He will help you."

These were trying times for his parents, particularly his mother. Sacha met them both here, regularly, and Suzy never failed to come back refreshed, her heart at peace, at least for a little while. It felt like having a gentle massage applied to her heart, to her emotions. He hoped the same effect was in store for Deborah.

A minute later two men in clerical collars came to their table. Deborah stood up and left without a word. She couldn't stand the idea of saying goodbye.

Sacha closed his eyes. He had inspected the room already. It was impressive.

They sat him in the very center of the round chamber. Directly in front of him sat his principal accusers. An empty lectern with discreet light above it awaited the chief prosecutor and the devils advocate, with room for their assistants on either side. They all filed into their assigned places in total silence. The assistants were the representatives of all three faiths. Higher up sat the three judges, each also representing one religion. On both sides of the judges, though a little lower, sat the twelve jurors. Four Christians, four Moslem and four Jews. After thousands of years democracy was creeping into the Office of the Holy Inquisition. It was necessary. In case something went wrong.

On the outside of the inner circle were three rows of pews, stepped, one tier behind the other, filled to the last seat with men wearing black, white and scarlet robes. There were many of them. Still farther behind, some men in clerical collars manned cameras of close circuit television. If all went well, the proceedings would be broadcast *urbi et orbi*. After suitable editing, of course.

"I must be some kind of celebrity," Sacha muttered, a vacant smile playing about his lips. He found it all profoundly ridiculous. "But necessary, I suppose," he sighed.

Yet, there was more to admire.

Behind the three rows of gloating ecumenical conspirators, on the periphery of the magnificent rotunda, there was a circle of closely spaced alabaster columns—silent sentinels, or perhaps petrified witnesses, of previous crimes committed in the same chamber.

Finally, high above them a renaissance artist must have spent the better part of his life painting a series of frescos depicting scenes from the life of the Apostles. Long, flowing robes in vivid color made one think of Roman Patricians rather then poor, emaciated bearers of the Good News. But this was the Church's image. It commanded more respect. The truth was of little import here. The scenes of the early days had been gently lit from below. No natural light came through the upper story, undercutting the dome. Not even a glimmer of the setting sun. It was dark already. Such works as they had in mind were better served at night, when fewer people might identify those present. For Sacha it did not matter. He had no interest in the proceedings.

"In the name of the Father, and the Son and the Holy Ghost," intoned the chief prosecutor.

He'd earned his position. Since Anno Domini 1233, when the Holy Father commissioned his Dominican predecessors to investigate the Albigenses in the South of France, his Office carried out its vital responsibilities without fail. The responsibility for prosecuting the guilty, and punishing them according to the Law, rested upon Its broad shoulders. In the name of the Church. In the name of God. Today he had to share his privilege. They would take turns in carrying out their duties.

Sacha hardly listened.

The problem is that all religious fanatics, or even just deeply religious people, invariably search for a yes or no answer. Their world is black and white, devoid of shades, colours, nuances. They seem totally unaware that heaven is infinite. Not just beyond time and space but infinite in its potential. Nothing, nothing at all lies beyond its scope. Nothing beyond its possibilities. Perceptions of good or bad, of better or worse, are all relative. Only the law of balance

*seems unrelenting. All extremes fall, sooner or later, dissolve
into their opposing components. Only the potential remains.
Eternal, unchanging. All else is recycled in infinite
possibilities, infinite relationships, infinite attempts to cross
yet another horizon, to master yet another unknown.*

This alone is the earthly truth. On Earth even truth is
relative. There are no absolutes in this reality. The
changeability of Earth is complemented and balanced by the
unchangeability of heaven.

*The religionists claim infallibility. They think they know
all the answers. The truth is that no one even knows all the
questions. No one ever would.*

We all make mistakes.

"*Errare humanum est,*" Sacha muttered under his nose.

"Then you admit your guilt?"

The long silver beard of the withered rabbi swung
forward, as the black suited man was sure he'd caught him.
But Sacha had not even heard him. The rabbi adjusted his hat
and continued the enumeration of Sacha's blasphemies.

The other learned men, the witnesses, swayed from side
to side in the great outer circles. The rabbi has been close.
Very close. How they all wished they were given a chance to
ask their own questions. As in LA, there was a circle of red,
of white and of black. They were kept well apart by those
determined to stick this out together. There would be no
infighting within the lower ranks. It was important for Unity.
It was good for business. Their fine apparel contrasted greatly
with Sacha's dark shirt and a suit, which had seen better days.
He maintained his silence as a succession of speakers took
turns enumerating his transgressions.

"Shalom," intoned the man, in order to silence the
murmur of voices that swelled like a wave around the
rotunda.

It's inner peace you must search, my friend. Would Verdi have composed the magnificent chorus in Ernani if Austria hadn't invaded Italy? Everything has its purpose. Italy is now no longer under the Austro-Hungarian whip, but Verdi's music lives on. Beauty is often born out of pain.

"And God created the world..." said the rabbi turning to the first page of Torah.

Anyone can create a universe. We all do it. All the time. The universe we live in is of our own creation. Some in our imagination, some in our thoughts. Even animals do it. It is only a question of our perception of reality. But only those we call gods can sustain those realities. That is why, no matter how wrong, there is such an enormous resistance to change. We feel that when we give up our ideas, traditions, our reality will collapse. Not so. They will sustain the part we share with others. We can contribute our own unique perception to that which is. Our universes are transient, ever on the brink of dissolution. A billion years is but a blink of an eye in the Undiscovered Realm. Not even that. We must lower our finger into the outer boundaries of the Far Country before we can experience the transience of time. A billion years is as nothing. This, physical, objective universe which we share is sustained by billions of people in this reality and billions upon billions more in other realms.

"*Visibilium omnium et invisibilium...*" promulgated a tall man in a resplendent crimson robe. A massive cross of pure gold adorned his chest. He looked like a true prince. An aristocrat.

It's not teleportation. I never left the podium. I've always been visible though not to your blind eyes. Yet in another way, you are right. I was never here. Or there. Or anywhere. None of us are. Our experience of earth-life is but a dream. It is real for only as long as we are asleep. Once we wake up, the reality changes to a state of being, rather than becoming. Becoming, by definition, is transient.

Aren't we suppose to live our dreams, you might ask?

Of course. But few of us realize that living a dream is still a dream. Once we remember that, our problems are over. Gradually we learn to wake up at any time. We can even sustain our physical body's awareness, or what we recognize as awareness, while we rise in our true consciousness...

"Thou shalt not kill..." The white robed man enumerated all the commandments from the Book. Later he, too, would count Sacha's transgressions.

Have I killed anyone? Death, mass death in wars, holocausts, are of little consequence. The body dies, its elements are transformed and metabolized into other living organisms. Including human. The crime lies not in the termination of biological functions—nature strives on eat or be eaten—but in the mental anguish which is caused by this act. Anguish that is brought back embodiment after embodiment, fomenting, often augmenting and magnifying, and generally exacerbating the original error. That is why some Eastern philosophies have postulated that the Golden Age of eons ago had been succeeded by the Silver, Bronze, and now the Iron Age we live in. All three religions teach the expulsion from Eden. We live in the darkness of the goddess Kali. In the last phase of the present mindset. The shelf life of a mindset goes on for countless ages. If it weren't for the fact that we are immortal, the whole process of becoming would be meaningless.

The conclave of judges was ready to interrupt all statements Sacha might make with quotations from the New and Old Testaments, and from the Holy Koran. Only Sacha hadn't spoken. Not for some time now.

"Bismillah ar-Rahman ar Rahim. La hawla wa la quwwata illa billah," recited a man adorned with a beautiful

turban. His stern face regarded Sacha with disbelief. Why would he risk his life to make a point, he wondered? Back home he would be dead by now. The Ayatollah would have seen to that.

Indeed the Whole is compassionate and merciful. As for strength and power?

If what so many people regard as God were the embodiment of Power that directs our lives, then such an entity would have to be the most cruel, hateful and uncompromising tyrant the human mind could invent.

In no reality I ever visited have I encountered any such evil. In fact, I've encountered no evil at all. It is self-evident that we, and we alone, can give evil reality. And then we build our own selves, our egos and personalities unto the image and likeness of that which does not exist.

Look at the impoverished in Calcutta, Columbia, the cruelties in parts of Africa and so many other countries, cities and groups. Unto whose image have their oppressors been created? Look at the back alleys of your own towns and cities. No, my friends. We alone create ourselves in the image and likeness of our own twisted, perverted, depraved egos. And egos have nothing to do with divine creation. It is what keeps us apart from it...

"...a time to be born and a time to die," a grave man spoke in a grave voice.

Time is a dimension of only the lower realms. If you are destined for greatness, it might take you a few embodiments to realize it and a few more to do something about it. When you do, it is called self-realization. You realize your purpose. And by the way, we are all destined for greatness. Only greatness is not measured on the scale of material success. That is transient. Ephemeral. Your greatness lies in your indispensability and is anchored in immortality.

The world is set on automatic, but the results of the setting are not always predictable. Yet you are not of the world. You are the creators of your kingdom. In it you will find solace, in it you will taste of pain. Why can't they understand my words?

No man can deny his destiny. Do you think I have no power to make myself invisible and walk out of here unharmed?

A time to live and a time to die...

Die, die, die, diediediediedie..... Sacha could sense the thoughts of his judges as though they'd been spoken out loud. They reverberated under the dome, resonated in their hearts and poisoned their minds.

I wonder what method they will choose to dispose of my body?

If we don't dispose of him he'll destroy our power... we shall become as nothing... we shall lose everything... we shall be as the masses...

diediediediediedie

He must die. Die. Diediediedie

...you are saying that I must die so that you shall live. But I say to you, that by disposing of my body you will kill the spirit within you.

diediediediediediediedie

If you kill me, I shall become more powerful than you can possibly imagine...

But no one listened any more.

And they wouldn't have heard his thoughts. There was no point talking out loud either. Their hearts and ears were closed. The decision had been made before the trial began.

They've studied the evidence of the media. They've run through the tapes of hundreds of interviews. The man before them was the most dangerous man in the world. He threatened their welfare. He threatened the seat of their power. Divine power. The culprit has been growing in power exponentially. People were beginning to question the authority of the Church. Of all the churches. They couldn't wait any longer. The only problem remained how to dispose of this uncomfortable evidence. The doors had been locked. But... walls had ears. They couldn't kill him and they couldn't release him. They had to play for time. And guard him well. Very well. He had the power of the devil.

God will help us, others thought. After all, aren't we doing His work? Aren't we protecting the Holy Words He'd given us in all the Holy Scriptures? It must be done.

"The trial is over."

The Chief Prosecutor made the announcement. The presiding Cardinal of the Office of the Holy Inquisition slammed his gavel on a round polished stone blessed with the Holy Water. He also rose to his feet and thrice hit the floor with his staff. This was the sign for others to arise. The cardinal was proud that his ancient Office finally found, once again, a worthy cause. His eyes almost misted when he thought of the good old days when all you had to do was to tie a sinner to a stake and set fire to it. Now? Now there was no justice. He worked all his life for the Church. He pored over the scriptures till his back hurt. The Holy Bible allowed punishing men who broke the Law of God. To punish them without reprieve. And now?

"There is no justice," he murmured under his breath, and wiped a tear of remembrance. "Oh, for the good old days..." But there were men who would help him. He had contacts. They would need a little money but no matter. It was a worthy cause. A Holy Cause. Money well spent.

He wiped his brow with a silken handkerchief embroidered with tiny crosses.

"…and now the trial's over. Had they only left it to me, I would know how to deal with such a charlatan. I would have him drawn, skinned and quartered in no time at all. No one would even know. But they? Especially the new generation? The goody-goody do-gooders? The holier-than-thou deacons and acolytes? Some of them were as likely as not listening to the ravings of this madman. Why, some of them even wanted to suspend the office of the Holy Inquisition. My Office! If they had it their way, they would reprimand this maniac and let him go." He gritted his teeth. "Over my dead body! Not one of them has the guts to carry out justice. They don't punish the guilty any more. At best, they excommunicate them. Big deal! As if that scared anybody."

There was utter silence in the chamber. The cardinal glanced as his own colleagues with ill-concealed disdain, as if he couldn't believe his own eyes.

"They would slap him on the wrist and let him go." A lopsided sneer distorted his features. "Well, not if I can help it. I, too, have friends. And my friends are higher up. Much higher up. And they know how to keep their mouths shut."

The verdict was a foregone conclusion. The Churches spoke with a single voice. That was what Ecumenical Union was all about. You make your decision, then you go through the motions. The Cardinal had been a young cleric, still reading law at the Universitad di Roma, when he'd learned that you never ask the accused a question to which you didn't already have an answer. And the answers to all questions were guilty. Guilty as charged. There would be no point wasting money of the prosecution otherwise. They told him, there were other, more worthy causes. He wasn't quite sure about that.

Normally the jury would retire to deliberate. But not here. Here they were guided by the Holy Ghost. Here the guilty would be taken out and wait the pleasure of his betters.

But it wasn't necessary. Each of the man sitting at the judges' dais had already reached to their left for a black skullcap. They held them in their carefully manicured hands ready to cover their aging heads. The verdict would be unanimous.

The chief prosecutor hit the floor with his staff three more times.

"You have been accused of blasphemy, of corruption of the Word of God, of misleading the children of God by leading them astray. May God have mercy upon your soul. How plead you?"

The lengthening silence was interrupted not by Sacha's words only by his laugher. The question had to be asked. So the protocol demanded. The inquisitor took a step forward and asked again.

"Do you have anything to say before judgment is rendered?" He could hardly contain the rage mounting in his voice. His face now matched his scarlet robe and skullcap. It didn't help. Sacha was laughing even louder.

"He's mad..."

"It's the devil in him..."

The room was replete with whispers. Some on the outer rim stamped their feet.

"Why are you laughing, my son?" This was the chief judge speaking. The word 'son' was adding insult to injury. Then he turned on his own audience.

"*Silencia*," he barked.

And, except for Sacha trying hard to hold back his laugher, the chamber once more sunk into silence.

"There is nothing in the Hebrew, Christian or Islamic scriptures that allows you to kill me. By what authority do you intend to do so?"

After the outburst of laughter Sacha's voice rose barely above a whisper. Yet everyone present heard his every syllable.

"You will kill me if you find a way to do so with impunity."

And Sacha closed his eyes again. For him the burlesque had run its course.

"*La comedia e finita,*" he muttered. He almost laughed again.

The three presiding judges donned their black scull caps.

"Let the Will of God be carried out," they spoke in unison. Only at this moment none of them had any idea how to get rid of this pest. What an ungodly nuisance.

I wonder what dad and mother are doing? I'm glad none of this was televised. Not for general release. They probably still wouldn't understand. Nor would Alicia. Wonderful Alicia. Look well after my Debbie, Grandma. I know she'll look after you in return.

I love all four of you. And Joan. I'll look in on John for you. You were both so kind to me. I'll miss you, too. I shall miss you all. That is the problem with this reality. As I once told Alicia, grief is the price we pay for love.

It won't be long now.

The twelve men in fancy suites rose simultaneously, their jaws set in stern grimaces of the responsibility they carried on their shoulders. In fact, they had nothing to do. They were there in case the judges failed to reach a conclusion. It had to be unanimous or by the majority of jurors. But the judges had done their duty. Inspired duty.

One by one the ecumenists filed out through the door behind the raised podium. Except for the three tiers of witnesses, Sacha remained alone, smiling. He was glad they didn't call any more witnesses from outside. It will be easier for them to overcome their karma. Although, most probably, the Office took their depositions beforehand. To cover their tracks—if necessary.

"You poor, poor people. You have no idea what you have done," he spoke in undertone but those in the nearest circle heard him. A strange shiver passed over their spines. As though they'd walked over a grave.

The question was... whose grave?

And with these words Sacha raised his consciousness to the Undiscovered Realm retaining but the most tenuous link with his physical form. A silver cord so fine as to be almost meaningless, though necessary that his destiny might be fulfilled. Yet even this modicum of life that remained with his physical body was enough to cause a solitary tear to form in his eye and flow slowly down his sallow cheek.

Even his body was crying for his accusers.

***

25
The Destiny

From a great distance, an airplane, or a passing spy satellite, he would look as though he were resting. Perhaps sunbathing? Lying spread-eagled, virtually motionless. His body was indeed relaxed, though his arms and legs had been secured to the stakes driven deep into the hot desert sand. Only at the hub of all three religions could they really count on each other's support. After all, here, except for political struggles, most of the time they'd been cooperating with each other. Lately.

That is why it is called the Holy Land.

Only the top echelons of the Triune knew where Sacha had been taken. They couldn't trust their own rank and file. They would never have agreed. They'd grown soft. But the men at the top knew their responsibility. They wouldn't kill him, of course, but with God's help, nature would take her course. For now, the important thing was that Sacha be taken out of circulation. Let things cool off a little, they said. Later... well later, we shall see, they said. God acts in mysterious ways.

They'd taken precautions, of course. They already knew that Sacha had the devil's power to become invisible. No saints ever did that. And only the devil was usually invisible. Holy men had nothing to hide. To make sure that Sacha would not disappear, the four chains binding his extremities had been cast of formidable steel. Not one could be broken by the strongest among the guards. But they also played safe.

They posted guards around the prostrate body of the prisoner with their machine-guns drawn. To protect him, of course. It wouldn't do if Sacha's followers stole his body and claimed that he'd liberated himself. No, that wouldn't do at all. But the four iron chains were powerful enough. They gave the guards a chance to get some sleep.

This was the third day since Sacha had been tethered to the stakes in the desert. They still didn't know how to dispose of his body. Particularly since he was still alive. They were hoping for God or Allah or Yahweh to help them. Something always turned up in the desert.

It did. It came in the form of a scorpion.

Since late morning yesterday, Sacha's body began experiencing visions. This is what happens when the link with your self becomes so very tenuous. The body heard the plaintive crying, perhaps from a dessert minaret... *therein are rivers of water unstaling... rivers of milk unchanging in flavor... rivers of wine... of honey purified...*

Or maybe just water?

Water?

His tongue clang to the roof of his mouth. His throat burned with the fire of the desert. There was sand in the air. His guards wore scarves, but the face of Sacha's body was exposed to the elements. Most of the time he'd spent in the Undiscovered Realm, waiting to be liberated permanently from his physical prison. He felt that he should not do it by an act of his will, though he also was reasonably sure that he'd already accomplished his mission. Yet there was a nagging emptiness in the pit of his stomach that wouldn't let go. And it wasn't hunger. His body had experienced hunger before.

And then his eyes saw the scorpion.

...rivers of water unstalling... of milk and wine and honey...

The scorpion got closer.

...and therein for them is every fruit... the voice sang in Arabic—it must have been from a distant minaret.

Only then did he realize, dimly, that whatever else he might have left undone, it would never do to let his body die of thirst or hunger. The scorpion wasn't large, but it was food...

It was only after he felt the sting that he realized that he'd been hallucinating for some time now. Total dehydration. They'd given him some water. Perhaps the few drops sufficed for the Bedouins, for the men of the dessert. His body wasn't adapted to desert life...

The next instant the Undiscovered Realm dissolved and Sacha became fully aware of his plight. Still invested with the resplendent light of his true home, he transferred all his power into his physical body. It was too late. It wouldn't respond. With a superhuman effort he attempted to free his body from the shackles. There was a clap of thunder. The soldiers rose to their feet waving their machine-guns.

The prostrate body began shining with eerie light. Then, in deceptively slow motion, it rose and stood up on its feet. The shackles had melted away. Literally. They remained on the sand as little pools of melted metal. The next moment Sacha's body began to shimmer and rise above the ground. The guards had been warned. They emptied their magazines into the air where they'd last seen Sacha's body. But this, too, was too late. Only a shallow depression of a human form outlined in the fused silicone remained. It was as though Sacha's body still lay there—only pressed into the desert sand. Their eyes deceived them.

Their prisoner was not there any more.

Sacha had never done this sort of thing before. Although it takes but a minuscule fraction of eternity to translate his higher state into physical awareness, he didn't have that fraction at his disposal. He'd acted as a body of light, pure light, to liberate his physical remains. He'd failed. He'd only succeeded in converting the mass of his body into pure energy. An energy which could sustain him here, in this reality, until he fulfilled the remainder of his mission. Whatever it was.

Whatever it might have been?

That was all the information he'd managed to extract from his physical embodiment. Not what to do, but that there still was a fragment of destiny unfinished.

He had a little time. He'd learned long ago, from Eastern Mystics, that one can sustain ones physical body in the form of energy, on Earth, for up to forty days. He was sure it would be enough to remember the last part of his dream. The dream from Bardo. It wouldn't do to leave such a great mission unfinished. In his last life, all he had to do was to give his all to help people. As a physician. He now sensed that it was not the healing that was of importance. It was the act of service. He now knew that we couldn't help ourselves unless we helped others. It had to do with one's awareness of Oneness.

He thought of himself in the human form. And in that instant his body assumed contours of his former self. A little transparent, but even as he looked at his arms, they became more opaque. Only he was naked. He couldn't do much in this condition.

"How can I get some clothing?" he wondered.

He need not have worried. While the desire for some sort of covering was still formulating in his mind, his body became wrapped with the suit he'd worn at his trial. Or one exactly like it. The last memory, he thought. He assumed that what he'd worn even later, when tied down in the desert, got burnt to a crisp. Vaporized.

He tried moving his arms and legs. They worked just fine. He wondered if his body would still have to eat and sleep, but he doubted that. He was on Earth, but the body he now occupied was the product of his mind. It had nothing to do with biological evolution. It was more like a holographic projection. Only he, himself, was the projector.

Finally, he looked around.

He was standing on the familiar sand of Solana Beach. "Sand to sand," he muttered, enjoying the coolness below his feet. "It seems that subliminal desires are also fulfilled in this body…" He was learning fast. The next moment he was in LA walking the familiar streets. He was no longer barefoot. He glanced at his reflection in a store window.

"Not bad. I now look like a regular Joe." He hopped up and down. "It will be fun to see what people are saying," he thought.

He now had a body he could use for that purpose. To find out.

And people were saying a great deal. Although he no longer commanded the front page of every national daily, in every newspaper he looked he found heated arguments regarding his heritage. About ninety percent of people demanded to know what happened to him after the Los Angeles Convention. There were rumors, which the authorities neither confirmed nor denied, that he had been drugged and waylaid by people who found his views uncomfortable. There were also direct accusations against the leaders of the principle religions that also remained ignored.

"I wonder how they'll explain my real disappearance!" He laughed out loud.

The lady at the newspaper kiosk gave him a strange look, then shrugged and moved away. Sacha forgot that he had recreated his body in the image and likeness of his previous appearance. To all who met him, he was Alexander Baldwin, Ph.D. The man with a golden mop.

There was one other tremendous advantage in being what he now was. He needed neither busses nor airplanes to get from place to place. In his present form, his body responded to a reality much closer to the Home Planet than planet Earth. Whatever he imagined—just happened. He had to keep reminding himself that this was a new reality for him, and that he must be careful not to make mistakes. He had about thirty-nine days left to learn the rules. Later, it just wouldn't matter.

He wondered also if he should visit his parents and Deborah. He decided against it. It was possible that they already went through the period of mourning. Four weeks must have passed since his original 'disappearance'. Whatever Suzy and Alec and Debbie and Alicia suspected, they must have been, at least partially, reconciled to the worst. Even his nearest and dearest regarded liberation as 'the worst'. How little they knew. Perhaps if they announce my death officially, I could drop in on them. Sufficient unto the day is the evil thereof, he quoted one of his learned accusers.

There were other things he had to do.

Like his father before him, he made a whirlwind tour of South America. He didn't make appointments. He materialized his body in various churches, synagogues, mosques, lecture theaters, university auditoria. He found controlling people's mind was much easier than before. But he didn't abuse his power. All he did was to instill in their minds a notion that he was not a crank who invaded their minds under false pretenses. Then he spoke as he had always spoken. He shared with people his perception of reality. No more and no less. He did not impose his views. He let every man and every woman make up his or her mind. He did that for just over two weeks. He had about three weeks left. He was on the way to repeat his performance in Europe, when an Arabian TV station announced that even as four soldiers had been guarding a man in the desert, the prisoner had suddenly disappeared. Sacha's name wasn't mentioned. It probably never would be. What could be better for the Ecumenical Authorities, the Holy Triumvirate, than having him disappear? No evidence, no body, no one to blame. God is on our side, they announced. But only within the walls of the Vatican. The rest of the world already knew that. Or so they thought.

Their opinion changed somewhat when Sacha has been reported seen in a number of churches in Rome, apparently dressed like a priest, a rabbi or an imam, doing his own agenda. The reports became more troubling when they arrived simultaneously from Rome, Paris, London, Amsterdam, Berlin, Warsaw, Moscow and some three dozen other towns, all reporting on Sacha preaching at various locations. This was not accurate. Sacha never preached. Nevertheless, for the Triune the matter was becoming serious.

"Mass hallucinations" was the official dictum, *ex caterdra, urbi et orbi*. The top men in control of the Ecumenical Trio had undersigned this sentiment. The Ecumenical Triad—the next best thing to the Vedic Trimurti, or other mythical Triune. Poor Arjuna, Sacha thought. He must have his own problems.

When Sacha had finished planting the seed in Europe he had three days left.

It was time to visit his family.

"Do not be afraid," were the first words he spoke to them.

He appeared in the living room where Suzy and Alec and Alicia and Deborah were sitting around the table. There was some food served, but no one was eating. Even after he spoke no one moved. They all heard his voice in their dreams, often on the Home Planet. His voice was nothing new to them.

"I am here, with you," he advanced a few steps towards them.

Deborah was the first to jump to her feet.

"Don't get too close," he advised. "I am not used to this body. I don't know how it functions on contact with biological life form."

Deborah's mouth fell open. Suzy was on her feet and she too pulled short in mid step. Alec held her for balance. Only Alicia remained seated.

"Are you really here, Sacha?" she asked in her clear, precise voice. Grandma had nerves of steel.

"I am with you in every way that counts," he assured them all. "But my physical body was... actually it was and it wasn't destroyed in the desert..." There was no clear way to explain this. "Please sit down. All of you. I am taking this precaution because two men who touched me got inadvertently burned. Some sort of electrical shock, I think. They are all right, but it must have hurt like blazes."

During the following two hours, Sacha described the essentials of his activities since his now famous disappearance from the LA auditorium. They, in turn, had news about him, apparently about him appearing all over Europe and South America, sharing his concept of reality. People were going wild. Especially in Brazil.

"But I left Brazil over two weeks ago!"

"No, you haven't. They showed you speaking from the podium in Sao Paulo. Actually it was rather funny. All the people were staring at a point on the stage that was empty. Later they swore that they saw you and heard every word you said," his father assured him.

"Evidently this body is capable of a lot more than I ever imagined..." Sacha confessed. Arjuna had told him that such a body as he now occupied could be incredibly powerful. He wondered what else it might be capable of doing.

"But we can all see you, darling. We can all hear your every..."

"Yes mother. So could they, but..."

"But we mustn't touch you..."

"Would you rather I hadn't come?"

Deborah rose again. She walked up to Sacha and stood a foot away from his body.

"I will never disobey your wish, Sacha. But if I were to touch you, would I go with you?"

"No, darling. We all have our own path to cross. Your time will come. Believe me."

"Then I shall wait. Especially since your father taught me to see you on the Home Planet."

"So you'll never miss me," he sounded relieved. He was.

"No, Sacha. I shall never miss you." And then her voice fell to a mere whisper. "But I shall miss your body..."

An hour later Sacha said he had to go.

They all got up and remained standing. Suzy's eyes filled with tears. Deborah hardly looked at Sacha. She was half way to the Home Planet where she could touch him all she wanted. Alicia took a few steps towards him.

"You won't forget about Desmond and your grandfather, Sacha. Promise me."

"I promise, Grandma. And I'll never forget about you, either."

"And my parents too..." It was all Suzy could manage.

"I will, mother. You know I will."

Alec made as if he wanted to embrace his son, then he just waved his hands.

"I'll see you, my son. Probably tonight." His voice was hoarse. "If you're free tonight son..."

"I shall always be free. Even as you are..."

And even as he spoke his body grew fainter till it dissolved in the evening light.

I'll see you, they all heard. But they couldn't see him any more. Only an eerie light lingered in the room for some time. Then, that too was gone.

He went to India to say good-bye to Arjuna. They spoke on the Home Planet, but somehow this was different. He asked Arjuna's permission to leave an echo of his perception within the ashes he'd once visited. It was a sentimental visit. He owed a great deal to that time in his life. It gave him the confidence he lacked before. Arjuna was the only man Sacha had met in his quarter century on Earth that understood fully what Sacha was talking about. And vice-versa. They shared so much more than just friendship. They were united by their love of the same reality. Of the Undiscovered Realm.

And Arjuna had good news for Sacha. It had been years since the Government of India had officially dissolved the cast system that victimized, especially the Untouchables. Arjuna had thought of a way to remove the cast system from people's minds and hearts. It might cost him his life, but nothing would give him greater joy.

It was time to make his last visit. Sacha was surprised to see the same faces all gathered together in the same room. The same semi-darkness; the same scarlets and whites and blacks—with skullcaps and turbans and yarmulkes. What not one of them wore was a happy face. Not one. All that they'd done went for naught.

"What else could we have done? Killed him right here right then? With our bare hands?" They racked their brains.

"He's the devil himself," one elderly bishop confessed. "You cannot kill the devil."

"You are a devil! I could kill you!" Another assured him.

"Gentleman, gentlemen. Please! Is this the way for the inner circle of the Holy Triune to behave?"

Of the more than two billion believers, only about three hundred were present here. The man who acted as the principle judge at Sacha's trial rose to his feet.

"We must find a way. We had problems before. We solved them. We shall solve them again."

"I suppose you will invoke the Holy Ghost for inspiration," a turbaned dignitary asked with a sneer.

"If need be, my friend. If need be. But God gave us brains that we would use them. Let us..."

He stopped dead.

Only then he noticed that lower down, on the chair in the center of the rotunda a man was sitting as though dozing. His head was down, concealing his face, but the hair, the mop of brilliant golden mane, was unmistakable. The Chief Justice couldn't even sit down. With trembling hands he began drawing a sign of the cross in the air.

"*In nomine Patris...*"

He couldn't say any more. His throat was as parched as Sacha's had been after three days in the desert sun. The rest of the men forming the inner circle were equally as stunned.

They all sat motionless, frozen in the bizarre infinity of suspended time.

There was no doubt that Sacha had united the Churches. The many, or at least the Three became One. The three principal religions became a single organism determined not to fight each other. At least, not on theological grounds.

It was equally as evident, that the unification of the church leaders was quite another matter. Even on *St-Laurent*, in Montreal, there were some people he couldn't help, who were too far gone. He sensed a similar mindset here. On the outside, they still performed their duties in accordance with an imposed unity. Behind their hardened faces a different brew was stewing in their derailed minds.

When Sacha felt his earthy vibrations waning, almost forty days after they tortured his body, he attempted to look on the New Vatican of the New Era. He returned here for one final time to bid farewell to all who fought each other for so many years, centuries. Now they sat united, brother akin to a brother, with long wiry beards, others clean-shaven, still others hiding they hair under exuberant headwear, many clad in most delicious garments with twenty-four karat accoutrements hanging around their necks—yet... all one.

Finally, all One.

During the last few hours, on the way to the Rotunda, Sacha saw hundreds of clerics, like ancient scribes busy at their computers, recording for posterity the great ecumenical event. Others were rereading the ancient scriptures to find infallible confirmation of the new era in the words of the ancients, in the words of God Himself.

They'll find it, he thought. *There is nothing you cannot find in the scriptures, if you try hard enough. Surely my work is done here. The rest is up to the Source that had inspired me to come here to start with. I have nothing more to do here.*

Then why this inexplicable disquiet?

The New Believers had all gathered at the New Vatican, the Vatican of the New Millennium. The Triumvirate decided to start the calendar from year One. *Anno Eccumenico Primiero.* To be announced in all languages of the Earth. To all the faithful of all religions. Because they now all belonged to the First and only Ecumenical Union. Even if they hadn't joined it yet. The Triune wielded such power that no one would dare to oppose them. So far, no one did. Except for one impostor who was giving them trouble. A small fry. But no one here believed in ghosts. This was no Hollywood.

Sacha watched them for a while. He'd scanned the matrix of time and saw their struggles to make one religion acceptable to all. No matter what the compromise, no matter what the ancient scriptures said. As of now, for these few, unity was the most important thing. After all, they all agreed there was only One God. And therefore there could only be one religion.

And unity meant Power. With a capital 'P'.

And here they were. The infallible, the most reverent, three-in-one Holiness. Three—yet speaking with a single voice. One for the Father, one for the Son and one for the Holy Ghost. Like in the old days.

"In nomine Partis et Filii et Spiritus Sancti... BEGONE!" the same frail voice commanded. The exhortation had been so successful in Los Angeles. This time nothing happened. Nothing at all.

"Are you addressing me? Sacha spoke directly to their minds. As in LA, they all heard him in their own language.

No one answered.

"I thought you didn't like parlor tricks, father..." This only one man had heard. His Chief Prosecutor.

Another man got up to speak but Sacha moved one hand and the man fell back grabbing his throat.

"This is what it feels like after three days in the desert sun, my friend."

Without moving his head, he scanned them all. Their minds hadn't changed. The undergoing vibrations kept repeating a death wish. His death. His alone.

"I came to help you," Sacha said quietly. This time he spoke in English. "You rejected me. I came to forgive you, and you still wish me badly. Then I shall leave you..."

Sacha felt the energy he'd confined to the periphery of his body seeping away. It was time to leave.

He rose to his feet. His body was glowing. The light grew until the round chamber was filled with a billion suns. When the light waned, he wasn't there any more.

Over the last forty days, Sacha's conscious construct of a physical body was gradually giving back its deficit to the reality he'd sustained with his attention. As he spoke in different parts of Europe, Americas and the Middle East, there had been reports of a rise in temperature of the room in which he'd appeared; some that witnessed his presence had suffered from temporary blindness. The radiation that seeped from him went far beyond the visible range. At last, the time came when he could no longer maintain this arbitrary contrivance that was his self-made tangible presence. The laws of physical reality demanded its dues.

Only the last remnants of his rarefied structure remained when he appeared in the midst of his oppressors. But those last remnants still obeyed the Einstenian formula defining the conversion of matter into energy. Even the last residues of the particles held by his will, had produced an immense amount of free energy, especially when released over a very short period of time. Absurdly, the final conversion took place in absolute silence.

Next morning the handsome guards, magnificently attired in their medieval Swiss regalia, found no one to bear witness to what had transpired in the Rotunda. The outer walls of the Rotunda were slightly blackened. All that was neither stone nor metal just wasn't there. Those in adjoining

SACHA-The Way Back   361

rooms were in a state of shock, akin to a deep coma. They
lived but lost their eyesight. The light had been so intense that
it burned their irises through the eyelids. Strangely, the few
who survived in areas adjacent to the Round Chamber have
been the representatives of lesser religions, those not
empowered to vote on the matters of the Triune. They were
just the observers. They would observe no more. They
became blind. Totally blind.

It has been written that you cannot see God and live.
That the light emanating from God would convert your body
to ashes. Sacha would have smiled, had he seen the Rotunda
that morning. He always thought of himself as so very
insignificant. And anyway, there were no ashes. It was as
though no one had ever been there. Here and there, there were
little hardened puddles of gold or some other metal on the
floor. All else was gone. Vaporized? No one knew.

Sheep are said to be lost without one they could follow;
with no one to show them the way. So far, they'd all been
fairly good sheep or, at the very least, they were sheep. Now,
as of that day, there was no one to show them the way. No
shepherds. The churches, the synagogues, the temples grew
even more empty. Deserted.

Even the clergymen were missing.

In the days that followed, some attempted to revive
interest in religion by quoting the epistles of Paul to
Thessalonians and Corinthians and the gospel of John, in
which a great Rapture, they said, had been foretold. A
Rapture in which Christ returns for His Church, and those
that have been faithful would have been "caught up together
with them in the clouds to meet the Lord in the air..." and
taken bodily, intact, into heaven. They warned that soon, as
prophesied by Zechariah and foretold in the Revelations of
John the Divine, the Church will be in Heaven and during the
next seven years the antichrist and the Jewish False Prophet
would rise, and the world would plunge into Great
Tribulation. Then, and only then the Millennium would

begin, as prophesied by Isaiah. After a thousand years of Messiah's Kingdom, they said, the Earth would be dissolved, even as the gold chains and crosses had been, reportedly, dissolved in the Rotunda.

But it didn't work.

People no longer believed the fundamentalists' interpretations of scriptures, and most preachers would not risk God's wrath by preaching them. No one knew for sure what really happened in the Round Chamber. Would anyone ever really know?

People were worried. It was darkest just before dawn, they said. They were right.

***

The
Epilogue

"Man supposes that he directs his life and governs his actions, when his existence is irretrievably under the control of destiny."

Johann Wolfgang von Goethe

By now, you must have guessed. I, Alec Baldwin, Sacha's father, put together this account of my own struggles, and then of my son's short life on Earth. It's hard to believe that it had all began when I, at the age of thirteen, saw the Sandra's reflection in my bedroom window. The rest, as they say, is history. The last part of my story is based, in part, directly on Sacha's notes, but most of it comes from our meetings on Home Planet. Suzy helped a lot. While I remember the facts well enough, she supplied the emotional content. She knew my son's heart better than I. Women always do.

Once again, the three of us met on the Home Planet. Sacha did smile when he heard from me what had happened.

Only there and then, at long last, Sacha finally and fully understood his real mission. He was never intended to unify the churches. He'd dreamed of unifying the people. Sacha came back in his ethereal body for the one final look at the Earth he'd inhabited and loved for almost twenty-six years. It seems that he was right. For the first time in human history people decided not to be sheep any more.

And don't worry about Alicia and Deborah. They are happy together. Maria still looks after them. I'm doing my best to teach them access to the Home Planet. And now it's time to say, so long.

"Beam me up, Scotty," Sacha said, his voice filled with laughter. He was on the way up—we would descend to Earth.

And if anyone had eyes that could see, they would witness a shimmering globule of light gently rising above the ground, hovering momentarily amongst the clouds, and then spin a little dance of pure joy.

Sacha was going home.

***

Acknowledgments

I would be remiss were I not to thank Madeleine Witthoeft in particular, and my many friends in general, for their diligent editing and proofreading. As always my gratitude to my wife, Bozena Happach, who, having put up with being a grass widow for weeks on end, offered me her inimitable insights.

Sincerely,

Stan I.S. Law

A Word about the Author

An architect, sculptor and prolific writer was educated in Poland and England. Since 1965 he has resided in Canada. His special interests cover a broad spectrum of arts, sciences and philosophy. His fiction and non-fiction attest to his particular passion for the scope and the development of Human Potential. He authored more than thirty books, most of them novels and short stories.

Under his real name he published seven non-fiction books sharing his vision of reality. He also composed two collections of poems in his original native tongue in which he satirizes his view of the world while paying homage to Bozena Happach's sculptures. His poetry in English, as well as a number of articles and short stories, can be seen at Authors Den: http://www.authorsden.com/Stanislaw

If you enjoyed this story,
please write a brief review on Amazon

I'll be seeing you...

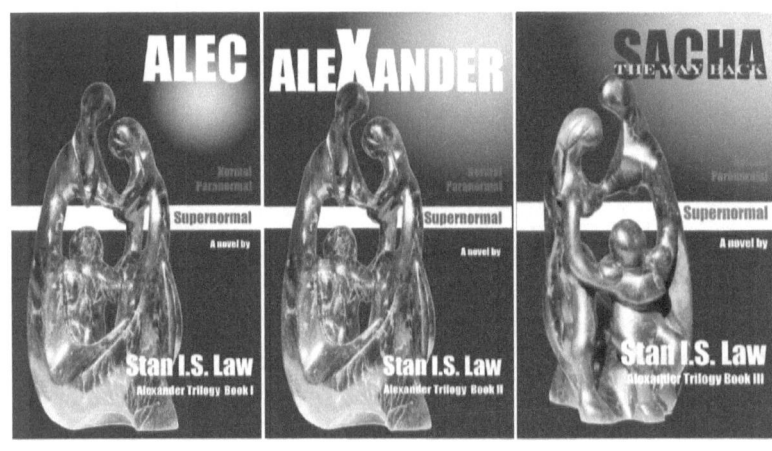

INHOUSEPRESS, MMONTREAL, CANADA
http://inhousepress.ca